THE CHINA SAND WEDGE
A Family History of China

A Novel by

Michael Willihnganz

First Edition

vi

Marshal Lee placed a shallow box on the table and put several stones and some sand into it. "Think of the box as China, the rocks as the old institutions and the sand as the people. The sand was held in place by the rocks and the rocks would not move for the sand. Only by a violent revolution, which would shake the box, could the sand wedge under the rocks to throw them out of the box and allow the people to be free."

In Memory of My Parents

Robert and Mae Willihnganz

x

Contents

Table of Maps and Drawings

Preface

Growing up in America, during the "cold war" era, my generation knew little that was actually true about China.

The Chinese Nationalist Party, called the Kuomintang, had successfully lobbied and propagandized their way into the Washington power structure, during the Second World War years, and received a large share of our "foreign aid" for their own purposes. The American press and several authors adopted the cause of the nationalists and had influenced their American readers to back China's Generalissimo Chiang Kai-Shek.

The Communists took control of China in 1949, to the horror of the American Government and the ousted KMT which had been sent packing to the small island of Taiwan. The knee-jerk reaction, in the U.S., was to ignore the realities of China and to deny its recognition in the U.N. for several decades. Factual information about the country and its people was filtered through a propaganda screen "to protect our national security interests".

That concern for national security led us to witness the McCarthy Era excesses, scandals of involving politicians who didn't follow the party line, diving under my desk at school to avoid the radiation from atomic bombs, and endless nights as a member of the Ground Observer Corps, watching every plane in the night sky for that one "Ruskie Bomber" that we knew would be coming to get us -- that was *national insecurity*!

However, the more subtle and more damaging distortions to our understanding of this fifth of the world's population were the omissions in information about the history and current events in China that was covered-up by the Chinese for their own "National Security". Fifty years after the fact, I read how 30,000,000 people in China died by starvation --

that was approximately three times the number killed in all of WW1.

To travel in China today, it is more than just helpful to have an understanding of the flow of its history -- otherwise China is just so many tall buildings with gift shops.

To help you understand that flow of history, I have invented the Wen family which lived in three eras which led to the Communist State of today. The Late Imperial era of decaying civil control through a central government; The Warlord era, that decentralized power for personal gain; and the New China which followed the revolution, the civil war and the Communist take over.

I drew my characters from literature cited in the suggested reading list and tried to frame each of the family in their time to show how they were motivated to do what they did. I have tried to view life from their perspective and context. The historical frame work is as true as I could make it and names of historical persons are left unchanged to help the reader to do further research of his or her own.

I hope that my readers will find that framework, the historical flow of the times, and get a feeling for the influences which drove that history.

Michael Willihnganz

Acknowledgments

This book could not have been written without the patience and encouragement of my wife, Wendy. Traveling with me to the distant reaches of Yunnan Province, through the back streets of Shanghai and the endless museums and Cultural Centers in China, she has, as always, my undying love and admiration.

The historical framework, which supports the story and motivates the plot and interactions of the characters, is public record. Much of it was acquired and verified by cross references between sources found in the suggested reading list and information available through the internet.

The Wen Family, shown in the family tree, is a figment of my imagination, but it was drawn from the personal histories of many people. When a theme was found in several biographical works, which followed a similar path, I felt free to grant its authenticity as historical fact and have taken the liberty of incorporating it in basic story line.

The maps and charts which I redrew, identify the cities, rivers and political boundaries that might be difficult to find on a more complete map. Several of the pencil drawings were rendered by my son-in-law Michael Stanek. The cover artwork was ours or shot for the book by my friends Gerry and Lori Pas and their daughter Olivia in Milford.

Thanks are certainly due to friends and family for their input during the early stages, and to the editors and publishers who, later on, added their critique and guidance. Finally, I am grateful for the encouragement that I received from the members of the Huron Valley Council for the Arts, in Highland Michigan, as well as the Village Fine Arts Association, in Milford, Michigan.

xx

Author's Notes on Spelling and Pronunciation

Representing spoken Chinese, in English or any other phonetically written language, has always been a problem for those of us who try. What a word sounds like depends where you hear it and even on the context in which it is used. Just as the Bostonian "park the car" sounds more like a nasal <Pack th' caw> to someone in Jersey City, who speaks from his throat, who might say <Par 'u kau>. But, beyond all of that, entire words change from one dialect to another. Even more confusing, the names of places change, and nicknames are commonly preferred; many cities are referred to by their historical antecedents.

In writing this book, generally, I have elected to use the official Pinyin transliteration system. However, the older Wade-Giles system is sometimes still used owing to the age of the referent. Also, the Chinese are proud of their memory and of their own history and often refer to a city by its role as an ancient capital of a past kingdom. And some people, like Sun Yat-sen, is as known well by his Japanese pen name, which he used in exile, Nakayama (middle mountain) or its Chinese equivalent, Zhong Shan.

Titles are also affixed to the family name or are used in lieu of a proper name. From time to time, one of my characters may be referred to as Shao Wen (Young Wen) or Wen Xiansheng (Mr. Wen - or, literally First Born Wen) or even Lao Wen (the elder Wen). A man could be addressed simply as Xiansheng. Any young girl could be addressed simply as Xiaojie (little sister) with or without the family name.

In the final analysis, in China, names and titles are flexible; they take much of their meaning from the context of the situation and reflect the flavor of spoken Chinese.

Map of US vs. China

Geography: China vs. USA

The Maps on the facing page point out an interesting fact -- China and the United States are almost the same size. What is not evident is that there are four times as many people in China as in the US.

The capitals of the two countries are almost the same Latitude. If you were to overlay a map of China onto a map of the US, Beijing would sit near Gettysburg, Pennsylvania, about 120 miles to the north of Washington DC.

For historical reasons, Beijing means "North Capital" and Nanjing means "South Capital". Nanjing would be found on the west coast of the peninsula that forms the Chesapeake Bay, south of Washington about the same distance and about the same latitude as Richmond, Va. And, Shanghai would be just on the east side of that peninsula.

Wuhan, the center of the Civil war, that ended the Imperial era, is south and west of Beijing and, on our overlay map, would be near Jacksonville Florida. This triangle is important to understanding the great Taiping Rebellion -- China's almost-Civil war which happened before and during our own American Civil war.

The southern provinces are in the same latitude as the Gulf of Mexico, placing Hong Kong and Canton in the area of the Yucatan Peninsula of Mexico, around Cancun.

My Wen Family starts with the birth of Wen Fulian in the mountains of central China, in southern Shaanxi Province, south of Xi'an -- on our overlay map of the US, that would be just about Montgomery Alabama. But instead of being 230 ft above sea level, we are introduced to Wen Fulian on a farm above 5,000 feet. His son Zhenli would later serve in the Imperial Army out in the far west, which would be about the middle of Idaho, on our overlay map.

Nick Remos, the protagonist of the story, meets his
Marshal Lee in the far north east Province of Heilongjiang,
slightly north of the tip of Maine, in our overlay map.

Map of China with Indexes of Provinces

North East Provinces (Old Manchuria)
1. Heilongjiang
2. Jilin
3. Liaoning

East Central Provinces
4. Hebei
    Beijing
    Tianjin
5. Shandong
6. Shanxi
7. Henan
8. Jiangsu
9. Anhui
10. Zhejiang
11. Hubei

Territories and Tributaries

25. Inner Mongolia
26. Taiwan

Southern Provinces
12. Jiangxi
13. Fujian
14. Guangdong
15. Guangxi
16. Hunan
17. Guizhou
18. Yunnan
19. Sichuan
20. Hainan Island

Western Provinces
21. Qinghai
22. Xinjiang
23. Gansu
24. Shaanxi

27. Tibet
28. Mongolia
29. Korea

The Family Trees

The charts on the following page describe the two families which are at the heart of the story of The China Sand Wedge.

The Imperial Family

The last of the Qing Dynasty is not one of direct decent. Controlled by the Dowager Empress Cixi for the last forty-eight years, new bloodlines were introduced to reinvigorate the line of succession -- too little, too late. The Dynasty had just become irrelevant.

The Wen Family

The Wen family history also grew by extension - some times to its advantage and sometimes to its great chagrin. The family fortunes were many -- land, a network of commercial enterprises, money in the bank, and indeed, banks themselves. But most remarkable of all were the network of relations with men of influence in their time. The New China, as the old China, grew and survived at the expense of its lower and middle classes. In the end, the fortunate family members were the ones living outside the Peoples Republic of China.

Illustration of the Family Trees

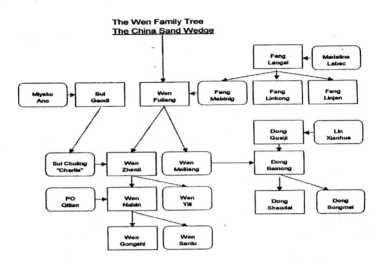

The Wen Family Tree
The China Sand Wedge

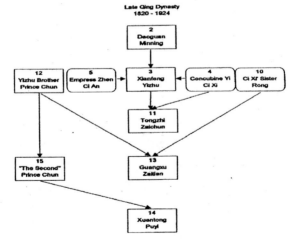

Late Qing Dynasty
1820 - 1924

Dramatis Personae

Note: All named below are Fictional Characters
Note: Family name is first, followed by the person's given name
Note: A Wife retains her natal family name, children the father's
Note: A family name, alone, refers to the eldest in that scene
Note: 'Lao' before the family name indicates an older male
Note: 'Xiao' before the family name refers to a young male
Note: 'Xiansheng' following a family name is Mister.
Note: 'Xiaojie' following a family name is Miss.
Note: 'Furen' following a family name is Mrs.

Deng Weili 1834 - ?: Magistrate of Xiangfan, schoolmate and protégé of Wen Fulian

Dong Bainong 1854 - ? : Printer, Married to Wen Meiliang and father of Shaodai and Songmei.

Dong Guaiji 1825 - ? : Printer, Married to Lin Xiaohua and father of Bainong

Dong Shaodai 1885 - ? : Son of Bainong and Meiliang, commercial agent for Zhenli and undercover agent for Sun Yat-sen

Dong Songmei 1892 - ? : Daughter of Bainong and Meiliang.

Fang Laogai 1798 - 1873 : Farmer/Banker/Teacher, married to Madeline Lebec. Father of Meixing, Linkong and Linjen.

Fang Linkong 1832 -1857 : Soldier, Eldest son of Laogai and Madeline. Served with Qing Imperial Forces in Beijing.

Fang Linjen 1836 - 1856 : Soldier, Youngest son of Laogai and Madeline. Served with Qing Imperial forces in the Nanjing area.

Fang Meixing 1834 - 1893: Teacher/Farmer, Daughter of Fang Laogai and Madeline. Wife of Wen Fulian, mother of Meiliang and Zhenli

Fang Meliang 1856 - ?: Printer, Married to Dong Bainong and mother of Shaodai and Songmei.

Kong Bang DOB? - ? Head Coolie at the Xiangfan Facility

Lao Gai DOB? - ? Farmer/scholar Mentor to Wen Fulian

Lee Dayi 1912 - ? : Marshal PLO, uncle of Xiaoli, commander of force in NW Manchuria on the Russian Boarder.

Lee Zhenzhu 1951 - ? : Student, (Red Guard Want-to-be)

Lin Xiaohua 1827 - ?: Printer, Wife of Dong Guaiji, mother of Bainong

Madeline Lebec 1803 - 1863: Teacher/Farmer, wife of Fulian, mother of Meixing, Linkong, and Linjen.

Magistrate Hon DOB? - ?

Master Deng Gaoxi DOB? - ?: Commissioner for Education in Xiangfan and mentor to Wen Fulian

Master Lu DOB? - ?: Teacher, Village School Xaohexi

Miyaka Ano DOB? - 1862: Mother of "Charlie", wife of Sui Gaodi

Nick Ramos 1939 - Present: The author's alter ego, he tells the history of the Wen Family.

Po Qitian DOB? - 1862: Farmer, Wife of Naixin, mother of Wen Gonshi

Shan Quiping DOB? - ? Taotai (mayor) of Zhongxian Vilage

Sui Chuhng "Charlie" 1861 - 1951: Sing-song girl/farmer/ Landlord, Wife of Wen Zhenli, Grandmother of Wen Gongshi, The Sailor.

Sui Gaodi DOB? - ?; Pirate/bar owner/enforcer/dope dealer, Father of "Charlie".

Tong Gaolin DOB? - ? Town Carpenter Xiangfan

Wen Fulian 1832 - 1909; Farmer/Kwan A5/Industrialist, Progenitor of the fictional Wen Family.

Wen Gongshi 1939 - Present: Landlord's son/Farmer/Sailor, introduces Nick to the history of China as seen by his family.

Wen Meiliang 1856 - ? Teacher/Printer/Revolutionary, Grand-daughter of Fulian, sister to Zhenli, Wife of Dong Bainong, Mother of Shaodai and Songmei, undercover finance agent for Sun Yat-sen

Wen Naixing 1891-1959: Teacher/Landlord, Grandson of Fulian, Father of Gongshi

Wen Yili 1884 - 1951: Farmer/Landlord, sister to Naixin

Wen Zhenli 1855 - 1929: Farmer/B7 Kwan/Police, son of Fulian and Meixing, Father of Naixin & Yili

The China Sand Wedge

A Family History of China

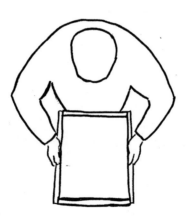

Michael Willihnganz

2

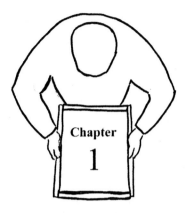

Nick's Tale

***

A New Situation

"Coffee, Sir...? Would you like some coffee? Sir...?"

The voice was insistent, so I suspected this was not the first time he had asked.

"Oh! Coffee, yes please!" Coffee sounded good, but I had almost forgotten what it tasted like; I hadn't had any real coffee since I landed. And, I couldn't really remember how long ago that was. Days seemed to have blurred together. It had been enough just to get through them one at a time.

I could hear the rattle of a service tray being set up and a small deck table being dragged over next to my deck chair. I opened my eyes and could only see the blanket that covered me from my head down to my toes, which were still pretty numb.

"Will there be anything else, Sir? If not, I'll see to your cabin." With that, he gathered up his things and was gone before I could pull back the blanket.

"Thank you," I mumbled, trying to sit up. The sun cut through the folds and burned my eyes. I decided to stay inside -- just a little longer.

"Are you all right, fella?" It was a man's voice, maybe Norwegian, and he sounded sympathetic. Well, that was worth a look! But I was blinded again by the sun and only caught a glimpse of white, tooled leather shoes and knickers. A woman stood by his side, her coat flapping against the breeze. But they were just silhouettes that blocked the sun.

"When the soldiers brought you on board, this morning, we couldn't figure out if you were a prisoner or a patient. The Captain had us all wait in the dining room, with our life jackets on, even while we were in port, and we weren't allowed back on deck 'til we cleared the port. Bad business, that! We just wanted to make sure you are all right. Enjoy your coffee." With that they left, walking away toward the warmth of an inside room.

"Thanks!" I called after them, but my attention was on that steaming cup on the table next to me. Beyond the table was the railing of the fantail and beyond that, the flat hills of Manchuria, turning from black green to powder blue as they were sucked into the changing perspective. The engines droned steadily as the ship shouldered into an endless series of waves. A dissipating plume of smoke drifted to the east, while I sat up and sipped at my coffee.

After a while, a crewman appeared at my side and said, "Your cabin's ready for you, sir; if you would just follow me." With that, he picked up a bundle of things next to my chair, which I now recognized as my clothing, and walked smartly toward a door on the starboard passageway.

This cabin was even smaller than the one I had had on the freighter coming over from Japan, but it was much cleaner and was set up as a single room. Obviously, the crew on a cruise ship enjoyed a better life style! For one thing, there was no smell of fuel oil and old sweat. Oh, that was rank! This was a proper cabin, clean and well lit; it even had a small porthole. At one end was a door that opened onto a real bathroom. Then, I caught a glimpse of myself in the mirror; a face I was sure was not my own! I could hear my mother's voice inside my head saying, "What a rag bag!" I turned on the faucet. Oh my God! Hot water! I hadn't seen running hot water since I got here. I leaned against the door and just laughed. Real soap and water! God, it felt good!

There was a knock at the door, which I opened, and found the Vietnamese cabin boy who had first wakened me, standing there with a stack of terrycloth towels, a robe, and slippers -- all with the ship's crest embroidered on them.

"Have you any laundry, Sir?" I looked over at my pile and laughed again.

"Give me a few minutes and I'll bag up what I have. Thank you! This is fantastic!"

"No problems, Sir. If you wouldn't mind then, just hang the bag on this hook by the door and I'll take care of it straight away." He turned and left me shaking my head -- what in the world had I stepped into this time?

I turned my attention to the bundle of clothing on the floor next to the bed. Everything I had was stuffed into my sheepskin coat, with a rope through the sleeves so I could sling it over my back and tie it across my chest. It was all wet and stiff, and smelled of road dirt from my long trek down from the north.

OK! There was a bag for laundry and a list of clothing items with numbers to circle. So, I thought, two pair of Levis; I guess that would be trousers, one shirt, one sweat shirt, two underpants, and two unmatched pair of socks. The boots and jacket I would have to clean myself. That done, and now striped naked, I furtively opened the door and hung out the bag on the hook in the hall.

Exploring the bathroom, I found it stocked with complimentary toiletries! Wow! What luxury! I embarked on an hour-long removal of a month's patina -- amid lots of steam and loud singing.

Once clean and shaved, I donned the robe and slippers and ate my way through the complimentary basket of fruit, breads, and jams. Totally relaxed, safe, and comfortable at last, the rhythm of the boat quickly lulled me to sleep. A knocking at the door wakened me to brilliant amber light, as the setting sun filled the room "Ahh! Clean duds!" I thought, and sure enough, there was a brown paper parcel hanging from the hook where I'd left my laundry hours before. My underpants and socks had been replaced with new ones from the ship's store. And in a large envelope, I found my money pouch! Wow! I almost forgot about that! Opening it, I found my passport, traveler's checks, and my good old American Express credit card. Things were defiantly looking up!

Down the hallway I heard the musical chimes announcing the evening meal. And was I ready to dress for dinner? Oh yeah!

Wearing my better pair of blue jeans, shirt and boots (with most of the mud scraped off), I walked into the main dining room. Conversation stopped in the foyer as I entered and I could feel eyes following me as I walked across to the bar. Everyone else was dressed in "dinner attire" or sports clothes. I took a stool and scanned around the room as heads turned back to their groups and conversations resumed. I asked the bartender if my credit card was acceptable. He just smiled and said "No need, Sir."

At that point, a waiter stepped up and said, "The Captain has invited you to sit at his table, Sir." Without waiting for an answer, he turned and led me across to the head table.

The Captain had a chair pulled out for me and a place set at the table. With a grand wave, he indicated where I should sit, next to him. "Well, you have caused quite a stir!" he said, then regarded me for a long time. I looked around blankly at all the faces looking at me. "Do you remember what happened and why we had to make port at Luda?" the Captain asked.

"I guess Martial Lee had them stop you." I blurted it out. "I was half expecting that they would throw me into the sea. I'm really sorry if I caused you a problem." The Captain laughed, rolled his eyes, and leaned back in his chair.

"You know, I've been at sea a long time and today is the only time I have ever been forced into port at the point of a gun! They signaled us out in international waters and told us we had to go into port. Of course, I tried to object, but they had a gunboat and quite an attitude. Not a talkative lot! So we radioed our home office and told them what was going on, then we followed them in. Next thing I know, armed soldiers came up the gangway with you in tow, put you on a deck chair and waved us out of port. As soon as the Harbor Master gave us the word, that is just what we did. Now, I think you need to explain this so I can write it up in a way that will not cause an international incident."

"I am sure that I cannot repay you and your company for making an unscheduled port call." I said. "I'm not even sure I can afford passage on this ship." I started picking my words, hoping I wouldn't have to wash dishes for the rest of my life. "But I may owe you my life and I am very thankful. I'll do what I can."

"I guess you might start by explaining how you got in with the Chinese? And, how you rate having some Marshal pirate a ship off the high seas for your transport?"

I was feeling a little uneasy before. Now I felt like a bug under a magnifying glass -- and the sun was getting very hot! Faces around our table and the tables within earshot were all turned toward me. I looked back at the Captain and said, "If you don't mind, sir, this may take some time. Could I get a beer?"

***

The Plan Was …

"Oh, this trip was not my first choice, I can assure you, Captain. I was supposed to set up some equipment in South America, but it didn't quite work out that way. You might say I was Shanghaied to Shanghai. It's what I get for going to church!"

That is where I met Reverend Karl McDonnal -- in his bible class. He stood six-foot-four and had a shock of red hair going to white. He loved to hug you and he smiled a lot. But most of all, he loved to talk about the Bible and all the good works that that book could do.

Sometime, many years ago, Karl McDonnal had been a Peace Corps volunteer in South America. He got a little too involved in the 'down trodden Indians' and shifted from ministering to their spirits to working with their political problems. Next thing you know, he was hiding rebels from government troops. Soon after that, he was a partisan, smuggling ammunition till he fell down a ravine, fracturing his hip, and getting himself tossed out of the country. There was a flim-flam story in all the local papers about the rescue of a missionary padre. But it was American advisors in an unmarked helicopter who snatched him off the mountainside and flew him out of the country – never to return.

The good Reverend looked back wistfully at all that and said he had gotten the message; he was given a new direction. But there was still a rebel living inside him, who wanted to do good works. His chance finally came in the mid 1970s, when he was able to get back in contact with some of his old friends in the mountains. There was less of a need for bullets by then and more of a need for food, medicine, and employment. Rev. Karl was up to speed in no time. He was consumed with raising funds for the needy in the mountains.

His fundraising was very successful, and by the time I came into the picture, Reverend Karl had already made arrangements to purchase a mobile hospital, commissary and a machine shop. He also arranged, through one of the church deacons, a retired parts manufacturer, for materials and a contract to assemble wire harnesses for compact cars. The equipment was ready to be shipped and all he needed was someone to take it there and set it up. And, happily, there was money for that as well!

The Reverend dropped that long arm over my shoulder one day and drew me toward him. "Hello, Nick!" he said. "I understand you speak Spanish. Is that true?" I nodded, guardedly.

The plan was simple. It would take me a couple of weeks to finish the project that I was working on, then I would fly down to San Diego, meet with the equipment dealer, and inspect the equipment before it was loaded on a ship. At that point, I was free to spend three weeks hiking the West Coast trail. Then, when the equipment got to port and was transported inland, I would fly down, take charge of setting it up, and getting it working. For this I would make $10,000 -- darn good money for three months work! Since it was a better deal than the job I had, I turned in my notice and started packing for my little adventure.

***

Out West

The flight to San Diego was long and bumpy, but it was my first glimpse of the Grand Canyon and all that. Of course, you couldn't recognize any of it looking straight down. As soon as we landed, I called my contact, the equipment dealer, to arrange our first meeting. He was expecting me, more than I knew. First he told me to look for his driver by the airport taxi stands. He would take me to "my hotel" and I should wait for him there. I hadn't really expected a hotel room; Rev. Karl had given me traveling money and the tickets. But hey, why not enjoy the moment? So I found the driver and he took me to the hotel, which was a bit less than three star, you might say. And I noted, as we unloaded the bags, that his driver was using a rental car.

About five thirty, I got a call from the desk that a Mr. Clark Henderson was there and would meet me in the bar. I cleaned up and went down. It was a typical hotel meeting place with a spotlighted miniature indoor waterfall and pool stocked with tropical fish.

Mr. Henderson met me at the doorway. "Well, quite an adventure you've gotten yourself into, young fella," he said, shaking my hand jovially. We proceeded to a table, off to the side. "I hear you're already a world traveler," he continued as we sat down, "Germany wasn't it?"

"I was in the Army," I answered. "They sent me to France for two years. But I did see some neat places on our USO day trips. And…."

"Well, this is going to be a bit different than all that, you know! You will be on your own in strange surroundings and there won't be any sergeant to tell you what to do. You think you're up to some real adventure?"

"I think I have a pretty good idea from what Reverend McDonnal told me. He has a list of…."

"Yeah, well, eh…." He was holding up his hand with a curious short waving motion. "That plan, I don't know if you had heard, but it's been changed some. We had to shuffle things around. Another deal came up and we had to redirect our assets to take advantage of the opportunities as we saw them. The plan is pretty much the same; the need is the same, you know, poor people all over the world need help. What we got lined up is the same thing only different, if you know what I mean."

Well I didn't know what he meant and I had a creepy feeling that the more he talked, the more I wouldn't like it.

"We have an adventure that will knock your socks off," he continued. "Listen to this! You know Nixon opened up China? Yeah, well, we're getting in on the ground floor of a whole new China trade thing! And you are a part of it! That stuff the preacher bought got sent off to our new partner in China and they'll need you to set it up there just like you were going to do in South America. What do you think?"

"I think I'm confused. I'm here as an agent for Reverend McDonnal and you're telling me you just shipped his things off to China? I'm not sure I like what I'm hearing!"

"No! No! No! Don't get me wrong!" he said, wiping a needed napkin across his mouth. "This thing with McDonnal and South America is still going to go through. We just had to jump on this deal in China before we lost the opportunity. Hell, South America will still be there when you get back and there will always be a need. The Reverend saw what I meant. We got all that worked out! Don't worry. He's being taken care of. It's just that we had to do this first. His Indians have been up there for years! They can hold on a little longer. You can rest assured of that!"

Rest assured? What the hell was he talking about? I took a deep breath and sat back to consider my options. I had money enough for a ticket home; I could go tonight. I didn't need Henderson and his 'knock your socks off' deal. First, I had to hold off till I checked in with the Rev. When I looked back; Henderson's mouth was moving a mile a minute. "I'm sorry, what did you say?" I leaned forward.

"I said we'll double the deal he gave you! We will pay you $20,000 up front and pay all your travel costs. Just rest up here for a couple of days. We'll get the paperwork in order. You can fly over and catch the ship in Yokohama Harbor before it goes on to China. You'll have what you'll need with you and our contact in China will have the rest prepared for you when you land." He slid his card across the table with three hundred dollar bills. "Just be our guest and enjoy the city, OK?"

"I'll enjoy it more when I've had a chance to talk with Reverend McDonnal and think this thing through," I said reluctantly. He took his hand off the money as I reached out and pulled it toward me.

"Good, then!" he said, with a big smile. "I'll start the paperwork on the visa and I'll be back in touch in a day or so." With that, he reached out, shook my hand, and slid from behind the table.

I looked at the bills and the card still lying on the table before me. "What just happened?" I asked myself, shaking my head. Gradually, I started smelling the heavy cigarette smoke of the bar and hearing the soft music drifting down from the speakers above the table. As I turned, I caught a glimpse of the ample frame of Mr. Henderson, almost skipping out the door and into the lobby.

When I talked with Reverend McDonnal the next day, I learned he wasn't sure what had happened either. He had been contacted by the equipment company and told that there would be a delay because of "equipment problems", but not to worry. The equipment company would take care of me until things were resolved. When I told him about the plan Mr. Henderson told me, it didn't reassure either one of us, especially because McDonnal didn't recognize the name Clark Henderson. He said he would check into it and get back with me.

By mid week, I hadn't heard back from the Reverend. Henderson's driver called up to my room and told me we had an appointment downtown. We went to the Chinese Government Travel Office where I filled out a lot of forms. I got photographed and was presented with a new visa, which was pasted onto one whole page of my passport. "We told them you were escorting military cargo to China and you had a flight to catch," Henderson's driver said. "It costs a bit more, but you can get things done faster that way. A little payola works wonders." As we headed to the hotel, he asked, "Are you all packed? I wasn't kidding about that plane. It leaves at 5:30 tonight!"

**

The China Option

The ship's Captain brought me back into the moment. "Then, it wasn't the Chinese that got you into this mess?"

"No, it was that damned equipment dealer who sent me over here," I answered. "He hustled me out of town before I really understood what was going on. When I got back to the hotel, there was a packet of paperwork waiting for me. The first thing I saw was this certified check for $20,000 made out to me. Well, you know that got my total attention! I got that into the bank before we did anything else. I took out enough for spending money and bought some travelers checks, but the rest was tucked away. Then there was the flight, leaving in just a few hours -- about enough time to clear my room and leave. Next thing I know, I'm in Japan looking for the ship.

The freighter didn't actually get there till three days after I did. But, that was OK. I had a blast just wandering around the harbor and watching them loading and unloading the ships. At first, with all those container boxes on their decks, I couldn't imagine why they didn't just tip over on the first wave. But seeing how much stuff was under the decks, I understood how they have enough ballast to roll with the seas.

I checked with the Harbor Master's office every day till I finally got to see 'my ship come in'.
"There it is, there!" he said, pointing out a speck on the horizon and handing me a pair of binoculars. The glasses didn't help a lot; it was just a bigger speck. Then, when it did get into port, it had to lie off for two days, till they got docking space. Each day, I went out and looked it over. It seemed older and rustier than most of the ships and was very low in the water. Like all ships, the bilge pumps were working all the time and brown oily water spilled continually back into the brown oily water of the harbor.

When they finally did get it docked, I was allowed on board, but was sent directly to a "Passenger's Cabin" and told to either stay in the cabin or get off the ship. The decks were obviously no place for a novice like me. I moved my things down from the hotel and peeked around as many corners as I could, but I couldn't see anything that looked like my equipment. When I asked, they said my stuff was down there somewhere.

Each night, the hums and clunks of the ship's unloading noise would lull me to sleep. During the day I could look down into the hold under the huge hatch covers. Vast layers of sub-flooring held level after level of small cargo and large cargo chained down. Piece by piece it was hauled up in a net or on a hook and chain rig. So much stuff! Finally, the process was reversed and more things were loaded back into the hold. Still no sighting of my stuff! The hatches were closed and the large container boxes were stacked on top. I would not see my equipment till we got to China.

The next morning, the bow lines were slipped off the mooring posts and slapped against the hull of the ship, just behind the painted name of the ship 'Kyori Maru'. I found out later that was the name of the shipbuilder's youngest daughter; she was probably a grandmother by now. Then we backed up to release the stern lines and we were under way. Slowly we backed into the harbor, accompanied by our tug tenders and a lot of noise from the ship's horn.

The sun was warm, but there was a cooling breeze. I stepped out of my cabin for a walk around. On the deck below, I could see a table with some machinery and tools. It looked interesting and there was a ladder, so I climbed down to have a look.

***

The Sailor

"Wei Shinma? Sheia?" I turned to see a Chinese sailor sitting in the shadows next to the bulkhead. He was holding a half empty bottle of beer. "Ni guo lai! Lai, lai, lai!" He waved me to come toward him with that 'fingers down' gesture, clawing the air, that they use.

"I'm sorry, I can't speak Chinese." I said as I approached him. His oily hands and forearms were recently wiped with a not too clean rag that lay across one leg. I could see that he was muscular and seemed as weather-beaten as the ship he lived on.

"Oh, you dat crazy American gunna take those trucks to China? HA! They gunna eat you alive! You outta jump ship right now while you can still swim to shore. You crazy as they are. China's no place for you! No place for anyone!"

"Oh, come on, how bad can it be?" I retorted, looking down at him.

"You don't wanna know how bad it can be!" He looked intently at his beer for a moment, and blew out a wispy punctuation as his eyes glazed over and his face collapsed into three horizontal folds.

"Don't you still have family over there?

"Hell No! They all starve to death; long time ago. I lucky to get out at all."

I slipped down and sat next to him, but his mind was somewhere else. "God, I'm sorry," I said.

"Everybody in my town starve to death. Crazy people over there! Crazy! You'll see!"

His name was Wen Gongshi and he filled my three-week passage with his stories, histories, memories, and a picture of the China that he knew or had learned about since he ran away."

The Captain sat back and put the tips of his fingers together, patiently. "OK, but how does all this get you on my ship?"

"I'm sorry, the short answer, I guess, is that I saved the life of Marshal Lee and he was saving mine by getting me out of China. The Marshal was a friend of Mao and he pulls a lot of weight, even now, two years after Mao died. He is an old man but very well connected. I hope you can write this up so he doesn't get into trouble with the new rulers. You see, he really became my friend, too."

"All right, then, how do you get from running into a sailor to being buddies with a friend of Chairman Mao Tse-tung, the headman of all China?"

By this time, the tables had been cleared and some had been pulled up around ours. I have to admit, the ham in me was coming out. I had an audience, a story, and all night to tell it.

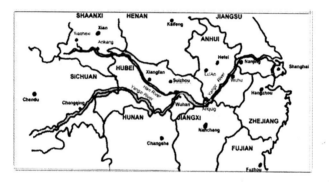

Map of River Trade Routes

Chapter

2

The Sailor, Wen Gongshi

***

Memories of China

"Let me start by first telling you about the sailor, Wen Gongshi. This is all based on what he told me as we sailed from Japan to China in the spring of 1978.

His earliest memories were of long robes hanging in a dusty closet; the smells of old spice and floral sachets had faded over the half-century since they were last put away. And the closet was where his sister would most often find him when they played hide-and-seek in the farm house where they lived, in southwest Anhui Province, south of Beijing and west of Shanghai.

The long black robes belonged to his Great Grandfather who had been a Kwan, or Mandarin, and was a county magistrate in the last years of the Qing Dynasty. The term Mandarin came to China from Malay in the fifteenth century by way of the Portuguese traders. The Malay word 'mantri' meant counselor or minister of state. The Europeans had generalized the term to refer to any of the members of the bureaucracy of the empire. The formal black silk robes were embroidered with a silver pheasant and the cap had a crystal button. That was the insignia of a fifth-level minister, in a system of nine levels. It seemed to hang there as if waiting for him to reclaim it in some after-life. On the floor were boxes of photographs of the old man, Wen Fulian, Gongshi's Great Grandfather, and his son Wen Zhenli, his Grandfather. The boxes also held a treasure trove of medals, sashes, and swords.

In the old days, these relics of the past would be displayed in some special room of the house, where they were venerated so their spirit could direct the lives of the family. But, these were not the days of the past. The realities of Gongshi's youth were civil war and uncertainty. He was born ten years before the Communists had taken over the government and proclaimed the Peoples Republic of China. He was only eleven, in 1950, when Chairman Mao Tse-tung proclaimed The Agrarian Reform Law and life in the Wen household was turned upside down. When the Communists came to power, a sense of euphoria swept over the peasant class. Chairman Mao had promised them that they would all be the owners of the land they farmed and that the landlords and warlords would be held to account for their past treatment of the people. Rebellions had always promised this; but this one had actually won!

***

A New Freedom

Madness bloomed across the land. Ad hoc committees hauled civil authorities, old Kuomintang heroes, and landlords out into the public streets for easy justice and retribution. Many died on the spot; many were tortured and beaten. The catharsis ran long and many died by their own hand to avoid the mob. On the farm where Gongshi lived with his family, they locked themselves in the house. Roving bands of peasants swept over Anhui Province and attacked those peasants who still worked the fields for supporting 'the feudal classes.' They stole everything they could carry and all of the animals that were left outside.

Inside of the house, Grandmother was the undisputed head. She broke the hand of some man who tried to reach in and unlock the kitchen window. And she stood ready to lay waste to anyone else who would try to enter. Anti Yile took after her mother in most things, but didn't have her mother's resolve for hand-to-hand combat.

Wen's father, Wen Naixing, was a teacher in the local school who was more sympathetic to the new government. He had actually read the writings of Mao, Zhou Enlai, and the others. He understood the new vocabulary and, to a degree, the revolution.

Wen's Grandmother did not care to understand. And, even though the house and lands would someday come down to Naixing by inheritance, he did not feel that he himself was a landlord. His wife, his sister, and even his daughter were treated just like any other peasant servant. Grandma made sure they all knew their place. Every day, Gongshi went to the school with his father, and studied there as long and as hard as he could.

But, throughout the winter of 1950, the family stayed close to the farm; the school was closed. In late March, a group of people came into their front yard and pounded on the front door. "Come out! We are the Revolutionary Town Housing Committee!"

"Go away!" bellowed Grandma, through the locked door.

"If you do not talk with us, you will be in much trouble."

Naixing went and opened the door. Recognizing some of them as his neighbors, he said, "I know you and you know me. I teach at the county school. How may I help you?"

"Wen Xianshang, we must talk with you and all of your family, outside, now!" The man had worked for a neighbor, who was a friend of Naixing.

"Please wait here, just a moment." He turned and went inside. "Mama, we must all go out into the front yard and speak with them. Most of them live close by and I do not think that we need to fear them."

"And the rest? They are all peasant bandits. I do not trust a one of them!"

"We have to go out there and face them. Come on, everyone!" He turned and stepped out of the door; one by one, the rest followed.

"This is my family!" he said to the leader.

"Who else lives in the house? Do you employ servants?"

"No, we live alone." Naixing was hedging just a bit. The two servants who had lived with them had actually run away the day before.

"Six people in such a large house is a waste! We will bring some more people to live with you. Many have no housing at all! The land will be divided up and you will have a plot to raise the crops that you need."

"What are you saying?" Grandma shouted back at him, her face turning red and her hands defiantly on her hips. "This is our house and this is our land! Our family has always lived here. You cannot just give it away! What kind of bandits at you?"

"We are not bandits of any kind!" The leader of the group replied threateningly, moving to stand directly in front of her and matching her glare for glare. "This is the New China and everything is owned by everybody. You are no better than anyone else. As a mater of fact, you are less. You and your whole family are landlords and soon you will feel the pain that your class has made the rest of China suffer!"

"Get off my land!" She screamed, right into his face.

He smiled and walked back to his group, then turning to face her again, he said smugly, "Make room for at least ten more people. They will be here within a week. Resistance will only get you in more trouble." They left.

***

A New Reality

Inside the house, Grandma broke down, sobbing uncontrollably. "They can't take it all away! Xiao Wen, you won't let them; will you?"

"Mama, the new government has promised a new distribution of everything in China. The country has always looked forward to the day when the tillers of the soil would have their own land to work for themselves. We are an anachronism. We will bend with the change -- or we will break."

"But, how will we live? With no rents, we won't last the year. Your earnings couldn't support us all. Must I sell your sister so we can eat?" She fell, exhausted by her tears, into a chair.

"You can't sell Yili!" Naixin reminded her. "The new laws forbid arranged marriages and concubinage. She is free to choose anyone who will have her" He looked at his sister. "Although, as a 'landlord' you might have a problem finding a match." His sister was older and plain, if not slightly..., well, just say plain. She had long ago planned to never get married. She had thought of becoming a Buddhist nun. Now, that was a lost hope as well; the Communists were against religion of all sorts. She sat next to her mother and they cried together.

For three days, the family didn't talk about it. Every time Naixing brought it up, his mother ran from the room. It came to a head when a large group marched down the road and into their front yard.

"We are here for the redistribution of your house and lands!" they shouted, pounding on the door and looking in through the windows. Naixing opened the door, and the committee walked in and started looking around. There were sixteen people with bundles of clothing in the front yard.

"What are you thinking?" Grandma ran into the room pushing everyone aside. "Who are all those people? There is no room here for all of them! Send them away!"

Two men near the door took her by the arms and forced her out into the front yard. "Everyone out except the committee!" the leader shouted, and briskly ushered out the whole family. "Stay out there! We will determine how much room there is here."

Naixing held his mother by the arm as the committee rifled through the house. The windows on the second floor were thrown open and clothes, lamps, books, and all sorts of furnishings flew out. There was a whoop and a voice called out, "Look at all this stuff! Feudal Pigs!" There was a pause, then out of the same windows came the robes, pictures, and treasures of Gongshi's Grandfather and Great Grandfather. Naixing closed his eyes and held his mother back with all the strength he had left in him, but she broke free and ran into the house.

There was a great deal of yelling and scuffling inside. A window at the back of the house broke open and Grandma came tumbling out, falling into the vegetable garden under the kitchen window. The family ran around the house, finding her dazed and trying to stand.

"Mamma, stay down! Don't try to get up."

A clock and a small table came out of the same window and landed on her shoulder and on her knee. She cried out in pain as her family dragged her away from the house. Her lower lip was cut wide open on the right side and blood was flowing freely from her nose.

"What kind of men are you? My mother is too old to be treated this way!" Naixing yelled.

"Shut up, Landlord! She is only starting to feel the pain that we have known at her hands for years!" More things flew out of the windows and scattered out around the house. "Now, we will measure the house and see how much room there is for everyone. There may even be some room for you." There was a laugh and some rude comments from inside.

Grandma's right eye was getting puffy and a red sack of skin formed below it. She had several cuts around her face and on her arms, and couldn't move her left hand without pain. Naixing picked up a blanket, from one of the heaps of clothing jettisoned from the upper floor, and wrapped it around his mother.

From inside, voices called out measurements of the rooms and hallways. Then, silence.

The head of the committee came out the front door and looked over the group that had come with him. "What is the largest family here?" he asked. They gathered themselves into family groups and each family looked around at the others.

"We are six," one man said, holding his hand up.

"Good, you will take the large room upstairs on the front of the house."

Two other men held up their hands and called out, "We are four!"

"This family will take one of the rooms in the back upstairs," the headman said, pointing. "You will take the other. And this couple will live in the large room in the front of the house, but you will have to share it with everyone else during the day. The small room downstairs will be the office of the Communist Party District Chief, when he comes."

Then, he turned to Naixing and his family, a twisted smile curling across his lips. "Well, I guess there is room for you after all. In the back! But keep your things out of the kitchen. That belongs to everyone in the house."

Grandma's eyes were wide behind the puffing lids. She grabbed Naixing by the arm. "That is the store room! We can't live there! There is no room for us all. We will die!"

The headman sneered at her, "If you don't like that, you can sleep with the rest of the pigs outside!" He turned to the committee and waved his arm. "Let's go!" And they did.

The sixteen newcomers went into the house. In a momentary hushed silence, they looked around at the inside as though they were in a museum.

"Painted walls!"

"Pretty pictures!"

"How clean!"

"This is the way the landlords live! While we lived in sheds, no better than animals! This is what they bought with what they stole from us! This is the life that they stole from us!"

A man ran from the house with saliva streaming from the corner of his mouth, his eyes wide with fury. The veins on the side of his head were bulging and his skin was flushed and sweaty. "You are the landlord scum! This is what you took from us – all my life. You are my enemy!" He careened wildly toward Naixing and his family, stopping only when he tripped and fell to his knees coughing up a mixture of blood and mucous.

His wife ran to him and threw her arm over him, "Lou, Lou, calm yourself. They will be dealt with soon enough." She glared at the family cowering before them. "You will die! They promised us that! You see what you have done! And you will pay for it!" She spit at them and helped her husband back into the house.

Niaxing's wife went around the house and assessed their possessions lying in the yard where they had been thrown. She retrieved several blankets and a duvet, and was walking toward the family when a woman from the house ran out and ripped the items from her arms. "These are not yours! They belong to all the people!" She slapped Naixing's wife and sent her tumbling to the ground. Laughing, the woman went back into the house.

"There are strangers in my house." Grandma said it without emotion.

Throughout the afternoon, various people came out of the house and picked through the things that lay around on the yard. Naixing went around to the back of the house where the side door stood open. He could see the inner door to the kitchen was left wide open. The shelves were empty and the crocks were all opened. The newcomers had taken as much as they could of the oil, the salt, and the rice. The wheat and oats were not yet milled, so most of that remained. He closed the inner door and scooped up the spilled salt and rice. As he went outside, the sun was setting and the noise inside the house was diminishing.

Naixing helped his mother to her feet and led her around to the back door, where she sat in stunned silence on a stack of wood. Then he and his wife circled the house and picked up any clothing, robes, and table linens the others had left. He also picked up the military-dress long and short swords and two commemorative daggers. "At least they won't kill us with these." he muttered to himself. His wife had found one unbroken oil lamp, but no matches. They spread the clothing around on the storage room floor and covered themselves with tablecloths and an oilcloth liner for the table. Before he closed the door, and lost all light, Naixing jammed the swords, still in their scabbards, between the shelving and the wall to block the door into the kitchen. He used the short swords in the same way, to hold closed the outside door. Exhausted and uncomfortable, they passed the night.

Naixing and his family woke to the sounds of the others banging into unfamiliar walls in darkened hallways. They quietly opened the outside door and left immediately for the fields. There was an area on a rise overlooking the fields they had long used for family picnics. On the hill above were six markers where two brothers, and a sister were buried, next to their parents. Beside the sister's grave lay her husband, Wen Fulian. There was also a memorial plaque to Grandma's husband, Zhenli (the Magistrate's son), who had died in the civil war. On the grassy knoll, someone had made a fieldstone fireplace for cooking. There were matches and charcoal and a few supplies. They boiled the rice Naixing had gathered off the storage room floor, and they ate it from a common bowl.

"We will starve," said Grandma.

"We will survive," said Naixing.

"I will glean the fields," said his wife and, taking the children, set off.

Naixing's sister, Yili, cleaned Grandmother's cuts and bruises. "How can people be so heartless?" she wondered aloud.

Naixing started looking over the area and thinking out loud about building a shelter. "I think we could make something out here, away from the house." he said.

"Maybe we should just leave and move up into the mountains." his sister answered.

Naixing's wife and the children came back with a small bucket. "Look what we found!" She held out the bucket, which was half-full of clean rice. "The workers must have taken some rice and hidden it at the edge of the field. There is more!"

"Good! Let's save that for later," Naixin said. "Right now, we should think about where we want to live. I am not sure that we are safe at the house, and Yili thinks we should think about moving up into the mountains. Whatever we choose, we'll have to do it before it gets cold outside again tonight." He looked back at the house. "Oh, no!"

***

A New Justice

A half-dozen figures were coming up the path toward them and the family all stood right where they were, trapped.

"There they are! Landlord pigs! They would kill us in our sleep! Now they will get what is coming to them!"

A man at the head of the advancing party was someone they had never seen before. "You are the family Wen?" he asked, puffing from the climb.

"Yes, we are. This is my mother, whom these people have already abused; my sister, my wife, and these are our two children."

"You are the Teacher Wen?

"Yes, I teach the children in the school west of the village."

The man had finally caught his breath. "I am Sergeant Lee Laoxi of the Peoples Republican Army. I am here to arrest you as landlords and to take you into town for your trials."

"What? We have done nothing wrong! We were the ones thrown out of our house. What are the charges?

"You and your family are landlords! You have stolen everything you ever had from the people. Your crimes are many and you will answer for them. Now come along!"

"Wait!" said one of the men from the house. "What about the swords and knives that they were hiding? They meant to kill us all in our sleep!"

"All of that will come out at their trials. Come on now! The rest of you get back to the house and start your organizing. You are now tillers of your own land and it is your duty to make the land productive as soon as you can. Now go on!"

"Not yet!" screamed a woman running toward the fire. "Look, they have stolen the people's rice again!" She snatched up the bucket and swung it at Yili's head.

Yili ducked the blow and stood by her mother's side. "We didn't steal it. We gleaned it from the fields."

"Liar! Rice so clean? You didn't get that out of those old fields!"

"Bring it along." said the sergeant. "It will all be shown at their trial."

The whole procession moved down the hill and past the house. Various people leaned out of the windows or stood in the yards hurling insults and small rocks at the family as they passed. It was a long walk to the village; one Naixin had walked daily with his son, these past five years. For the others, numb with fear, the journey seemed to take an eternity.

"I am going to have to let you stay in the schoolhouse," Sergeant Lee said. "There won't be any school for a while. Remember, it is officially your prison. If you leave the yard, you can be shot on sight. Do you understand?"

"Yes, thank you!" said Naixing.

"I think they might have killed you back at the farm. You're probably safer out here. Someone will be sent each day with food. You have a pump. Just don't show yourself outside till I come back for you."

"Thank you again, Sergeant. Really, thank you!" called Naixing as the soldier walked off toward town.

The schoolhouse was slightly larger than the living room of the farm house. There was a kang bed in the back room, where the previous teacher had lived. It was a brick structure with a fire box at one end with lids that could be removed to place pots close enough to the fire to cook. The fumes from the fire were drawn through passages between the bricks toward the chimney. At night, it was the only heated area in the building. Hanging on the wall were an old torn oilcloth rain slicker and a tattered quilt. They all crowded into that back room and fell asleep on the floor. Grandma slept on the kang. It had been an exhausting day.

***

The Trial

The Sergeant returned three days later with two soldiers carrying rifles. "Everyone outside!" he shouted as he opened the door, the soldiers standing on either side. The family came, squinting, out into the bright sunlight.

"Thank you for the food, Sergeant!" Naixin began, "We really want to tha ...."

"You eat the same food as everyone else. Today, we will start your trials. Today, an officer will hear the charges against you. He may ask you questions; you may not! When he is done, he will draw up any formal charges and hear your confessions. Admission is your best defense. Forget your arrogant pride and accept the will of the people. You will live in contrition the rest of your life and be thankful for that."

They walked in stony silence into town. The main square was full of people; few faces were familiar, none were friendly. They were again subjected to catcalls and small objects thrown at them. A table was set up at the end of the square and three military men were seated behind it. The family was lined up in front of the table and forced to kneel facing it. A soldier at the side of the table read the charges in high, sing-song imperial Manchurian Chinese accents. The charges were being a landlord family, stealing food from the people, plotting to assassinate citizens, and holding weapons while not in the army.

"Does any one of you deny these charges?" asked the officer in the middle.

Naixing stood up and was immediately knocked down by one of the soldiers.

"You can speak from there," the officer said.

"I am Wen Naixing. I am a teacher in the village school. My wife works in the house for my mother and these are my children. None of us are landlords."

"Are you saying that these two women are the only landlords in your house?" the officer asked, smiling.

"I am saying that my family and I are not landlords. We live by my stipend, which I receive from my appointment as the local teacher."

"Then you say you are a benefactor of the warlord class, the Kuomintang? You might want to choose your friends more carefully! Aren't you related to these two women?"

"Yes, this is my mother and my sister."

"Are you not her only son?

"Yes."

"Then you are all landlords! That is settled."

"Sir, may I answer the charge about the swords?"

"All right, but we already know that you had them. Don't deny that!"

"Yes Sir. The swords and knives were family heirlooms. I only took them back to keep them out of the hands of the people who had taken over our house. We wanted only to keep them from killing us."

"You were keeping them to protect you from these peasants who were assigned to your house by the people's committee? Did you plan to kill them if you thought that they meant you some harm?"

"No sir! I never meant to harm anyone. I just used the swords to hold the doors closed while we slept. See how they are bent by being forced into the shelving? They can't even be pulled out of their scabbards. When we left the house we left them there; we had never planned to use them for anything else."

"I will recommend to the People's Safety Committee that that charge be reconsidered. However, you say that these were heirloom pieces which your family secretly worshiped. These are the relics of imperialism and the subsequent warlord oppression! You will be instructed by the Peoples Safety Committee to renounce such ancestor

worship and to find value in the future of our New China --
to reject this decadence of the past!"

"Sir, may I ...?"

"No! The Wen Family is found guilty of being of the
landlord class and I leave your instruction to your village
People's Safety Committee. This trial is closed"

The three officers stood up and walked away from the
table. Then some one shouted, "Down with the landlord
class!"

Gongshi and his sister were knocked to the ground and
people swarmed over the family.

"Teach the landlord what it feels like to be one of us!"

Gongshi remembered only a great deal of pain and noise in
the moments that followed. The noise faded away into
numbness, but one pain was followed by another, as feet
and fists hit him again and again. At some point, his mind
went limp and all the pains became one. When he regained
consciousness, his mother was leaning over him, crying.
Her face was bloody and dirty. Her clothes were torn and
pulled out of place.

"You must get up!" she was saying. "We are going to go
now."

There were people standing around them, hate-filled
people. He could see they were yelling things at them, but
he couldn't hear anything except a loud ringing in his ears.
Slowly, the noise of the crowd came into his ears in waves,
and he started hearing his mother crying, "Come, we must
go!" She was pulling at Naixin and holding the limp body
of his sister. "Get up, please!" she cried as she kept pulling
at him.

Naixing started to move. Blood dripped from his mouth as
he rose up on one arm. Someone in the crowd kicked him

again and he fell back on his face in the dirt. Gongshi's sister also started to move and softly started crying. His mother pulled the two of them closer and kissed them, rocking on the ground. Again, Naixin rose on his elbow. He spit out some blood and looked around at the crowd. He caught sight of his wife and children and dragged himself toward them. Someone spit at them and insults and jeers filled their ears again.

"All right! That is enough for now!" The sergeant stood over them and waved the crowd back, away from them. "Get up!" he shouted at the family. "You have a long walk ahead of you." With his boot, he shook Grandma and her daughter. "Get up you two! Get used to your pain! It is your new life!" He laughed and shook them again.

The two women stirred and tried to get up. "Oh, what have you done?" Grandma groaned. One eye was closed and blood drooled down the older woman's cheek. She pointed an unsteady hand at the crowd and said, "In your next life, you will know such ..."

At that point, two women jumped on her with renewed punching and kicking that drove her onto her back.

"Enough!" yelled the sergeant. "She will learn to enjoy the pain soon enough." He laughed and pulled the two assailants off of her. "Go on; let me get them back to their prison."

Grandma and Yili dragged themselves up and the family started limping out of the town, toward the schoolhouse.

"You are not my son!" Grandma hissed. Her voice was rough and she lisped through her swollen lips. "What kind of son steps back so quickly when his own mother is attacked by the mob? What kind of son turns his back on his sister when the court calls her a criminal? You have not earned any merit with Buddha today. The kitchen god will ..."

"Oh Mother, stop it! We all were treated badly today. Not one of us did anything to you. I had to protect my wife and children. That was not a bad thing! I stood up for the truth; that is not a bad thing. I defended all of us against false charges."

Naixing paused to catch his breath. He felt a broken rib or two. He couldn't take a full breath. The incline slowed them all down. They marched the rest of the way in silence.

***

Re-education

For two days, they moved as little as possible. The man who brought their rice was not supposed to talk with them at all, but he did.

"I didn't hit any of you. I am telling the truth. Many of us didn't do it. They said you were all bad because you have always taken your portions out of our labor and paid the Emperor his tax before any food went to the peasants. We were supposed to show our contempt for the landlords because they always held us down. I don't know what that means. You have always helped my family. Your school has always been open to our children even though we could not pay. We don't know why they hate you so much. Please forgive me, if you see me in the crowd."

"I know you didn't!" Naixing assured him. "We saw that they had outsiders there to make the people struggle against us. We know all the people in the village and we could see what the officers were doing. I don't understand it either. They have our property; now they want to destroy our family and our souls."

The next morning, a large number of the villagers came up to the schoolhouse. With them were several of the revolutionary cadre, the outsiders who were instructing the villagers on the art of rectification of the reactionary class (i.e., landlords, merchants, intellectuals, and anyone else who had a stake in the power structure before the civil war). The mob was beating on pots and pans and carrying banners written in large characters, 'Struggle Against The Landlord'.

"Naixing," they shouted. "Come out and face your crimes!" The door opened and Naixing stepped out, shielding his eyes against the bright morning light.

Two of the cadre stepped up next to him and hung a sign around his neck; 'LANDLORD ENEMY OF THE PEOPLE'. They kicked at the back of his legs till he dropped to his knees. "Confess your sins, landlord!" they shouted. "Confess your sins to the peasants that you have robbed all of your life."

One of the men from the cadre grabbed hold of Naixin's hair and pulled his head back while he screamed into Naixin's face, spittle and sweat spraying all over Naixin's head. "You have starved the people so you could eat your full! You have watched as these peasants suffered through long droughts and floods. You fanned yourself cool while your neighbors labored in the hot fields. You read your books and sang your songs while these people brought you food and drink like lowly servants! No more! Today you will answer for these crimes!"

Naixing looked fearfully through his tears at the mob of his neighbors and friends -- empty faces, not believing what they were seeing, not understanding what they were saying. "I am sorry!" he pleaded. "Please! I never meant to take anything from you."

"What? Speak up! The people must be able to hear your false confessions!"

"We didn't steal anything. We helped ...."

"Lies!" The man from the cadre yelled in his face. He grabbed Naixin's sleeve and held his hand up high over Naixing's head. "This hand is soft!" he shouted. "You have never shared the work that supported your way of life. You are fat and pampered at the expense of these peasants who stand before you. Beg for their pardon! Plead for your life, for your very life was a gift, forced from them. The people demand revenge!"

Niaxing's lips were trembling and his pants were wet and soiled. "I am sorry for anything like that that I did without knowing it." He wailed.

"Lies! You have lived these lies so long; you don't even know what you are saying. You are not sorry for the injustice of your life! You really believe that they should be peasants and you should be a scholar! They should make the things that you consume? Raise the food that you eat? Starve to death when food is scarce and you eat from the stores that you have withheld from them? Don't you see the hypocrisy of your life? Landlord, you are a criminal! You are a criminal so deeply in your heart that you cannot even understand your own crimes! But you will! Before you die, you will know your crimes against the people."

With that, he shoved Naixing's face into the mud before him. Then, putting a foot squarely in the middle of Naixing's back, the man from the cadre lifted his own arms over his head and called out, "Death to the Landlord Class!" and the people were exhorted to repeat the chant over and over.

"Death to the Landlord Class!" "The Peasants Will Lead the Democratic United Front!" Over and over they yelled these slogans.

"Get up, landlord! Stand and face the people!" they shouted, and drew him up and thrust him forward, stumbling into the crowd. "Show him to the whole village!" they yelled. And the mob turned and marched, with Naixing at the front, down the hill and throughout the village.

Gongshi, his mother, sister, aunt, and Grandma cowered in the shadows inside the schoolhouse. It was late at night when Naixin finally returned home. He was spitting blood and had many marks all over his body. Mama had boiled some water and had prepared bandages for his return. His rib was broken again and he was exhausted by the events of the day.

In the morning, terrified, they again heard the banging of the pots and pans as the villagers came back up the hill to the schoolhouse.

"Oh, no!" Naixing called out. He rolled over against the wall and wept.

***

Retribution

Bang, bang, bang! The noise grew louder and the chants became more rehearsed and more in unison. "Death to the landlord class!" and "The Peasants will lead the Democratic United Front!"

Mama opened the door.

"Wen Furen, come out and face your crimes!" the leader called out.

Mama stepped out into the front yard.

"Not you! The Old Landlord!"

Mama stepped back in through the doorway.

There was a scuffling inside and Grandma was shoved out of the door. The men of the cadre grabbed her by her hair and forced her to walk up in front of the crowd. They kicked the back of her legs and she dropped to her knees on the stone walkway.

"Old Lady, your crimes are more than your son's. You have stolen all that you have from the people. You have always treated them with disrespect. Your husband was an officer in the service of the warlord monster, Chiang. Your generation was active in the suppression of the peasant class. Many have died at your hand. Many died at the hand of the dealers of opium that you supported with your taxes. Those taxes were stolen from the very peasants who stand before you. Even now, you smear your face with paint and ointments. Have you <u>no shame</u>?! You will learn to hate yourself and your life and then you will die. Speak to the people, if you dare!"

She lifted her head and glared at those closest to her. "You would all have died long ago if I had not run the farm so that you could eat. You should thank me...."

A boot kicked her on the cheek and she fell on her side in the mud, off the side of the path. The mob set on her without any provocation from the cadre. They kept it up till she lay still, like a rag doll.

"Get some water!" the leader of the cadre said. A bucket was pumped full from the well and poured over her head. She opened her eyes and spit out some blood.

"Stand up, Old Hag!" One of the cadre men kicked her, while the other dragged her to her feet and hung a sign around her neck that read, 'Landlord Enemy of the People!' "Your trial is just begun!" he screamed into her face. She tried to spit at him, but he twisted her head away and drove a fist into the back of her rib cage. "She still doesn't understand her crimes!" he called out in mock surprise. "Shall we teach her?"

The mob yelled, "Yes! Let's teach her!"

Some thick sticks were gathered and the villagers took turns striking her when she refused to admit the charges against her. They railed against her all afternoon till she could no longer stand. When her bruised and bloody legs finally gave out, she was tied to a chair. When they couldn't revive her with water, they left her there, tied to the chair. "Do not take her inside tonight." they warned the family. "We'd better find her right where she is in the morning!" And they left.

The sound of the pots and pans came earlier the next morning. Grandma tried to move, but the ropes were tied too well and she was too weak to move very much.

"Let's see how much the old hag remembers!" called out the cadre leader. "What are your crimes, old lady?"

Grandma couldn't make much of a sound. They threw cold water on her and tried to get her to stand, still tied to the chair. She fell backwards, knocking her head on the stones in the path.

"Looks like she needs a walk to wake her up!" called out one of the group and they took off the ropes. "Stand up, you old hag!"

She tried but was not steady. "Maybe she needs some help!" someone said, thrusting a long pole between her feet and lifting it up between her legs. Ready hands lifted up both ends of the pole and they jerked it back and forth violently. "Let's walk!"

The procession moved on down the hill to the village. That night, a cart came up the hill and dumped Grandma's body in the front yard. Yili ran out and lay across her mother, sobbing violently. Naixing, his wife and children huddled in the back room. In the morning, Naixing's wife came in and wakened him to tell him that his sister had hung herself from the tree in the front yard during the night.

The procession, with its pots and pans, came again, back up the hill. But this time, it stopped at the scene they found in the front yard. There was a moment of quiet, and then the leader of the cadre said, "Somebody bury these two." After a while, shoveling could be heard in the front yard and then muttered conversation.

***

Relocation

"Wen Naixing, come out!" a voice shouted. He managed to get to his feet and stumbled out the front door. He glanced at the newly filled graves and then at the group standing on either side of the path. "The village chairmen will interview you today," the cadre leader said. The procession then walked noisily back into town.

Wen Gongshi didn't see his father for many days. When he did return, he was a ghostly man, broken in body and sprit; compliant and submissive to every command. The family was 'sent down' -- away from the village and the school house -- to a very rural village in the south. They were not allowed to use their name, Wen, but were known as 'the landlords'. The whole family worked in the fields, planting, weeding, picking off insects, and watering the crops. Everyone they met knew them only as the landlords and had no meaningful conversation with them. The family was allowed to live, but they were the last to eat, the last to rest, blamed for every bad turn of the weather, and were never to be praised, under any circumstance.

During the Great Leap Forward of 1959, crops were planted more tightly together to get a higher yield; many such experiments ended in failure, but the official reports were exaggerated to claim even higher yields than promised. The reality, however, never met the promises; food was not just scarce; it was not there. The people harvested what they could, but it was never enough. Anything that looked like grain was included in the figures for the provincial tax. Phony bookkeeping made it look like production quotas were being met. In actual fact, they were only about two-thirds of the amount needed to pay China's debt to Russia. The people ate roots, until they had killed off all the plants. They ate the dogs and cats and rats, and any bug that they could find. They ate bark until most of the trees died. They ate dirt until it clogged their intestines and they died. In the end, they cannibalized each other and their babies. During 1959 and 1960, 30,000,000 peasants and "counter revolutionaries" were starved to death. In the end, bodies littered the fields and road sides. No one was left to bury them; no dogs or rats were left to eat them.

Wen Gongshi saw his mother and sister die with bloated stomachs and pus-filled sores. His father was a walking bag of bones; and still they persecuted him. Naixing's last day was spent in a field holding up a long pole with a rag on the end; he was literally a scare crow, protecting any seed still left in the fields. His guard was in no better health but was determined to keep 'the landlord' and his son busy in the fields, chasing away the birds. When Naixing finally dropped, face down, in an irrigation ditch, Gongshi ran. He ran as hard as his skinny fifteen-year-old legs would carry him -- away from the guard who stumbled across the field after him. He ran on joints that threatened to fail him on every furrow in the field. At last, the field ended at a stream and he fell in. Thrashing about in the water, his arms landed on top of a half submerged tree that was floating with the current.

Gongshi laid his cheek against the rotting bark, in a crotch between two broken branches, and they floated together down the stream. As he floated along, he started drinking the water and bits of bark floated into his mouth. Decayed as they were, they were easy to chew and they filled him. Under the bark were white worms or grubs; and he ate all he could. The river merged with a larger river and between the rest and the food, Gongshi grew stronger.

***

A New Life

After several days, the river flowed into the largest river Gongshi had ever seen. He avoided people and stayed in the shallows by night. One day, he saw some men cutting bamboo. They bundled it up along the bank and then got some more. When several bundles were tied together, they made a sizeable raft. The men made a fire and boiled water with rice in one pot, and parboiled fish in another. The fish was laid on the rice, in bowls made out of split bamboo sections, and they sat down for dinner.

Gongshi swam along the side of the raft to a point where he could reach between the bundles. He snatched one of the bowls and ate it greedily.

The man above on the raft jumped to his feet. "What the ...?"

His friends across the raft laughed and said, "Must be a rat!"
"Damned big rat!" he said. He grabbed a stout bamboo pole and jabbed it at the hole where his meal had gone. Gongshi shoved the bowl back through the hole.

"Looks like he wants seconds!" They were doubled over with laughter. The man refilled the bowl and watched as a hand reached up and took it again. "That is one hungry rat!"

An arm came over the side and caught Wen by his waist sash and pants. "Come here, Rat."

And that became his name.

"Rat" became their mascot and helped them bundle the bamboo and bind it into rafts. When several rafts were made and tied together, the whole group climbed on, and poled them out into the open water beyond the marshes.

The open sea was something "the rat" had never seen before. He had an initial fear when he could not see the shoreline too clearly. But the men soon stopped rowing away from the shore and all laid down on the raft and went to sleep. The hot sun and gentle rocking soon put Wen to sleep as well. He woke with a start at the sound of a ship's horn and saw a great wall of the ship next to the raft.

The men on the raft started talking with the men on the ship in a language Wen could not understand. They seemed to be arguing, but in the end, several men came down in a boat and gave the leader a packet full of money. The raft men took five large pieces of bamboo and made a small raft to get back to the shore. Rope lines came down from the ship, and the men from the ship tied off the rafts, which were then pulled one-by-one onto the ship. The raft men talked again with the men in the boat, and then explained to Gongshi that he could go with the ship if he wanted to. He would be well fed. They all encouraged him to go, and in the end, he did.

"He had been at sea almost twenty years when we met in 1978, on that fantail of the cargo ship going from Japan to China. He told me about his China – the land of his childhood memories. He also gave me a copy of a book that he had bought in England. It was a scholarly history of the civil war in China which contained his father's 'confession' to the village chairman, supposedly detailing the family's history of guilt by involvement in imperialism, militarism, and landlordism.

Wen Gongshi could not read English with any facility. So, during the passage to China, on evenings when he was not on watch or working in the machine shop, he would sit with me while I read from the book. He would often interject his own memories of his family history, as it was told to him at home."

***
The Histories

I glanced around at the passengers who had stayed to hear Wen's story and noted the time. It was late, but there were still questions and I could see how this could last well into the night. I looked over at the Captain and apologized that I might have taken too much of his time.

"No, not really!" Captain Eller replied. "I think I will be able to write-off the unscheduled port call as a humanitarian event, like rescuing a sailor in distress. But, this story of your friend and his family in China.... That has possibilities. How would you like to continue this tale till we get to Honolulu?"

We finally agreed I would 'work my passage' by giving extemporaneous lectures on Wen's family in the main lounge each evening for those who were interested. Even though Wen's book, detailing his family history, had been confiscated from me in China, I freely lectured on all that I could remember, and embroidered the rest as best as I could.

Map of Taiping Rebellion

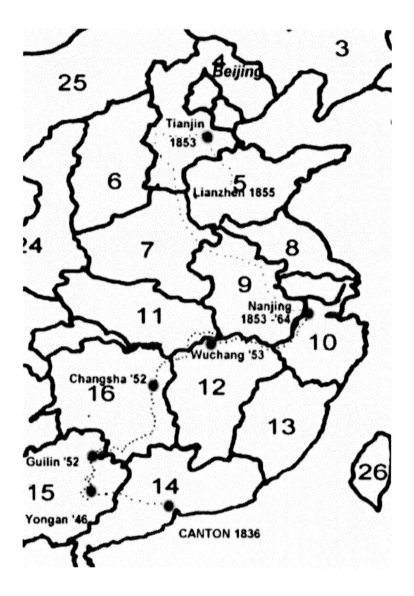

Great Grandfather, Wen Fulian

Part 1 - The Mud Scholar

***

Origins

"Wen Fulian, the unlikely founder of the family linage, was born in 1832, the third son of a peasant who worked the land on a large estate in the mountains of southern Shaanxi Province. One day, the landlord passed by. Normally he would not have noticed the small boy squatting by the side of the road; children in the country seldom used anything we would know as a toilet. But this day, the landlord caught a glimpse of his own name scratched in the dirt in front of the boy. It so surprised him that he stopped his horse and dismounted to have a closer look. Fulian was afraid and reached out to cover the marks in the dirt.

"No! Stop!" the landlord said. The poor boy stood, afraid, and at the same time curious – he had never spoken to any adult other than his own parents. "What is this? Did you write this?" the landlord asked. Peasant children did not write, at least not any that the landlord knew. "Did you really do this?" Fulian fixed his stare somewhere between the characters and his feet. "Here, take this stick and do it again." The boy took the stick and methodically made the scratches in the dirt just under the others.

The landlord snatched up Fulian, set him on his horse, and rode up to the house above the road. As they passed the entrance, Fulian pointed to the signpost by the gate where the landlord's name was written. The man laughed and went on up to the house. He set the boy on a stool next to a table in the yard. "You wait here!" he said and excitedly ran into the house. He was back in a short time with a sheet of paper, a brush, and an inkpot.

"All right then, watch me." He picked up the brush and dipped it into the ink, holding it vertically between his thumb and the tips of his fingers. With a deft flick of his wrist, he shook off the excess ink into the pot. His left hand drew back his right sleeve and then held down the sheet of paper. Magically, the pen touched the paper and a dance began. The lines and dots, the practiced hooks and daubs. Fulian was mesmerized. Each element found its place and the familiar faces of the characters emerged like old friends.

"Would you like to learn how to do that?" the landlord asked. Fulian reached for the brush. "No! Wait! Writing is not a game! If you would learn to write, you will be expected to do much! First, you will learn to prepare yourself; writing is an honor and an obligation. You must first remove the dirt of the fields. Do that, and come back here in the morning."

The next day, Fulian came to the house with clean hands, but little else. When the landlord came out, he laughed at the boy's appearance, and called to his first wife, "Lianmei, come clean him up and get him something to wear. He should at least look like a scholar."

Fulian was marched to the back of the house where he was brusquely stripped and set in a laundry tub used earlier for the clothes. Methodically every inch of the rough-cut peasant child was burnished into the semblance of a student scholar. As Fulian stood shivering in the morning air, Lianmei rummaged through the cases of old clothes her own boys had worn. Presently, he was taken back to the front of the house, looking new and determined.

The third son of the landlord came out of the house and watched warily as his father showed the boy how to hold the brush and how to make several basic strokes. "Do that till you have filled the page. " he said, and turned to his son. "Bring out your writing kit and let's see if you can teach Fulian how to do it." Third son was not amused.

If the new boy were to be adopted, the three sons would lose part of their inheritance. Under Confucian law and custom, a father's estate was equally divided between each of his sons; there was no primogenitor, though respect always went up, toward the elder. In this way no one son could waste away the family fortune, or take away from his brothers' opportunities to determine their own futures through education, investment, or bribes. One fourth is less than one third, and that prospect was the first thing the third son thought of. The only way to great wealth, without physical work, was either by education and appointment to an office, or through success in the rising merchant class through great cunning. But the landlord's sons had all become lazy in their studies and work; they probably would have to survive on their inheritance. The father rented the land but made his money in trade, selling what the peasants raised on his land or what was made in his shops. He was not a school-educated man, but he was driven to work, he was guided by Confucian principles, and he liked to read the histories. Not so with his sons.

Later in the day, Fulian's own mother was amazed to see him return with the landlord. He scrambled down off of the horse and ran to her with papers flapping. "See what I did!" he cried, holding the papers out for her to look at.

"The boy will come to live at the house," the landlord said. "He will not work in the fields as long as he is a serious student. And your rent will be less while he is away. Come, boy!"

***

Basics

The work at the house was harder than the play he was accustomed to. But once or twice a week, the landlord would take down the writing table and rub an ink stone with a black stick of ink and water. Then Xiao Wen would learn to make the characters, each one within a square, almost always starting at the top left and ending with the line across the bottom. The order of the strokes was as important to the form as rhythm is to music. Each character was like a face; subtle differences changed the meaning. Quickly, Fulian learned to recognize each new character and its meaning as he would the face and moods of an old friend.

Originally, the crude characters depicted physical things; birds, fish, numbers, night, and day. Shaman priests would use the characters to divine the weather or coming events, like the outcome of wars or the guilt or innocence of an accused. Developed over a history of 5,000 years, some characters still maintained vestiges of their original forms. As the science of writing progressed, and as the instruments changed, the forms were modified; but still, many texts that are 3,000 years old can be read by scholars today.

Spoken Chinese changed from place to place, as local accents reflected something of the nature of the people. Sometimes, the spoken language became different enough from that of another area that it was called a separate dialect. But the consistency of the written form helped maintain a continuity of the grammar and usage, so that writing itself held the country together.

Each character has its own sound, usually a single syllable. But there are only a limited number of single syllable sounds, so four accents were added to differentiate one homophone from another. Beyond that, the meaning of a spoken word was identified by the context in which it was used, (as we can tell 'to' from 'two' or 'too').

Varietal forms of single characters, called radicals, were combined to form new characters. For example, the word 'good' is represented by combining a variation of the character "nu' (female) with a variation of the character 'zi' (child) to form a new, single character, which has the sound 'hao'.

Modern dictionaries list characters by the number of strokes in their 'underlying radical'. The new character will be listed in a subsection, containing characters which require the same number of additional strokes. There is no order of presentation and each new character must be found by sight recognition.

***

Application

Wen Fulian's first lessons began on the day after his scrubbing and continued for the next ten years. The dabs and drips of his early works soon, with practice, became the elegant strokes which formed the radicals that determined the meaning and sound variations of each character. From the 214 basic radicals, representing things and actions to more complex concepts and relations, 80,000 characters could be formed. With the words came the ideas and the theories and the histories that were Chinese traditional education. The wealth of learning from over 5,000 years came to Fulian through these classics.

Lao Tzu, "the old one" (near 500 BC) wrote the Tao Te Ching, which spelled out the Daoist Way and its expression; but the words are vague and the meanings can only really be learned at the foot of a master. For example: 'The emptiness of a bowl is the important thing; without it, it could not hold anything.' 'The height of anything starts at its base.' 'The good of anything is measured by its opposite.' 'Nature is of two natures; and, both are necessary for there to be meaning.' 'Yield to the mysteries and forces of nature.' It is an old view of life, dating from the stone ages, which saw spirits in every physical thing; honoring the spirits of the dead became the foundation for ancestor worship.

At about that same time, Confucius was a traveling scholar who earned his living as an advisor to the warring Dukes who ruled the remains of the second empire, and as a teacher to the scholars who would serve the Dukes when he moved on. Confucius believed that each man owed a duty to his fellow man and to the state, and that each man's innate honor and virtue should be enough to motivate him to do his duty as administrator, teacher, or in any other assignment. Even the Emperor, Confucius taught, must prove he deserved the Mandate of Heaven or he would lose it. Floods, crop failures, plagues, or corruption were evidence of imperial failings that could allow a man of "higher virtue" to rise to Emperor and justified the ending of a genetic dynasty.

In order to become a scholar, according to Confucius, an educated man had to know the histories, which recorded the successes and failures of the society and the events that led to both the successes and failures. Only by knowing the histories could a man be expected to lead the nation. The more thorough this knowledge, the higher degree and class rank at graduation, the better able a man was to participate in the government and consequently, the more authority and responsibility he was given. The scholar would also have to learn and participate in all the rituals which showed respect to other scholars and which bound them all together. Of course, Confucius' teachings were addressed to the upper levels of a society, to those who could get an education and could rise to the occasion. But the system of learning, examinations, and appointments that resulted from his teachings became the model for the bureaucracy during the following two thousand years, through all the changes in succeeding empires and invasions.

The histories were rooted in the oral traditions of Paleolithic China. Actual writing began as symbols, drawn for Shaman divination, using a stylus on bones, shells, and bamboo strips in the earliest Shang dynasty (1523-1027 B.C.). The script of that period was the forerunner to modern Chinese script, but it was more curved and idiographic. Use of the brush pen came later, and changed the look to what we are familiar with today.

The Chunqin, or Spring and Autumn Chronicles, described the history of the state of Lu (722–481 B.C.), which was ruled by the Zhou dynasty (1027-221 B.C.). Later, the History of the Warring States (403-221 B.C.) covered the beginnings of the Qin dynasty, the first Empire to rule all of known China. Then, as ambitions grew and collapsed, The Three Kingdoms period (220-265 A.D.) recalled the "chivalry" of that period, much as we think of the Crusades in the West.

***

Other Lessons

Wen Fulian the student usually had to yield to Wen Fulian the household servant. There were chores around the big house and in the many out-buildings scattered throughout the landlord's holdings. Sometimes there were seedlings to set out for planting by those who worked the fields, or crops to be harvested before they rotted in the fields. There were never enough hands for all the work, but whatever the crop, the produce had to be stored, processed, or taken to market before it could spoil. There was, for example, a wine-making operation to ferment fruits and grains into jars of liquor. There were drying sheds for straw and tobacco and smoke houses for meats, as well as a mill for grinding and malting soy milk into tofu, (which, literally, in English, means decayed soy).

On one of those days that Fulian liked best, he and the landlord took a cart filled with produce to town. The water buffalo was hitched to the long cart, and when it was loaded with that day's produce, the owner would come out and look over the list that Fulian had prepared and checked off. Then they would clop off down the road and the old man would talk on whatever subject he had chosen for the trip. This day, it was one of the histories of the Warring States, with an analysis of how different things would have been if they had listened to Confucius. But today's trip would have a different lesson.

As the buffalo slowed on an upgrade in the road, Fulian noticed someone in a bright yellow robe sitting on a large pile of rocks ahead of them, off the side of the road. Beyond him, three men were walking toward them, coming from town. They were loud and were singing and laughing. When they drew near the figure on the rock, they stopped and said something to him. The small man in the yellow robe stood and bowed to them with his hands pressed palm-to-palm in front of him. Then the three rushed toward him! The one on the right was swinging a box of tools in a menacing way. But when they got to a point about three feet in front of the robed man, he stepped forward. His left foot was planted firmly on the large rock behind him and his right foot flew up into the center of the man's chest. At the same time, the robed man grabbed each of the outer men by their sleeves and pulled them forward, then around behind him. All three fell in total disarray among the rocks. The man in the yellow robe then bounded up to the road and stood right in front of the cart, smiling broadly.

"Would you like a ride to town?" the landlord asked. The man in the robe jumped up onto the cart as it passed the men and picked up speed on the downward slope that followed.

"Thank you," he said, drawing a string of beads from his sleeve, which served as a pocket as well. "I should not be pleased with that." He nodded back toward the rocks.

"It looked to me as though you had no choice!" the landlord said, looking back at the three men, who by this time were fighting and pushing each other on the roadside.

"True, but I have earned no merit in the eyes of Buddha. I am too proud of self and too far from the middle way. I must journey to seek enlightenment and non-self."

"Who is Buddha?" Fulian asked, for he had no idea what the man had just said.

"Buddha is the enlightened one!" the man replied. "Buddha showed us the middle way to salvation from the suffering of this life. The Great Buddha has perfect knowledge of Dharma in this world. Through his teachings, we learn to act in conformity with Dharma. Dharma is the way of life, and to oppose Dharma is to fight reality; this is what causes suffering. We must learn to float in Dharma as you would in a raging river -- ride the flow over the obstacles and not into them."

"These are Four Noble Truths," the man continued. "Life is suffering, and the three causes of suffering are grasping for what you want, avoiding what you fear, and not understanding your life. The cessation of suffering comes only from learning to let go. And letting go can be done by following the eightfold path."

"But, where is the Eightfold path?" Fulian asked. The monk laughed and rolled his eyes.

"Oh, the eightfold path is within your grasp. It is the way to live that all men may choose. That is - right view, right intention, right speech, right action, right livelihood, right effort, right mindfulness, and right concentration. A Buddhist lives in these ways."

The landlord stopped the cart at the side of the road, overlooking a valley. Below was the town, but the road ahead was long and led back and forth down the slope. "I think this is where you get off!" the landlord said to the monk, pointing down the hill.

"But wait," Fulian cried. "How will I know which is the right way?"

The monk jumped down and turned back toward the boy with a smile. "How would I know?" he laughed. "I am just a student myself!" And he started off down the hill.

The landlord drove the buffalo on down the road, then looked into Wen's wondering eyes. "That was a Buddhist Monk," he said. "They live their lives searching like that. They have more lists than you can imagine. There are sixteen of this and twenty-four of that and no end of things they list. They came from India, over the western mountains -- and they could just as well go back!"

"What kind of work do they do?" Fulian asked.

"Nothing! They aren't supposed to do anything. They run around with a bowl to beg their food, and people give them free food so they can earn 'merit' toward some next life. They think that one life is not enough and that they will come back as a snake or a bird if they are bad -- or as a noble or a priest if they are good. He can't own anything other than his bowl, his robe, and his beads. He's a waste of time!"

"But what if he is right?" Fulian asked.

"When we get back, you can start copying the Analects. Confucius will help you know right! And, in the end, you'll be a useful and productive man in the real world."

Part 2 - The Village Scholar

***

Village Life

The village of Xiaohexi lay along the banks of the Mingshue River, which cascaded out of the mountains to the north and slowed to form a wide, clear lake in the valley below. Further south, the lake became a river again and meandered on for twenty-four kilometers before joining its blue-green waters into the great Han River. The Han flowed southeast to Wuchang, about five-hundred kilometers away, where it joined the Yangtze.

To Fulain, this was the wide world. Many buildings lined the street, which was tiled over with stones worn flat with the passage of time, carts, and weather. Strange people looked out of glass windows, under painted shutters that were hinged at the top and were propped open with sticks.

Men, in town, wore a long grey cotton smock, called a 'sam', with wide-cut sleeves that buttoned with string loops at the right shoulder, and black pants called 'fu' that tied below the knee to hold up white cotton socks. Their shoes were black cotton uppers sown to woven straw soles filled with sheets of paper, often as not torn from a Bible that passing missionaries had left. On their heads, they wore black caps with a braided queue running down their backs; these were the merchants.

Other men, in long pants and opened shirts, with their hair loose in the wind, were coolies (literally, cruel labor). Sometimes, they would also wear an under-jacket of loosely woven rice straw fibers that formed a net to keep their shirt from sticking to their chest. The shoulder area of the under jacket was woven extra thick, with indigo-dyed cotton or hemp as a pad for a carry-pole. The pole was usually made of bamboo, about two inches in diameter and six feet long. The ends of the pole were notched to catch a rope, from which hung baskets of produce or packages or children -- whatever had to be carried.

Younger Han women also wore the Manchu style samfu, but more often in coordinated silk sets of pastel colors. Some of the girls, from rich families, had bound feet and had to be carried by coolies from place to place in a sedan chair. Their maids ran alongside; they had large unbound feet and less colorful samfus. The binding of feet was actually a Han Chinese custom, dating from the Ming Dynasty; the Manchurian women never did it. Older Hakka women, like Wen's mother, wore the darker colored samfus, sometimes made from wool, with a short working apron made of woven hemp that was black on the bottom and brown on the top.

Wen Fulian had no shoes and wore only homespun pants, tied at the waste, and an overlapping shirt which he held closed with a sash belt. His head was shaved in front and his hair was drawn into the long queue-type braid. The queue was the style of the Manchurian tribes when they lived in Manchuria; the style became mandatory for every man when they conquered China.

In town, Wen Fulian was regarded as a farm laborer. But he knew there was a larger world that most farm laborers would never know, save the few who would make their way to the sea and take the voyage to "The Gold Mountain" called America.

Wen's thoughts were interrupted when a man came across the street toward them, calling, "Lao Gai! Lao Gai! Long time no see!"

The landlord called back "Master Lu, too long! Have you eaten?"

"Yes, but I would like a nice tea, if my wealthy merchant friend would buy it," the man answered, joining them. Wen surmised from the landlord's calling him 'Master Lu' that the man was a teacher. The three went to an open area next to a hotel where several tables and chairs were set about under tattered sun shades made of painted sheets on bamboo poles. The crossed poles were lashed to a center pole that creaked whenever a gust of wind moved them.

"Master Lu, this is Wen Xueshang. He works for me and is my student."

"Oh! Now you are a teacher as well? Let me see; Xiao Wen, can you write your name?" the man asked. Fulian picked up a feather and wrote his name in the dust on the table. "And do you know who the new Emperor is?" Fulian looked puzzled. Master Lu laughed and patted him on the back. "All right then, there is always something more to learn, isn't there?!"

"Have you thought of sending him to school?" Lu asked the landlord. "I have a class here at the temple and we have lots of room! Boys his age are already studying for the prefectural examinations. Last year one of our boys passed that test to become a Shengyuan (a government-sponsored student). If Xiao Wen studies very seriously, he may pass the provincial examination and become a Juren (a presented scholar) and get an appointment. In any event, he will have a life in the gentry which others will envy."
The landlord, Gai, sat looking pensively at his tea. "How much do you charge for a year of school?" he asked at last. Fulian stopped breathing as he caught the implication of the question.

Master Lu looked over at Fulian. "Have you learned the Rituals of Zhou? I fear how much we forget of our old ways. Why don't you let me work with him for a week or so. Then, next time you are in town, I'll let you know how much of a scholar we have here."

***

A Scholar's Life

While the men talked of his own future, Fulian's eyes glazed over and he tried to imagine the path which had just been opened for him. The two men, who sat before him, represented the two highest callings in China – agriculture and scholarship. For a Han Chinese, these were the paths. There was always a need for food, so the path of agriculture, with long years of hard work and good planning, could enable a man to amass a large estate and found a large family. On the other hand, the pathway of scholarship could lead to high governmental office and untold power and wealth.

The rest of the day for Fulian was a blur of unloading the cart and picking up supplies for the farm. But when Lao Gai, the landlord, headed the cart back up the hill to leave the village, Fulian and Master Lu walked the other direction, toward the old Daoist temple behind the town.

Wen followed Master Lu up a stone-step path, behind the buildings of the town, to the schoolhouse. When it was built, in the Ming Dynasty, the town was much smaller and the temple stood further away. The old slate roof still swooped up at the corners, but now sagged, more from age than design. A wall in the back had collapsed many years ago, but the roof still stood like an umbrella over the remains of the Chamber of Eternal Perfection. Much like the Daoist religion itself, perfection had not weathered well under the Manchurian reforms.

"Boys, this is Wen Fulian," Master Lu said. "He has come to us from one of the farms in the hills. He is not from an extended family, but he will become a member of our family here. You will have to help him learn and understand our ways, but I think you will find he has knowledge of things which will be of benefit to you as well. So, show him where we sleep and you may prepare the evening meal."

Fulian followed the boys to a back room where mats were lined up along a wall. Some clothing hung on pegs over the mats and baskets of smaller things sat next to the head of each mat. In the corner was a stack of unused mats; one was dragged down and he lined it up next to the last in line.

"No, no!" someone called out. Each boy who was younger than Fulian went to his mat, and one by one, they dragged their mat over one space. Then Fulian's mat was placed in its order by age. One of the younger boys brought a basket from a stack in the corner and set it next to the head of Fulian's mat.

"Let's make dinner!" the oldest boy said, and they all filed down to the master's room. They stopped at the doorway and knocked.

"Come in," a voice came from a back room that served as a closet and toilet. The boys entered the main room, which was used both as a bedroom and the kitchen. As the younger boys got out the pots, the older ones lit the fire in the stove end of the kang. At night, the master's bed would be made up on top of the kang, as it would be the only heated part of the building. But, for now, the fire which would heat it would be used to cook dinner. They put two pots of water over the holes to boil. Soon a mixture of soaked grains was added to the boiling water in one pot, while vegetables cooked in the other. Each boy got a bowl and two kuaizi (chopsticks) from a can on the shelf. When the food was finished cooking, they served the master first, then themselves, and returned to their own room.

As the boys ate, they asked Fulian about life on the farm; what were his duties, who were his kinsmen, what gods did they worship. Fulian, in his turn, was curious about them and learned that almost all of them belonged to one large, extended family. They all knew each other from birth and knew their place within the family structure. They all had the same great ancestor and all paid homage in the same great hall to the intervening ancestors.

To the younger boys, such traditions were a bother; but the older ones took the whole issue of ancestor worship as a much more serious business. They would have to dress and parade to funerals as their fathers did when older clan members died and were buried. In time, they would have to make the offerings and declarations at those funerals. The honor of the family gave them face, and they were in the school to protect and advance the good of the family. "How," thought Fulian, "can I compete with them?"

The boys woke up very early. Even on the farm, Fulian had not gotten out of bed before there was a trace of light in the eastern sky! He rubbed his eyes. The others were gathering their things together and going out into the yard, so he followed. By the light of the waning moon and some faint stars, Fulian could see that the boys were lining up at an outhouse and then running to the pump to splash cold water on their faces and bodies before dressing. They were wearing small pants under their fus and white socks like the merchants wore with straw sandals. Over the rest, they put on a sam and a skullcap. Fulian had only his farm clothes; no shoes or socks or underpants. He felt even more out of place, but fell in line to the outhouse. Under the squat toilet was a bucket; a local farmer would come by later in the day to pick up the night soil to be used as fertilizer.

Class work began early, after breakfast and by the first light of dawn, in the great hall. Each student sat on his folded legs and copied from a separate text. Throughout the morning, each one would be called to the master's desk to review the work he had done, and have a short discussion of the meaning and sound of the new characters that the student had just copied. Late in the morning, the students' completed pages were laid out in the sun to dry. The ink bottles were stopped and the brushes cleaned and dried. It was time for lunch.

In the middle of the afternoon, the students took a break for tea (actually just hot water flavored with some beach tree bark strips and bread from the local bakery; the baker paid his son's tuition in bread). Master Lu called Fulian out to the front of the building to receive a package. Before leaving town, the landlord had ordered a set of student's clothing for Fulian. Running to the back yard, Fulian took off his shirt and pants and washed in the cold water from the pump. He returned to the classroom in his new clothes, and everyone cheered and gathered around him to touch the new clothes and complement him on how nice he looked. "Hao! Hao! Back to your writing now," Master Lu said at last.

The straw shoes were uncomfortably tight and the socks kept falling out of the pants and gathering around his ankles, but nothing could take the smile off Fulian's face that afternoon. Before dinner, he went out to the pump to wash his old shirt and pants and hung them out to dry. He took off the samfu, shoes, and stockings so they wouldn't get wet. He left the small white pants on, due to a newly acquired modesty, and also because he liked them -- so light and tied in place.

Dinner was the same, that night and every night. By day, Fulian was given many of the same old texts he had copied at the farm. Only occasionally did he get a character wrong, but it meant his page had a blotch on it; there was no way to remove the ink once it was on the page. To fix it, he had to recopy the page anew, and that was what he did, often more than once. Master Lu was compassionate in his review of Fulian's work and his comments were encouraging. The teacher's understanding of the text and knowledge of every book gave the students a deep-seated respect for him.

Two weeks passed before the landlord came back to town. He stood outside, looking at Fulian at his desk – a real student among other students. When Fulian caught sight of him, he stood and bowed his head with a slight smile.

***
Spring Break

The winter passed in fleece boot socks, wooden sandals, and a heaver weight sam added over the samfu. The classroom was cold, but not cold enough to freeze the water at the pump. The mountains in the north and east formed a bowl that held the heat of the winter sun, while the mountains to the west sheltered the valley from any heavy snows. The boys would go out into the woods for firewood, and to burn off some youthful energy by throwing snow at passing squirrels, but throughout it all, the boys' page copying went on. The copied pages were collected and bound into books, to be sold for added income for the school.

Spring planting season required some of the boys to return home to actually work, while others used 'helping the family with planting' as an excuse, just to get back to the comforts of home. For Fulian, it was the former. Each year, the crops had to be set out, the irrigation systems repaired and expanded. New fields were made by building low walls from stone, mud, and straw to terrace the slopes further up the foothills. Then the water retention basins high in the hills were repaired with more stones and gravel. The loose rock walls were built, one stone at a time, across the natural cascade of water from the mountains to form small basins. More rocks and baskets of gravel were dropped on the upper side of the dam, and as the base was enlarged, they raised the lip by adding another rung of large stones to the rim. Over many years, the dam had raised the level of the lake so it could contain almost all of the rainfall and melted snow that fell in the mountains in the upper elevations. Then, through the year, a reliable flow would filter out through the rocks and gravel to feed the irrigation system in the terraced fields below.

One day, Fulian stood in the doorway of the owner's house and looked out, remembering all of the repairs to the broken irrigation ditches and putting back all of the stones that had fallen out of the terrace walls. Done was the early spring plowing, with the single blade dragged behind a water buffalo through a fine ice sheet over the brown muck. Now, through the morning mist on the terraced slopes, he could see a tinge of green over the mud. The sown rice had sprouted into new rice shoots that had been gathered and replanted in close rows. Now Fulian was ready for his other life. He had had his last hot bath for a while. His hair was plaited, his forehead shaved, and the skullcap pinned in place. His new samfu and straw sandals felt right and familiar. It was time to go back to school.

The long cart, overloaded with things to go to town, was in the yard. Gai Xiansheng, the landlord and ever the teacher, was going over the list of goods with a new boy in a slightly irritated voice. He looked up with a smile as Fulian approached, and winked.

"Oh, here is our honored passenger!" he said. The new boy dropped his eyes, respectfully, and took a step back.

Fulian was almost ready to accept the deference, but turned to Lao Gai and said, "I am in your debt forever; I am your student always."

Gai smiled and motioned for Fulian to climb up onto the bench seat at the front of the cart, then climbed on behind him. The new boy climbed up on the load and they set off for town.

In town, Fulian soon found his classmates and excused himself to be with them, rather than unload the cart. He had to take his things back up to the school, but the rest of the day he would use to catch up on what everyone else had done during the break and what news there was of the outside world.

***

The World Outside

Newspapers came up the Han River slowly. Though Wuchang was only 500 km to the south, it was 1500 km on the river -- and against the current. The opium war had dominated the news for the past eleven years. World views held by the Chinese Empire were at odds with those of the British Empire. The vast market that was China to the English was the last bastion of civilization to the Chinese. The Chinese didn't want anything from the West and had long ago closed their ports to sea trade. But the Portuguese had opened trade in Macao and Guangzhou, and were soon joined by the Spanish, French, English, and Germans. Some opium was smuggled in through the ports (under penalty of death), but most came in over the land routes from India. By the time Fulian was born, the British had turned the trickle into a flood, with imports of 1,400 tons per year. Opium was the poison of choice for China, the "Sick Old Man of Asia".

The problem came to a head in March of 1839. The Daoguang Emperor, Minning, appointed Minister Lin Zexu to stop the opium trade and punish those involved. With the full authority of the Emperor, Lin Zexu went to Guangzhou and rounded up and executed large numbers of the ministers, tax and duty inspectors, and tradesmen who were involved. Foreign nationals were blockaded from their ships and held hostage in their hotels. Lin Zexu then ordered all opium confiscated.

The foreign nationals refused and the blockade continued until a deal was struck with the British Minister of Trade, Charles Elliot. He had all of the foreign opium signed over to him, in the name of the Queen, and issued chits for its value to the traders. He then turned over all the foreign opium to Lin Zexu for destruction. With confirmation from the Emperor, Lin Zexu had all of the opium publicly destroyed in a solution of salt and lime, and then flushed out to sea. After saying a prayer for forgiveness to the gods of the seas, Lin allowed the foreign nationals to get back to their ships and leave. He told them in parting that trade in goods with China was acceptable, but opium was never again to be admitted.

The news was welcomed in Beijing. The Emperor announced that trade in opium had been stopped and that China would now start getting over its hundred-year addiction. In Briton, the news was interpreted much differently. The opium merchants, and the taxes that flowed back to London, convinced the Queen and Parliament that the Chinese had unjustly interfered with free trade -- and free trade was the life blood of England. The government's answer was to send a fleet of warships back to China to open the ports.

Even though the Chinese had invented gunpowder and developed functional cannon and explosives a thousand year before, the Manchurians had stopped their use for the last two hundred years to prevent a Han rebellion. The Chinese navy, with its lumbering square-rigged junks and outdated weapons, were no match for the British fleet. The Chinese Empire relied on its 'Celestial Mandate of Heaven' for protection and guidance, while in England, 'God Is My Right' was taken as the justification for British militaristic endeavors. The confrontations to come, and the results, were inevitable.

To improve the defenses of Guangzhou, Lin Zexu installed larger cannon and reactivated the Provincial Armies in Guangdong and Guangxi provinces. When Captain Bremer, the commander of the English flotilla, arrived and noted all of the preparations, he turned his fleet north, toward Beijing. Lin sent riders north to seven major forts along the route and to the capital, warning of the coming force.

In The Imperial Palace, the Daoguang Emperor, Minning, held council with his court of First Pin Kwan and other top advisors. Qishan, Viceroy of Zhejiang Province, reported on the destruction of seven forts along the coast, and on the size and power of the English ships; he advocated some course of appeasement. General Guan opposed any concessions, and proposed leading the Civic Corps, a Han militia, to join the Manchurian Bannermen regular army in an all-out resistance to the invasion.

The Emperor granted the activation of the militia and put General Guan in charge of the defense of Fort Dagukou which overlooks the mouth of the Haihe River, the gateway to Beijing. Raised Barbette platforms for cannon placed at the main fort, plus five big forts built during the Qing Dynasty and twenty smaller back-up forts, sealed the river from invasion.

Instead, the British war ships shelled the fortifications from the sea, a distance Chinese cannon could not reach. Within a matter of hours, the forts were decimated and overrun by the British troops. General Guan died in an explosion of the powder magazine.

When news of the battle reached the Forbidden City, Viceroy Qishan was appointed Imperial Commissioner to negotiate an end to the hostilities. He met with Captain Bremer and Charles Elliot on board the flagship, and presented them an offer of three million teals of silver and an end to hostilities. Elliot countered that England would settle for no less than six million teals of silver, the opening of five ports for free trade, and the Island of Hong Kong as a harbor for the British navy to enforce the terms of the treaty. The English, Elliott said, would occupy the island within ten days. If a signed treaty were not received within thirty days, England would consider the inaction a declaration of war. The document spelling out these terms became known as the Treaty of Nanjing.

Fulian and his friends knew little of this recent history. They had studied the histories of the dynasties and kingdoms of old. They knew the political and social lessons of China's long past, and participated in the rites and rituals of religion and custom, but they were removed from the current events of their own lifetimes. Fulian and his classmates relied on the stability of the Empire to take care of external affairs. But Wuchang was close, and the newspapers from there were filled with stories of rebellion and famine.

Wen Fulian was curious about that outside world and read as much of the newspapers as he could. Some of the stories had characters that were new to him and they talked of events that he didn't understand. He asked a sailor in town about these stories, but the sailor could not read, so Fulian read what he could and the sailor explained what he knew.

The foreign devils, the papers said, had attacked many of the fine cities in the east and south from their ships, but the Emperor had sent the Banner Army against them. There was widespread famine in the south and much unrest. The Emperor had dispatched the army to make investigations and to quell the rebellious peasants. Downriver, there were large numbers of roving bandits. The costs of fighting required higher and higher taxes. Several groups that called themselves the Tien Ti Hai (Heaven and Earth Societies) were killing landlords and government officials; they wanted to take the land and give it to the peasants.

Back at the school, Master Lu tore up the newspapers, and told the boys they should not pay attention to anything beyond the histories. "The Emperor will deal harshly with the rebellious peasants. Be thankful that you are scholars! You will soon enough be called on to defend the empire and to administer the civil laws."

But, Wen Fulian lay uneasily in his bed that night, and his mind wandered during the day as he tried to copy the text that he was assigned. The boys were forbidden from going into town and most especially from being anywhere near the sailors on the docks. The time for the first exam was coming and there was too much to learn. Wen was high in his class and could recite all of the histories and the rites. He was proficient in writing poetry and had learned to play a pipa, a stringed instrument that was held like a very small cello and plucked or bowed. His voice had changed and he loved to sing the reedy melodies of the northern sagas.

One afternoon, a new man came to the school to talk with Master Lu. The man wore a black silk cap with a red button on the top, and a heavy, brocaded silk jacket over a grey wool sam. His shoes were made of black leather and had hard heals that left half-moon marks in the dirt where he walked. The two men talked in low tones, so that the boys could not hear them, and then they left for a while. When they came back, Master Lu called out Wen Fulian and Dong Weili; they were the top two students in the school. The four of them went into Master Lu's room. The two men sat on the kang; the boys stood in front of them.

The new man explained to the boys that he needed someone to help in the county office of records. The rebellions had taken away so many young scholars, who had passed their prefect level exams, that he was willing to use someone who had not yet passed them, but probably would in the spring. He just had no time to wait for the spring exams. He said he could assist the candidate with his studies during the interim, but needed someone now. The boys looked at each other; Dong looked scared.

"I would go!" Wen said, impulsively.

The two men laughed and looked at Dong. "Is that alright with you?"

Dong looked relieved and nodded. Master Lu said, "All right then, Dong, you can go back to your work. Wen Fulian will go with Magistrate Hon and I will explain to Gai Xiansheng."

Part 3 - The Town Scholar

***

Down from the Mountains

The Magistrate was taken down the path along the river by palanquin, a covered sedan chair on long poles carried by two men. Wen Fulian followed on a short horse with supplies strapped to its sides. The trail down from the high country was rugged and, from time to time, impassable. They had to dismount frequently to climb over fallen rocks or trees or to ford some tributary cascading out of the mountains high above.

After several days, the river became deeper and moved more slowly. But still they walked along the old trails, as the river occasionally tumbled over great rock rapids and small waterfalls. Finally, they arrived at a large lake, where they transferred to a river raft. The horse pulled the raft along the shoreline by long ropes while Wen rode on the raft and held it away from the bank using a long pole to keep it out in the deeper water. At last, they arrived at the city of Ankang. Here they were able to leave the raft for a river steamer. It belched black smoke and moved much faster than the river. Although the boat would go all the way to Wuchang and the great Yangtze River, Wen and the Magistrate got off at Xiangfan, about half of the way down the Han river.

The city of Xiangfan seemed warm and damp to Wen, who had lived all his life at a higher altitude in the northern end of the Wudang mountain range. The first thing he saw was the large, ancient wall that surrounded the old part of the city. The huge grey wall was capped with a tier of white stones, which made it look very formal. Beyond the city, to the west, was the Wudang Mountain itself, towering some 5,000 feet above. The wooded hills leading to the mountain often were veiled with a fine mist.

Wen joined the Magistrate on the dock and they went into the city through a gate in the lower part of the wall. Inside, there was a long street leading up to the center of the town. On the left, buildings were built onto the wall. On the right, buildings were built onto the face of the cliff and followed the road up to the town. Soldiers watched as coolies off-loaded boxes from the boat and put them on large carts pulled by mules. The Magistrate went into an office by the main gate and talked with an army officer. Wen sat outside and watched the unloading.

Later, they went up the street to an empty building on the cliff side. This one building was larger than the whole village Wen had just left. Long hallways fed off into offices and storage rooms and indoor toilets. There was a large kitchen and great dining halls, all empty.

"This is your new home." said the Magistrate. "You will be responsible for many records and personal possessions of the great families to the south. You have enough room to keep all of the records and property of any family together. The military attachment will guard you and the building, but always remember that you are in charge. You will answer to me alone and you will have my complete authority while you are here. But, this is only because these are extraordinary times. You can make your life -- or lose it -- depending on how you conduct yourself.

"To help you in your studies," he continued, "Master Deng has agreed to be your personal tutor. He is a very accomplished Jinshi, who graduated in the top ten in his class. The Emperor has appointed him as the commissioner for education for Hubei and Hunan Provinces. Often he will be away, administrating the Provincial tests, but he will guide your studies and monitor your progress."

The Magistrate summoned an older coolie and introduced him. "This is Kong Bang, the head coolie. You will direct him where the boxes are to go and he will direct the other coolies. His face is important to him; he can only direct the others as long as you treat him well. In addition to his pay, you will have some discretionary funds to reward or withhold as you see fit."

***

Work and Study

As the winter of 1849-50 passed, each time Magistrate Hon returned, he brought with him more crates for storage -- and increasingly disturbing news. Each of the crates held some family's treasured possessions and the one-of-a-kind land deeds to that family's estates. The news from the south was of rebellion. Starving peasants were easily enlisted into service of one of the Heaven and Earth Societies that offered food, which they would steal by force of arms from landlords or city granaries. Some of these groups had attacked the Magistrate's shipments and some of his soldiers had been killed in skirmishes fighting to protect them.

The news from Beijing was no more encouraging. The Daoguang Emperor, Minning, had died in February. The new Emperor was his nineteen-year-old son Yizhu, who took the title Xianfeng, which means Universal Prosperity, more in hope than expectation.

Meanwhile, as Wen continued his studies for the spring exams, Master Deng used him to try out new questions on 'western learning' which had been added to the studies this year. Many in Beijing were unhappy with this movement and the Censors would be watching closely to make sure that the traditional education was not compromised; Wen was Deng's test subject.

One night, Magistrate Hon joined them for dinner and told them the news from the other provinces. One of the Triads, or Tien di Hui (Heaven and Earth Societies) that had fought the Emperor's Bannermen for two months in Guangxi, had killed the local Magistrate. They had joined forces with a religious fanatic named Hong Xiuquan. He was the leader of the Bai Shangdi Hui (Society for the Worship of God), a group that was attacking local monasteries and destroying non-Christian religious artifacts. His group was attracting a large number of desperate and starving peasants, religious zealots, and unemployed laborers. The army was restrained from attacking this "religious" group by the Treaty.

It was early spring of 1850, when Master Deng suggested to the Magistrate that, since he had already given Wen the examinations and his understanding was clearly certified, they should give Wen the title of Shengyuan (comparable to a Bachelor's degree) and appoint him a Ninth Pin Kwan. The Magistrate laughed at the idea, but he quickly saw more advantages for himself than for Wen. With the degree and appointment, Wen could begin taking over some of the tedious report writing to Beijing on the progress of the storage facility project.

So, that summer, Wen Fulian became the newest Kwan. It was Magistrate Hon's pleasure to order and present Wen with his 'Mandarin' robe with an embroidered long-tailed Jay on the front and back, a buffalo horn girdle clasp, and a cap with a one-inch worked-silver button on top.

***

Thunder in the South

Not so very far to the south, the rebellion had continued to grow. Three years previous, in 1847, Hong Xiuquan the religious fanatic leader of the present Society for the Worship of God, had left his studies under Reverend Issachar J. Roberts. Roberts was an American missionary who would not take Hong Xiuquan into his church, noting that Hong and his friends were "bent on making their burlesque religious pretensions serve their political purposes."

Now, however, by June and July of 1850, thousands of followers of 'Teacher Hong' had gathered in the south of Guangxi Province, giving up what little they owned to 'the

Sacred Treasury' and pledging to follow Hong to the death. Hong announced the establishment of the Taiping Tianguo, (The Way of the Heavenly Kingdom). The Qing Empire, meanwhile, was rushing fresh armies from Sichuan, Guizhou and Yunnan, to encircle the Hong bandits.

Magistrate Hon attended a formal dinner in Wuchang in June of that year, where he was presented to the new Provincial Governor, Chang Dachun, and several Generals. Hon was honored for his initiative in protecting the records of so many extended families, and was instructed to search out promising scholars from the spring exams to assist him. When he returned to Xiangfan, he gave this task to Deng, along with a conditional promotion to the Eighth Pin for Wen, pending his passing the Juren (provincial) Examination. Though that exam was not to be given till 1853, Magistrate Hon allowed that it would be up to Deng to make that determination.

Over the summer of 1852, the Qing armies chased the 'Heavenly Army' north, from Yongan toward the Guangxi capital of Guilin. Hong's followers had taken several cities along the Xiang River, but in passing the city of Quanzhou, his "south general", Feng Yunshan was killed by a sniper's bullet. In retribution, they sacked the city and killed thousands who had not fled.

Further up the river, a local militia ambushed Hong and killed ten thousand of the Heavenly Army. Those who escaped marched north to Guilin where Hong lost yet another of his principal generals. 'The West King, Xiao Chaogui, led several charges against the city gates but was severely wounded and died three days later.

Meanwhile, in Xiangfan, normal cataloguing and storing the chests of documents filled Wen's days, while the evenings were filled with reading and studying for the Juren (Masters Degree level) exams. It sped the time throughout 1851 and into 1852. Late in one of these afternoons, Wen was looking over the contents of a case from a farm in the Changde region. Much of the land there was delta silt from the Yaun River, which was runoff from the Wuling Shan Range. He was musing about how different the operation of this farm was from the farm on which he had been raised! And how similar the family linage was to those of his schoolmates in the mountains back home. The records were old and….

"A manifesto? They have the gall to write a manifesto!" Hon's voice echoed down the halls from his office on the floor below. Wen ran there as quickly as he could to learn what was wrong.

"That turtle spawn, that slime of a snail!" Hon shouted, just as Wen came into the room, in time to see Magistrate Hon tearing up a piece of paper and kicking at the pieces as they fell. Wen had never seen the Magistrate exhibit any anger before.

"The outlaws are writing manifestos now?!" The messenger who had arrived a few minutes earlier was cowering by the doorway and looked to Wen for protection.

"They drove the army behind the walls in Guilin and they think this fight is theirs? Now they are calling for the people to rise up against the Emperor! This is why we must struggle against ignorance!" he said, as he shook his finger at Wen and stepped on each torn piece of paper as though it were a bug. "Peasants who wouldn't know what to do with land if they had it are supposed to rebel against an empire that has led the world for thousands of years?! Stupid peasants! They can't read or think; what would they do with land if they had it? No more use than a dog fart! These outlaws will be the ruin of their own kind!"

Indeed, there were three "manifestos", dated June 13, 1852, all drafted by Yang Xiuqing, The Eastern King, their call to rebellion claiming to be under the 'orders of Heaven'. *"Buddhist Idols, the Monster King of Hell and the foreign devils are alike; they are all devils, the enemies of the people. The people must take up arms and slay the devils on behalf of Heaven!"*

The Buddhists had always given the downtrodden hope, but at the same time, kept them in their place. The Monster King of Hell was none other than the Emperor himself! The Qing rulers, according to one of the manifestos, had lost the mandate of heaven as shown by natural disasters that had caused widespread famine in the south and flooding in the north, as well as manmade disasters such as accepting unequal treaties with Great Britain that resulted in new taxes imposed to pay an 'indemnity' for the cost of the war. Even in Confucian terms, these were the sorts of evidence that justified a change in the imperial rule. The foreign Devils were, of course, the Europeans.

But the Qing forces were gathering. Again Hong's army moved on, this time attacking the Hunan provincial capital of Changsha. Unable to capture it, they descended to Lake Dongting and down the Yangtze to Hanyang and Hankou, the commercial cities that straddle the Han River at its mouth on the Yangtze. Across the river lay the Hubei Provincial Capital of Wuchang. On January 12, 1853, the rebels floated two bridges across the Yangtze and blew open a section of the wall. Wuchang fell and the Heavenly Army celebrated its first large success.

Like a snowball rolling down hill, the size of the army had grown at every turn. Peasants who were starving joined and were given food, taken from towns along the army's way. In Wuchang, they were finally able to stop, set up men's camps and women's camps, hospitals, the Sacred Treasury, and to form a navel flotilla of 10,000 river boats. To pay for all this, they confiscated the landlords' and officials' gold and silver, salt and food.

Hong's remaining generals contemplated their next step. Hong had become a senior adviser and the religious head of the movement, but he had agreed that military planning was better handled by his generals. To stay in Wuchang much longer would be a disaster as the Qing Armies could take back the city by an extended siege, for which they would have a decided advantage. The alternatives would be to either attack north through the mountains in the winter, or to drive east down the Yangtze and try to take Nanjing, the old capital city of China; then they could march north to Beijing the following spring.

Exploratory forces had been sent up the Han River valleys to the west and then north, while the decision was being made by the generals to go down river to Nanjing. The evacuation of Wuchang was carried out suddenly, for security reasons, and in February, a force of half a million swept down the lower Yangtze on either bank, with a flotilla between them on the water.

The exploratory expedition, which had been sent up the Han River, ran into the Magistrate, returning from one of his trips. During the ensuing battle, the Bannermen from Xiangfan joined the Magistrate's guard and the exploratory party was caught between them. During the battle, the Magistrate and several of his soldiers were badly wounded.

***

Taking Charge

In the storage facility that afternoon, unaware of the battle down on the river, Wen was looking for a particular book he had been studying. His was an outer office to the Magistrate's, which had its own passageway from the larger office to the main hall. Wen's office served as a buffer to the larger office. The walls in the Magistrate's office were lined with built-in shelving and cabinets containing books, vases, and statuary. Wen lit the gas lamps and looked over the books on the shelves. There were books of the Histories and Romances from the ancient periods. There were collections of maps and detailed sea routes from the Ming Dynasty. One large book listed all of the magistrates in all of the counties with their grades and degrees. A globe caught Wen's eye and he was surprised to see how small China was; he had thought of it as being much larger. Some of the vases were from the Ming period; one brass stand was from the Song era. On the shelves were hand-written verses from the Tang and Song periods, copied by the Magistrate himself.

On the desk, Wen finally found the book he had been studying, titled Da Qing Luli (Great Qing Laws). This book was not like any of the others; it had leather binding for a cover and the pages were organized into blocks of text with headings. This book had been printed on a press using ivory carved blocks. The 436 sections were grouped into books of laws and punishments -- everything from civil laws to military laws, marriage laws and laws and rites of ritual observances. Wen had started his legal training by reading every word; he was reading the book now for the third time.

Suddenly, he heard a great clamor in the street outside the window. He saw a squad of Bannermen soldiers helping to unload wounded men from farm wagons into the facility. From the blood and open wounds, it was obvious to Wen there had been a recent conflict nearby. Magistrate Hon was one of the wounded.

Wen rushed to the Magistrate's apartment, where they had set him on his sofa. "I'm all right!" he was insisting. "See to the men. I'll be all right. You are dismissed! Go!" Reluctantly, they left him there.

Wen brought a wash basin and a thermos of hot water. "Can I help you?" he asked, looking around for towels and dressings.

The Magistrate took off his outer garments and inspected several cuts, which were still oozing blood. "I'll clean these up! You should go out there and take charge. I'll be all right! Here, give me that cloth and tear up some strips of silk to bind these."

They worked on his arms until most of the cuts were stanched and bound. "Now, go out there and see what is going on!" the Magistrate said. "And let me know as soon as you can."

Wen ran down the hall to the front loading ramp where he found a farm wagon still loaded with soldiers who were badly wounded and moaning, crying out for help to anyone nearby. Other soldiers were tending to the wounded, helped by civilians of every class.

Wen asked what had happened, what was going on. The ranking Bannerman told him they were attacked outside the east gate by bandits who came up the river. "I think we killed them all, but we will have to go back and search that area to make sure there aren't any more out there."

"All right," Wen responded, "Leave a contingent here to guard the building and take your Civil Guard to help clear the East road!" Magically, the captain turned and did as he was told; the soldiers and guard ran off toward the East Gate.

Wen organized a makeshift hospital in the barracks and had local women tend to the wounded. Then he returned to the Magistrate's apartment and reported what had happened.

"Very good!" the Magistrate said with a smile. "You know that we have a military commander and that they will take care of military problems. We are civilian Kwan; we are above the military ranks here, but it is good to leave the military command in charge of its own duties. When they come back, let me know what they found," he said sinking back onto the sofa pillows and closing his eyes.

Wen turned down the gaslight and let himself out.

***

An Act of Heroism

The Captain of the Guard returned in the evening and reported to Wen that they had found several dead peasants and strangers in southern dress along the side of the road. The soldiers questioned three who were still alive and then killed them. That was in accordance with the law; Wen had just read it: Anyone who attacks a Kwan of the sixth rank or higher is to be beheaded immediately.

"Where did the strangers come from?" Wen asked.

"They are Hakka from Guangxi." said the captain. "They came up here to spread the terror from the south. They said they were in the Heavenly Army of the Taiping Tianguo."

The Hakka (Guest) people had been driven south centuries ago by the armies of the contending dynasties and by the invading armies from Mongolia. Still regarded as outsiders, they maintained their costumes and traditions, which separated them from the Punti (local people) and the Hoklo (men of the Hok, coastal lands southeast of Canton).

Wen thanked him and returned to the Magistrate with the news.

The Magistrate was restless and running a fever when Wen returned. "We must bleed your wounds," said Wen. "And you should drink a lot of hot tea!"

The Magistrate scowled at him and pulled the covers up under his chin. Looking around the apartment, Wen found a bottle of English gin. "Now we are talking!" Wen said, showing the Magistrate the bottle. Then he got some more bandaging strips of silk and pulled up a chair next to the sofa.

After much protesting, the Magistrate let Wen reopen each wound and wash it out with the gin. "Do you know how expensive that stuff is?" the Magistrate wailed. "At least get me a glass!"

Wen left the room and returned with a steaming pot of tea. "This will do you much better than gin," he said. "I have some cakes as well. What you really need is a lot of rest! I'll see you in the morning." He dimmed the light and went out to the street.

The farm wagon was now filling up with those who had died from their wounds and others who had killed themselves to ease the pain. Wen walked to the East Gate and looked over the wall. He could see lanterns moving among the trees and along the riverbank.

"We will have patrols out there all night", said one of the guards. "It seems pretty quiet, too quiet! We'll be on alert, just in case."

In the morning, the families who had lost their sons and fathers came for the dead. Each of the bodies had to be buried because the soul would only rest if the body was returned to the ancestral plot. Those who had died far from home would wander the world, hungry ghosts forever. Cremation and water burial were forbidden by law, though cremating Buddhist priests was an exception which was not contested. Wen made sure he was there to say something to the family of each man, even the rebels. And he walked with them to the gate; he felt it his duty to honor that final equality. His concern was genuine and it was a comfort to everyone.

Wen spent the bulk of the day with the Magistrate or touring the military fortifications along the wall. The Magistrate's fever had gotten worse and he shivered under his blankets. Wen had him drink hot tea when he was awake and dressed his bandages whenever he could. The next day was much the same, but the Magistrate had become delirious and couldn't eat anything. On the following day, his fever broke and he managed to eat some soup. Within a few days, he was sitting up, but it would be several weeks before he could return to his normal duties.

On the fifth day after the battle, a soldier from the East Gate ran into the Magistrate's apartment. There was trouble at the gate.

By the time Wen arrived there, many soldiers were on the top of the wall and a force had assembled inside, ready to repel an attack. Beyond the wall, Wen saw a small mob of peasants and two Hakka who were shouting slogans which the peasants shouted back in response.

"The land is yours!" they cried. "God has sent us to reveal the truth and help you take that which is yours. The Monster King of hell is killing you. This wall is his lie! It keeps you from eating the grain you have raised! Take it back, it is yours!"

Suddenly the mob stopped yelling and the Hakka turned to see what they were looking at. Wen had come out of the small door in the gate and was walking directly toward them. One of the Hakka picked up a club and started to wave it over his head. Someone in the mob pulled it away and threw it alongside the road.

"Talk to me, if you have something to say!" Wen shouted at the Hakka. "Talk to me if you have reason to waken the beast in the people. Have they not suffering enough without you! Talk to me with your maddening voice! You are a coward! Your cause is without merit and illegal. Talk to me!" He stood toe-to-toe with the Hakka.

"Your Emperor has failed us!" one of them said. "The people are starving and the Monster King of Hell bleeds the land to pay his debt. We will take the grain we have raised with our own hands. The peasants own the land and we will take what it yields! We are Hakka and we will lead the Army of Heaven to victory!"

Wen pushed him aside and walked into the mob. "I am Hakka! My mother and her mother before wore the black and brown apron of our heritage." His accent suddenly became that twangy dialect that he remembered from his home so long ago. "I have plowed the fields and I planted the seed. These hands put that grain into the stores. And, I am no stranger to the pangs of hunger that are the lot of the peasant. I know your life, because it was my life. I had the good fortune to rise above that life. Today I am a Kwan and I am your servant in that office. But, I cannot make food that doesn't exist. Nor can he! He would have you murder and steal. I would help you to survive these times to live another day. These men are not here to give anything to you, but take everything from you. They have nothing to sell but death – your death!"

Several men in the crowd had taken hold of the Hakka and Wen noticed a squad of soldiers, from the wall, was marching toward them.

"Who saw these men attack the Magistrate?" Wen called out. Several men stepped forward.

"No, no! Just one." said Wen.

A strong young man stood alone before the mob. Wen looked him in the eye. "You witnessed the attack on the Magistrate by these two men?" The man nodded and tears welled up in his eyes.

Wen turned to the Hakka. "I condemn you to death by the sword!"

The soldiers took the Hakka aside and forced them to their knees. Without further ceremony, the Captain of the Guard stepped up, unsheathed his sword, and cut off their heads.

"You, step forward!" Wen shouted, pointing at the young man. "For not reporting the attack, sixty blows with the bamboo."

Again the Captain of the Guard stepped forward.

"Lightly, if you please" Wen said quietly, as he stepped to the side. With the soldiers behind him, he walked to the wall and called out, "Open the gate!" Inside, a cheer arose and the gate swung open. Wen and the squad walked in and he said, "I think you can stand down the men, Captain."

Back in the Magistrate's apartment, Wen was faced with a beaming patient. "They tell me that you saved us all from the mob. That is the best medicine I could have received. You just marched in there and turned it all around. Amazing! Well done!"

Wen was flushed with the moment and started to notice some trembling in his legs. He had to sit down and took a glass of water. "I didn't know what else to do. The chaos and anger were growing and I had to stop it. If they had attacked the gate, they would all have died. It just had to stop; so, I stopped it. "

"This will go on your record and I will bring it to the attention of the Governor," the Magistrate said proudly. "When I told you to take charge in my absence I hadn't expected so much." They sat there in a glowing silence, savoring the moment.

In the morning, when Wen looked in on the Magistrate, he seemed stronger, and waved Wen into the room with a broad sweep of his arm and a warm smile. "Come in! You have to hear this! The post rider from Commissioner Xiang Rong in Wuchang passed this message on to our rider in Suizhou."

> *The Taiping have left Wuchang with a massive troop of peasants and ships. They are heading down river toward Shanghai. They have left no military presence in Wuchang and we are encountering only spotty rear guard units. We will pursue and engage as the opportunity arises.*
>
> *There is fighting all along the lower Yangtze and we hear that the rebels have taken Anqing and they are on the gates of Nanjing, if they haven't taken it already.*

Map of Taiping Rebellion

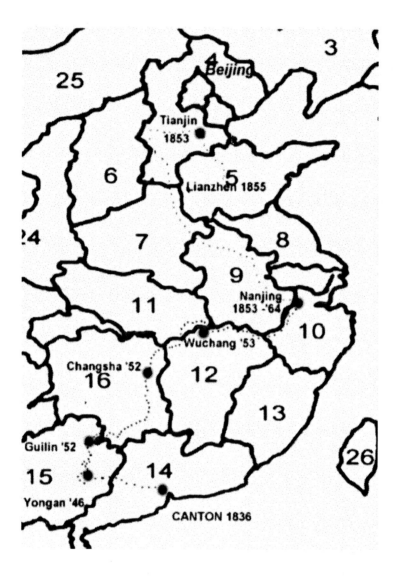

Life in a Time of Rebellion

***

The Merchant Farmer

Somewhere on a main road running westward out of Lu'an in Anhui Province, north of the Dabie Mountains that separated him from the Heavenly Army, was a farmer named Fang Laogai. The cold March winds blew down the north face of the range and he had to keep reassuring himself that it was all worthwhile. With him was a caravan of sealed wagons, filled with rice and corn. Protecting them was a detachment of 150 soldiers, members of his tuanlian (private army).

Lao Fang had grown successful and powerful on his fertile farmlands west of Nanjing. But the news of the rebellion had chastened him. His two sons were already assigned to commands in the Qing Army. The grain, which would normally be sold on the Shanghai market, was now subject to confiscation by the Qing Army -- or worse yet, by any number of bandit organizations which were operating to the east of his farm. So, Lao Fang was heading west in search of a decent return on his harvest.

News of the arrival of armed troops from the east had caused a mixture of panic and hope in Xiangfan. The gates to the East Road were closed and with the approach of the tuanlian, the city's soldiers rushed to their defensive posts on the wall and in the trenches outside the main gate. As the caravan drew nearer, however, it became obvious to the guards that the approaching soldiers were not an attacking force, but an escort.

"But what person would have such a procession?" "Surely, it must be someone of great importance!" "Where is the Magistrate?" "He is still healing from his wounds!" "Where is his second – the Kang, Wen?"

Wen put on his official robe and cap, and ran to the East Gate to welcome whoever the important person was at the city gates. The caravan halted, out of range of any gunfire, and a single mounted soldier came to the gate. After some conversation with the guards, the gate swung open and the caravan advanced. Once inside, the gate closed again, and a line of soldiers on either side of the street watched as the contents of the wagons were inspected.

The Farmer stood by his wagon as Wen introduced himself and welcomed him. Together they led the wagons through the town and down to the facility at the south end. Wen went up to the Magistrate's apartment to tell him about the caravan.

"Grain? That is as good as gold!" the Magistrate replied to the news. "I guess we can store it as well as any other valuable. I don't have silver enough to buy it and we can't really confiscate it without authorization from the Governor. You look after it." With that, he turned onto his side and went back to sleep.

Wen returned to the Farmer and explained the operation of the facility. What he proposed was holding of the grain as a family asset. After settling the grain question and making arrangements to billet the Farmer's escort, the two men went to the hotel in town, the Long Meng, for lunch. Lao Fang was very interested in Wen's military reports from Nanjing.

"My farm is not far from there!" he cried. "They could take us over any day at this rate!" He decided to return directly to his farm and bring his family back to Xiangfan. He and his soldiers left town early the next morning.

Lu'an city, at the east end of the highway, was experiencing its own problems. North of the farm, the Imperial Banner Army had stronger control, but even that was slipping away. The Nien rebels, a group unrelated to the Taipings, lived north of the Yellow River and were fed up with the lack of response by the Qing government. Flood damage suffered two years before had left thousands of victims along the Huang He River. They had received no assistance from the Qing because of the war in the south and the treaties with England that had drained the treasury.

Open rebellion also limited the markets. Shanghai, the gateway to the rest of the markets, was in the grips of the Short Sword Society, a group closely related to the infamous Triads (gangsters from the southeastern provinces). They had taken over much of the Chinese part of the city, and were disrupting all merchant traffic except opium, which had grown steadily.

The Fang Farm stood on the open plain, west of Lu'an -- a collection of buildings, houses, barns, and sheds, about four hundred kilometers west of Nanjing. It sprawled over hundreds of acres cultivated by long-term tenant farmers. Lao Fang ran it as a loose 'grange'. Fang did the financing and marketing, operated the storage facilities, and taught anyone who wanted to learn how to farm. Some of the surrounding fields had been planted with winter wheat and sweet potatoes that grew year round, but the bulk of the land was not yet cultivated -- and wouldn't be, in view of the unstable political situation.

At home, Fang was pure Chinese; when he entered a room, all else stopped. He wore a black silk cap, a formal silk sam over his winter samfu, and leather farm boots. His face, wrinkled from years of sun and laughter, would light up any room and reassure everyone around him. He was direct in his speech, but perceptive beyond his mild exterior. His ready apologies for the state of his farm were typical -- and just exaggerated enough to attest to his modesty. His office in the house, however, contained shelves lined with books, maps of the world, and memorabilia from his travels around the globe.

Fang's private soldiers had their own barracks, which looked like any other barn from the outside. They went to these quarters immediately now, after the long march from Xiangfan. Lao Fang's wife met him at the door, his daughter, nineteen-year-old Meixing, at her side. Meixing took her father's coat and boots to clean the road dirt off of them. Her mother went into the kitchen to prepare some food for her husband, and soon returned with a tray of tea and cakes. But, her sunny disposition seemed to change in the few steps from the kitchen area.

"What is the mater?" she asked her husband. "You are so quiet. It is not like you to be so. Did I miss something?" She poured tea into the cups and sat across from him.

"Madeleine, we have a problem," he answered softly, laying his hands palms down on the table. "I have disturbing news about the Taiping rebels. They have taken Nanjing. I feel that we may not be safe here anymore."

"What would you have us do? Move the farm to higher ground?" her eyes began tearing up.

"Oh, Mama. Calm yourself," Meixing said, coming to stand by her mother. "The farm will always be here."

Lao Fang looked out at the flat land, beyond the windowpane, beyond the limits of 'home' that his family had known for five generations. He struggled with the thought that the farm might not 'always be here'. They could take it all away! He knew that this Qing dynasty was only one in a long history of dynasties -- and this one was certainly on shaky ground. His wealth was invested with the Europeans because they did have a better banking system. But his family history, the family investment, could all be plowed under with the bones of those who had come before. There are things that you just cannot control, he told himself. Better to protect what you can and move on. He rubbed his eyes and went to hug his wife and daughter, wrapping his arms around them reassuringly.

"I just think that it would be better if we moved over to Xiangfan 'til the Emperor's army settles the rebellion. Let's try to think of it as a vacation."

"I would rather vacation in France!" his wife retorted, walking to the window. She looked west toward Xiangfan, and the tears ran freely down her face. It was not an idle fantasy; Madeline Fang was born and raised in France. She had met her husband in Paris, where she was teaching French to foreign students in the 1820s. She remembered their first date; they attended the premiere performance at the opera for the German composer Beethoven's new Ninth Symphony. The production had to use the newly extended stage in order to seat the new, larger orchestra. After the performance, they had walked the banks of the Seine till sunrise. It was a time for romanticism everywhere in Europe. They had spent the next day in the Louvre, at the exhibition of Delacroix, luxuriating in his fantastic use of color. Sometimes, she could not remember why she had come to this wide, pitiless land.

"We will need some larger wagons," Lao Fang said, and went to the barracks to talk with his men.

It would take a few days they told him, but they could use the wheels and undercarriages from existing wagons and just build clean new boxes to transport the family possessions.

Three days later, a caravan of five carts, loaded with books, household possessions, and important papers, set out for Xiangfan with a complement of two hundred and thirty of the tuanlian, their personal army.

***

The New Magistrate

Meanwhile, back in Xiangfan, Wen was awakened by a knock on his door. He opened it to find an obviously upset Bannerman soldier outside.

"Sir, the Capitan of the Guard told me to get you. It is the Magistrate; he died last night!"

Wen ran down the hall to the Magistrate's apartment and stepped in next to the guards who had gathered when they heard the bad news. "What happened?" he asked, as he walked to the bedside.

"He died in his sleep. We came into his apartment this morning and we couldn't rouse him. He said he wasn't feeling well last night, that he just wanted to sleep. We didn't hear anything from him; nothing till this morning. Sir, I am very sorry."

"Did you call his doctor?" Wen asked, then looked up at the astonished faces around him. "No, I mean, we have to determine a cause of death. I can see that he is dead!"

The Magistrate's personal doctor came and determined that a blood clot from one of the wounds had passed up into his brain; nothing could have been done to prevent it. "I will write up a formal report for the Governor," the doctor said. "And I guess you will have to take on his duties until a replacement has been found." Wen asked about a funeral. The Doctor said he would make the necessary arrangements; they would ship his body back home.

As he was about to leave the apartment, Wen turned back. "Oh. I don't know whether you've heard," he said. "Governor Chang Dachun died when the Taiping retook Wuchang! You will have to send the report to the new Huguang Governor, General Zhang Liangji. He is over the Hubei and Hunan Provinces, at Changsha."

Wen returned to his own apartment, laid on the bed, and stared at the ceiling. Tears ran down the sides of his face as he recalled his mentor and his friend. Sometime later, he dressed and went to his office. Though it was familiar, it felt strange to him now. He stopped at the doorway into the inner office; it was, of course, dark but warmer and reassuring.

He lit the gas lamps and began looking over the unanswered correspondence that had accumulated since the Magistrate was wounded. One of the papers, not yet filed away, was a copy of the report the Magistrate had written to the Governor describing Wen's act of heroism with the mob and his administration of on-the-spot justice. There was also a letter of response from the Governor, which suggested that Wen be given broader authority and recommended that he continue his studies toward the Jinshi (Doctorate) degree.

Later, Wen walked over to the offices of Deng Gaoxi, the examiner. They sat and talked about their friend and longtime acquaintance for most of the rest of the day. They agreed that Wen should perform the duties of the Magistrate until he was relieved. The sun had set, and finally, Wen felt the exhaustion of this long and difficult day.

The next morning, Wen submitted his personal memorial on the passing of the Magistrate to be sent with the Doctor's to Beijing. Then he returned to the office -- and to the sad business of removing the Magistrate's personal effects for storage, with the things from his apartment, till they could be sent to his family.

By afternoon, Wen's mood was brighter and he began thinking about his own role as the new acting magistrate. For the moment, the soldiers had cleared the area of the Hakka resistance, and had sent patrols downriver, where they found that the danger, for the moment, was over. "What if they came back, in force?" Wen thought, and began to consider the defenses of his little city with more interest.

For the next few days, Wen toured the city with the military commander, a young man only three years older than himself. Kong Beifu had always wanted to follow his father's career in the army. He had studied, and received his own military version of the Shengyuan (Bachelor) degree; it was far less academic than the civilian version, but included many more practical subjects. Together, Wen and Kong made up a wish-list of improvements to their defensive preparation; at the top of the list was larger troop strength. They decided that Wen would work on raising funds from the local merchants and Kong would gather recruits.

The Fang family arrived that week, and Wen was happy to play host, get them settled in the Long Ming Hotel, and show them around the town. Wen drew Lao Fang into his project of fundraising for the new civil guard; it gave them both a chance to meet and get to know all of the merchants and craftsmen in the town. In the evenings, Wen enjoyed the company of Fang's delightful wife and their daughter, Meixing.

***

Settling In

Very quickly, Madam Fang became something of a celebrity. Known as 'the French lady', she was at once both exotically French, yet very accessible, as her Chinese was understandable. Within days, she had met almost everyone in town. She and her daughter moved freely in and out of the shops, and regularly held court in the park in the center of town. Madam was sought out for her knowledge of the outside world, certainly, but also for her perspective on all sorts of current events. "Who are these Christians and what do they want?" "How can the Europeans presume to tell the Chinese anything about their own lives?" the people asked her. Even, "How is French poetry structured and what subjects does it deal with?" It filled the time, separate from the men, and bonded the mother and her daughter even more closely.

More and more, there was pressure on Mama to explain the western ideas that were changing lives, even this far back in the hinterlands. However, she could not. She had spoken with Lao Fang and he advised her to talk only about the Empire and the stability it had developed over thousands of years. The European countries were, after all, younger even than the current Qing Dynasty, and the uprisings of hungry peasants were older than history.

Wen found a friend in Lao Fang. They spent many afternoons on the open veranda of the hotel with Master Deng, talking about the educational system in flux throughout China. Lao Fang was a Jinshi who had graduated high in his class, but not so high as to get caught up in a ministerial assignment immediately. His father had little use for "that gang" in Beijing, and quickly sent him off to England to further his education. He studied Political Science at Cambridge and worked in a local bank that served the Chinese community there. After graduation, he moved on to Paris where he met Madeline, a teacher of French to foreign students. They had an intensely romantic courtship in that most romantic city, where art and history were part of everyday life. Later, they moved to Heidelberg for a short time, so they could learn German, and he could study the mathematics and mechanics of the emerging Industrial Revolution. But China was home, and eventually, they came back across the Atlantic, down the east coast of America, through the jungles of Central America, and by ship across the Pacific, home to the farm.

One evening, the conversation centered on rural customs and Daoist influences in the home which limited girls' activities and opportunities. Before Wen had realized it, Meixing had joined their conversation and was sitting in a chair next to his. She was particularly irritated by the education of women students; there was none! Girls her age were still thought of as property of the family. Throughout most of China the only education girls received was, almost exclusively, valued for its usefulness in running the home. Unlike her contemporaries, Meixing had a mother who could teach her and they had read widely all of her life.

"How would you have the system change?" Wen asked.

"For girls, it is like an avalanche is in front of them. They have to climb over all these boulders in their path, just to get to the trail that the boys walk so easily. I've been talking to the girls in the town and there are a lot of very smart ones out there. But, they talk with words that they cannot write. If they could read and write, they could use books that would lead them on to a much richer understanding of the world. There are no books for girls. Boys have the histories presented in written form, and can use that form to help them memorize the lessons. For the girls to learn without writing is like insisting that they walk gracefully on one leg. I think, ideally, girls should have schools and the time to go to them, just like the boys."

"All right, let's say that is the goal!" said Deng. "But to get there, you have to make small steps. First, you have to know what the student knows. Then, only teach that next step."

"My daughter is a dreamer," Fang said. "But it's a start. Now you have given her a challenge. Watch out! What is possible, Meixing? And what will you do to make it happen?"

Meixing sat quietly a moment, looking up at the hazy afternoon sky. Then she nodded her head slightly. "I'll let you know. You make a good point." Looking now at Master Deng, she mused, "I wonder if they are all at the same level. I will have to see about that."

The men's conversation then returned to the plan that Wen and Kong had drafted. Kong was selecting young men and housing them in one wing of the military barracks. The recruits had to be willing workers; in peacetime, they couldn't just draw wages and do nothing. He also was eliminating anyone who used opium or large quantities of alcohol. The men would be a part-time military and part-time civil service, to be called The Civic Guard. What he needed, next, were rations and uniforms substantial enough to attract recruits of some substance, not just the riffraff.

"I think we have the same sort of problem as Meixing," said Lao Fang. "We have to find out what we have to work with first. Let's see what kind of men Kong has found."

Wen went by the barracks on his way back to the office and found Kong interviewing half a dozen young men. "The word is out," Kong said, "And I'm getting a good idea of who is available. Two of the men who were here earlier were miners. I didn't even know we had mines around here. They say there is a zinc deposit to the north of us, and iron and coal are both available to the south, around Yicheng. Some of the craftsmen in town, they tell me, use the zinc for making dinnerware and food storage vessels. The coal and iron ore could be useful if we made a melting furnace…. But that is a big undertaking."

"Let's see if anyone is skilled in making weapons," Wen suggested, "Maybe the blacksmith, or the furniture maker in town. Surely they could make bows and arrows. We could set up our own armory!"

Wen and Lao Fang next paid a visit to the furniture shop in town. The yard in front of the shop was filled with chairs and tables that the carpenter had made but not yet sold. The building had a porch that was overhung by a short roof that slanted down in front and covered the front room, where he lived. To the back, the roof was high and pitched slowly down, allowing a high space for a work room. The back yard was a clutter of cut logs, saw horses, boards aging in stacks, and wood shavings everywhere.

"Tong Gaolin, have you eaten?" the two men greeted the carpenter. The old man shuffled out from the back yard. He wore a folded felt hat that was flat in the front and had sides that joined at the top -- it, too, covered everywhere with shavings and saw dust. He had a dark wrinkled face with wispy white hairs floating around it.

"Ah, Your Excellency! Two visits so soon, he said. "Did you come back to buy one of my chairs?" His toothy smile was yellow and wide. As he approached them, he wiped the dust from his hands on his loose pants, which were held up with faith as much as with the rope that ran through the holes around the waistband. He wore wooden clog shoes that he had made himself and dragged them around the yard as he walked.

"We may have some business for you," Wen answered. "You remember Fang Xiansheng?"

"Of course!" he said, bowing his head slightly. "What can I make for you?"

"We are interested in bows and arrows. I understand that you know how to make them as well as furniture and other things. Is that true?"

"Of course!" the old man answered. "They are not an item I have made in a long time though. As you know well, they are illegal for my normal trade. Would these be for you? For hunting, maybe?" he asked, deferentially.

"We are thinking of a military application," Wen said, openly addressing the issue. "They would have to be strong and rugged. We were hoping you could help us to make many of them. The city would pay you a fair price, of course."

"I haven't made any in a long time... and it takes a long time to make one...," the old man said hesitantly, then added, "I don't know if I can do what you are asking, but I will try, of course."

"I understand the problem," Wen assured him, but we will help you with workers and equipment. What we are most interested in is the design and the techniques involved," said Lao Fang. "Could you make one and teach our soldiers to make others like it? We will set up the equipment to make many more."

"With your authority, I will start today," the carpenter agreed. "But it is a process that will take several days."

"That is fine," said Wen. "I will have some soldiers come by and watch you, if you don't mind. Then when the methods are established, we will build machines to make them on a large scale." Wen set a small sack of coins on the table next to Tong. "One more thing," he added. "This is not to be talked about in town. We need to keep anything related to military matters out of the public eye. Do you understand what I am saying?" Wen asked.

Tong nodded vigorously and snatched up the sack of coins. "Good," said Wen. "We will be back in a day or so." He raised his hands in a cupped salutation.

As they walked back into town, Fang muttered "I wonder if we can trust that old thief?"

"He is the best thief we have!" Wen chuckled grimly. "But, you know, I do have my spies around town. Nothing gets said or done here that doesn't filter back to the Magistrate."

"I hope you're right!" Fang answered, but didn't sound very reassured.

***
The Civic Guard

Over the next few days, Wen and Fang met with Kong and his new recruits. "Most of them were farmers and transient workers without families," Kong told them, "But they're young and strong. And they eat anything you offer them. I have fifty-three of them so far. They're billeted in the barracks, and during the day, they're working with my men on repairing the wall. Some of them have trade skills, too, and we are looking at other projects, like fixing up some of the buildings inside the city."

"What kind of trade skills are you finding?" asked Fang.

"They all do carpentry and masonry, but some have worked with blacksmiths and in wheelwright shops. One worked in Canton, on the docks. He is awfully good with levers and ropes. Talk about ropes, we have two weavers. And one dyes cloth."

"The fellow from Canton, why is he so far north? Is he Hakka?"

"Oh! No, no. His family were boat people, from the Hok, the seacoast around Fujian Province. For a while the family worked on the docks, but the local Punti, and even the Hakka, wouldn't have anything to do with them, so they worked their way up the Bei Jiang River. He ran away when the Triads came to steal boats and take young men for pirate work. Then he just kept heading north until, he said, he 'got cold'."

"How about the fellow who worked with a blacksmith? Does he know enough to set up a forge?" Lao Fang asked.

"Why do that?' Kong asked, "We do have a blacksmith in town!"

"Yes, but his things are ornamental and domestic," Fang answered. "I was thinking about spear points and battle axes. We might even get into founding cannon and swords."

"Good thinking!" Wen responded, his mind was taking the idea even further along than anything they had discussed. "Rather than expanding what we already have in town.... That would throw a lot of change at these people who are all right with the way things are. It just occurred to me that we should be setting up a whole new town! Think about it! We could take that land to the northeast and create a town based on the military. We could farm the hills, train and house the Civil Guard up there, and have all the room we need to set up any manufacturing facilities; all this without changing life in the town, directly."

"That is a huge idea!" Kong said, staring at Wen. "How could we afford it?"

"We can't!" he answered blithely. "It would have to be self- sustaining from the start. We are already 'employing' these new recruits on the town's payroll to repair the town wall. Why not start, right away, with a separate accounting. We charge for their 'labor' and 'services' and cover their expenses out of that income." Wen sat back, smiling, and looked at the others.

Fang was still staring at him, now even more intently. "I agree with what Kong just said. 'That is a huge idea'! I'm trying to imagine creating a whole town based on the work that we could supply, repairing walls. Either it would be a very small town -- or we need to find a lot of work for them."

"OK, let's think. Here is our little city," Wen said, cupping his hand like a bowl. "If it produces more than it consumes, it will flourish and expand. If it consumes more than it produces, it will wither away. Right now, our little city is fifty-three guys living in 'rented rooms' and getting paid with room and board. In return, it is providing manual labor. But, it is self sustaining, right? What do we get from it? In addition to some badly needed repairs, we have available a Civic Guard under our direction -- and the possibility for growth. What do they get from us? They are fed and have a room to go to each night. Can we afford that? Sure! The city has money enough for that -- and we had a need to get those walls fixed anyway."

"Now let's up the ante just a bit," he continued. "Let's have them dress in minimal uniforms and train like soldiers. Can we sell the merchants in Xiangfan on the idea that our Civic Guard provides them with further security from the civil war that is raging around us? And, could we have the merchants subscribe to a fund that would sustain the Guard?" Wen looked at Lao Fang.

"Well, that is how most tuanlians are funded," Fang responded, beginning to get the idea that was brewing in Wen's mind. "It depends a great deal on how well you sell the idea and what you have to sell. Will they have weapons? Will they have sufficient training and the authority needed to be effective? That is all part of the package."

"I think that the two will grow together," Wen said. "Initially, we will run the funding out of the city treasury under the rubric of civic works. We can start with something as popular as repairing the east road. And, Kong, you said you had some ideas for repairs to buildings inside the city? That could be another revenue stream."

Lao Fang offered another idea. "If we used the men's mechanical abilities to make tools and equipment that the local population doesn't generally have, the Guard could offer services that would help the farms along the highway as well as within the city. The Civic Guard could even farm, plant cash crops that don't compete with what is already being raised, and provide other services like I did in Anhui."

"What sort of services were those?" asked Wen.

"I ran silos and grain marketing for my tenants; the larger the load, the better the price. Then I would bring market goods back from Shanghai, better seeds and fertilizers. There is a lot of know-how needed for running a large farm, even when it's just a lot of small farms working together."

"Well, I think that it's the scheme that we can grow with. Kong, you keep recruiting and deploying the new members of the Civic Guard, and we will work on raising the funds," Wen said. "I would like Lao Fang to set up the books so that we can keep track of the money flow. I'm sure that someone from Beijing will audit them one day and I like to have documentation."

For the next few weeks, there was a flurry of activity along the East Road. Land was cleared and some of the logs were used to construct a large building. Squads of men rotated on the ends of two-man saws, ripping trees into rough planks which were then stacked for drying. The huge piles of chips and branches were covered with reeds and mud. Then, as the mud dried under the sun, more was added 'til there was a layer several inches thick. The workers left one hole, about a foot in diameter, in the mud layer at the top, and another at the base about the same size. They shoved dry branches through the hole at the base and set them afire; a squad of men rotated to keep the roaring flame going. After two days, the mud began to steam. A few days later, the steam lessened and the mud cover became hot. The men kept the fires going at the base and soon the fumes coming out the hole at the top changed from white steam to a thick, yellow column of fumes. A torch held up to the column of fumes burst into a column of flame that lasted for two more days, as the material inside changed from wood to charcoal. When the flame of the tower finally flickered and extinguished itself, the workers covered the top hole and plugged the air holes around the base. This process was repeated each time another substantial pile of wood accumulated, and the charcoal produced was stored as winter fuel.

In town, Tong Gaolin, the carpenter, was working with a special squad of Bannermen soldiers to develop techniques to produce large numbers of bows and arrows. A hand-crafted bow that Tong made was used as a template for many more to come. Boards of the clearest heartwood were gathered from the project north of the East Road. These, in turn, were rip-cut into two-inch-by-four-inch strips and stacked to dry. The dried strips were sorted for straightness and lack of twist. The best were cut to five-foot lengths that were to be milled.

The blacksmith fashioned a two-edged tool, which spun on a shaft powered by a tread wheel. The fast-spinning tool could cut away wood from boards into the rough shape of the bow. The finished shaping and surfacing were done by hand, but the high speed mill did the bulk of the work.

The arrow shafts were made from the shorter pieces not used for bows. They were turned on a lathe that rotated the wood against a cutting tool guided down the length of the shaft. Bundles of arrow shafts were then heated in an oven to fix their straightness and finish drying them. One end of each shaft was notched and trimmed with feathers.

The final step in the arrow-making process involved mounting the point. The idea came from the shop that made dinnerware. The shop used zinc, poured from a ladle into molds to make plates and vessels; between pours, liquid zinc would drop on the floor and form small circles. These small flat circles of thin zinc could be folded in a half-moon shape and were used as scrapers. When the circle was folded up on four sides, simultaneously, it could be crimped over the end of an arrow shaft into a four-bladed point. Done at high speed in a hot press, the points were held fast to the shaft and their edges could be filed sharp.

By late spring, the Civic Guard was easily recognized in town by their blue shirt and grey fu pant uniforms. They were paid a regular, though very small, allowance, and were well policed by their own sergeants. The Bannermen soldiers of the regular army became their trainers and drill instructors; both groups seemed to become more cohesive and civil.

The barracks in the military town now housed more than two hundred and fifty of the Civic Guard. Most were employed in engineering projects. One group, in the foothills to the west, was constructing an aqueduct to carry water from the mountain streams west of the river to the rich farmlands on the eastern side of the river. Another group was clearing that same land for extended farming. Lao Fang directed his tuanlian soldiers in the conversion of one of the older buildings, built into the wall along the river, into a grain silo. And still another group was dredging out a docking facility for trade, at the river's edge which, Wen had assured the merchants in town, would surely follow.

The military training of the Civic Guard ran concurrently with these projects. The recruits were trained in the base camp area in hand-to-hand combat, individual as well as rank-by-rank shooting with the bows, and larger scale maneuvering under possible battle conditions. As their ranks grew and the terrain became more familiar, the recruits did more and more of their training downriver on extended expeditions. On one of these, they captured a scouting party from the Wuchang area who were river pirates pressed into service by the Taiping and now very far away from their Guangxi home turf.

Wen ordered the captives held in an old warehouse that had been converted into a prison. Even though the group's loyalty to the 'high and mighty' Taiping was questionable; they all claimed to know nothing about the larger movement which had come back up the Yangtze. They knew that the Taiping had taken back Hankou and were battling for control of Hanyang, but they said Wuchang was still held firmly by Qing Imperial forces.

Wen decided to take a different tack in the interrogation of the prisoners. Dressing as one of the Hakka who had been taken when the mob came to the gate a few months before, he had himself locked in an adjoining cell. Using his best Hakka accent, he asked the prisoners, as a fellow southerner, for information.

Almost as if bragging, they opened up, describing a plan that made Wen pale with a combination of fear and anger. The Taiping general Shi Dakai, the Wing King, and three of his generals had come to retake the upper Yangtze. Shi was heading south to establish extended supply lines into Guangzhou; the others were to retake Wuchang and go on upriver.

The most disturbing part of the plan was that the Taiping were going to march north, around the Dungbai Mountains, to ship those supplies from Guangzhou to their armies that were marching north to attack Beijing. To do this, they first had to take the city of Suizhou, which blocked a valley in a range east of the Han River. In order to attack that town from both north and south, the Taiping would be sending soldiers up the Han River to take Xiangfan, and then go around the mountains north of Suizhou. The plan was only awaiting the arrival of the shallow-draft steamships from downriver.

Wen signaled the guard, and he was taken out of his cell. He went to his apartment to clean up and settle his nerves. All of the histories and tales of battling kingdoms had not prepared him for this! He carefully dressed in his official robes; as though, by looking the part, he could get through what had to be done. He sent a messenger to the hotel and to the county office building to invite Lao Fang and Master Deng to a meeting on the veranda.

"Gentlemen," he began, "I just had a meeting with the enemy!"

***
War on the Doorstep

The three went over the revelations of the river pirates and discussed their options. It was a long afternoon. In the end, it was still up to Wen to make up a plan and to make it work. He spent that night at his desk, pouring over the maps and drafting a plan. In the morning, he called the commander of the Guard into his office. They agreed that the paramount concern was secrecy. A joint operation of Bannermen, Fang's tuanlian forces, and the Civic Guard would carry out the plan. Basically, it consisted of three separate operations which would have to be coordinated in battle but, for security, kept isolated from each other till then.

On the map of the city and environs, Wen had laid out three areas for the three parts of the operation. The Han River flowed east, past the city which lay to the north, and then turned abruptly south just beyond the city. The first area was upriver, where the heavily wooded foothills grew close to the shore. The second area was east of the city and after a bend in the river to the south, along the hills on the eastern bank. The third area was on the southwestern side of the river, inside the bend, where a small farming community had grown up along the end of the Yicheng road. An antique ferry service joined the southern bank to the larger city of Xiangfan.

The ferry relied on a submerged iron chain that lay on the bottom of the river. With a hand crank, the chain was lifted and fed, link by link, through a cog-wheel box, drawing the boat from one side to the other. At best, only six people or one cart could cross at a time. It required a strong arm and about ten minutes of cranking to cross.

The Bannermen built a larger raft with a rudder on the upstream side. A long, stout rope was attached to a tree, upriver, and tied off to the raft near the rudder. By pushing the rudder to the right, the current would propel the raft to the left, quickly taking twenty soldiers across at a time. A second raft was attached with a long stout rope to the opposite bank further downstream. With no pressure on either rudder, the rafts came to rest, one on each side of the river

The most recent recruits to the Civil Guard were the least-able fighters, so they were assigned to tree cutting along the river in the first area. The massive logs were tied loosely with jute rope into rafts. Bails of smaller branches and twigs were stacked on each raft. As each raft was completed and tied off to the bank, that team of workers moved up the river and started making another. Soon more than fifty rafts were waiting to be released.

In the second area, along the east bank of the river, past the bend and up the hill overlooking the tow path, the engineers had built and installed small catapults, capable of throwing explosives and incendiary bombs down on the steamships in the river below. The Bannermen dug trenches and barbette platforms for the catapults and cannon. Bannermen sharpshooters with cap-lock rifles were deployed in the trenches and took firing practice with the Civic Guard archers at targets across the river on the western shore.

In the third area, west of the river and south of the village, under the title of physical training, the main body of the Civic Guard had to learn to run to the river from the woods, west of the fields, with fifty pound sacks of sand on their backs. Then they would walk back to the woods and run again. When they were able to do that, each guardsman added a bow and rack of arrows. Now, when they got to the river, they threw down the sack of sand, lay down behind it, and fired at targets that were high on top of sticks on the other side of the river.

A little further downriver, south of the field, a special squad of Bannermen had laid the old ferry chain across the river bottom, where it was secured to a large tree on the western bank and to a large log on the eastern bank. The log on the bank had holes drilled through the ends. It had been floated down the river and drawn up onto the eastern bank, directly across the river from the tree. The free end of the chain was drawn through the hole in the downstream end of the log and secured to form a loop.

A second large log, with holes drilled through the ends, was floated down and raised up to lay on the bank directly above the first log. The two logs were loosely joined, at the upstream end, by several loops of strong rope. A third log was then raised onto the bank above the first two and tied to the second log at the downstream end. Then a fourth was floated into position, raised, and tied, and so on. By joining alternate ends of the logs, a log boom was formed which was long enough to span the river at that point and could be anchored at both ends.

In the midst of the preparations, Master Deng returned from the country with six young scholars. "Before he died," Deng said to Wen, "The Magistrate ordered me to select six of the brightest of this year's scholars to work with you."

***

A Staff of Six

Wen looked confused. "What do I do with them?" he whispered to Deng.

Deng put his hand on Wen's shoulder and said philosophically, "It doesn't matter. This is how you advance yourself. A good Kwan learns to use all the available resources to empower himself, so that he can do more good for everyone. If you aren't ready for that step, then you won't want to see what I have in this package... Do you want it?"

"Of course!" said Wen, taking the package with a broad grin.

"You had better get rooms for them at the facility first, and open this in your apartment."

The suspense was palpable and Wen hurried to get the new young men settled. Each one had a folder with Deng's recommendations. He took the folders to his office and left them on his desk, then went immediately to his apartment and opened the package.

Inside was a new cap with a worked gold ball on top. Beneath the cap was a new robe with a quail embroidered on the front and back. These were the insignia of an eighth-level Kwan. Between the two was an official scroll announcing that Wen had been awarded the Juren (Master's) Degree, by the authority of Deng. In a second scroll was a letter, under an official seal, from the old Governor, Chang Dachun, appointing Wen as Deputy Magistrate. Beneath the scrolls was a letter from Magistrate Hong:

> *Salutations and congratulations on your advancement. You are honored both for your ability and for your timing. Your ability has gained you the knowledge to receive your new degree. You should know that the new appointment is because we are serving the empire in very difficult times. The Emperor needs your best service and has approved your appointment. I trust that you will honor me and yourself in the conduct of this new responsibility.*

The next morning, Wen appeared in his office in the new robes and wearing the new cap with the worked gold button. He welcomed the new scholars. "I am acting Magistrate Wen and I welcome you to this new assignment." The words were round and full in his mouth. "I will expect from you your best efforts. Initially, I have decided to have each of you inventory a room and its contents, and to check the records for any discrepancy. These valued items are here under our protection. We pledge on our life and the honor of our families, indeed the honor of the emperor himself, that those families who have deposited their wealth and records with us shall never suffer a loss."

Wen then moved in among the group for personal introductions, greeting each young man individually. One surprise: Dong Weili, the boy who had been reluctant to try this position three years ago back at school in Xiaohexi, was among them. Of course, they were all bright and willing and represented a broad area from the north.

For their first assignment, while five watched, Wen and Dong demonstrated how to recheck the contents of a room for inventory and how to confirm or question the record sheet. When they were done, Wen looked at the other boys and said, "Is the record complete?" Nothing!

"Did anyone notice anything missing that was listed on the record?" No one moved or even looked up.

"Did anyone notice anything that was not listed that was in the room?" They all looked furtively around the room. "It is important that these records be accurate," Wen said. "Even those things that you see as not valuable must be recorded. Look again in the room and tell me one thing that is there that is not listed on the record."

"The crate is not listed on the record," one boy said.

"Very good! Is there any thing else?"

"The carry poles?" another boy offered.

"Yes! The poles and the ropes are not listed. They should be! Everything in this room is a possession of the family that sent it here. It does not matter how common or insignificant it seems to us; each and every thing that is put into this room must be accounted for. One more thing! There is a space at the bottom of the record sheet for additional comments; use it. This pole has a crack in it and may have to be replaced before it is used again. The ropes are frayed. Pay attention to details like this and you will avoid a lot of problems later on."

The procession then went to a second room and so forth. At each door, and whenever a door was opened, two security guards would stand and watch. Nothing new was taken in or taken out without it being recorded. Stealing anything from the rooms was punishable by death. And each guard was responsible for the other. Any guilt was mutual and they would both die. Qing justice was uncomplicated and pitiless.

At the end of the tour, the records were filed and each of the new boys was assigned two guards, a new crate, and a new room. "Take all the time that you need to do the inventory correctly," Wen said. "I will be here to answer any questions. The room numbers are already marked on the case and on your record sheets. Kong Bang will have the cases delivered to your rooms and you will have him mark the delivery on your record with his chop (inked stamp). When you are done, return the records and you will be through for the day."

Feeling somewhat remiss in his duties, Wen had made plans to have lunch on the veranda overlooking the river with Fang, his wife, and daughter. They were able to spend the afternoon in pleasantries and social conversation -- and would only occasionally be interrupted by reports from the young scholars at the facility and updates from the river.

As they talked, Wen was again pleasantly struck with the fact that Madam Fang shared her strong but delicate facial features with her daughter. Every now and again during the conversation, they would even lapse into French. Fang was quick to insist that they keep it in Chinese. For Wen, it was a delightful interlude and a chance to get away from his duties.

"How are you coming with educating the girls in town?" he asked when Meixing's parents wandered to the opposite side of the veranda for a moment.

Meixing looked at him with mock surprise. "Haven't you heard about the new 'Girls School'? I have six girls already," she said proudly.

"Wonderful! What are you teaching them?"

"Reading first! I listed all of the characters that they knew on a board and we are using them in a game. I point to a character and to one of the girls. She says the word and then uses it in a sentence. Then she picks out another character and another girl; it rotates around the group. Soon, they will all know the same basic set of characters. We have almost one hundred."

"Can they write them as well?" asked Wen.

"Not yet; but soon! We are looking through the Confucian book of three hundred and eleven poems to find ones that use characters they already know. If they could hear the ancient, 'unruled' poems that Confucius selected for his 'Book of Poetry', they might see it as a more serious exercise. They seem to like the simple four character lines and rhyming the last sound of every other line."

"That's a good way; rhythm and rhyme have always been good guides for memory." said Deng. "But, for writing, there is nothing to equal to practice and review. I had to copy the three hundred and eleven many times before I did it without a mistake. Now I think I could do it in my sleep. It is a pity that his 'Book of Music' was lost in the Great Destruction (221-211 B.C). We could have sung them as well."

"That's right!" Meixing looked at Wen. "I heard that you play the pipa and sing, too!"

"Oh, where did you hear that? I am the worst among amateurs! Do you play?"

"Not the pipa. Mama taught me to play a little on the piano. We had to leave that back at the farm. I hope nothing happens to it." She looked down and swallowed hard.

"We'll get you back there as soon as we can. Maybe you can use all that emotion to write poetry of your own. 'Til then, this school looks like it might help you as much as it helps the girls in town "

"Oh, oh," Meixing said, lowering her eyes with a bit of a blush. "Mother is gathering her chick to roost. We'll talk again, soon."

"Yes, I'll look forward to it." Wen watched her walk away across the veranda, and caught her mother's eye -- looking at him.

Wen spent the rest of the evening with Lao Fang, reviewing the plans and trying to imagine the realities of the war that was moving toward them. Scouts and communications were in place to warn them in time to set their defenses, and the soldiers and Civic Guard were in a high state of readiness to be deployed. If things went well, they might prevail, but neither of them had any first-hand experience, so the weight of doubt lay heavily on their shoulders. It was up to the other side to attack, hopefully in a way that they were prepared for.

Fang had been working throughout the fall and winter to make a foundry for cannon. The low heat available from charcoal was just not enough to cleanly melt the iron ore that they could get from Yichang. So, they built a larger cupola and switched to coal. By mixing lime layers between the layers of coal and ore, they were able to create a fire so hot that the rusty rocks broke down into liquid iron. Once separated from the sludge and dross, a clean flow of liquid iron ran down the chute into the mold amidst a shower of carbon sparks and popping sand. When it had cooled, the sand was broken away and a rough cannon emerged. The small bits and flashes of metal that stuck out from the finished casting were removed by hand, chipping and scraping and grinding.

The next problem was the inside of the cannon barrel. Roughly cast as a tube, the inside had to be ground out using a spinning rock on the end of a pole. The barrel was rotated on its side as the rock was spun inside while being drawn in and out in a stream of water. When the bulk of the grinding was done, a finish-grinding rock was used to smooth the surface and size the barrel. The finish-grinding rock was chipped to look like a sausage, a very symmetrical sausage. As with the first stone, the cannon was laid on its side and turned while the finish-grinding stone inside was spun and drawn in and out. A steady flow of water ran through the barrel during the grinding to cool the rock and to clean out the grinding debris. When the smooth barrel was the right size, the fuse hole was drilled and the cannon was test fired.

***

Engagement

The months passed slowly, as if to trick them into letting down their guard. Wen had to keep stirring the pot, moving soldiers from area to area to avoid lethargy and to work off the chill that had settled over Hubei. Finally, on April 28th they heard a clattering of hooves up the Yichang road. A messenger from the advanced scouts brought word that two shallow-draft steamers were working their way up the Han River. The boats carried soldiers of the Taiping Army on both decks and on the top; each boat bristled like a porcupine with their rifles pointed toward the shore. They had passed Zhongxiang, the messenger said, and would probably be in Xiangfan in two days.

Wen gave the order for the final preparations. Two kegs of coal oil were added to the top of each of the rafts. Fresh gunpowder and exploding cannon balls were taken to the west bank trenches. Small cannons along the river were fused and loaded for their first shot. The soldiers who would fire them and reload them would be in adjacent camouflaged pits. In the morning, he would deploy the troops.

A messenger woke Wen with the news that a signal had been passed up the river and they would soon be ready for him to take command of the operation. Quickly, barracks emptied and selected soldiers from the wall left their posts and reported to their groups. One group was marched east, along the old tow path, to the cannon site. The rest were shuttled across the river by the swing ferries. Fang had deployed his tuanlian army throughout the city to take the places of the missing soldiers. The town was now locked down, and the people slowed and listened, anxiously.

Across the river, the soldiers fanned out like a seine net to gather everyone from the fields and woods into the village. Everyone was identified as a local; they found no spies or strangers. The peasants were then obliged to sit in rows in the middle of the village, under guard. Most of the Civic Guard and their Bannermen officers went south along the Yicheng Road, next to the river, until the head of their column stopped just north of the tree that held the chain. Then they turned away from the river and marched west, in a line, across the fields and into the woods. There, out of sight from the river, the soldiers spread out and sat on their sand bags to clean, load, and prime their rifles. The Civic Guard strung their bows and checked their arrows There they waited, as a small detachment dressed in farmers clothes went out to work in the fields -- as would have been 'normal' for the day and time.

Wen and his scholars stood on a promontory north of the river bend, where they could look west at the squads standing by to release the rafts, and south at the wisps of smoke from the approaching boats.

The smoke from the steamboats gradually became more defined and darker. Wen watched intently as they approached. "There it is!" he said, as he caught the quick flash of light signaled from a reflecting mirror on the bank downriver. Two of the scholars flipped over long, thin sand-filled hourglasses and silently counted seconds. They waited.

"There is number two!" said Wen. The second pair of scholars flipped over their hourglasses and silently started counting the seconds. The first two had marked the levels of the sand in their glasses and reset them. They wrote down the time interval as indicated by their hour glasses and the counted seconds.

"There is number three!" said Wen and the first pair of scholars flipped their glasses again, and again started the silent count. The second pair wrote down their counts and reset their glasses.

"There is number four!" said Wen, and the process repeated. The numbers were averaged and the speed of the boats was calculated. Quickly, they computed the time it would take until the boats would be in the trap, and at what point the release of the rafts should start.

The first boat entered the trap and the Taiping soldiers were plainly visible, bristling along every inch of the rails of the top and bottom decks. Their guns pointed outward and every eye was on the shoreline.

"Release the rafts!" Wen said to the signalman and flags were raised in a relay along the north shore. Slowly the rafts were set adrift in the river and pushed off to catch the current. As one left the shore a second one was released, and then a third, and so on. As each raft started moving down the river, its squad would run up the river to release another, till they were all parading on the current toward the bend.

When the second boat loaded with soldiers entered the trap like the first, the 'farmers' in the field started walking toward the tree that had the chain attached. When the lead boat noticed the first raft coming around the bend, it slowed and blew its horn. The second boat slowed as well, to avoid a collision. The raft floated toward the lead boat and the second raft came around the bend, and then the third. Unnoticed, behind the boats, the 'farmers' had dragged the chain out of the water, allowing the logs on the opposite bank to roll in. The log boom obligingly floated across the river. Soon, the boom was anchored from shore to shore and the rafts were held by it. As more and more rafts came around the bend, the two steamboat captains brought their boats to a standstill in the river. The rafts quickly surrounded their boats and still more rafts came, choking the river and pinning the boats between the banks. The captain of the second boat blew his horn furiously and tried to maneuver around the left of the lead boat, quickly running aground as soon as it left the channel.

"Open fire!" Wen yelled out and the flags were raised. The cannon aimed at the lead boat and fired, exploding balls directly into the middle of its engine room. The cannon on the hill were quickly reloaded with grape shot and fired on the men at the rail who were scrambling for cover. The sharpshooters had moved into their positions and raked the decks with their highly accurate rifle fire, while the Civic Guard showered the boat with flights of arrows.

Over on the west bank, the soldiers hidden in the woods took up their sand bags and ran with them on their backs to the edge of the river. There they threw down the sand bags and lay behind them with their rifles and arrows firing at the Taiping who were jumping off the boats onto the rafts. The sky filled with a shower of arrows. Explosions started breaking up the rafts, turning them into a tangle of logs that crushed anyone who would walk on them. The bullets from both banks broke open the casks of coal oil, and fire leapt from raft to raft on both sides of the boats. The cannon fell silent and the sporadic rifle fire slowed as the supply of available targets were exhausted.

Wen and his scholars packed up their instruments and walked back to town. The townspeople were on the wall and atop their houses trying to get a better look at the source of all the commotion on the river. Black smoke wafted up toward the town, but was swept harmlessly away by a gentle breeze from the west. Wen walked to the middle of the park in the center of the town followed by a wave of people who had been on the heights. When the curious had gathered, he spoke to them.

"The bandits and thieves who would have stolen your life are dead! The glorious Qing Army is, today, victorious! As the Heavenly Mandate helps us to govern in peace, it requires us to be brutal and unforgiving in war! The Bannermen and Civic Guard will finish their business on the river, and I warn you not to venture near it for a few days." Off in the distance, an occasional shot was heard and the crowd stood listening to the sudden silence.

After dispersing the crowd, Wen walked to the hotel and up to the veranda, where Meixing and her mother had been watching. They greeted him with troubling news. Meixing's father had gone back to bed, complaining of feeling weak and nauseated.

"It was too much excitement," Mama said. "He was too active, too tired. Perhaps if you would tell him that everything is all right, maybe he would be able to rest quietly till he comes back to himself."

Wen went quickly to their apartment. Lao Fang lay like a ghost on the white silk sheets, but struggled to a sit up when he saw who his visitor was.

"It is over and we won!" said Wen jubilantly. "You would have loved it! The plan worked without a hitch and now they are just cleaning up. I will be anxious to hear the reports. Your cannons helped win the day. They couldn't have done it without you. Now you must take it easy. I will keep you informed."

Lao Fang lay back in the bed, some color returning to his face. "Good, very good! I think I can rest now. Thank you for letting me know. It was just more excitement than this old man could take." Wen patted his hand and left the room.

As evening fell, reports did indeed start coming in. "We counted more than two hundred dead!" said the Captain of the Guard. "There are many more inside the boats, hiding behind things, but I am sure if any more are alive they will be dead by morning. I set up a receiving area for information and confiscated weapons. We will clean and oil the weapons tonight, before they get rusty. What shall we do with them?"

"There are only so many hands here that can use them. Perhaps we should ship the excess over to Suizhou. That is where the fighting will be." He sat back and rubbed his eyes. "I would like to know of any information you recover from the bodies -- any plans or maps."

"We'll be working through the night, but I hope that you will rest. Your plan worked well. We only lost six of our own. The men thank you."

By morning, there was news of more recovered stores and weapons. The boat crews had come out from hiding and were held as the only prisoners. The count of the dead had gone over three hundred and fifty and would go higher; they were straining to dig the mass graves needed for even that many.

There was also a wealth of information found on the bodies of the dead Taiping officers. Their maps indicated the rebellion was now a war between the Qing government and the Taiping government – as equals -- in their minds. But, most importantly, they discovered battle plans that left less than a week to transfer the confiscated arms over to Suizhou! A caravan left the East Gate that afternoon.

Throughout the day, work continued on clearing the logs and rafts from the river and salvaging everything possible from both of the boats. The shoreline became a tent city for recovered items: clothing to jewelry, weapons to medical supplies, food to tools. The second boat hadn't been so badly damaged in the fighting and was floated off the sand bar. Then work began replacing damaged boards and rails where needed. Additional cannon, found in the boats, were mounted for action on the upper deck and sandbag redoubts were assembled all along the upper and lower rails.

Wen looked over the list of recovered items. "What is this about cases of new rifles?" he asked Kong Beifu, Captain of the Guard.

"Yes, there were six cases of brand new rifles and twenty-four boxes of some sort of cartridges. I don't think they knew what to do with them, any more than we do." He held out a booklet. "All we know is that they are brand new, in the original cases with instruction books to show how the guns work. It's some new kind of mechanism and we can't understand it -- and the books are European. None of us can read them."

Wen opened the booklet to a page that had a drawing of the mechanism inside the gun. "Where did they come from?" he asked. "It is strange they would have something so modern!"

The Captain smiled and said, "According to the manifest, they were captured on a French boat, bound for the Imperial forces that were defending Nanjing. But the Taiping got there first and sent the whole boat back up the river to Hankou to help in the battle to retake Hanyang and Wuchang, which they had lost last summer. They must have just passed the problem on to the bunch in this party. And now, on to us."

"Let me see if Lao Fang can help us," Wen said, putting the book in his pocket. "I'll be seeing him for lunch."

***

A New Technology

After lunch and some relaxing conversation about the progress of the new girl's school and the recent battle, Meixing and her mother excused themselves, to read the books they had recently bought in town. Wen took Lao Fang off to the side.

"I just got a book on a new machine, but it is written in German and I can't understand it. Could you perhaps help me read it?" Wen asked Fang. He pulled out the instruction manual and handed it to Fang, who glanced at it and then over at his wife. "Very interesting! But, could we go over this in your office? We'll see you ladies later, all right?" He ushered Wen quickly to the door.

As they scurried across the street toward Wen's office, Fang asked in hushed amazement, "Do you have such a weapon?"

Wen nodded.

"I have read of such rifles in articles in the technical journals that I get from Shanghai, but I didn't think they had any in China. This is the latest technology. How did you come by it?"

Wen kept walking and they talked in whispers. "We recovered two cannon and several boxes of these in the battle on the river. It seems the French sold these to the Qing government for the defense of Nanjing. But before they docked, the Taiping took control of the river and seized them for their forces in the fight to take back Wuchang. Instead, those troops sent them on up here for the assault on us."

"No wonder you haven't seen anything like this. This is the new German Needle gun technology. This is practically a Prussian state secret. Someone must have made a big mistake selling this to the Qing government in the first place. I can't wait to see them!"

In the office they poured over the text of the instruction books. As Fang read the German and translated it, Wen wrote furiously in Chinese. The afternoon passed and the sun had set when a messenger from the hotel came over. "Madam Fang wonders when you might come back. They are preparing to eat dinner."

Fang laughed and went back with the messenger. He told Madam that he and Wen were just engaged in a very interesting project, and he would like to get back to work on it some more, that evening, if the ladies wouldn't mind.

"There is something strange going on here!" she said, waving a finger in his face knowingly and pulling on his chin hairs. "You go back to your men's games. Meixing and I will read."

After dinner, and late into the evening, the two men worked out the text and selected existing characters which would approximate the meaning of the new German words.

After breakfast the next morning, Fang went directly back to Wen's office. Wen was already compiling yesterday's translations into characters that less-educated foot soldiers might understand. Without much conversation, they returned to their translation. Fang returned to the hotel only for lunch and dinner, but again didn't get back to his apartment till much later that evening.

The translations went on throughout the next day until late in the afternoon. A room had been set up for the young scholars to make several copies of the book. Satisfied with the translation, Wen and Fang went across the river to see the real thing. The soldiers had erected tables, wiped off the sticky Cosmoline, and washed the bolt-action rifles down with light oil.

Fang picked up one of the rifles and lovingly stroked it, working the bolt action. "May I try it?" he asked, as he reached for a cartridge from its box.

Wen nodded and said, "See if you can hit that tree over there."

"Do you see where the branch was broken off?" asked Fang. He raised the rifle to a proper firing position, took aim, and fired as though he had been doing it all his life. A soldier ran over to the tree and pointed to a hole in the broken stump of the branch. "With this rifle, you can kill a man at two hundred meters. No problem! The Taiping in Wuchang, must have had no idea of what they had!" Lao Fang said, shaking his head. "This rifle is five times faster than the muzzle-loading cap-locks that they are using against us. See how the cartridge is loaded in the middle of the rifle and held in place with this bolt?" he asked, demonstrating for Wen. "Instead of a cap on the outside the rifle, there is a cap built into the cartridge. The needle is contained in the bolt and strikes the cap through a hole in the front of the bolt when you pull the trigger. Just open the breach by moving the bolt, like so," he said, continuing the demonstration, "Put in a new cartridge, with the bullet attached and close the bolt like so. Now you are ready to take another shot while the other fellow is still trying to tamp down his cartridge, wad, and ball. And then he still has to find a fulminate of mercury cap to put under the hammer!"

"Another thing," he continued, "I don't know if you noticed but -- the bullet on the end of the cartridge is not a round ball. It is tapered to a point in front and has a hollow base that expands to engage the rifling inside the barrel. That insures the projectile will spin, which makes it go straight. It's called a mini-ball after its inventor, a French Captain named Claude Minie."

Wen, and the soldiers around him, listened to Fang in amazement.

"I keep up on such things, as you can see!" he laughed at their surprised faces. "There is always time on the farm, so I read everything I can get from Europe, especially the technical publications."

"How would you like to train my soldiers to use these?" Wen asked.

The Bannermen soldiers were quick to line up for lessons on the operation of the new rifles. The new technology was a hot topic amongst the troops and a source of competition. Only the best shooters were allowed to actually fire the weapon due to the limited numbers of cartridges. But soon, these new cartridges would be produced in the shops of the military city.

Life, Death, and the River Trade

***

A Flourishing

Lao Fang had become a very busy man. In addition to the new military classes, cannon foundry, and accounting for the Civic Guard, he was also overseeing the new farms cleared by the Guard along the river to the north of the city. The first crops were coming in and filling the silos he had built into the city wall. Food was less scarce now, and quietly, prices decreased; this was the best defense against rebellion. New farms along the East Road were being cleared to provide for the growing population and anticipated trade.

The city of Suizhou sent an emissary and trade mission: "To officially thank our neighbors for their help when we were under attack by the Taiping, and to purchase grains and goods, if such are available."

The emissary had with him a chest of five-hundred silver tales to compensate Xiangfan for the timely arrival of their troops and the gift of the rifles, powder, and shot which they had sent after the battle on the river. The Taiping had marched from Hanyang along a valley on the far side of a small range of mountains at about the same time the steam boats were making their way north along the Han River toward Xiangfan. They had set up a siege around the southern side of the city and planned to wait for their own troops to come down from the north after they had taken Xiangfan. Instead, of course, the troops that came down from the north were Bannermen and Civic Guard, well armed and fighting against the Taiping. Their route put a halt, for the moment, to the Taiping plans to go north around the Dabie Shan range.

The merchants who accompanied the trade mission were introduced to the merchants and artisans in and around the city. The trade missioners were assured that Xiangfan would help them with whatever they needed 'at a fair price'. They took back with them three of the grain wagons that Lao Fang had in storage -- at a fair price. The need for food had overwhelmed the few farms that were still operating, though marginally, in the south. Taxes and outright theft by official and unofficial bandits had made farming an unrewarding business.

When the guests from Suizhou had left, Lao Fang hosted a dinner party at the Long Meng for the whole town. All of the merchants, artisans, and many common laborers were fed and entertained; the streets filled with people well into the evening. "If we can maintain our Civic Guard as an instrument of expansion," Lao Fang said to Wen at the height of the evening, "We stand to make a lot of money!" He was beside himself with expectation. The serious planning would come later, but for the moment, the wine flowed.

In the days that followed, Lao Fang and Wen met with many of the merchants and artisans in the town, and they decided to have an open meeting to discuss trade prospects which Fang knew lay ahead for them. He understood the principle of venture capital and corporate mercantile operations better than anyone -- and he knew from his schooling and experience that they would need financing on a large scale. Once again he was grateful for his father's insistence on continuing his education before going into farming. After receiving his Jinshi degree in Shanghai, Fang's father had sent him to London to study. He learned English, worked in an English bank, and eventually received a Master's degree from Cambridge in Political Science, which included the new study of economics.

The Long Meng hotel dining room again hosted the occasion. The banquet for the evening included sixteen dishes and two soups. Two pipa players on the balcony at the head of the staircase greeted guests with their music. Wen had made sure everyone who had a business or trade was invited. The Fang family, Deng Weili, and the Taotai of the town all sat at the head table with Wen.

After dinner, Wen stood up and announced to his guests that the city would offer the services of the repaired steam boats, under the protection of the Civic Guard, to implement a commercial project being organized by Lao Fang.

Then Fang took the floor and proceeded to turn the announcement into an impromptu presentation on the English trade model. "What we are proposing," he said, "Is a unified way to sell our goods to the larger market of customers down along the Han River. Items which you have had in stock for a long time and have not sold, overstocked items, and items that you would like to sell more of are the sorts of things we will be handling. For example, I will be sending grain that I brought from Anhui."

"Things get stolen downriver!" one man called out. "Why should we put anything at risk?"

"For profit!" Lao Fang answered him immediately, with a broad smile. "The time is ripe to trade with the towns that have suffered the pillage of the recent Taiping rebellion. They need things we have in abundance and can sell to them."

"They only pillaged the rich and powerful!" someone called out in a southern accent.

"Not entirely true." Fang said. "In the wake of the rebellion many innocent poor families lost their use of the land. Regardless of what the Taiping claim, many are starving in their own homes, afraid to have anything for fear of loosing it to bandits who are on the loose because the imperial armies are tied up fighting the Taiping. By helping these families and these towns, we will be spreading peace and stability. Well-fed people do not throw away their lives to follow people like the Taiping."

"Where will they get the money to buy our products?"

"Some have hidden money; others will need our help till they have money. But it is still a world of opportunities. Look at how we have created wealth here in Xiangfan!"

"Who will sell our goods for us?"

Lao Fang looked over the faces before him. "We will form a corporation," he said, "A business in which we all are the owners and the world is our marketplace."

"How is that possible?"

"The corporation is just an agreement between ourselves to jointly sell our goods," he explained. "We each put into the venture what we are willing to put at risk in the anticipation of a higher profit than we would normally expect. The price and the number of potential sales are greater where the need is greater. Where the Taiping have ravaged the countryside, there is a need awaiting our products. Where they have taken away the food, we can sell food, which we have in abundance. Where the cities have been decimated by the conflicts, we can sell building materials, which we have in abundance. Where the farms are in ruins and the seed grain has been eaten, we can sell seed and tools, which we have or can make in abundance. We have what they need! This is our opportunity to enrich ourselves and to help our neighbors at the same time. The coming peace will bring us prosperity."

Fang looked over the faces before him and saw one or two nodding in agreement. "All right then, do you already make or can you make more than you can sell? Would you sell more, if you could?" With each question, more heads moved in agreement. "How about the person setting next to you; did he sell all that he could?" Heads turned and talk between the tables rose from a murmur to a roar.

Fang waited for the room to still, then he continued. "We each decide what and how much we are willing to put at risk. No one is forced to participate. There are no quotas. Those who want to participate offer a list of merchandise they are willing to contribute. A bill of materials is drawn up from those lists and we agree, among ourselves, what the prices will be for each item. The value of each merchant's contribution determines the size of his share in the venture. Now, a share is like a slice of flat bread; the bigger your contribution, the larger your slice is. We are all entitled to shares -- according to our contribution. The larger our risk, the larger will be our share of the profits of the venture."

The room again broke into talk and arguments. "What if someone wants a bigger share than his stuff is worth?" A man asked from a table at the side of the room.

"This is all based on agreement between us. If someone will not adjust his price to a fair market level, as seen by the rest of us, then he is out! He is free to keep his stuff in his shop and not participate." Fang had to take a deep breath and remind himself that he was more teacher than organizer in all of this.

"What if my things don't sell, downriver?" asked a man in the back.

"If your things don't sell at the price that we had agreed on, then you have three choices. You can lower your price and accept a smaller share of the venture, or you may take back your things and relinquish your shares, or you may sell your shares to someone else. The form of the investment, for each of us, will change from the materials, into shares. The materials that each of invests will still be there, but we will not own them any longer. What we own will be our shares in the corporation -- it, in turn, owns the materials. The shares can be bought and sold just like material things, but they are more fungible, that is, able to be sold for its own value on the open market. Let's say, I am the only investor. And, I invest my grain in the corporation in exchange for stock. We know what the price of my grain is, so that is the value of my stock. Now the corporation owns the grain and I own all of the shares in the corporation. The value hasn't changed."

Fang regarded the serious faces in the audience to make sure that everyone had taken that first step. "Now, the corporation puts the grain on Wen's boat and he takes it somewhere else - a place where they don't have much grain. Someone there is willing to pay a higher price for it than it had here. A sale is made and Wen comes back with the money he got for the sale. Now, the corporation is worth more than it was when he left. But wait! This is important. I owe Wen a fee, to cover his costs for the boat and his Civic Guard for taking it to market. So, the corporation pays Wen for his expenses. If the stock is still more valuable than when I bought it, the difference is profit. That is why I send my things down the river for sale."

Looking again at the faces, Fang made sure they all were still with him. "We will always make a profit if we include the expenses and the investment in the sale price. There are still risks of loss, but we will always protect ourselves by protecting the boats and the cargo. That protection, provided by the Civic Guard, is another expense that must be included in the sale price of anything."

The evening continued with similarly animated questions from the guests and reasoned answers from Fang. Not every question could be asked or answered, so it was several days before the first merchants signed up.

Lao Fang placed one of his wagon loads of grain into small casks to be sold individually. The carpenter put up a lot of unsold tables and chairs that he had in his front yard. A few merchants contributed sewn shoes and cooking utensils, candles and clothing. It was a start. The value of each item was calculated and, when everyone agreed, shares were issued in proportion to the investment.

Wen went along on the first cruise to assess the prospects. His cabin was fortified with a sand-filled wall, against the possibility of small arms fire. The boat was impressive from the shore, but intentionally slow so it could be seen by any prospective customers out there. Wen could sense the presence of people, back behind the tree line, as the steamboat slipped along the river, but he couldn't see anyone for the first few days. On the third day, they sighted some people foraging along the shore. Wen had the crew anchor the boat in the middle of the stream so he could talk with the people.

As it turned out, they were a family displaced from their home north of Zhongxiang, a trading town halfway down the river to Hongzhang. There had been many others, they told Wen, who fled when the Taiping came through the town.

"They were like crazy people!" the father said. "They took whatever they wanted and would have killed the taotai, if he hadn't run away. But they left us and went up the river. We thought this was their boat and we were afraid they had come back to kill us."

"Well, it was their boat!" said Wen, "But we killed them and took it for our own use. We are from Xiangfan and we are here to help people like you. We want to help set up farms and towns along the river."

"We have nothing!" the father said sadly, shaking his head in despair and disgust at how their lives had changed. "We cannot buy or farm. We left everything back in Zhongxiang."

"Are there many more out there?" Wen asked waving at the flatlands to the east.

"Yes, there are small groups of families who have built houses; not so big as a town, but they are out there."

"Good! Then this will be where we build our first store."

***

The Merchant Marine

The Bannermen surveyed the area and proposed a spot for the store on the higher east bank, where the ground was firm enough to support a building. The surrounding area was low lying, good for farming but too soft to support horses, so it would slow down any attacking rebels.

From the bamboo thickets along the river, Wen had the farmer and his family gather enough materials to construct a raised-platform building; in return, they were fed from the stores of grain. The Bannermen staked out the land to be tilled and planted, and they measured out enough seed to plant twelve lee, about two acres. After building the store house, they selected a supply of various hand tools. Leaving three of the Civic Guard to build the store and direct the planting, and leaving enough grain to feed the people for two weeks, Wen and the steamboat crew headed out again.

Further downriver, they came to the town of Zhongxiang. The town itself was almost two kilometers east of the river and seventy meters above it. Wen beached his boat at an area along the riverfront where the local boatmen tied up. The Bannermen sent a scouting party into the town, and found it quite recovered from the passing Taiping. The taotai, Shang Qiuping, came back to the boat with the Bannermen to personally greet the Magistrate from Xiangfan.

"Ah, Your Excellency, we are greatly honored by your visit," Qiuping said. "How may I be of service?"

Wen stepped down from the gangway and greeted him warmly. "I am relieved to see you well! I had heard that the Taiping passed this way and we were concerned for all of our people in the area. We have brought some things to trade with you, and to establish closer ties with all the towns along the river."

"We have survived the Taiping, but I understand that you have defeated them in battle. We are in your debt." He bowed, then added with a small smile, "And, I see that you are making better use of the steamboat than they were."

Two palanquins arrived and Qiuping gestured an invitation to Wen. "Yes!" Wen said, "I would like very much to see the town and meet your people."

The two men got in and were carried side-by-side up the pathway to the town. As they rode, they exchanged stories of the war. The taotai was able to confirm that the town of Suizhou had recovered well and had sent troops of its own out to secure the mountain pass through which they traded. Although they were still fighting skirmishes with bandits south of them, near Anlu, the main force of the Taiping Army was fighting the Hunan Army, under Zeng Guofan, a local landlord and high Imperial official.

Wen and the taotai spent the day touring the shops and facilities of the town, and ended the day with a very good dinner at the best restaurant in town. Wen returned to the boat that evening. They had sold some of the furniture and a few utensils, but no grain. The town's grain stores were well hidden and had survived the Taiping. Wen would have to go further south of Zhongxiang.

The boat drifted on the river in a wide path of shallow silt till another landing was spotted at Jukou. Here, the land was less fertile. Again they stopped and toured the village, offered their wares for sale, and left with only moderate success. Further south, they stopped at Shayang with similar results. Then, the river picked up speed and passed quickly through a series of bends. They stopped at Zekou. Wen decided not to continue any further down the Han when he heard of a Taiping gun emplacement on a bluff, only a few miles downstream.

Zekou itself wasn't much, but a trader there said he had dealings with a much larger town, Qianjiang, which lay two kilometers upstream to the south. Because the tributary river, the Xiaojiang, that went inland was too small for the steamboat, the trader could use a skiff to negotiate the trip, he said, and eagerly proposed to buy everything they had for a very small price. Wen declined the offer, but suggested an alternative. Wen would have his men build a store on the south bank, at the mouth of River, to sell their stock to the trader at a ten percent discount for sales in Qianjiang. The listed price was double what the materials would have commanded in Xiangfan. After the stocks were off-loaded, three of the Civic Guards were chosen to remain behind to act as agents and operators of the store. They would also take orders for other materials to be delivered on a subsequent trip. Most of the grain stayed on board, because it posed too great a temptation for local bandits and the trader indicated he could not sell rice at their price.

On the trip back up the river, they stopped at each of the towns they had visited on the way down, and sold more of Lao Fang's grain at each stop. When they returned to the site of the first store, Wen noticed several more families had come out of the woods; some were working in the fields.

"They begged for food and we couldn't refuse them," the Guard-proprietor told Wen. "But we insisted they help cultivate the fields and plant the seeds that we had. Now we're running out of seed and food. The seeds they planted aren't ready for harvest yet. What should we do? "

Wen ordered the rest of the grain off-loaded and the farming area expanded. In time, the seed would replenish itself. "Try to get them to start a permanent town," he told the Guard. "We'll need a good base population in the area to make this work."

***

Home Port

The boat steamed northward again, back toward Xiangfan. When they arrived, they were astonished by how much the work had progressed along the banks of the river. A trench more than twice the length of the boat had been dug parallel to the river on the north bank and about a boat's length inland. The trench was lined with rough-cut boards. The soldier supervising the activity had worked in the harbor of Canton and was clearly in charge.

Lao Fang met the boat at the river's edge and greeted his protégé with a raised cupped hand salutation and a broad smile. "We have an ambitious project for you here! They are digging the forms for a coffer dam that will be the back-side of our new docking facility. And over there," he said, pointing at the opposite bank, "They are working on a dry dock to repair out fleet." He climbed aboard on the gangplank which was swung out to the shore, and took Wen's hand in a hearty shake.

Wen smiled weakly. "I am sorry, but I don't know that we'll need any more boats," he said.

"Why?" Fang asked, "What is the matter? What went wrong?"

"We didn't sell it all!" Wen said disconsolately. "In fact, we didn't sell most of it!" Wen looked down at his feet, fighting with himself to keep control. "I am afraid that I've failed you and all the merchants in town."

"Look at me!" said Fang, leading him back into his cabin. "Look at me, straight in the eye. Stand up and tell me; what did you do.?"

"We couldn't…. "

"No! Don't tell me what you didn't do! Tell me what you <u>did</u> do!"

Wen recounted the trip and the attempts they had made to sell the goods entrusted to him. "We had to leave most of the merchandise out there, unsold."

"And you did it for good reasons! Don't loose sight of that! Every decision you made was based on what you found. All right, it wasn't what we had imagined here, so far away. We didn't know! You didn't know! They didn't know! You found what you found and you decided to do what you did. There's nothing wrong in that! You do not need to apologize to anyone. You will have to explain why things turned out the way they did, but give yourself credit for making the decisions that had to be made."

"I wish that we had been more successful."

"Of course you do. But things change. So you change with them! Now look forward. Yes, some of the merchants will be surprised and disappointed that you are not putting sacks of money in their hands as soon as you land. But that's the reality. Some people may even get angry because things didn't go as they expected. So what? Let's just be ready to face their anger, if and when it happens. First of all, you must be firm in your conviction that you did nothing wrong and that you couldn't have done anything better. We can save apologies for something more worthy of apologies."

"Yes, Lao Fang, I know you are right. But they will want their money today. And I don't have it!"

"That's all right! Let's think this through. This was always a speculative venture -- they knew that going in. They knew that bad things could happen, remember? 'Things get stolen down river,' they said. They knew they could even have lost everything. Right now, it's not lost; it's just unsold."

"Well, we did sell some of it. Maybe we could give them some money."

"No! Don't even start thinking like that. The agreement was that the costs would be paid first. Did you get paid for the use of the boat or the pay for the soldiers and guardsmen? Of course not! The accounting is the last thing. Right now, it is a work-in-progress. You can report that you did set up two outposts and a farming community. And you established good relations and mercantile commitments as far downriver as you could go. You are a success! Glory in that! This is only a start."

"I don't feel successful."

"Well, don't go out there till you do! You did a courageous thing; like when you walked into that Hakka mob. You put yourself in harm's way for duty's sake! This is no less. You didn't know what was downriver. This boat could have blown up underneath you. A lot of things could have gone wrong. But you went; they didn't. You got the job started. I dare say none of them would leave on such a venture. Now get ready to meet your public. You are a hero!"

Wen went back out onto the deck with Lao Fang, and waved at the cheering crowd that had gathered. They walked down the gangway over to the site of the dock construction. The soldier who had taken charge of the dock project was presented to Magistrate Wen, and explained the plan he was bringing into reality.

The large trench would be filled with rocks and cement, and would serve as a back wall of the slip where the boats would load and unload. At the ends of the back wall, two other walls would be built, angling out both upstream and down. Then all the dirt, from the walls to the river itself, would be dredged out for a harbor. He talked with so much enthusiasm and urgency -- so like that of Lao Fang -- Wen was sure it was due to his friend's influence on the men.

There was, of course, a welcome-home banquet at the Long Ming. Wen presented a summation of the trip's events and carried the whole thing off with remarkable ease, even announcing another trip to be made upstream in the near future. The merchants, who had all been invited to the banquet, seemed to take whatever disappoint they may have felt in stride; there were no problems for Wen to deal with after all. Following his presentation, many of the guests adjourned to the veranda to watch the sunset and talk into the night.

***

Civil Pursuits

Wen looked for Meixing among the banquet crowd, and finally located her trying to look inconspicuous by a table of cut fruit. She could not have been any less inconspicuous to his eye. She wore, he found out later, her first European-style dress. Her mother had sewn it by hand while he was down river. He turned and bumped into a server from the hotel staff. Taking a deep breath and excusing himself, he headed directly toward her. "Well, how is your school coming?" he said as nonchalantly as he could.

"My school is work!" she said with a rueful smile. "I didn't think it would be so hard to find things to learn. We ran out of common words. -- and it was getting a little boring anyway, just talking about words. They need a context!" She fiddled with the necklace her mother had given her. "So I've been re-reading from the Book of Poems, and trying to find ones that use the words the women know. The words they used back then are not the words that we use today. These women just don't talk that way. I think I will have to write new poems or stories to...."

"Monsieur?" Meixing's mother interrupted their conversation with a light tap on Wen's sleeve. She was standing surprisingly close. "May I have a word with you, please?"

They excused themselves and crossed to an unoccupied table at the other side of the hotel veranda.

"You seem to have taken an interest in my daughter, non?" she began, "Alors, that is as it will be. My husband has also taken an interest in you. But I know them both! Do I not? What I know is that in the end, we will all be most happy if this courtship is done properly. Is it not so? That is all I have to say on that." With that, Madam rested and sat back in her chair.

Wen also sat back in his chair and rolled his eyes. "Madam you speak with refreshing candor. I would have it no other way! I would be honored to join our families, but as you say, there are proprieties. And as a Chinese man of letters, I have studied them. I have never lived them. But in time, I am sure that they will be our best guide."

"So!" she exclaimed, and sat up in her chair, "That being said, let us return to the others, d'accord?" Wen stood, held her chair, and they walked back to the other guests.

"What was that about?" Meixing asked from behind her fan.

"I think I love your mother," he whispered. She slapped his arm playfully with her fan.

***

Expanding Trade

During the months that followed, Wen went north to Ankang and stopped at the cities along the way, making contacts, writing contracts, and shuttling passengers and cargo. The profits paid for repairs to the second boat and it was pressed into service. The harbor at Xiangfan became a busy place, so much so that a second harbor was constructed across the river with larger machinery to load and off- load cargo.

Wen's companies also started expanding in all the towns where they docked. His construction company was overwhelmed by requests for new docking facilities and bridges. His boat building facilities started work on a floating dredge and work platform to make new harbors and river improvements.

Lao Fang was also getting busy, starting his own bank, Merchants Bank Group, with the home office in Xiangfan and several branch offices along the routes of commerce opened by his new son-in-law. Oh, yes. Wen and Meixing were married -- in between all the business dealings and expansions -- and even took a week-long voyage downriver as a honeymoon.

The honeymoon trip, in a commercial steamer on a business passage, was a sweet-sour joke among the family. Mama had always wanted to show them Paris and the Danube. But, most regrettably, Meixing's brothers were still stationed with the Qing Army fighting the Taiping and could not attend the ceremony. Her older brother, Linkong, was up north, near Beijing on General Senggelinqin's staff, while her younger brother, Linjen was in the Great Southern Encampment, between Nanjing and Shanghai, with General Xiang Rong.

But, it was 1854 -- and the rebellion was affecting everyone's lives. Millions were dieing, untold numbers were homeless, destitute and crushed by the passing armies. In Hunan Province, south of the lake and the Yangtze that fed it, Zeng Guofan, a High Kwan who was the Vice Minister of the Board of Rites, had formed an army, petitioning and receiving Imperial sanction to act on his own with the authority formerly reserved for the emperor alone, despite the fact that Zeng Guofan was Han Chinese. He set up a spy network throughout the southeastern provinces, rooted out criminals and criminal bureaucrats, and conducted trials and executions in the name of reestablishing justice and the rule of law. Among the Heaven and Earth Societies, who were largely river pirates and local bandits, he became known as 'the head chopper'. After a year of fighting, and problems back in Nanjing, the Taiping armies left the western region and went back downriver, pursued by his Hunan Army.

Throughout 1855, trade along the river continued to expand. Meixing had their first baby, a boy named Zhenli. Wen had taken up his studies again with Deng Gaoxi and received his invitation to take the Jinshi (Doctoral) exams in Changsha in June. Three weeks later, word came to Xiangfan that he had passed third in his class, and was promoted to seventh pin Kwan status. He received his new formal assignment as The Magistrate for the county from the Governor General himself.

With the war moving down the Yangtze, Wen and Fang were able to expand their operations into Wuhan, as it was now being called. The three towns at the intersection of the Han and Yangtze -- Hankou, Hanyang and Wuchang -- were now incorporating into one city. Port sites and harbor facilities were purchased, and outfitted with local money through the organizational abilities of Lao Fang. Day-to-day affairs in Xiangfan were now being handled by Dong Weili, who had passed his Juren (Masters) exams and was made Deputy Magistrate.

Lao Fang, however, was showing signs of slowing up the expansion of his banking empire, and had a suggestion for Wen and Meixing. "I was thinking I would like to settle down again and have a small farm, maybe up along the East Road. How would you like to build me a farm? Maybe you two would like to join us and have an adjoining farm?"

The thought of moving out of the city and their cramped apartments was all the motivation the young couple needed. Wen took two forty-acre parcels off the books and assigned them to himself and to Fang. By the spring of 1856, the houses and out buildings were finished and stocked, and they had a staff of loyal Civic Guardsmen, who had "retired" to take on the day-to-day duties of running the farms. Meixing soon announced she was expecting their second child in the fall, and Wen returned to a long-postponed study of Tang Dynasty poetry.

***

Fang Linjin

Meixing's school had grown; it was housed now in an older house on the northeast side of town. Classes were open to all girls, but still did not receive governmental support as the boy's school did. The books to be copied had to be borrowed from someone's personal library, and there was no state support for the teachers. Meixing now employed three teachers and paid them out of her own allowance. The elegance of the girl's script was strikingly feminine; it became an art form, more akin to painting as it reflected the emotions and scenes described. The girls read the histories and poetry of the Song and Tang eras; the lessons of the Warring States period were less interesting to them, as were the terse aphorisms of Sun Tzu's fifth century B.C. book on The Art of War, which were standard texts in the boys' schools.

In June of 1856, the war itself crashed down upon the family. Fang Linjen, the younger son of Fang and Madeline, younger brother to Meixing, died in the fall of the Great Southern Encampment, which wrapped around the east wall of Nanjing. Ten thousand Qing troops died in three days of intense fighting. Imperial Commissioner Xiang Rong also died fifty days later from his wounds in the town of Danyang.

Word of Linjen's death was brought, with his body, to the farm in Lu'an. One of the peasant farmers who worked on the farm, a man who knew and loved the family, made it his business to personally bury the body on a hillside west of the farm -- a place where, together, the family had enjoyed many picnics watching the setting sun; he then rode the five hundred kilometers to Xiangfan to notify Lao Fang.

Wen had never met Linjen or his elder brother Linkong, but he grew to know them as though they were his actual brothers. The family could not go back to the farm in Lu'an because the Taiping were still active in the area, which had changed hands from imperial to rebel control several times. But Madeline and Meixing recounted the lives of the brothers over and over after Linjen's death. Lao Fang drifted in and out of depression and waved off any consolation. He took long walks with Wen and retold his sons' lives in memories. Wen thus became the repository of the sons' history and felt, at last, a real member of a larger family. Wen had thought much during these walks of his own family, who had passed away as he grew and lost touch with his mountain home. Now, he mourned his own loss of family and linked it with the passing of Linjen. Together, they mourned as one family.

***

Taiping Tianguo

In April, the Taiping had come back up the Yangtze River. They overran the stores on the southern end of the Han River and members of Wen's Civic Guard were fighting alongside Zeng Guofan's Hunan army, which was now Wen's primary customer for food and clothing. What none of them knew at that time were the strange happenings going on downriver in Nanjing.

Hong Xiuquan, a self-anointed minister, was the "Heavenly King" and leader of the Taiping movement. But, there were five young men who joined him in the realization of his movement. They were his five "Kings" and had run the movement for the last six years. But now, Hong was under attack by his own subordinates.

The story of the Taiping rebellion is so integral to the Wen family that I must digress here for a short explanation of the roots of this largest of all civil wars. The advent of the sweet potato and extensive farming in corn supplied the food to forestall the normal death rate by starvation and to nourish a Chinese population that had tripled in the fifty years since Minning became Emperor in 1820.

Opium had become the slow poison of Confucian governance and the underlying cause of its moral degradation. Easy profits from the illicit drug trade had cost the heads of many mid-level Kwan officials who participated. The opium wars were the failed attempts by the Chinese to extinguish the trade and to expel the foreigners involved in it. The wars were lost to superior European armies. The 'indemnities' were settlements imposed by the victors on the losers for resisting colonial aggression -- millions of dollars were assessed and collected, depleting China's cash reserves and bankrupting the government.

With no funds to operate, the government was incapable of performing its normal duties. The countryside was awash with lawless, starving, and unemployed peasants, as well as tradesmen and soldiers who decided to take what they needed from those who still had something. The result was The Taiping Rebellion.

Hong Xiuquan was only thirty years old in 1844, when he started his own form of Christian ministry in the Thistle Mountain area in Guangxi Province. He was a charismatic person who believed that he was the second son of Yahweh, the god of Moses and Abraham. This made him the younger brother of Jesus. His mission was to rid the world of the devils who were starving his people, and to destroy the false religions that supported them. His teacher, the American missionary, Reverend Issachar Roberts, refused to accept him into his church because of Hong's "burlesque" ideas, which were skewed to fit the politics of poverty.

Hong's ministry became increasingly militant and, in the end, brought together millions in his cause. Among them, five young men were brought to prominence; they were his 'Kings'.

Feng Yunshan, was a twenty-two year old neighbor of Hong's, who accompanied him into the mountains of Guangxi in 1844. After a few months, Hong returned home to continue his ministry and to write, leaving Feng to organize the Pai Shang-ti Hui, the God Worshipers Society. During the three years of Hong's absence, Feng grew the membership of the group from one hundred to twenty three hundred. He had also started revolutionary activities that got him arrested twice in 1847 and '48. Feng was arrested and jailed by Wang Zuoxin, a powerful local landlord, who correctly saw the Society as more a political than a religious movement. Hong went to Canton to seek help to get Feng's release.

Yang Xiuqing stepped up into the leadership, claiming to speak for God himself. He had been a farmer who tilled the soil of others. He also had a side business of making and selling charcoal; and for a short time, he was a porter on the wharves in Canton. Despite his lack of education, however, he was a born leader. He organized a fundraising campaign among his fellow charcoal sellers to raise enough money to bribe Feng out of jail.

Xiao Chaogui, also a young, poor farmer in eastern Guangxi, joined the movement, eventually claiming to channel the voice of Jesus directly from heaven. Xiao was particularly good at preaching, as well as at training and directing men. He was, however, given to excesses of loyalty and courage.

Wei Changhui joined the movement for his own reasons; he wanted to get revenge on another landlord. He sold his property and gave over the proceeds to the Heavenly Treasury. He was a manipulator, but a good one, and took charge of supplies and distribution.

Shi Dakai was an outsider for several reasons. He was of half-Hakka and half-Zhuang ethnicity, came from a landlord family, and was educated. He was liked by everyone and brought with him recruits with backgrounds in mining, tunneling, and explosives. He also brought in business clerks, pawn brokers, and merchants who could run the Heavenly Treasury.

During 1851, Hong changed the name and the mission of the organization to the Taiping Tianguo (The Heavenly Rule of Great Peace) with the goal of ridding the land of the Qing government and of all foreign influence. By this time, over a hundred thousand had gathered in the foothills of Tzuchingshan, Guangxi.

At his side, were;
The South King, Feng Yunshan, fiercely loyal;
The East King, Yang Xiuqing, in charge of all military operations and highest among the other kings;
The West King, Xiao Chaogui, steady and courageous;
The North King, Wei Changhui, materials and treasury; and
The Wing King, Shi Dakai; Hong made him his Assistant.

These six young men, 20 to 35 years old, gathered together an initial following of 10,000 of the starving and disenfranchised peasants from Guangdong and Guangxi Provinces in south China, to face the army of the Qing Empire. Weakened as it was, the imperial army still had the funds, organization, and Confucian moral authority to hold most of the country under its sway. Forces from the adjoining provinces of Yunnan, Guizhou, and Hunan had been called in to join the repression of this 'peasant uprising'.

The battles swirled around in the mountains of southern Guangxi Province with tens of thousands of casualties on both sides. Along the march, Feng Yunshan, the South King, was shot and died. The peasant army was passing a small city and had no intention of fighting there; but the sniper's shot that killed Feng Yunshan turned loose the Taiping in a slaughter of everyone in the town. It was a rage they would come to regret and vowed never to repeat. They would kill millions of 'Devils' in the imperial structure, but pledged thereafter not to kill the innocent and submissive. In a later battle to take Changsha, capital of Guangxi, West King Xiao Chaogui died leading a charge.

Despite the massive losses, the Taiping Heavenly Army grew. Whenever it moved through an area, thousands of people in the depths of poverty joined the army to obtain food and hope. The Taiping took from the establishment and fed the massive army; people living in constant despair saw this peasant army as their only chance for a life. By the time they overran Wuchang, the tens of thousands had become five hundred thousand. This was the Army that swept the Yangtze from Wuchang in February, 1853.

Now, settled in Nanjing for just a few years, one expeditionary Army had been sent north to attack Beijing, and another back out west to gather supplies. Personalities festered in the luxury of calm as Hong took to his chambers to 'correct' the Bible. Yang Xiuqing, The East King, was still the anointed commander of all the Armies, but he was plotting and agitating for position and consolidation of control. He sent Shi Dakai, the Wing King, to the western and southern provinces for supplies. He sent Wei Changhui, the North King, to reestablish military control of the Yangtze River cities. Using his 'voice of God', Yang rebuked and humbled Hong Xiuquan, establishing himself nearly as Hong's equal.

On August 3, 1856, Hong Xiuquan sent a letter to both the North King and the Wing King. In the letter, Hong told them the East King, Yang Xiuqing, was out of control and had to be killed. Spies were everywhere, but with remarkable security, the main body of the army under the North King, Wei Changhui, slipped out of its encampment and raced down the river to Nanjing. Entering the city unnoticed in small groups, they took control of the palace of the East King, and proceeded to kill almost everyone inside, including Yang.

Hong made a public announcement that the East King had been killed by the North King. But, because the North King had used excessive force, he would be publicly flogged in a large arena used for religious rallies. Five thousand of the East King's followers flocked inside to witness the beating. As they entered, as was the custom, they left their weapons at the door. When the count reached 350 strokes, upon a prearranged signal, Wei's troops charged in and killed over two thousand or so unarmed spectators.

Shi Dakai arrived two days later and entered Nanjing. Going first to Hong Xiuquan, he was told that indeed the East King and his followers had been and were still being killed by Wei Changhui, the North King, in and around Nanjing. Hong was incredulous at the news of the murders; he had only sanctioned the execution of Yang Xiuqing. Wei had clearly lost his mind -- and there seemed nothing that Hong could do.

Shi went to confront Wei to see if he could put a stop to the madness. His visit was short, and as he left, aides whisked him away and out of the city. Wei's troops proceeded to surround Shi's house in the city and killed his family and everyone inside. Wei then sent his commander, Qin Rigang with fifteen thousand soldiers, to get Shi. Qin and his men left the city, but instead headed north to fight the

Qing forces. They would let "the Kings" settle their affairs between themselves.

Shi called for volunteers to return the Taiping movement to its proper course. An army of nearly one hundred thousand answered the call. Shi sent a messenger to Hong, in Nanjing, demanding the executions of Wei and his subordinate, Qin Rigang. In the alternative, Shi would attack Nanjing and do it himself.

Inside the city, Wei had turned his attention to Hong Xiuquan. His remaining force of only two thousand surrounded Hong's palace, but was caught between the fiercely loyal women guards inside and a reconstituted force under General Fu Xuexian. Wei was killed, dismembered, and his head was sent to Shi Dakai in his camp outside the city walls. Wei's troop commander, Qin Rigang, was summarily turned over by his own soldiers, and his head was also sent to Shi Dakai. Shi reentered the city a hero in December 1856.

Hong had promoted his own brothers to political positions just below the 'king' level, for which they were still woefully ill equipped. Shi Dakai was over them, in charge of administrating all of Nanjing. But, after six months of in-fighting born of petty jealousies, Shi Dakai had had enough. On July 2, 1857, Shi Dakai left Nanjing with a force of two hundred thousand and headed back inland toward Guangxi. Most of the towns upriver had already fallen back into Qing control.

***

Fang Linkong

A packet of letters arrived by overland courier at the home of Lao Fang in Xiangfan in March 1857. They had been sent from an army camp somewhere along the Grand Canal. Fang Linkong, the older brother, had been in the heat of battle in the north since May of 1853. The cover

154

letter apologized profusely for the lack of communication. "I kept writing to you in my diary everyday, but we were not allowed to send any letters due to the sensitivity of our position. I have been in the command tents of our Imperial Commander, General Senggelinqin, since we came to the field. We always thought that it would be over sooner, and that we would be able to send out something. But the months have become years and only now can I tell you about our victories in the north." The diary and letters were filled with the details of the long campaign against the Taiping in the north.

The Taiping had managed to come within 360 km of the capital. The royal family, with about two thousand eunuchs and servants, made a dash for the hunting preserve at Jehol, in the mountains about a hundred kilometers to the north beyond the great wall. After three years, Senggelinqin had been able to turn the Taiping forces back to the banks of the Grand Canal. By building a system of dikes, they forced a flood of cold mid-winter water to inundate the rebel camp, leading to their total defeat and annihilation. Imperial forces, further south, were also successful in containing and eliminating the last of the northern expedition supply lines.

For Linkong, his war was over. The winter campaign had been bitter, matching the winter itself. In their rush to end the Taiping threat, Linkong joined other staff officers on the front lines. Unaccustomed to the line-soldier's life and ill clad for the extreme cold, Linkong's feet suffered frostbite. He was facing some hard truths as he wrote this letter to his family from a field hospital bed in Shandong. The smell of gangrene was seeping through his bandages; the infection had gone up his legs. This would be his last letter.

He apologized for his lack of attention to his own health, and to his father for not being there to help run the farm and perpetuate the family. He apologized to his mother for not being safe and with her. "I wish I could take your sadness with me." He apologized to Meixing for missing her wedding and never meeting his new brother-in-law. Finally, he told them he had made arrangements to have his body delivered to the farm. And then, he was gone.

"We will be going back to Lu'an," Lao Fang said, "I have to bury my boys." He was beyond despair and Wen knew better than to even try to advise him. The two men walked together without talking that evening and many to follow. Meixing stayed with her mother all of that first night, in the living room of the new house. How vast and vapid all of the family's recent successes seemed; how unreal and distant they felt from the things of this world, this Xiangfan interlude. Reality was a smelly old farm in the flat lands of Anhui, and they longed to return there and rebuild their lives.

Wen made the arrangements. The caravan, however, was light; they took only the coach and a small wagon for necessities since they might not be able to stay. Deng Weili would take care of the town while they were gone. The businesses would conduct themselves. The crops would grow and life would go on. Even Wen looked back on the town with detachment.

The trip went slowly, up the East Road to Suizhou, then north through the pass that separates the Dungbai Mountains from the larger Dabie Shang range; east then till the bridge at Yeji, then onto the flat farmland and on toward Lu'an. Finally, the farm appeared on the right side of the road and the pace picked up. Familiar to most of the tuanlian, if not the Civic Guard, the soldiers rode on ahead of the caravan to make sure they were not getting into the midst of the war. They found farm buildings had been vandalized but still stood. The commander of the tuanlian rode back to tell them the farm was empty but the buildings had been occupied and damaged during the recent fighting.

The coach, carrying the family, slowly drew up to the old house and Lao Fang helped his wife down and through the overgrown front yard. "Nothing!" Madeline said at the door. "They took everything that we left, even the curtains.

Look, there is no glass in the windows! What kind of people are these?"

The Civic Guard put together boxes and covered them with straw mattresses to make beds in the old main room. Wood was brought in and the fireplace came alive. Madeline lit a fire in the kitchen oven and got a pot of water boiling, while Meixing hung towels over the windows to stop the drafts. Hot meals were made and they all got their first good night's sleep in a week. The soldiers went out to the old barn, which had been their quarters before they left, and settled in there.

In the morning, Lao Fang and Wen took some of the soldiers to town and asked about Linkong. Indeed, his body had been delivered, but because no one knew when the family would return to the farm, they had buried him in a plot outside of town. Fang had the soldiers dig up the body while he ordered matching markers for the boys. Then they returned Linkong to the farm. They located his brother's grave and buried Linkong next to him.

The next day, Lao Fang went to town and brought home the two matching monument stones; they were of polished marble with the names and dates of the two brothers' births and deaths. The family stayed for a week at the farm, but it needed too much work to make it their home again. Instead, they agreed they would leave ten of the Civic Guard there build furniture and fix all of the broken doors, windows, and walls. The rest of the caravan would return to Xiangfan and come back in a month or two with all of their normal household things.

Over the following months, however, Madeline and Lao Fang talked less and less of returning to the old farm and settled instead on returning to Paris before they grew too old to enjoy it. But, that too would have to await the suppression of the Taiping in the lower Yangtze. The farm was left in the hands of the Civic Guard; they were to plant crops and improve it as they saw fit. Meixing returned to her school for girls, and Wen traveled up and down the river, keeping tabs on his little empire, which sustained them all.

***

A Poem

The war had moved well downriver. Trade was able to expand, moving food and materials freely throughout Wen's system of stores and shipping facilities. Many of the families who had sent their valuables to Xiangfan came to reclaim them. The Bannermen soldiers were sent off to more active duties in the east. The town residents looked forward to more normal times.

Wen Zhenli was fussing for attention at Meixing's feet, while she sat nursing a new baby girl. Zhenli's feet were inside quilted booties that made it hard to walk, an art he had only recently mastered. The house was not cold, like outside, but there were drafts, so he still had to wear the booties over his pull-up pants. So many problems being one-and-a-half years old!

"Baba" was away, again, and Grandma was busy cleaning and washing. "Mother, you don't have to do all that" Meixing said, an admonition that required no real response. Grandma liked to keep busy and there was just more than her daughter could handle at this point in her life. She knew that to be a fact. So she kept right on sweeping and dusting.

Wen Fulian was in his office, a room on the second floor, where most of the heat went. The office had a large window that looked out over the military city toward the bend in the river. The town of Xiangfan was off to the south. He could see the back side of the Long Meng Hotel where they had lived three years ago, as well as the East gate in the town wall.

A plume of white steam rose from one of the new smoke stacks. Bricks were the order of the day in construction, and the brick factories ran around the clock. During the war, many of the homes and businesses were burned out. Although wood was plentiful in the surrounding mountains, brick walls were the new look. Bricks sold well downriver, as well in all the old and new cities. Barges for bricks were being made and loaded continuously, the loads so heavy the water lapped at the bottom of the stacks. And of course, where there are bricks, there must be mortar. The limestone kilns ran continuously as well. Stacks of broken limestone, iron ore, and coal were fed into the huge pipe. Lined with firebrick and fired with coal gas, it was always yellow-white hot on the inside and rolled on massive, pillow block rollers. A small steam engine drove a massive chain and it rumbled day and night. White steam and dust raced up the high brick chimney and the fine white gypsum powder poured steadily into a chute that filled one gondola cart after another. As the carts went around the track and cooled, they were tipped and the gypsum dumped into a hopper that fed a bag-filler.

On the far side of the military city were the really dirty, noisy industries; cast iron stoves, grates, and andirons were cast in sand molds. The burned binder that held the sand forms together smelled like bad molasses. Huge piles of dark brown, broken sand molds were dumped in the valley to the north. New white sand came from an excavation pit about three kilometers further down the East Road. The sand was mixed in small batches with water and cornstarch till it was just damp and sticky enough; then it was poured and tamped down over the cope or drag forms. Later, the forms were removed and the molded sand forms were dried, first in the sun and then in an oven, till all the moisture was gone. Then the two halves were held in their frames, face-to-face, making a cavity in the shape of the thing to be made. The white-hot cast iron melt was then poured into the fill port till it flowed back up the riser holes. When it cooled, the sand mold was broken off and the hot metal was cleaned and cooled. Everything that was not the casting had to be broken off in a loud clanging process with sledges and then any sharp bits were ground off. The plant could never make enough; the market was that good.

Wen Fulian smiled at the distant operations; such contentment, he thought, had to be written down. He took out a new sheet of paper and mused how the poem would look against the blank page. The eye would lead the mind from character to character -- idea to idea, along a proscribed path of repeated tonal patterns and parts of speech.

The modern p'ai-lu or 'arranged rule' poem uses five or seven characters per line. Every other line rhymes and no character may be used twice within the same poem. The lines are written in parallel form, that is, each pair of lines is matched in the sequence of parts of speech. A line having noun, adjective, adverb, verb, and direct object would be followed by a line having noun, adjective, adverb, verb, and direct object. Both lines must also maintain the same rhythm of accents – High/even, falling, low/even, low/even, and rising tones must be mirrored in the following line.

Wen had an Imperial Rhyming Dictionary that arranged characters first by tone and then by rhymes, but he no longer needed to use it. The words flowed, almost as quickly as he could draw the characters on the paper. The time-consuming part was making the strokes; they not only had to clearly follow the character, but had to deviate ever so slightly to reflect the emotion of the poem. It was the sort of inflection a mischievous smile adds to a familiar face. He had to carefully load just the right amount of ink on the brush so one character might be intruded into the space of the next. He would write the poem only once, but it would be viewed and enjoyed many times. The advantage must be to the viewer.

Writing poetry was an old discipline, and one so respected it had been a required part of the Imperial Examination system for hundreds of years. Writing poetry reflected intelligence by demonstrating a grasp of vocabulary and style. But it is a visual art form, and even among Chinese themselves, is almost never recited as a train of words. This is even more true when the writing is done, not with a subtle well trimmed brush, but with a rough handful of grass. The result is a form known as 'Grass Hand'. The characters take on a wild and primitive appearance as the grass is dragged throughout the character with a minimum number of interruptions between strokes, which points up the emotion of the poem. The instrument was, at one time, just that – a hand full of grass. Now, the writer uses a brush with courser and longer hair. The effect lends itself more to the unruled Daoist poetry of the Song era.

When the poem was done to his satisfaction, Wen cut and split two pieces of Bamboo, just a bit longer than the width of the paper. He then slid the top edge of the paper into the slot and bound it closed at each end with a thin string. He then repeated the process for the bottom edge. The poem would be hung on the wall from a slack string, spanning the top piece from end to end; the bottom piece provided just enough weight so the paper would not curl. Eight lines, five characters long were written top to bottom, right to left. His signet 'chop', a carved stone stamp in a stylized form of his name, was added in red ink to finish the work.

Lao Fang, was upriver at one of the smaller branch offices of his Merchants Bank Group. 'Branch office' was the family joke; a branch office was a cash box in any local restaurant that would participate. Lao Fang would travel like an itinerant preacher, explaining his program to anyone who would listen. The program centered on a cooperative for buying and selling whatever was made or grown in the area. No money was held, but a record was kept of transactions, credits, and debits. Products and produce would be taken on board one of Wen's boats for credits; seed, tools, or supplies were delivered against debits. Fang had enough money of his own to back the liberal credit which he offered.

Larger purchases of equipment, which would be used by all the members of the co-op, were owned by all members and debited proportionately against each of their accounts. Lao Fang also talked to groups of farmers or merchants about the benefits of bundling their sales for better profit and of using Wen's boats to expand their markets.

Taxes, based on these transactions, were assessed and recorded on the program's records, which were public to all members of the co-op. No 'clever minister' could get his hands on the money or add a 'fee' to be put in his own pocket. The taxes were held by Wen, as Magistrate for the area, until a replacement for Tao Enpei, the Hubei Governor was named. The Governor died on April 3, 1856, when Wuchang fell for the second time to the Taiping. Wen also levied an 'appreciation' tax to help in the reconstruction of the capital when it did come back under Qing control.

Aside from merchandising, Lao Fang also promoted information. Wherever he went, Fang would arrange for some public place -- a wall or a fence, for the posting of news and information. The notices could be small, "I have something to sell." Or large, "Taiping attack another city." Either way, the postings did two things: they gave the people access to communication, and they encouraged people to read and write.

On this particular day, Lao Fang was on his way back down river and noticed a dispatch, on a wall, from Wuchang. "Imperial forces open trade through to Shanghai." The article covered the Imperial Army's victory over the Short Sword Society gangsters in Shanghai and the cooperative efforts of the foreign and Chinese soldiers, under the American soldier of fortune, Fredric Townsend Ward's, "Ever Victorious Army". Mr. Ward fought alongside of his men and had been killed in an attack against the Taiping. His Command was taken over by the British Commander, Charles Gordon. But, between the Imperial and foreign forces, the joint action had indeed cleared the way for some trade and travel through to the port of Shanghai. The article also covered the news of the victories in the north against the Taiping, but downplayed the Nian rebellions further north and the Muslim riots in the west.

It was the news that Lao Fang had long waited for. He could, at last, take Madeline back to France. By the time he returned to Xiangfan, Madeleine had also heard the news and was preparing the chests of clothes. Wen was readying one of his steamers to accommodate the whole family in safety and comfort all the way to Shanghai. Flying the Imperial flag, with his Civic Guard aboard in uniforms closely resembling those of the Bannermen, Wen's boat set off in January 1858.

An Overdue Vacation

***

Shanghai

On the way to Shanghai, Wen's boat stopped at Wuhan; for once, Wen had some pleasant official business to take care of with the new Governor, Hu Linyi. Hu had led the Imperial army in retaking Wuchang when the North King's son, Wei Jun, had heard about his father's death and abandoned his command, last holding Wuchang, on December 19th.

The Governor was surprised and delighted to welcome his subordinate, especially so when Wen off-loaded several chests of silver teals in payment of back taxes and his 'appreciation' levy. Wen explained his family situation, and the Governor sent a six-man honor guard to accompany them on their journey, adding his banner to Wen's, which gave them added protection.

The voyage to Shanghai was uneventful despite quickly steaming past the Taiping fortress at Nanjing. The batteries on the hills had had the recent misfortune of firing on

British warships carrying diplomatic personnel upriver to meet with the leaders of the Taiping movement. The British had returned fire and destroyed the offending gun emplacements. It caused the Taiping to hold their fire and to make sure they were not engaging the wrong parties. Their delay was enough to allow Wen's boat to hurriedly slip past unscathed.

Though Lao Fang had frequently traveled through the area before the Taiping, this was the first time he had ventured into it as hostile waters. On his trips selling the produce from his farms, it was an easy passage; on this trip, he only looked out from the safety of the cabin. Every now and again, he would point out some landmark along the shore, but as an imperial ship, he knew there were always sharpshooters hidden behind the tree-line.

At last, the river opened into a wide bay and Wen's captain followed along the shoreline on the right-hand side till they came to the mouth of the Huangpu River. Following the river inland for another twenty kilometers, they entered the bustling harbor of Shanghai. Tall ships were anchored along the river. The family all noticed the unhealthy odor, loud noises, and many transient workers camping on the German Bund, the street that faced the harbor. The city had grown as trade increased. Many Chinese were living inside the foreign nationals' concessions, out in the open, for their own protection. Outside of the concessions were tenement squallier dwellings, tong control, and every sort of vice, all overseen by a corrupt and largely ineffective police force.

Madeline recognized a French sailor by his uniform, and called out to him. In a flurry of rapid-fire French, the sailor told her there was a French ship that would be able to take them on their first leg of the trip back to France. For a small consideration, the sailor would help make the arrangements. Fang quickly stepped into the conversation and offered a fixed fee for them to lead Wen's boat over to where the French ship was anchored; they would make their own arrangements.

The Dame de Marseille was an older, three-masted warship, retired to commercial service. They arranged a meeting with its captain and went aboard, while Meixing stayed on the smaller boat with the children. Later, at dinner, Wen told her about the accommodations for her parents on the big ship and the plan they had worked out with its captain. Being a commercial ship, it would sail to one port after another, working its way along the southern coast of China to Formosa, then back to the mainland at Kawloon and the island of Hong Kong. After that, there would be a long, open sea leg till they reached the ports in Malaysia. Finally, there would be another, even longer, leg around India and across the Arabian Sea; going up to the end of the Red Sea, until disembarking at the city of El Suweis.

Fang and Madeline would then travel north by caravan to the Mediterranean Sea. "We hope to see some of Greece, travel up through the Italian States, and see Rome. From there we'll sail to Marseille. I have read that the trains are working all the way up to Paris and home." Meixing followed this narrative of her parents' proposed journey, looking at a map spread out on the table before them, and she started to softly sniffle.

"I wish we could go with you," she said and held her mother. "Maybe another time," Madeline crooned in response, as they held each other and rocked back and forth.

***

A First Parting

Just outside the bay, the Dame de Marseille settled on the waves of the open sea like a bird come to roost on its nest. The last of the sails were unfurled and the northeast winds listed the bark to its starboard side. Wen and Meixing stood on the upper deck of their little steamboat, which had followed them out of port, and rolled with the waves as they watched the huge ship recede toward the southern horizon. They followed in its wake, until they passed the Nanhui lighthouse and then veered westward along the shoreline into the Hangzhou Wan, the bay that would take them to Hangzhou. Marco Polo had called Hangzhou the "most beautiful and luxurious city in the world." Wen wanted to see it for himself after reading about it so many times in the poetry of the T'ang Dynasty. For Meixing, it would be the honeymoon that they had never had.

Two hundred and fifty kilometers south and east of Nanjing, Hangzhou was the starting point for the Grand Canal which crosses 1,764 kilometers of lakes, rivers, locks and open farmland north all the way to Beijing. Started in the 5th century, it is the largest manmade waterways in the world. It provides ice-free, north-south inland passage for trade and military goods, year 'round.

From their boat, at the docks of Hangzhou, to the center of town was only a short ride in a rickshaw and they took rooms at the Ling Hotel on the east bank of West Lake with a magnificent view of the sunsets. Further down the east shore is the five-story Leifeng Pagoda. North across the lake is the Baoshu Pagoda Tower. The two landmarks bracketed the view of the irregular hills beyond the western shore.

The next day, they wandered along the lake shore to feed the koi fish, and stopped at the tea shops to enjoy dumplings filled with sweet lotus root paste. Later that week, they took a day-trip and walked through the terraced Meilongwu Tea plantation, where they purchased a large quantity of tea and had it delivered to the boat to take back home. In town, they went to a silk vender and bought several bolts of Suzhou silk and silk brocade. One evening, they sat in a park listening to a flute player. They bought two of his instruments as souvenirs, so they could try to learn to play them themselves. They also visited the Lingying Buddha Temple with its carved stone statues that, fortunately, had not been destroyed by the Taiping.

After so much sightseeing, Zhenli, now two-and-a-half years old, was getting fussy, so they reluctantly returned to the boat for the trip home. As they pulled away from the dock, they recalled the old saying, "Paradise is in heaven, but on earth, we have Hangzhou and Suzhou." Sadly, seeing the canals of Suzhou would have to wait for another vacation.

Wen stopped at Wuchang on the way back, both to drop off the honor guard and to have a more formal visit with the Governor. He brought with him intelligence reports from the commander of the new Southern Encampment, which hemmed-in Nanjing on the south and east.

To Meixing and the children, the pressures of travel had been exhausting. She was happy to see the farm house on the East Road again; at the same time, she was saddened to see the empty house next door. In their absence, the Civic Guard had maintained both houses and the crops were in the fields, but her parents being so very far away left her with an empty feeling. To compensate, she threw herself back into work at the girl's school with renewed energy, taking the children with her every day.

Wen needed to make another inspection tour of the facilities and stores along the river, and had promised the Governor several shipments of grains and animals for Wuchang. The supplies would be needed if the Taiping decided to mount a siege of the city.

***

Les Voyageur

The first letter from Madeline came in April. The postmark and stamps were from the city of El Suweis, Egypt.

"I hope that you will forgive us for the recent series of postcards," she began. "We thought that the artwork said so much more than we could, so I kept our comments short.

The real details are in my diary and I hope to share that with you when I get home and can look back with a better perspective. We are just too new to all this. We haven't traveled this much since we were married."

She went on to elaborate on the cities that they had stopped at and the people in the ship's crew. But the cards she referred to actually came the following week. They had been bundled by a postal worker in Wuchang; low-cost cards went by packet boats on a much slower pathway. The artwork she referred to were hand-colored ink drawings of harbor and street scenes.

Lao Fang added his observations of shipping on the high seas, the ports and facilities, as well as on the sheer size of the ocean between Europe and China. He had also been digesting the newspapers and talking extensively with other passengers who were more current with world affairs.

China, it seemed, was not regarded as a high priority issue in the world at that time. China's rebel wars were just one of many issues in the world of free trade, but of little interest beyond that. Europe was interested in Europe; and local news of the Middle East and China was seen in terms of how it would affect the Europeans, as both were areas of colonial influence and domination. The French and Germans were contesting for influence in North Africa, while the Turkish Ottomans were losing theirs.

In the Port of El Suweis, Fang noted how the Dame de Marseille was able to get berthed and unloaded while ships of other national registries were still waiting. It was a game of pressure and profit. The Dutch would pay no more than the standard duty and fees; the Germans waited their turn and were upset when someone else got in ahead of them. The French paid for the advantages they received and worked on relationships; they also had more war ships in the area than anyone else. The Egyptians, who ran the port, were running from one loud conversation to another with their hands full of documents and making assurances in five different languages.

Somehow, their baggage was unloaded, identified, and delivered to the other side of town, where a caravan would take it across the desert. The agent for the caravan arranged for a carriage to take them there, and to transfer their bags to the larger coach for the trip. The coach was a Spanish overland design, large and heavy, but comfortable. They took rooms for two nights while everything got organized and they got rid of their 'sea legs'.

"That will be all from us, for a while," Madeline wrote. "The next leg will be a lot of jostling and dust, I should suspect. Kiss the children for us. And write to us in care of Le Hotel George Cinq in Paris. I hope I haven't forgotten anything, but it is getting late and we will be off at first light." The letter was posted back on the ship, the Dame de Marseilles, for its return trip.

While the Fangs were in El Suweis, they were delighted to find that books and newspapers were again available in many languages, scripts, and formats. They, of course, purchased more than enough to read for the rest of the trip, and set about doing so as their things were loaded on camels for the trek north.

Once on their way, the coach bumped and swayed and it was more difficult to read. The hills along the way never got higher than twenty meters, but the roadway, where there was one, still pitched them violently from time to time. It was hot. It was dusty. And the sand blew into everything.

"Is everything to your liking, Mem Sahib"?" An obsequious little man in a filthy turban, bouncing along on his donkey, poked his face up to the window next to Madeline. His breath knocked her back with surprise.

"We are doing just fine!" Lao Fang called from the far side of the seat. And they rolled on. Off to the right, they could see the dry Bitter Lakes, salt flats from another geologic time.

The road finally came to an end in front of the Abu Benha Hotel in the city of Bur Sa'id. The carriage lurched to a stop and woke Madeline and Lao Fang from a deep numbness, not unlike sleep. Outside the carriage, the drivers and herdsmen were talking excitedly to the people from inside the hotel; the animals had to be taken around to the pens in the back. The street was a jangle with voices, each instructing the other.

"Now, you come down, please." The turbaned driver waved his crop toward the entrance to the hotel, which was just behind a series of pillars that were linked by arches across the front of the building. Another man, in a white European-style suit, came bustling out of the hotel, waving off the driver and speaking Arabic in dismissive tones.

"Qu'est ce que c'est ca?" asked Madeline.

"C'est votre hotel, Madam!" the man in the white suite answered.

Lao Fang helped Madeline down to the dusty street and the suddenly bright light. Behind her, a boy had already climbed into the carriage from the other side, and was handing down their small traveling bags. Their larger cases and trunks were taken upstairs and stacked to one side of a fairly large living room in a suite of rooms on the second floor of the hotel. Fang was generous with his tips, especially on long trips in foreign countries.

"We will need two baths as soon as possible," he told the head porter.

"Toute suite, monsieur," the man answered.

They had just located their clothes and changed into light robes, when there was a knock on the door. They were led to tiled bathing rooms at the back of the hotel. The tubs were filled with very warm water and two buckets of hot water sat beside both of them. On a rack were several thick cotton towels. Next to the bath tubs were tables with soaps, ointments, and oils of all sorts.

"Will you require any help?"

"I don't think so," they grinned at each other and dismissed the young man. Despite the heat, the clear hot water in the tub looked like a truly welcome oasis. They hung up their robes and enjoyed a good long soak.

The hotel concierge was able to arrange their bookings to Athens on a German ferry boat. He also directed Lao Fang to the Bank of England branch nearby. The neighborhood catered to Europeans, but could not keep the youngest of its poor from begging at every opportunity. The clerks at the Bank, on the other hand, went out of their way to accommodate the 'Chinese gentleman'. With a letter of credit and the appropriate passwords, Fang was able to identify himself and to make a withdrawal of enough money to see them well on their way into Europe.

A few days later, they were notified that their ship was in port, and that they could have their things moved on board as soon as they liked. Their journey would take three days, so they booked first class accommodations, which included all meals at the ship's first- class restaurant that boasted an oom-pa band and an open bar. It would be an interesting crossing.

When they arrived at the docks, they saw that the ferry boat was much larger than the name implied. The first thing Madeline noticed, however, was the presence of soldiers along the rail of the upper decks. Not only were they armed; they had cannon.

One of the other guests noticed her concerned look and whispered, "Pirates! Out there." and she pointed out at the horizon.

Madeline gasped. "Oh Lord! Did you hear that?" She took hold of Fang's sleeve.

In their cabin later, the ship's purser explained about the pirates. "Actually, we know of pirates operating in these waters. But they are not such a problem for a ship so large like this," he said. "They are quite common in the area, so we must show them that we are prepared to deal with them, should any cross our path out on the open sea. There are no police here, versten sie? So, we are the police. You will enjoy. Ya? Gotentag."

And, enjoy they did. The German cuisine at dinner that night featured sausages, boiled potatoes, sauerkraut, and pastries 'mit ien shlag' of whipped cream.

It rained sometime during the night and the morning decks were wet. The sun sent shafts of powder blue down between the distant clouds and the water sparkled as far as they could see. They were midway across the Mediterranean when they began seeing islands and smaller boats out fishing. Occasionally, they would still see a lateen-rigged dhow, far from its home on the coast of North Africa; but, most often the vessels were the brightly painted, high-bowed trawlers from the fishing villages on the islands. By evening, they could see the mainland of Greece. Tonight would be one last chance to try the saurbratten and dumplings, potato soup with dark brown bread, and dark brown beer. They joined in singing some of the songs they had learned in Heidelberg so long ago -- and some they didn't. They slept quite well! And the ship slipped into its berth before they woke.

The port of Athens was snug, surrounded with bluffs fifty meters high and a gradual main road that led up to the historic town. Once they were settled in their hotel, they set off on the first of a series of several city tours. Descriptions of the ruins of the Acropolis, the Parthenon, and the several amphitheaters around the large hill, filled Madeline's diary. She tried to sketch some of it but wound up collecting small artworks and prints instead.

They enjoyed a day of rowing along the coast, in and out of the caves that had been washed out by the tides. They took day trips to the islands, and long walks through narrow streets and fishing villages. It was too much! Finally, they both had to admit to the limitations of their age. It was a cycle that would be repeated several times as they worked their way across Greece to Italy, and finally on to Marseille and Paris.

***

Reconnaissance

After the first few days in Paris, at the George Cinq, they took a lease on an apartment on the right bank, between the Louvre and the Notre Damme. Their tourist phase was gearing down to a slower pace, now that they were on familiar ground. Lao Fang wanted to see la Sorbonne, the school where they had met, and to walk the Left Bank. They kissed again in the garden behind the church, St. Germain des Près, the oldest church in Paris. But, Madeline needed to face her childhood; she had to revisit her home outside Paris, in a small town called Saint Cloud.

La Ville de Saint Cloud lay high on the left bank of the Seine, downriver from Paris. Left is, of course, a relative term; it is based on a barge floating down stream. Looking ahead, in the direction of flow, the left bank is on the left. Thirty years had passed since Madeline had seen the old town. As the taxi-boat neared the town, she strained to look over the bank for a glimpse of something that she might recognize. Later, as they walked through the town, there were things she remembered -- some of the older churches and graveyards.

Turning a corner, she stopped suddenly when she saw it, her childhood home. It was still a bakery. And she could tell from the laundry line strung out of the back windows that some family still lived there. Though her heart was pounding, she made herself keep walking toward it; there were ghosts in there for her. Her mother had never approved of "cet chinois" and had died several years after

Madeline went to China. Her sister married and moved on to Germany, only to be lost in a carriage accident in the mountains.

Stepping inside the door, a bell tinkled over her head. That sound and the smells were as familiar as the walls of the room. Through a doorway in the back, she could see the ovens that her father had made. Then, the baker's face popped into the doorway, "Oui Madam?"

At first, she was startled; his wasn't the face that she had half- expected to see.

"Oh, I am sorry!" she said, a bit embarrassed. "I used to live here. My father, and later my mother, was the baker here years ago."

"Henri? Qui et el?" A woman, perhaps the man's wife, entered from the top of the staircase that led to the upstairs apartments. He shrugged and raised his eyebrows.

"I don't know! She said that she once lived here." He wiped his hands with a towel that was stuffed into his apron. "We bought this bakery from the bank. Now, it is ours!"

"Of course!" Madeline said. "I was just looking up old memories. You see, I grew up in this house. I had hoped that you would not mind if I looked around, just a bit."

The two couples talked at length as Madeline recalled bits and pieces of her early life. There was a shadowed outline still on the wall where her grandfather's portrait had once hung; he was affecting a very patriotic pose, wrapped in the new tricolore flag of the revolution. Her Grandfather was an advisor to Roger Ducos, one of the five Directors who were the executive branch of the Consulate, the men who had encouraged Napoleon, then the first consul, to lead the armed coup d'etat which ended the French Reign of Terror and brought him to power. Her grandfather had later fought at the Battle of Austerlitz, was decorated, and given a field commission, but had to retire with a wounded leg.

Madeline's own father had joined the Grande Armée when Napoleon marched to unite the kingdoms of Italy, and then marched north to bring together the Southern German states into the Confederation of the Rhine. Her father later died in Austria, leaving her mother and the girls to run the bakery with grandpa -- until Madeline ran off to teach in Paris.

"I was only eleven when the Restoration gave us back a king," Madeline said. "But, the Napoleonic Code remained the law of the land. Under those laws, girls like me could go into school. When I graduated, I took a job in Paris at the Sorbonne, teaching French to foreigners. This is how I met my husband."

She looked around the kitchen and the back yard. But she was closing that chapter in her memories; seeing it all was a relief for Madeline. The dread of confronting her memories dissipated and the afternoon sun now seemed just a bit warmer for it. They walked around the town and finally settled in a local cafe in the main square of Saint Cloud for a light lunch. Fang was, again, involved in reading the news in *Le Figaro*. "Nothing here about home," he said wistfully.

"You should read the notice board down at the China Club," a voice rang out from under the awning at the next table.

"Hello, I'm sorry, I didn't see you there. Do you mean we have a Chinese Embassy in Paris?"

"No, just our student social club. I am a student at the Sorbonne studying Far Eastern Political Science."

"Really? What are you hearing about today's history?" Fang looked into the curious face across from him. "You do realize that we are making more history every day!"

"Of course! I just hadn't thought of it that way. I have been reading about the government of the Song through Ming Dynasties. The Qing is fairly recent history."

"But it is part of the same story -- probably the last chapter of that story. You would do well to see how the story ends, as well as how it developed."

"I take it, then, that you are Chinese," the young man said. Fang nodded. "Well, I don't want you to offend you -- but I would like to ask you some questions. I don't understand the current politics. Your country doesn't seem to be able to police your own peasant class, and yet you are reluctant to take our help."

"Help?" Fang stood up enough to square his chair to face the student directly. "Did you really say 'help'?"

"Well, yes!" the young man countered. "We sent missionaries and trade missions. We even sent ships and soldiers to fight the river bandits that seem to be running amuck in Nanjing."

"Oh Lord, what are they teaching you in that school? What you call help is the very root of our problem. China only asked to be left alone. Our history was bumpy enough without your 'help'. Opium was a problem that the French and English only made worse by exploiting that weakness of our people. When we tried to stop the trade, your navies invaded our country with your military power -- no moral justification! It was mercantile greed and colonial mentality that bankrupted China. Those 'river bandits', as you call them, are poor people driven further into desperation by your cheap goods. That is what killed our local industries! Then, the people were led to mistakenly follow some missionary's teaching; that is what led them to steal and kill. Millions have died from your help!"

"I am very sorry, monsieur!" the young man said. "Perhaps I do not understand. Please accept my.... "

"No! Wait; this is not a minor 'not understanding'. This is 'not understanding' on a very grand scale! Our two countries, and many more, are paying the price for this 'not understanding', and will continue to pay it for centuries!"

"Cheri, non! This is too much. Please!" Madeline soothed him, patting his shoulder.

"Well, when will it stop if not with the new scholars?" Lao Fang was shaken.

"Perhaps Monsieur could help me to understand," the young man said. "I can listen. Maybe you could tell me how your country would have developed differently if we had not 'forced ourselves on you'."

"We probably would not have 'developed' at all, in your western sense. We would have followed the ways that we have known for thousands of years -- building on our own history. The Dynasties that you referred to all lived within the model that Confucius laid out for us over two thousand years ago. The histories would have directed our future and we would have remained content to be the center of culture. Those who came to learn our ways would be welcomed. Those who did not like our ways were free to return to their homelands. Little would have changed because little change was desired. The barbarians who surrounded us were always kept away by a wall, by a sea, or by armed soldiers. We did not change for them nor did we go out to change them to be like us. We probably would not have changed at all."

"But Europe has so much to offer you! Why would you not want to have all that?"

"What, these clever devices to make more things that we don't need? Machines that can take you ever faster to other places, when you could stay just as comfortably where you are? Progress is a matter of perspective, young man! Real progress is done within each man. A true scholar learns from the past and honors the ancients. China has much to offer to you, but you are too blind and self-involved to realize it!"

"Laogai, please!" Madeline cautioned her husband. "The young man is not his country – my country. Suet gentil!"

"I am sorry, young man. My wife is right. I am sometimes too 'Old China' for my own good."

"No, by your leave Madam, this perspective is new to me. And we students realize that the old-guard in our government and our press have closed minds on these issues. We should hear this side of the history. What can be done?"

"Nothing! The history is written. China once saw itself as the quiescent center of true culture. We had no real need that we could not fill. Your traders, your opium, and your priests have fragmented our culture. And China will continue to harm itself until we are, once again, of one mind. That is not an easy thing for a country as large as ours."

Madeline stood up and announced. "I think it is time for us to continue our little tour. Come, my love." With that she started gathering her things. Fang looked at her with resignation and said good bye to the student. "This has all been very interesting, young man, but our time on this vacation is limited."

"I am sorry, my love," said Fang "I am weak in the face of such false beliefs; like a coward, I bluster and rail against the evil of ignorance when I fear that it is bigger than me. I must relearn the principles of letting go. I may become a Buddhist!"

"I doubt that," Madeline chuckled. "You are a passionate man and I love that about you. That poor boy will have some tale to tell in class tomorrow. Enough about all that! How would you like to go to Versailles? I saw a horse trolley in town that goes there twice a day. We can stay there overnight and go back to Paris tomorrow."

It was actually only thirteen kilometers between Saint Cloud and Versailles and took less than an hour by trolley, time enough for Fang to cool down and enjoy the passing landscape. They entered the town from the northeast and without noticing it, passed by the hunting lodge where Marie Antoinette enjoyed her excesses. The magnificent grounds of the Royal Palace had become overgrown for lack of attention during the last sixty-five years. Despite the fifteen years of the Bourbon Restoration, upkeep was too large a cost, even for the regal Louis XVIII, 'King of France'. Louis-Philippe, 'King of the French', who followed him to power for the next eighteen years, was too much a populist to engage in any such extravagance. What the Fangs now rode into was a commercial town with a corrupted and discredited past. They were only able to look in through the rusting, gilt-painted gates at distant buildings with trees growing out of the windows and birds nesting in the chimneys. They were disappointed and there was no reason to stay, so they found the coach line that ran directly to Paris and caught the evening run.

***

A Lecture Series

Paris was lighting its gas lamps when they stepped down from the coach onto the Place de l'Etoile, the circular drive around the Arc de Triomphe. An evening rain fell lightly and they enjoyed it on their faces like a young couple in love. They had dinner at Le Boeuf Sur le Toit and walked down the length of the Champs Elysees to the Place de la Concorde.

"The obelisk was a gift from the Viceroy of Egypt to Louis-Phillip." Fang said knowingly.

"You just read that somewhere!" she mocked him.

"True," he shrugged. They passed the obelisk and walked under the trees along the paths in the Tuileries Gardens till the rain picked up and they hailed a Hansom Cab for a quick ride back to their hotel.

"I think the boy was right," Fang mused as they rode. "I'll go down to this China Club in the morning and see if they have any news."

When they arrived at the hotel, the manager was able to get an address for the club, 78 Rue de L'Université, and in the morning, they took a walk across the river from the Tuileries and down a couple of streets; not so far.

The club was in an old wing of the university. The guard at the gate was suspicious of this older Chinese gentleman. "What is your business, here?" he asked, his arms crossed.

"I am Chinese," Fang explained, "And I want to see if you have any news from China. There doesn't seem to be much in the newspapers here."

"Are you Taiping?" the guard asked him, pointedly.

"No, I am not!" he answered vehemently. "My sons died fighting that evil. Now, my son-in-law is the Magistrate for Xiangfan in Hubei Province. We are loyal to the Emperor. Now, let me in."

The door reluctantly creaked open.

The 'news' on the board was only slightly more recent than what they knew when they arrived. They went into the Reading Room, but there was nothing of interest there and only a few hand-copied classics for restricted circulation.

They were actually on their way out when they heard a familiar voice. "That is the man! Sir, could we talk?"

Fang turned and saw the boy from the day before with several of his friends and an older student-teacher. The group introduced themselves to the couple, and then led them out into a garden at the back of the building, where they passed the morning answering questions about China. The older student asked whether Fang had ever lectured or would consider doing so.

Initially, Fang was flattered, and told them he would think about it. This led to an interview with a Fellow of the college later on that afternoon. The university suggested they would pay a small amount for a guest lecturer,. Fang suggested he would prefer no pay and an open forum with interested students, just to see what their interests were.

Three days later, Fang was invited to the University for an Informal Discussion with interested students. When he arrived he was directed to a small hall, with seats in tiers. The audience was bigger than he anticipated, but he felt ready. He kept his opening remarks brief, and invited the students to ask him about China. As the discussion went on, Fang could hardly believe what he was hearing. The questions were nothing more than requests for confirmation of the official French position on Colonial policy. Fang's response was tempered so as not to stifle their questions. "We live in a world of differing viewpoints." he thought to himself, "but this is just nonsense!"

By the end of the day, Fang had almost filled his notebook with ideas for a lecture. He had decided to not take the small amount of money that the University offered but to accept, instead, the use of a free lecture hall and to sell his own tickets to his lecture, which would pay him much more than the university offered. On the appointed day, Fang took the stage with almost every seat sold.

"China is a real country, with real people," he began. "It is a country every bit as reasonable and legitimate as France. What I have heard from students at this university does not reflect that truth!" Within 15 minutes, disgruntled students refused to hear him out and a third of the seats emptied as students left the hall. Fang and the rest of the students held out for three hours as he finished his lecture -- mixing history with politics, economics, and religion. The hesitant applause at the end was not a ringing endorsement of his views; but the students had, at least, stayed to the end.

The University sent a note to Fang at his hotel "We would like to extend to you an offer to continue your lecture on the state of China. However, before you fix the content of the lecture, we would like you to present your views to our faculty for review."

Fang wrote to the University in response: "Please thank the Gentlemen for their kind offer of the 13, October 1857. I would be reluctant to have your faculty 'review' my lecture, since they have already presented their views, through their students. I will not, in turn, present their views, but my own. I wish to be clear on that. I propose to again sell tickets, and will make myself available on a date which would be mutually acceptable to address those students who wish to attend." The letter received no immediate reply.

While they awaited some response from the University, Fang and Madeline were becoming well known on the streets of Paris. Some offered polite salutations, some derisive comments, and some simply averted their eyes and made no contact at all.

"It is good for sales," Fang laughed to Madeline. The couple regularly had lunch at the same cafe on the Champs-Elysees. Madeline would write post cards or entries in her diary; Fang read the newspapers and engaged in conversation with anyone who stopped by their table. The trees were beginning to turn color and leaves wisped about in the chill air. "Oh my!" Fang laughed one day as they sat at an outdoor table. "I've made the editorials. There is a letter here about 'a subversive Chinois who is denigrating the Church and France in his lectures to students.' I wonder who that could be?" The article went on, almost as a call to arms. "When has France deserved less a lecture from a citizen of such a failed society -- deportation would be too kind."

"I wonder, what they will say to my editorial." He looked far off at the obelisk at the Place de la Concorde. *Le Figaro* printed his letter to the editor the following week. It read, in part, "Ignorance and arrogance often are found together; it is regrettable that I find them at such high levels of this society. Since my detractors have drawn their heads deep into their shells, I trust that I will not see any of them at my continuing lecture series." A week after that, the university made him an offer to hold a second lecture, but with the restriction that they could stop it if it endangered public safety.

Fang took out a half-page ad announcing that; "The next lecture will be November 2, 1857 at 19:00 hrs Hugo Hall; students 5ff, non-students 40ff."

On the evening of the lecture, the hall was filled to overflowing, standing room was crowded -- people were actually lined up in the entrance way!

"Throughout my education at Cambridge University," Fang began, "We were encouraged to study and attend Christian services. We 'Chinois' were closely watched to insure that we received the full benefit of the Christian doctrine. I respect the tenants of that religion in all of its variations. I wish I had met more Christians who had taken equal time to understand the teachings of Confucius. They are out there I am sure; I doubt that they are in this hall tonight."

There were boos and catcalls, but it just made Fang more determined. He left his script, time after time, to relentlessly define and expand on his message. The three-hour lecture lasted five-and-a-half hours, but no one left.

In a follow-up letter from the university, the Rector told Fang they would no longer be able to host the lectures. The Board of Regents had decided the university could not be seen as a sponsor of Monsieur Fang's controversial views.

"Views? I'll give them a view!" He stormed out as Madeline came into the front room -- just in time to see the front door close and the letter fall off the coffee table and onto the floor.

Fang went directly to the offices of the *Figaro* newspaper. "Yes!" he said fiercely to the clerk. "I want a full-page advertisement with this copy!" Titled 'A Free Lecture', the text of the ad presented facts of history and arguments which detailed 'why these facts led to these results', why colonialism is detrimental to the colony, and how the zeal of Christian missionaries blinds them to the real needs of the societies which they disrupt.

When he returned to the apartment, Madeline was already packing. "I think it is time for us to visit England," she said.

***

Several Crossings

The Pas de Calais is called the 'English Channel' on the other side; not so in Calais. The white cliffs of Dover are the white cliffs of Calais; the same limestone, broken away to the south. The seas here are torturous, as wind and current contest for domination of the surface. The Fangs' boat rocked wildly and none but the very experienced were able to control their stomachs. Even in the Dover harbor, the sailors found it hard to tie the boat down tightly enough to keep the gangway from slipping into the water, yet not so tight as to tear apart the pilings with the weight of the heaving boat. The passengers were tethered by a line from the ship to the dock and helped, one-by-one, to the dock. The luggage was lifted off by a jib crane. Even by local standards, this was a rough crossing.

They checked their chests into storage in London, and lived out of their suitcases. By carriage, they visited the ancient structures at Stone Henge and many similar formations in the area that predated written history. From there, they went on to Wales, with its endless collection of castles, green hills and slate mountains. Across the Irish Sea, they toured Dublin and explored sites along the coast. They were more welcomed there, by the Irish, as China was seen as 'being on the same side' of colonial struggle against England. French colonialism was ignored by the Irish, as they were, after all, Catholics. Then, one day, they found themselves in the harbor town of Southampton, where they would retrieve their chests, shipped down from London for the trip to the Americas.

The American Civil war had not yet started, but the issues and sensitivities were just under the surface. Even among the relatively urbane passengers of the transatlantic steamer, the Fangs were a 'mixed race' couple and were warned they might be in some danger in America. It was beneath contempt, but something to be reckoned with, nonetheless. To avoid any trouble, Fang made reservations with a Spanish ship as soon as they landed, so they could continue their passage by sea to the jungle route across the isthmus named New Granada that lay between North and South America. Another ship, on the Pacific side, took them on to Manila in the Philippines. There, they would transfer to a Japanese ship for the return leg to Shanghai.

But, the Shanghai they returned to in March 1858 was much changed from the city they had left. Even though the war between the Taiping and the Qing sporadically continued in the countryside, life in the city ignored it. The news from Hong Kong and Canton was that the English and French were engaging in a much more powerful and directed war of colonial intimidation. Fang was advised to take the next boat upriver, to pay whatever ransom or bribe was needed, but to get out of the area as quickly as they could. They made good time, arriving in Xiangfan in early April.

They surprised Meixing when they arrived in town, in the middle of a bright spring morning. She was teaching classes outside, as their carriage came up from the docks. Meiliang ran toward the carriage so quickly, the horse shied to the side.

"Are you all right?" Madeline called out through the window.

"Oh, Mama, I love you!" she called back and they held each other's hands through the window of the carriage, crying and laughing at the same time as it came to a stop.

"How are the children?" Madeline asked, ever the beaming grandmother.

"They are fine! Step down and come see!" The couple disembarked, completed hugs all 'round, and went quickly inside to the back room, where a nursery was set up and where each of the girl students had to take turns watching over the two youngest while trying to teach Zhenli to write his characters. He often resisted and played with the toys instead, or begged to be outside with the other boys his age, who were not yet in school.

Fang came in and picked him up, throwing him toward the ceiling, as Zhenli squealed in delight. "How is my little guy?" Fang asked.

Zhenli loved their game, being thrown into the air and dropped so near the floor. But, Meixing was horrified. "Father, you'll drop him, one day! Stop it!"

"Oh, not often!" Fang laughed. "Where is Wen?"

Meixing's face clouded over. "He had to go to Beijing with the silver."

"What silver?" Now Fang's face clouded over. "Where did he take it from?"

"Governor Hu Linyi sent a messenger demanding that all silver be taken directly to The Emperor. Hu Linyi said the Emperor was dying from fear, and that only the sight of massive amounts of silver would set him right. Wen took all our assets, plus whatever was in deposits in the local banks. He took most of the soldiers with him and left last week."

"I'll have to see the bankers as soon as I can," Fang said. "I hope your Confucian scholar hasn't taken us into bankruptcy!"

"Father!" Meixing objected. "Not in front of his son!"

"I really should go right now...," Fang muttered to himself.

"Of course, my dear," said Madeline with a smile. "I've been seeing too much of you, anyway. And Meixing and I have a lot of catching up to do."

When Fang met with them, the bankers were remarkably understanding, and reminded Fang that business had been very good over the last few years. Things would get back to normal soon, they reassured him. They knew the asset value of all the trade in process and of the stocks on hand throughout the system, so they were not afraid of anything. They warmly shook hands with Fang, but 'counted the rings on their fingers'. Removing the silver from the banks was unnerving; silver had always been the measure of wealth. But, the new system, of value measured by corporate shares, debits and credits, and the massive amount of physical assets in the system was always made clear to anyone who would listen. It was a currency of confidence. Still, it would be unnatural if Wen's action were not a shock to the system. The merchants and the bankers could do nothing but hold on to the belief that it would all work out -- and hope they were right.

Over the next few weeks, Fang worked his charm up and down the river, making sure that business was brisk and assuring the merchants that the silver would be replaced as soon as possible. He was exhausted when he returned home.

"The Governor could only send about a tenth of the tribute that went to Beijing. It has almost all come out of our pocket." he told Madeline.

"We'll have to trust Wen to get the best advantage for the tribute. But I'll admit that it bothers me," said Madeline. "He has never had to deal with that kind of people before."

Chapter
7

An Imperial Tribute

***

Arrival

Wen's first impression of the city of Beijing was a blur of many buildings and people. Coolies were everywhere, with their carry poles bending under the weight of baskets loaded with everything from sacks of grain to children, naked and grinning. He saw two men carrying a live pig in a woven tube-shaped basket, slung like a hammock under a pole. A flock of ducks scurried in front of a boy with a long bamboo pole. Vendors, under their rickety three-pole sun shades, hawked their wares. Tradesmen's shops were open to sharpen knives, make clothing and shoes to order. Even bakers, who would cook a meal for those without a fire. There were letter writers and sing-song girls offering their services outside the wine shops. And, everywhere he looked, were people dressed in the clothing from different regions.

His caravan of wagons and soldiers entered the city from the west. Wen rode just in front of the four mules that pulled the lead wagon. Behind that wagon were six more, heavy-laden with the bars of silver. Surrounding Wen and the wagons was a double ring of mounted soldiers. The inner ring held their lances at the ready, while the outer ring held their unsheathed swords in their hands -- looking menacingly at the crowd as they passed. Ahead of them, Wen could just see the tops of the lead soldiers, a block or so away, clearing people off of the street, followed by a phalanx of his Civic Guard. As they moved into the city, Wen saw a red wall in the distance, beyond the trees that lined the street. Only at the last block, could he finally could see the top of the wall.

"It's the Forbidden City!" said the Bannerman soldier riding alongside Wen. "The wall is more than ten meters high and almost that thick at the top. See how the wall slopes down to the water in the moat? It is larger at the base; it was built that way to resist cannon balls and assault by ladders. The moat itself is six-meters deep and fifty-two meters wide. It goes all around the whole compound.

North to south, the wall is over a thousand meters; east to west, it is seven hundred and fifty meters. There is a gate in the north wall leading up to Jing Shan hill. It is good feng shui; 'A mountain to the north'. That hill was made bucket by bucket from the dirt they took out of the grounds inside the wall. They laid in fifteen courses of paving stones, half a meter thick each. They didn't want anyone to tunnel in under the city! It is the best fort in the land. We will be going to the side gate."

At the side, near the front, there was a small gate and a bridge. The guard told them to stop there and dismount. After a while, several large men in black gummed silk uniforms came out and looked over the wagons with the silver. The coating on the silk helped keep it from absorbing anything and gave it a uniform look.

"They are the household eunuchs," the Bannerman told Wen.

A table with a sun shade and a chair were brought out and set up between the wagons and the bridge. A Kwan, of the fifth rank came out with his second, who carried a record book and several forms. "Who sent this tribute?" he asked, looking over at Wen.

"Governor Hu Linyi of Hubei Province sends the tribute!" Wen answered, trying to sound as official as he could.

"Who conveys the tribute?"

"Magistrate Wen Fulian, of the City of Xiangfan, conveys the tribute," Wen answered.

"How much is the tribute?"

"One hundred sixty-five thousand teals of silver and twenty-three bolts of silk," Wen said proudly.

The Kwan, who had been writing the information onto a form, stopped and looked up, his eyebrows raised and his mouth not quite closed. "How rich is this Governor?"

"The silver was raised from all of the merchants and towns along the Han River, as well as from the Governor," Wen answered. "We all want the best health for our Emperor."

The Kwan shook his head and muttered something to his assistant. He wrote the number down and said to Wen, "We will have to count it out here and the eunuchs will take it inside."

The Chief Eunuch, Shim, led out a parade of other eunuchs who were carrying heavy wooden trays with handles on each corner. They set one tray by each of the wagons and started to unload the silver onto the trays. Chief Eunuch Shim was a curious looking fellow; he had round eyes, like a monkey, and a flat nose. His eyebrows twitched as he watched the silver stacking up on the trays.

"You are the Magistrate Wen?" he asked, coming to stand directly in front of Wen, and maybe too close for comfort. Shim had no insignia of rank and Wen had to believe that his bearing was based on his position within the Imperial Household.

"Yes, I am the Magistrate from Xiangfan in Hubei Province," Wen replied.

"May I presume that you have never been at court before?"

"Yes, this is my first visit." Wen answered, feeling a bit uncomfortable.

"You have conveyed a great gift to our Emperor, possibly greater than you know. While you are visiting the court, I would like you to call on me if there is anything that you need." He turned and walked back to supervise the unloading of the silver. Then the loaded trays were removed, taken through the door. Later, the trays were returned and the process was repeated until the wagons were empty.

Finally, the Kwan at the table put away the forms, except one which he put into an envelope. Holding it out toward Wen, he said, "This is the receipt for the silver and the silk."

Wen looked blankly at the Kwan, "Should I do something else? I don't know what is expected."

"You will be contacted in a few days, when all of the tributes have been received. Then there will be an audience, probably with one of the ministers." He and his assistant picked up their things, went over the bridge, and through the door.

Wen stood outside, contemplating his next move, when the door opened again. A younger eunuch stepped out and approached him.

"I am An-yan, personal servant to the Lady Yi," he said. "She wished me to thank you for her, and to help you get settled for your stay in the capital."

"I am unfamiliar with the capital and I have no idea what is expected of me," Wen said honestly.

An-yan smiled and came closer to him. "You will be honored by the court. You may even receive a personal audience with one of the ministers. I don't think you realize how great a gift you have delivered."

"I know it is a great deal of money, but I just did what the Governor demanded of me. It was my duty, my privilege."

"You were well schooled in the Confucian Way," the eunuch said respectfully. "But few Kwan fulfill their duties as you have just done. It will be seen as exceptional and it is appreciated. The foreigners have stripped the treasury bare and the Imperial household is without many of the things that made life comfortable in the past. The Emperor is heartsick to be on the Dragon Throne in such a time of stress and humiliation. We really do fear for his life."

"What more can I do, then? What should I do with my men and where should I stay?"

"Oh, you will not need all of these soldiers here," An-yan explained. "In your position, you should have a company of no more than twenty personal guards. It would be expensive to keep all of the rest here with you. You should probably send them back to Xiangfan."

"Good! I can send them back right away. But, I'm not sure I can afford to keep even twenty. We gave almost all of our money for the tribute."

An-yan laughed. "Ah, you are a treasure! Pick out your honor guard and tell the rest to return home. I will make arrangements for you in the city. Wait here." And he went back inside.

Wen gave the receipt for the tribute to the captain of the guard with instructions to return the soldiers and the receipt to Lao Fang. He also sent a short letter, telling his father-in-law just what had happened and his plans, as best he knew them.

Wen and his 'honor guard' were sitting under the trees when An-yan returned.

"The Chief Eunuch Shim maintains several households in the city for visitors. There are accommodations for your guard as well. He has instructed me to give you this purse of money to cover your expenses. He will send a tailor to you later today to make clothing for your reception in court. If you will follow me, I will take you to your accommodations."

They went south, into one of the better business and residential sections of the city, and were shown into a compound with a large house and guard barracks behind a high wall.

"This will be your residence for the duration of your stay," An-yan said. "I have taken the liberty to employ a young man from the neighborhood to help you find your way around. If you give him a very small amount of money from time to time, you will find him quite useful. The tailor should be here this afternoon. If you will pardon me, it would be good to bathe before he arrives, so he will not be distracted from his labors."

"Thank you," Wen said ruefully. "You are quite right to point that out. We all need to get cleaned up."

"Here comes your boy now. Bingzi, this is the gentleman I told you about."

***

An Audience

An-yan left them to work things out and returned to the Forbidden City. Wen and the soldiers looked around the compound, the barracks, and the house. They decided on security measures, but it seemed that a single guard at the front gate and another in the house would be all that was required most of the time, so they settled in.

The tailor came and took his measurements, but for the rest of the day, they explored the neighborhood and the local restaurants. The new clothes were delivered two days later, with two sets of new Bannerman uniforms for each of the soldiers. An-yan stopped by from time to time to inform Wen about the court, its protocols, what to say, and how to address various people.

The Lady Yi, his mistress, was an Imperial Consort of the fourth rank. She was also the only one of his wives to have produced a boy child, the two-year-old Zaichun. "She will try to arrange an audience with you," An-yan said, "And, if he is well enough, the Emperor himself. It is not just to thank you; she is building an alliance of men that she can count on if the Emperor should die. You will never hear this spoken of again. Do you understand?"

"I see. And you are close enough to make such arrangements?" Wen asked.

"I speak for her as she asks me to. I make such arrangements as please her."

"And the Emperor, is his condition as grave as they say?"

"He is a man exhausted with the pressures of his rank. His father died having seen the beginnings of our confrontations with the English and the French. Things have only gotten worse since his death. The Taiping have caused twenty million deaths over the last ten years. Fully a third of them were our soldiers; practically all of them were Chinese." An-yan paused, his expression growing more serious. "His Majesty feels the pain of his people and would happily die for them if it could stop the rebellions and the invasions," he said.

When he returned the following day, he was visibly upset, not at all the smiling, upbeat manner of his prior visits. "The Lady Yi will be unable to arrange an audience with you," he said. "She has directed me to let you know how much she appreciates your tribute, but she would like to know how your Governor raised such a sum. These are lean times and there are rumors and accusations of corrupt bureaucrats bleeding the public treasuries for their personal gain. His Majesty has, just this week, issued an edict to send inspectors to audit the books in all the provinces, and to take the heads of those who have violated the trust of their office. Your tribute bespeaks a loyalty and commitment to Confucian principles that she finds remarkable in such times."

"I am honored to know that we are of interest to Her Majesty and that we have her trust," Wen said solemnly. "We wish to be ever her loyal subjects in any way that we can. The tribute came from the Governor Hu Linyi and, by his order, from the merchants and people of the Han River Valley. We have depleted our liquid cash reserves to make the tribute, and did it willingly. Along the Han River, we have established manufacturing and agricultural associations which are productive and prosperous. We have supported Zeng Guofan's Hunan Army, as well as his navy along the Yangtze. We have raised tuanlian forces for our own protection, and have maintained a public repository for the land records that were sent to us from all of the southern provinces. We wish only to remain strong and loyal subjects of the Emperor."

"Well said!" An-yan said, smiling once again. "I will convey your words to Her Majesty. She will wish to make a more meaningful response, I am sure."

Wen didn't hear from the Forbidden City for several days. By now, he and his guard had walked almost every street in the outlying city of Beijing. To fill the time, Wen had purchased and started to read Lin Zexu's collection of articles on the Europeans. One afternoon, a messenger arrived from the capital with the invitation he had hoped for; he was to present himself the following day.

Bingzi was delighted to be a part of anything relating to the Forbidden City. His family was one of the neighborhood poor. They had a small shop, which was part of the network of small shops making up the local economy and supplying the trade goods and manpower that made things work. Today would be special for him, though he had just a peripheral function. He brought with him a small trinket, a bracelet. Wen had no interest in jewelry, but Bingzi insisted he take it with him. "The family of Lady Yi lives just two streets away, but they cannot see her because she is now part of the Royal Family. If you have a chance, just show her the bracelet and Lady Yi will know that you are in contact with her family. It will be useful for you." Wen took the bracelet and had it on his wrist when he went for his audience.

The tailor had done his job well. Wen's new Kwan robes and hat were the latest style for his appearance before the court. Bingzi accompanied him on the long walk to the front doors of the huge red south wall and, on the way, acted as his tourist guide.

"The City was built by the Third Ming Emperor, Young Li, over four hundred years ago," he told Wen. "When the Manchurians took over China, two hundred years later, they had to take it back from the peasants who had revolted against the Ming. There is still a tree, up on Jing Shan hill, where it is said that the last Ming Emperor hung himself when the peasants overran the capital."

As they walked around a corner, they entered a large park. Ahead of them was a huge gate.

"Do I go in there?" asked Wen.

"Oh no," Bingzi laughed. "That is just a ceremonial Gate; you see, the wall ends over there and over there. It is called the Da Qing Men, (The Great Qing Gate). It used to be called the Da Ming Men, but times change these things," he said with a laugh.

Further on up the path through the trees, the great red wall spread across their view. "The main entrance is in the center," Bingzi said, pointing. "The two large buildings flanking the gates and crossing the moat house the guard and serve as part of the fortifications which guard the gates. There are three entrances in the south wall," he continued, pointing ahead. "In the center is the Wen Men (Meridian Gate). It is used only by the Emperor and his family when they are with him. On either side are two smaller gates. You will go in the one on the right. These gates are for the ministers, visiting diplomats, and high governmental Kwan. You will present your letter to the eunuchs inside."

Wen looked to the left; high above the wall stood a three-story watchtower. It was larger, itself, than the Long Ming Hotel back home. Inside, suddenly darker, Wen was confronted by a tall eunuch in his black gummed silk outfit. "Give me your instructions," he said, without preamble.

Wen handed over the yellow silk packet. He strained to look inside beyond the gate, but could only see a large courtyard lined with stones. "You will wait, over there," the eunuch said and left, taking the packet with him. Wen sat on a stone bench and listened to muted conversations in the distant offices behind him. He could hear some wind chimes in a nearby tree that moved to a gentle breeze.

At last, An-yan entered the hallway and greeted him warmly. He handed the yellow packet back to Wen with both hands extended respectfully, and showed him through the doorway to the inner courtyard. "This is just the entrance." he said as they passed through.

Everything was gray stone except the white carved stone balustrades that ran across the yard. Through the balustrade fence were three bridges that corresponded to the three gates and crossed an artificial river. "The River of Golden Water is an extension of the moat," An-yan said.

"It runs from the north moat through the private gardens of the residences and across the courtyard here on the south end of the complex. It is for the Feng Shui; 'a mountain to the north and water to the south'. We will be summoned when it is our time."

Wen looked north at a large wall. In the center, up on a raised platform, was a building almost twenty meters high. On either side, about half way to the outer wall of the courtyard, were two smaller buildings. In front of each were large staircases. "That is the Gate of Supreme Harmony," An-yan said. "It is just the entrance to the next courtyard, the one that leads to the Hall of Supreme Harmony. Beyond that, there are other Halls and palaces where the royal family live. Today, you will be publicly honored by the Emperor. Say nothing unless he commands you to speak; then, be brief. He is still very tired and we are lucky to have an early audience. But, for now we must wait."

Soon they saw the tall eunuch emerge from the right-side building, shuffle quickly down the steps, and cross the court yard. "You must enter through the Gate of Supreme Harmony," he said. "You will use the staircase on the right. Go up to the top and down the stairs on the other side. When you are announced, you will walk behind the ministers to the center of the room, and fall to your knees for your first set of nine Kowtows. When you are done, walk across the courtyard to the base of the Dragon staircase, and again drop to your knees and do your Kowtows. Remain with your head on the ground till you are told to rise. Answer only when told to do so and leave when you are dismissed -- the same way that you came in. Remember to bow as you were taught."

Wen mounted the stairway on the right to the top and crossed the room under the enormous roof. Below him was a larger courtyard, filled with the ministers standing in rows. As he descended the stairway on the other side, Wen kept his eyes down and concentrated on not tripping or making too much noise. When he reached the bottom step, he waited to hear his name. Peeking between the plumed hats of the upper level ministers who were gathered for the morning audience, he tried to be as inconspicuous as he could. Across the courtyard was another wall with large staircases; the middle one was ornately carved with dragons writhing down the center. Above the stairs was a building with people standing in the center, but they were too far away to really see well.

Suddenly, he heard a clash of the gong and someone announced him: "Wen Fulian, His Majesty's Magistrate for Xiangfan City, Junxian County in the Province of Hubei. Raise and attend the throne!" Wen walked behind the ministers to the center and started the ritual entrance. When it was complete, he remained kneeling, with his forehead pressed against the cold marble floor at the base of the Dragon Stairway.

"We would see your eyes." The voice came from the top of the stairs; it was a woman's. Wen stood and looked up.

He could see the Emperor, lying on a divan, with two beautiful women standing behind him. The one on the right was evidently speaking for the Emperor. "His Majesty is pleased to receive his servant, Wen. Your record of gallantry in battle and performance of duty has been noted. His majesty awards you the Rank of A5 with a peacock feather and confers on you the title of Commissioner of Trade for all of Hunan, Hubei, and Kiangxi." One of the ministers stepped to Wen's side and presented him the feather. When Wen reached out to accept it, the bracelet on his wrist was exposed and the woman on the right noticed it. He could see it in her eyes, but she said nothing.

"The Commissioner Wen is excused!"

Wen repeated his bows and walked back between the rows of ministers, across to the side stairway and up the staircase. As he crossed the room under the enormous roof, he could see the city beyond the outer walls, but he watched his step and made his way down the other side and over to An-yan. "He gave me a feather!" Wen felt like a child, buoyant and suddenly very hungry. "The tailor will have to make another visit," An-yan replied.

"Did you know about all that?" Wen asked. An-yan just smiled and led him back to the gateway.

"Did the Lady Yi see your bracelet?" he asked. Wen nodded. "Then I will be seeing you soon, I am sure."

***

The Family

Bingzi was waiting just outside the gate. "Your saw our lady? And, she saw the bracelet?" he asked excitedly.

Wen nodded. "Yes, I think so. There were two women standing behind the Emperor. One of them seemed to recognize the bracelet when I exposed it."

"The shorter one? The one on the right? She is the one."

"Yes, she saw it. What did it mean?"

"It showed her that you are in contact with her family. Would you like to meet them?"

"I think that I must, with all of this signaling you have me involved in!"

They went down the street toward their own neighborhood, but took a detour a few blocks away. There was only one house decorated with royal banners and bunting. At the door, an older woman stood waiting for them. "Nimen Hao!" she greeted them and waved them inside to a closed atrium in the middle of their compound. "You have seen my daughter? And, the Emperor, how is he?"

Wen sat down and started to describe the events of the day and all that he had seen. Members of the family sat in rapt attention. Another much older woman joined them. "This is Sister Song. She isn't really my sister, but a friend of the family. Oh my, you haven't met them. Pardon me, please! This is Orchid's brother, Kuei Hsiang, and her sister, Rong." She noticed the question on Wen's face. "I am sorry, Orchid is the Lady Yi's family name. To the Court, she is Lady Yi. The other woman that you saw is the Lady Nuharoo. She is the Empress, first wife to the Emperor."

"They are both very beautiful women!" Wen said politely.

"Of course they are beautiful," Sister Song. said. "The beauty is necessary to stimulate the Emperor to plant the Dragon Seed. And a beautiful woman is a healthy woman, they say. The Lady Yi has the only child of the Emperor, the Crown Prince Tung Chih. "

"Not yet!" Mama corrected her. "He is the only son, but he has yet to receive the title. His father is in such bad health…. We need him to say the words that will make it so."

"Your daughter is fortunate to live in such style," Wen said. "I was raised on a farm in the mountains, and remember all too well slogging around in a rice field behind a water buffalo. It makes me appreciate any luxury that I have today."

"She also came from more humble beginnings than you see her in now. My husband was, at his highest, the Taotai for Wuhu. But he was brought down by scandal and killed himself. Orchid grew up among the Chinese people, ate rough food, and never liked the Manchurian ways. But, when they came around looking for beauties to marry the young Emperor, she saw her chance. Sister Song taught her the ways of the court; she had been a lady-in-waiting to one of the concubines in the old court."

Even before Wen had seen inside the Forbidden City, his curiosity had him searching for any maps or books that would tell him more about it, but he found none. The security of the city rested, in no small part, on its remoteness. And few people, outside the walls knew it as well as Sister Song. The large courtyards, which he had already seen, were not even a quarter of the area inside those walls. Miles of walks, parks, and gardens surrounded the densely laid-out private living quarters and administrative buildings behind the courtyards. Millions of teals of silver, gold, and jewels were encrusted on the buildings and garments housed there. The kitchens prepared foods that few would ever experience. The luxury of indolence inside the Forbidden City was meant to be a nest for great vision, wisdom, and power.

But, for Wen, it was enough to receive his new robes from the tailor. With them came a directive, written in the hand of Lady Yi, that he should return to Hubei, assume his new duties, and appoint his second as the Magistrate for Xiangfan. Wen thanked An-yan for all his help and tried to return the unspent monies; An-yan only laughed and sent him off with his promise to keep Wen apprised of how things were going at the capital.

*   *   *

The A5 Returns

It took the better part of a very hot May (even high in the mountains) to get back home. The farms looked inviting, but Wen just paused long enough there to see whether Lao Fang was at home. They then went on into town, to see him at the bank. As the horses clattered down the street, Fang ran out to greet the returning party.

They sent the soldiers off to the barracks to clean up and unpack their new uniforms, Wen and Fang walked to the school while discussing the tribute. Money had indeed continued to flow in, and new silver was coming back into the system from customers along the Yangtze. To Wen's relief, no lynch mob awaited him; in fact, he had become something of a legend. Everyone wanted to hear about his journey, but Wen needed to clean up and rest before any of that. He promised a banquet in a day or so.

Meixing joined the two men on their way home, and the three walked back up the East road. Madeline had already started a large dinner for them. They all had so very much to tell! But, saddle sores and tired bones had Wen yawning early and they all went to bed before the sun went down.

The next day, Wen and Fang had a lot to settle at the bank. Fang explained how tribute would pay their taxes well into the next five years. But, only by leveraging the stocks and raising new subscriptions had Fang been able to balance the books in the short term. Growth and sales were badly needed -- and Wen's new appointment would the key to all that. It would require him to travel a lot over the next few years, and he would miss his son and daughter growing up, he knew that. But, he felt that it was both his duty and his destiny.

Zhenli was three years old, one year older than the Emperor's son, and he didn't like it that his father was away so much. Meixing was also upset with the assignment, but tried to tell Zhenli how important it was for Daddy to perform this service for His Majesty. Baba Fang became Zhenli's father, teacher, and friend.

Dong Weili was understandably surprised to receive a letter directly from the Imperial Household. Wen, dressed in his new robes of a Kwan of the fifth rank, laid the yellow silk scroll on Dong's desk. "What sort of mischief was this?" Dong Weili thought. He looked at Wen for a clue, but Wen just laughed. "Read it yourself!" It took two or three readings for the message to finally sink into that bureaucratic mind. "Magistrate? How can I be the Magistrate?"

"Why not? You've been doing the job for the last year. You will have to get on with your studies, though. You really should have the Juren degree and be working on the Jinshi. But, I have been given a new title, Commissioner of Trade for three provinces. I will be gone most of the time. Deng Xiansheng will direct you and I will ask him to help you accomplish this as soon as possible."

Wen spent the next few days literally mapping out his next move. The rivers that he knew well were the large rivers. His stores were along their shores or at the mouths of the tributary rivers leading back into the mountains. But the people who ran the farms and would be his customers lived up those smaller rivers. The plan he developed was an exhausting search of supply and demand -- or "who has what and who needs what", as Lao Fang put it.

"Trade is just how the two get together," Fang said. "Where goods are plentiful, prices are low; that is where you buy. Where goods are needed, prices are high; that is where you sell. The difference between buy and sell provides the margin for profit. It is the economics of the trade routes. The caravans have lived on this principle for centuries."

Wen's boats and stores became his caravans. He took on rural scholars as both his students and his merchants. They were to explore the backcountry and identify, 'who has what and who needs what'. Wen himself would take the system into the adjoining provinces and tie the network together. The process was endless; the future seemed limitless.

***

The British

November 28, 1858. Wen was visiting merchants in the Wuchang area and was enjoying a game of Mahjong with the Governor when one huge ship and fifteen smaller ships sailed up river and anchored off shore, their cannon facing the city. From the ships, small boats filled with English soldiers were sent to the docks. The harbormaster ordered his soldiers on guard duty to not fire any weapon or unsheathe any sword. He alone walked to the end of the dock to receive the boats. The British soldiers, with bayonets fixed on their new Enfield rifles, took command of the docks and gathered all the Imperial soldiers into the center of the on-shore loading area.

The people of Wuchang had heard of the English, but this was the first actual encounter with the real people. News stories had come up from Canton and down from Beijing, but all of that was far away. They knew that, in the harbor of Canton, Guangzhou Province, back in 1856, a ship named the Arrow was boarded by Chinese Customs Services officers and several known pirates were taken into custody. The British, believing the ship to have been registered as one of theirs, protested the act as a violation of the treaty of Nanking.

It was one of those issues which had been blown out of proportion, to be used as an excuse to further British colonial goals. And, everyone knew that things would get ugly when the British plenipotentiary arrived from England in a few months. Though delayed by a fight in the House of Commons. Lord Elgin, son of the Lord Elgin who 'saved' the Elgin Marbles from Greece and sold them to the British Museum, was appointed plenipotentiary and arrived in Hong Kong in July of 1858, after being delayed a year by an uprising in India. The French plenipotentiary, Baron Gross, had also arrived with his force to settle a claimed murder of several French missionaries. The two forces jointly attacked Guangzhou, took the Governor General prisoner, and sent him off to a prison in Calcutta, where he later died. They then sailed up the eastern cost of China, shelling forts and taking the city of Tianjin.

The Emperor's fifth brother, Prince Gong, was sent several times to negotiate a peaceful settlement. But the Chinese were militarily weak and the foreigners were determined. Four separate versions of the Treaty of Tianjin were drafted, covering the 'rights' of the English, French, Americans, and Russians; giving foreigners residences for diplomats in Beijing, freedom for religious proselytizing, access up the Yangtze River for commercial expansion, and ten more ports for free trade. The treaty also called for an indemnity to pay for the foreigners' costs of the wars, further humbling and impoverishing the Qing government.

Lord Elgin then sailed back down toward Shanghai in October 1858, and turned up the Yangtze to Wuchang to assert the terms of the treaty relating to access. Despite messages sent ahead to Qing and Taiping alike, on November 20, Taiping batteries fired on the ship, and were answered and destroyed by the 68 pounders (cannon) on board the HMS Shannon and the other five ships of its flotilla. The British then sailed on up to Wuchang.

It was this flotilla which the Governor and Wen saw in the harbor when they came out of the restaurant from their luncheon. They were able to see the events on the dock and hurried down to find the English soldier in charge. Wen introduced himself and the Governor, as his English was better than the soldier's Chinese. The soldier sent a message by flags to the main ship and a reply was returned. Wen and the Governor were directed to get into one of the small boats and they were taken out to the large ship, the Shannon.

Wen and the Governor were overwhelmed by the size of the ship and the efficiency of its crew as their entire boat and its occupants were hoisted en masse from the water to the main deck.

They were then directed up a staircase to an elevated deck. A large table had been prepared, with five officers sitting on one side, their feathered hats and goblets of port at each place. There were documents already in the center of the table.

One of the gentlemen at the table could speak Chinese with some facility, and instructed them to take a place at the table, in front of the documents. He then introduced the officers in turn, starting with Lord Elgin, the commander of the fleet, the captain, first mate, and officers of the Shannon. The Governor, through the interpreter, introduced himself and Wen, as the Imperial Trade Commissioner.

"Good! I see that we have the right people on board and there should be no misunderstandings." Lord Elgin was all business, his business.

"These documents are the new treaty between England and China. This one is the Chinese translation of the official treaty, which is written in English. You will please read it in the presence of these officers. Then I will require your signature as proof that you understand the terms. Take whatever time you require."

Wen and the Governor sat at the table and began to read. The full document was nine pages long and contained fifty-six terms; it took some time. The Governor was upset and became more so as he read the terms. At the end, he looked up and said, "There is no signature page. Is this just a proposal? This is not a treaty till the parties ratify it!"

"They damned well better ratify it!" Lord Elgin said, "Or, we'll sink the whole of China!" He was red in the face and slammed down his glass of port.

The interpreter softened the commander's statement, but added, "The Emperor has one year to ratify it or there will be war. Until then, our ships and merchants will act in accord with the terms, as they are spelled out, as though it were already ratified. Failure to comply with these terms will be dealt with as indicated. Do you understand the terms of the Treaty?"

"I have read what is written on this paper; I have yet to see a treaty," said the Governor.

"You will sign it nonetheless!" Elgin stood by the table and menacingly leaned forward on his fists.

"My stamp is my signature, and it is in my office," the Governor said, ignoring the threat. "I must go there."

"Go then!" said Lord Elgin. "And we shall entertain your man until you return."

The Governor left the table without looking at Wen, and went directly back on the boat that had brought them.

Wen looked over the treaty and asked if he might speak to the terms. "It is an agreement for the terms of commerce, and I have recently been commissioned to promote commerce in the three adjoining provinces," he said.

"What do you know of commerce? You don't look old enough to know much!" said Elgin.

The interpreter pointed out the button on Wen's hat; it was clear crystal. "That means that he is in the fifth rank. Ninth is the bottom, and one is the top. The Insignia embroidered on his robe is a silver pheasant which means he is political, A5, not military. He probably has a Jinshi (PhD) degree. He looks to be about twenty-five or so."

"Actually, I am twenty-six, married, and have two children, Wen said nonchalantly. "I fought the Taiping, served as the Magistrate of Xiangfan for four years, and was recently promoted to my current position by the Emperor himself, because of my background in commerce."

"Well then, what do you make of the terms of this treaty?" Elgin asked, sliding forward on his chair.

"The terms are fair for business, between European states, but bad for China. We do not have your large manufacturing base. Ours is a handicraft economy; this trade will swamp our markets with your cheap goods and raise our unemployment. It is too much change for us -- we are not ready to sell that much to you."

"What do you think we would buy from you?"

"You will buy our silk, our tea, our spices, our fine porcelain, and our national treasures, like your father did in Greece."

Elgin slid back in his chair. "Well, he doesn't pull his punches, does he?" He smiled and rubbed his chin. "And how do you propose to get that all to England?"

"On the same ships that brought the cotton cloth from the midlands, and the metal wares from Birmingham, and all of that poison from India. I have thirty-seven steam boats trading up and down the rivers of the interior. We can bring it all to market, if you can stop the wars and give us a chance to earn a decent profit as well."

"Oh, yes! He is political -- not a diplomat, but certainly political."

"Oh, pardon me for not being diplomatic," Wen answered. "And yes, we know that we must follow your lead and trade like the Europeans trade. But it is not because we want to. Your trade has destroyed our internal economy, turned our civil administration upside down, and led to the death of more then twenty million of my countrymen. I will trade teal for teal and supply your demands as you supply ours. And we will do it your way," Wen said, pounding on the treaty. "But, it is only because we have no alternative!"

Elgin stood up, glaring at Wen. "I've had enough of this theater! Call me when the Governor gets back!" And he left the deck to his quarters aft.

The shadows of late afternoon were crossing the deck when the small boat returned from the dock, but the Governor was not on board. "He sent this letter, sir; said you would understand." The sailor handed a scroll to the Captain.

"What impudence is this?" said Elgin, coming out of his cabin. The Captain unrolled the scroll and held it out to the translator.

"He says that he can not put his stamp on the document since it may be misunderstood as his attempt to ratify the treaty which he is not empowered to do. 'I am acknowledging that I have read the terms of the un-ratified treaty and affix my official stamp to that statement. If you want my life for this act, I will be standing at the end of the dock.'"

Elgin looked out toward shore "What a blasted gall! Look, there he stands."

"I think you have made your point, sir," the Captain said. "The letter stands on its own."

Elgin turned to Wen. "Right, then! We have made a copy of the treaty to leave with you. See that you follow its terms and you'll find profit enough." He held out his hand. Wen bowed and walked to the boat. "Damned infuriating people! Why couldn't he just have taken my hand?" Wen heard Elgin mutter.

One by one, the British ships hauled up their anchors and turned downriver toward Shanghai.

Wen returned to his office in Wuchang, and copied the terms of the treaty into his own personal record before returning the original to the Governor's office the next day. "It would help," said Governor Hu, "If I could remember my grandmother's Daoist teachings, 'Follow the Way, for it is the nature of things that you cannot change.'"

"I don't know if Lao Tzu anticipated the English, but I do remember him saying 'The scholar is always on the side of virtue, so everyone around him prospers.' Maybe we can't get the rivers to go back up the hills, but we can distribute the waters to the thirsty."

"Always the pragmatist, eh? You are right. We must align ourselves with the Emperor and work to set virtue before us. What will you do now?"

"I will go back up to Xiangfan and tell Lao Fang about the new treaty. He knows more about the English than anyone else."

"May he live nine thousand years," said the Governor.

"Don't hex him!" said Wen, with a laugh. "I'm sure your Grandmother would have warned you about that." He left Wuchang that day and headed directly for Xiangfan.

The Commissioner of Trade

***

1858

In June of 1858, while Wen was delivering the tribute to the ailing Emperor and getting his promotion and commission, he was unaware of the political turmoil that was swirling around in the rest of the Forbidden City. His presentation of the tribute was an innocent act from quickly fading tradition -- more reminiscent of the Emperor's Grandfather's time.

Ministers and their memoranda were constantly contesting for the attention of the throne. At issue was nothing less than war or peace. The English and French were pressing for more and more colonial advantage. Using the Treaty of Nanjing and a two-year- old misunderstanding (The Arrow Incident), as a pretext. The English declared a violation of the treaty and had already invaded the city of Canton, taking control of Guangdong Province.

The French had joined the English with much the same motivation, using the execution of the French cleric, Father August Chapdelaine, in Guangxi Province as their excuse.

They joined forces with the English and sailed north to force a renegotiation and expansion of the Treaty of Nanjing and to extend its terms. They fought their way up to Tianjin, the gateway to the Capital, and that precipitated a contest of wills between the Emperor and his highest ministers, who were not all in agreement.

The Emperor's brother, Prince Kung, had negotiated a peace in the terms of a proposed Treaty of Tianjin for the Emperor. But, he was losing his influence with the Emperor to those ministers who would rather go to war than assent to the terms of the Treaty. Ratification of the proposed treaty was postponed for one year. Lord Elgin sailed out of Tianjin and down to Shanghai, then up the Yangtze. This was done to demonstrate and enforce England's presumption of the terms of the new treaty. And, that is when he met Wen.

The ministers, who counseled the Emperor to choose war, were emboldened by the recently signed Aigun Treaty with Russia. By this treaty, the Russians were committed to help the Chinese in any attack by the English and the French in exchange for a large tract of Manchuria. The Emperor had decided to fight the Europeans rather than submit to the terms of the treaty. The Mongolian General Senggelinqin was put in charge of opposing the foreigners. His Mongolian cavalry had been ordered to protect and strengthen the forts at Dagu on the Peiho River.

***

The River Trade

After his encounter with Lord Elgin, it took Wen took five months to return home, because he worked in as many port calls as he could along the way. He arrived in mid-November, to find Lao Fang sitting up in bed. He was wrapped in a robe and nibbling on a carrot, like a rabbit. After he had a chance to read the treaty, Fang laid it on the bed and said to Wen, "Well, you have to hand it to them.

They know how to kick the stuffing out of you when you're down. To their thinking, it is a fair treaty. Just open your doors and do it our way. They just can't get it through their heads that we don't <u>want</u> to open our doors."

"But, aside from all that, you <u>can</u> do business their way -- just never pay in silver! Trade with them, exchange at fair prices, but always pay in goods; never pay in silver. Let them part with theirs, if you can get them to do it. But, don't you do it. Issue credit only with their best collateral in your hand. Also, learn about their markets -- who they are selling to and how much they will get when they sell our goods when they get home. The only way to get the best price is if you allow them to make a reasonable profit. That's it!" He lay back in the bed and closed his eyes.

Wen pulled up Fang's blanket and sat back in the chair next to his bed. "I wish you were out there with me," he said wistfully. "I know how you love the chase. They will be opening concessions in Hankou and trading whole shiploads at a time. I've got to be there, but I wish you were there, too."

"If the doctors let me go, I'll be there. But, I guess the idea of being sixty years old hit me harder than I thought it would. I can't throw Zhenli up in the air like I used to. It is hard to breath the air out there sometimes -- I get this tightness across my chest, and I cough too much. I think, for the moment, that I'll just lie back and enjoy being pampered. By the way, I hope you brought something back for Meiliang's birthday!"

Wen smiled and showed Fang the doll set that he had picked up in Wuchang. "Eight Dolls of the Ethnic Peoples of Hunan." He had missed her birthday on November 2, but now that he was home, he was determined to use the time to advantage.

When he came in, from Lao Fang's house, he called out "Meiliang, come here. See what Daddy got for you!" She was standing in the hall with her arms outstretched. He picked her up and was caught by that hint of her mother's eyes -- deep black and flirtatious as any two year old, but with the roundness of the French in the lids. She had learned to snuggle, and loved to listen to her father's chest as he spoke. They sat together, wrapped in an Afghan blanket, as Wen told Meixing about his trips.

"The eunuchs were like regular men. You knew that they were not 'whole men', but men just the same. Most of them were not as aggressive as men on the outside; they were sly and cunning. The head eunuch, Shim, really uses his position. He could come and go almost any time he wanted. He was always doing some business on the outside, ostensibly for the royal household. But, I also know he has a bodyguard service called the Three Harmonies and several schools for martial arts. You could see his training in the way he walked. He was always 'on balance'. An-yan told me he even charges the concubines for the services that he can do for them, outside the walls. They can't ever go out, but they all have family out there who need favors."

"Were the women really as beautiful as they say?"

"The two that I saw were! They search for the most beautiful girls to be wives for the Emperor. They have to make sure that they are pure and don't have any family problems. Of course, the wives must be from Manchurian families, but the concubines are often Han. "

"And that is all you saw, beautiful women? Didn't they have any depth? Aren't they real people under all that makeup?" she chided.

"Of course they are," Wen answered. "An-yan is assigned to Lady Yi. He said she is really smart. Lady Lin, The Empress, is a professional beauty. She relies on her looks and her Buddha Beads; she doesn't care to know much. She sees her role as simply to please the Emperor. Lady Yi, however, is something of a conniver. She is educated and interested in politics. She is the real mind behind the throne, and if His Majesty dies, she'll be the one to deal with. She is the real mother of the Prince."

"Is she the one that you met?" Meixing asked.

"I only met with her family, outside the Forbidden City; I didn't communicate with her except to flash her mother's bracelet at my audience. She saw it and I could see she recognized it. But I never got to really talk with her. She spoke for the Emperor; he was there, but couldn't sit up and speak. He is really sick."

"Did you hear what my father did?" Meixing asked. "He got a message from the farm in Anhui. It seems they had a bumper crop this year, and Father sent it all up to the capital as his tribute. You are not the only politician in the family."

"He had better watch it or they will drag him into the government system. He never did serve, did he?"

"He lost two sons."

"I'm sorry. I didn't mean that," he said, pulling her into his lap. He held Meiliang and Meixing in a family hug.

"Why is Mommy crying?" Zhenli asked, pulling at Wen's pant leg.

"We were just remembering something sad," said Wen.

"Then, why aren't you crying?"

"I think I cry on the inside," he answered. "Mommy cries on the outside."

Beyond the windows, the snow was blowing and sticking to the windowpanes over the stove, then melting and sliding down, leaving a tear trail behind it. The sun had gone down behind the mountains and the dinner bubbled over on the stove. Wen vowed to stay at home that winter.

***

1859

All too soon, for Wen, it was time to return to business on the river. The spring of 1859 brought a late snow along the Yangtze, but the port at Hankou was busy with new construction. Wen's cranes were mounted to the new docks and swung over the empty births to deliver the cement that would line the bottom. Silt from the Yangtze would have to be cleaned out continually; if not, it would build up and boats would drag their bottoms on it. They were expecting a lot of ships and they didn't want any of them stranded on the silt. By building an estuary dam a little way upriver, much of the silt would drop out and be swept away by the current. The cleaner water would then be drained off and channeled through a slue to run continually through the slip across the flat cement bottom, to flush out any collected silt there back into the river.

The buildings on the shore and all of the utilities were nearing completion. Roadways and public buildings were being put in, at Wen's expense, in exchange for a twenty-year tax exemption. "Besides" Wen explained to Lao Fang, who had come down for a visit, "The city would never get around to finishing the plan. Ships would be held up forever waiting for a customs building to get built, or for the police to arrive over unpaved roads. This way, we will be able to start unloading in the Fall."

Fang smiled. "How will you be able to keep out the opium trade?"

"I have been working with the Governor on that. Even though the treaty makes trade in opium legal, it also says Chinese criminals will be handled by Chinese courts. The plan is basically to make it very uncomfortable for anyone who would buy or ship opium through the port. We will punish them for some other crime and ship them out of town. I am sure they will get the drift of our plan. Besides, we will have plenty to do just taking care of normal trade.

We do not want any part of the criminal element to take over Wuchang as they have in Shanghai."

Even before the port was officially open, the first ships started off-loading woven cloth, whiskey, and farm implements from England, and were reloaded with bailed raw cotton, wool, rice, and corn. The grain silos were large, efficient, and already stocked from the upstream stores along the Han River. The foreign goods went back up the Han to the local markets, in exchange for debits; more grain, wool, and cotton came down to Hankou in exchange for credits, with profit figured into each exchange.

New stores were opened up further west along the Yangtze River, and goods from both foreign and domestic suppliers found a ready market with payment in silver. Bankers trained in Lao Fang's banks followed the trade up the Yangtze, and trade increased even more with the infusion of available credit through Fang's banks.

In the midst of all his business affairs, Wen ran across an article in one of the English papers. In June 1859, the English and French sent a force of 21 ships and 2,200 men, with diplomats to demand ratification of the Treaty of Tianjin. Led by Lord Elgin's younger brother, the Europeans demanded passage up the river to Beijing. They were told the envoys could land, but could not have a military escort. The British engineers blew up the blockading chains and they attempted to sail on, to shell Fort Dagu. They were repulsed by 'very accurate fire' from the fort, which the British later suspected must have been directed by the Russians. After losing six of their ships, it was a 'neutral' American squadron under Commodore J. Tattnall which covered the English and French withdrawal. They would have to come back in force another day.

***
1860

Throughout the last year, the Qing armies, under the Qing General Senggelinqin, crushed the Taiping forces of the 'Northern Expedition' as well as their supply lines in Anhui. In the south, the armies under Zeng Guofan and Zuo Zongtang retook most of the cities downstream along the Yangtze that had previously been held by the Taiping. The danger, however, was not totally over. The Taiping were still fighting to hang onto and expand out from their base in Nanjing; they even dreamed of taking control of Shanghai.

Li Xiucheng, an up-and-coming Taiping General, was appointed 'the Loyal King' and, in the spring of 1860, started a campaign south of the Yangtze to take Hangzhou. The Qing army responded by rushing troops from its encampment around Nanjing to Hangzhou. However, the Taiping had doubled back, by forced march, and were reinforced by fresh troops from Nanjing for a successful assault on Suzhou. From there, the Taiping marched to attack Shanghai.

The foreigners living in Shanghai heard about the attack and raised what forces they could, joined by local Chinese. In the end, the Taiping were driven back to Nanjing, and any pretense of the neutrality of the foreigners was dropped. The French, Americans, and English were clearly on the side of the Qing in Shanghai.

In Beijing, however, the English and French, under Lord Elgin, who had returned to China from England, sailed north for a third time to gain ratification of the Tianjin Treaty by force of arms -- this time with a force of 173 ships and 18,600 men. They fought their way to Tianjin and marched toward Beijing. The British and French armies, armed with the newest breach-loading rifled artillery field pieces and new French mitrailleuses field guns, annihilated Senggelinqin's 10,000 troops and his 4,000 Mongolian Cavalry. The Emperor fled the capital and retreated to their hunting preserve in Johol in Manchuria, north of the Great Wall. He left Prince Kung to negotiate with the British Diplomatic Envoy, Harry Parks, and his small entourage.

But, in the confusion of the fighting, and with conflicting orders from ministers of opposing factions, the Qing Bannermen arrested Harry Parks and his team, and turned them over to the Board of Punishments. The British diplomats were detained, tortured, and three of his party died. To gain the release of the diplomats, the English took Beijing. In retaliation for the mistreatment and murder of the diplomats, the French and English soldiers decided not to sack the Forbidden City but rather march to on to the Summer Palace, strip it of its treasurers, and then burn it to the ground.

***

Back on the River

The news of the war up north did filter down to the Yangtze, but the great river had its own battles to fight. Its regional military maintained the civil order and the economy was growing and adjusting with increasing independence from the central government. For two years, the Emperor was too ill to govern and had removed the court to Manchuria, leaving his brother in Beijing to deal with the Europeans.

Zeng Guofan had initiated the transition from central to regional autonomy in the early 1850s. He was already a very high-ranking Kwan, The Vice President of the Board of Rites, when the Taiping movement was just becoming a recognized threat. Already highly regarded for his academic achievements, Zeng was one of the highest Kwan of his time, but he was not Manchurian. He was always seen first as Han Chinese.

On his way to his mother's funeral and in a state of mourning, when he should have had no governmental assignments, Zeng was ordered to raise an army in his home province of Hunan. He negotiated and won the Emperor's sanction to set up an army, free from the taint of the corruption from local ministers and generals, by enlisting the top classes of a local military school and their teacher as their leader. He was given unprecedented authority to root out corruption and conduct executions as he saw fit. To the local river pirates and Heaven and Earth Societies, he was known as 'Zeng, the Head Chopper'.

Soon, Li Hongzhang, Chang Chih-tung, and Zuo Zongtang, three of the leading Qing generals, were soon also operating independent armies under the loose and distant direction of the Emperor's staff; they were all buying and manufacturing weapons for their local armies.

Wen found himself living in one of the offices of the Port of Hankou during the construction period, as one problem or opportunity followed another. Even before the port was ready, ships were arriving with goods to sell and money to buy. Floating docks were built to accommodate the trade. The auxiliary supply depot was being used more and more as a repair facility for the ships that stopped at the harbor.

Two machinists from one of the passing ships had been thrown off their vessel due to an argument with the ship's captain. Though they didn't know Chinese well, they spoke enough to work in the depot, and in the end, took over the whole repair operation. Not only could they repair mechanical things, but they also designed and built machines to make the repairs -- machines that were better, in fact, than the ones Wen could get from Shanghai. Soon, they set up a manufacturing facility to cast and machine parts and to build whole machines for export. One such machine was a line-boring drill, which could make barrels for rifle, pistol, and cannon; three of these were sent back upriver to the military city in Xiangfan. Zeng Guofan's buyer for the Hunan Army also took an interest in the machining being done in Hankou -- he ordered several of these machines. Orders then started coming in from all of the Governors General in other provinces throughout China. Zeng was setting up an arsenal outside Shanghai.

In all of this, Spring of 1861 had come, and Wen vowed to spend at least some time with his family. The shops and the factories would just have to direct themselves. If he made good time, he would be able to get back home to Xiangfan in time for Zhenli's sixth birthday.

The trip home was shorter than he remembered it; the dredges had been doing their work well. Two sets of locks had also been installed to hold back the river, maintaining depth in areas where the terrain naturally dropped and the river had previously been nothing more than rapids.

When he arrived, the port at Xiangfan was bustling with activity. On the old city side, two boats were loading at the same time from the silos and by cranes. Across the river was the new city, with work in its dry docks throwing sparks and making all sorts of noise. Wen passed up the carriages and walked into town; his baggage would be sent to the house. He wanted to smell the old town and talk with old friends along the way home. He found the school closed for a spring recess; many of the girls had to help put in the next plantings at home. Dong had been doing a good job of running the town, Wen thought. He had kept it looking clean and prosperous. New stores had been added in the main area and there were now two smaller hotels along the streets leading to the docks. Wen walked on up the hill toward the farm and caught sight of his own children playing with some others.

Wen Zhenli was tall for his 'almost six years', but he ran with a grace and balance his father recognized; there was a bit of his mother there. He was flying, like a bird, over the yard between the houses. But, he stopped suddenly when he saw Wen walking up the street

"Papa! You home long time?" He called, running over to his father and jumping into his arms.

"Oh Boy, you have grown a lot this year!" Wen answered, noting his son's use of the local speech pattern. Or was it that he was now accustomed to the Shanghai dialect? They spun around till Wen was dizzy, then both fell laughing onto the grass. Wen looked up at the sky directly above him; it was blue with wisps of white. But off to the northeast, he could see a brown dusty haze from the military town's factories. Then he looked at the grass next to him; it, too, was dusty.

"Well! Home from the war, is it?" Meixing ran out of the house and helped him up off the grass and giving him a big hug.

"Yes, home at last! How is everyone?" Wen asked. Meixing's expression changed a bit. She looked more serious.

"Father still isn't himself yet," she said. "He keeps carrying on about how old he is. I think he is going to take that offer from the Shanghai bankers."

"What offer is that?"

"There is a group that is trying to buy up all of the credit along the Yangtze. I think if they offer enough, he might just go into retirement a rich man."

"He already is a rich man; he has us doesn't he?" Wen kidded her, as they walked across to Fang's house. Then he spotted Meiliang playing tea service with her grandmother in the yard.

Wen went over and picked her up. "How is my little girl?" he asked lovingly. She shot a look at her mother and wriggled down. "OK," Wen laughed, "But I think you will still like the English doll that I brought for you."

Lao Fang was napping lightly in the front room, with an open book on his lap. "Ah! The industrial giant returns," he quipped. "How are things along the river these days?"

"You should tell me," Wen tossed back. "Meixing says you are evaluating your own investments. What is this about a sale?"

"I was just thinking how nice it would be to return to the life of a country farmer," Fang mused.

"Are you thinking about going back to Anhui?"

"It is a possibility. But Madeline still wants to be near the children. Let us take them with us and we could make a deal. "

"I don't know," Wen answered. "With the Taiping falling apart and trade booming, this might be the time for me to sell off my shares and move onto something new as well." He sat down by Fang.

"Hold on, you two!" Meixing had come in with her mother and daughter. "Don't I have a say in this? I have investments here as well, you know!"

"I'm sorry. I thought you might like the idea," Wen said. He wasn't quite sure of his ground here; he had been away for a while. "Isn't that school of yours ready for some new blood at the helm?"

"Oh, the school could do without me, I guess," she answered, looking strangely pensive. "But I'm not sure that I can get on without it. Do you really think you could give up all that you built here and along the rivers? There is a lot more investment here than just money."

"I don't think any of you have thought this through," Madeline interjected. "Don't get so serious! Anyway, you just got back home! Wouldn't you like to like to clean up? We can discuss this over one of those Long Ming fish dinners."

***

Moving On

In less than a week, Wen was back out on the river. This time, his goal was to get some serious feedback on divesting his interest in the stores and banks. The small towns typically had only a few who used the extended boat service to sell their goods on the credit/debit system. The rest were local craftsmen and farmers who counted their wealth in physical things -- they traded at the dock. The algebra of finance was not within their realm. But there was always someone, in these small towns, who could read and write and could be taught to keep the books for a piece of the profits.

In the larger cities, there were several levels of interest, already established by some sort of guild structure. Older, more established trades would have masters and journeymen who controlled their segment of the market, their product line. They would trust a local merchant to act as their fiduciary and Wen's agent. So, without really letting go, Wen sold off much of his duty work and hung onto a substantial part of the ongoing profits.

It took him till late in the summer to wrap up most of these negotiations. But, when he got home, there was a message from the Governor requesting that he to go back down to Wuchang. It didn't seem desperately urgent, but it was the Governor.

When he arrived, Hu Linyi was in his favorite garden restaurant playing Mahjong with some friends. "Ah, Wen, guolai!" he greeted his younger friend. They went for a walk around the restaurant's large garden pathways. "I have a request from your friend, the Empress."

"What?" Wen stopped in his tracks. "What are you saying?"

"She seems to regard you quite highly! She has a special mission for you. "

"I only saw the Lady Lin once, and I didn't think that I made any impression at all."

"Oh, not her. No, no. The <u>real</u> Empress. Lady Yi."

***

A Summons to Court

"I thought Lady Lin was the wife of the Emperor and Lady Yi was just his concubine," Wen said, scratching his head.

"Then I have some news for you," the Governor answered with a wry smile. "I knew that the Emperor was about to die; that is why I sent for you. But today I received word that he passed away last month! The public announcement will be issued after the succession and all of the political wrangling is done. But my money is on the Lady Yi. "

"And she is the one who wants something from me?" Wen said.

"Yes. And that's why I am betting that she is the real winner in all of this. She has already put her men in place. And, you are one of them. I don't know exactly what is going on up there in Manchuria, but I know they will keep this power struggle out of sight. This is how I see it: The Emperor had two factions already vying for power. His brother, the Prince Kung, and the brother's father-in-law were the political realists. They got the Emperor to ratify the Treaty with the English and French. But, even with General Senggelinqin dead and gone, there is a faction that would have us go to war rather than live by its terms.

Prince Yee and the Grand Councilor Su Shun were the ones who had the British diplomat and his entourage captured and tortured till many died. All of this was in a letter that the Lady Yi sent to advise the Governors and to get our comments. She as much as accused them of treason and we think she is right. Also, the Lady Yi has the Emperor's only son. I think she is smart enough to pull this off."

"What does she want me to do? I don't have massive armies or much more treasure."

"Oh, no! She has many irons in this fire. Your job is much less dramatic. She wants you to take food to the people of Beijing and let it be known that it is from her. The last thing she needs, when they get back, is another rebellion. She also asked that you look in on her family. Do you know her family?"

"I met them when I was up there three years ago. What sort of shape is the city in? When I was there it was very busy, very prosperous by all appearances. And the court was resplendent. If the Europeans have run roughshod through there, the locals must need more than food."

"You might do well to take up some engineers who could fight if they had to. I don't know what shape their port is in, but anything that you can do to stimulate trade and employment would surely be the sort of help she is looking for. They should be back next month, so you should get started as soon as you can."

***

Return to Beijing

Wen commandeered two mid-sized steamer boats and filled them with rice. He assembled a crew from the Civic Guard engineers; the regular army Bannermen made sure they were well armed and had everything they would need for two months, then they set off, down stream. At Wuhu, Wen stopped long enough to pick up some Imperial Yellow silk. The Taiping, who had been dressing in Royal Yellow, which is reserved for only the Emperor, were no longer ordering it for Hong Xiuquan, so the local merchants were more than willing to trade their entire stock for a quarter of the rice in one of the boats. That evening, Wen's boats easily slipped downstream, past the guns at Nanjing and up the entrance to the Grand Canal.

As they headed north, they were boarded several times by the flotilla of small steam gunboats used by The Ever Victorious Army in their hit-and-run campaign against the Taiping. Their leader, an American soldier-of-fortune named Frederick Wade, had died fighting along side the Chinese troops he had trained It was his original band of military irregulars, The Foreign Rifles, that defended Shanghai against the Taiping. But, Wade only cared that the pay was good and that he was in the thick of it, whatever it was.

The canal took advantage of the low country and the local lakes, from the Yangtze up to the Yellow River and on to Tianjin. Along most of its course, it was wide enough to accommodate several boats, but some sections needed repair. Wen's engineers had to use all of their skills and equipment just to open up blocked passages and locks along the canal. The last leg of their journey was the Liangshui Canal from the Yellow River to the Port of Beijing, southwest of the city.

The Palace Eunuchs gladly accepted the silks and a large portion of the rice. Then, Wen took another large portion of the rice to General Zen Guofan's city headquarters, to feed the police and fire patrols. The headquarters was under the command of Guofan's assistant, General Sheng Pao. Sheng was Manchu and had served under General Senggelinqin in the defense of Beijing. He had no information about the status of the royal family, but brightened visibly when Wen told him that Lady Yi had sent him to the capital to distribute food in her name. Finally, Wen made sure that the bulk of the rice was sold cheaply on the open market under the name of Lady Yi.

Wen took four soldiers and a small portion of the rice with him to visit the family of Lady Yi. The house still had some tatters of yellow bunting, but the last three years had not been kind to the structure. The invading soldiers had shot down most of the decorations and left the bricks on the front of the house with chips from the bullets. Wen knocked on the door and was received by Lady Yi's younger brother, Kuei Hsiang. "Wen Xueshang, how nice to see you again. Come in. I'll get my mother."

Lady Yi's mother immediately recognized Wen from his previous visit and they talked at length about the family. Rong, the Lady Yi's sister, had married Prince Ch'un, the Emperor's seventh brother. They now had two children and were living in the country, for safety's sake. The mother knew nothing about the location or condition of her daughter and the Emperor. The subject was obviously distressing, but Wen declined to speculate.

The engineers had set to work on the outside of the city wall of Beijing, repairing major damage to the gates and port facilities from the cannon fire of the assault more than a year ago. Inside the Forbidden City, the eunuchs who had not accompanied the royal family or fled during the attack had done their best to prepare for the return of the Royal Family, but were grateful for any materials that the engineers could supply

Prince Kung had returned on horseback, ahead of a caravan that was coming down from the north, and was interested in meeting this Kwan, whose men were repairing the city gates.

"Oh, it is you!" he said, when he rode up to the work party. "I remember you from your tribute presentation. How is your commission working out?"

"We are busy all along the Yangtze and Han Rivers, and have made some progress inland as well," Wen answered, with a slight deferential bow.

"You know that the Emperor died two months ago, don't you?" the Prince asked.

"Yes, I received an order from the Lady Yi, via our Governor General, to bring food to her people in Beijing and to make what repairs that we could, in preparation for her return."

"Who knows about this?" the Prince asked, deeply concerned.

"I was surprised to find out that no one here seems to know about it. She just ordered the food and repairs, and I assumed the rest."

"For the new Emperor's safety, we have not made a public announcement quite yet. They should be arriving any day now. The body of the Xianfeng Emperor will be returned to the city and then taken to the tombs, about fifteen kilometers east of the city. But come with me. There is someone who wants to meet you."

Prince Kung led Wen back to the caravan, which was about to enter the city. There was a small troop surrounding a palanquin that stood on four short legs to allow the bearers to rest.

"Your Majesty, there is someone here to see you," the Prince said, speaking into a window of the palanquin.

The curtain pulled back and Wen fell to his knees. "Rise please."

Wen looked up. "Your Majesty!" he said in hushed tones.

"We are well pleased to see you," said Lady Yi. Her face showed the exhaustion of her trip, even though she was being carried. "I see your men are at work. And, the rice? Is it also at work?"

"Yes, your Majesty. It was put into the stores to be sold cheaply as your gift to the people. I also delivered some to the municipal workers and to Zeng Guofan's Headquarters."

"Is he there?" she asked, seeming surprised.

"No, Your Majesty. I gave it to General Sheng Pao."

She looked at Prince Kung, "Zeng is a fence-sitter. These Chinese Generals have their own agendas. I'm just as glad that there is a Manchurian in charge here." She looked back at Wen as though he had not been there while she spoke. "Prince Kung will direct you while you are in the city. It is good to see loyalty like yours; but I must get back inside." She slapped the side of the palanquin with her fan and the procession moved on into the city.

***

The Court Comes Home

Three days later, the 'Parade of Happiness' came down that same road with the new Emperor and his 'Mother', the Lady Lin After 230 kilometers of walking, the bearers of the palanquins were ragged and covered with road dust; their feet were bleeding through their bandages. Everyone was exhausted and entered the Forbidden City in silence. The Young Emperor was with Lady Lin. They went directly to their own palaces, deep in the recesses of the Forbidden City.

Two days later, the 'Parade of Sadness' arrived with the body of the Emperor and a surprise for those who saw its arrival. Su Shun, the Grand Councilor to the Emperor, was being carried inside a wheeled cage, like a wild beast. The Prince Yee, seven of Su's advisors, the Chief Eunuch, and the other eunuchs walked behind the cage in chains, like common criminals.

Ministers and Governors who were available were called to the Forbidden City to hear the charges. The same grand courtyard where Wen had been presented to the Emperor, between the Gate of Supreme Harmony and the Hall of Supreme Harmony, was filled with military, civil ministers, and Governors, all of the highest rank. At the top of the Grand Dragon Stairway, the Ladies Lin and Yi stood behind the nine-year-old boy-Emperor. The charge against the prisoners was Subversion of the State. They were all found guilty. Prince Yi was 'allowed to hang himself'. Su Shun was granted decapitation. The rest were whipped to death. The Lady Yi felt that some show of terror was needed.

Zeng Guofan, who in 1860 had been appointed Viceroy of Liangjian (the provinces of Anhui, Jiangxi and Jiangsu) and who was the highest of all Han Chinese ministers, took control of security for the capital and for the Imperial Family. Wen and his men were allowed to return to Hubei -- and to a more normal life.

234

Return to Lu'an

***

First Visit

Wen arrived home to find Meixing, her parents, and the children all getting ready to visit the old farm. "Always room for one more." she said. Soon, they were all packed up and set out for the old farm.

Despite the winter winds and the muddy roads, the journey was like a picnic on wheels. They sang songs and told stories about their trips. It was the first time Wen and Meixing had ever heard about Madeline's life, back in France. Neither of them knew about her grandfather's participation in the French Revolution -- nor, for that matter, much about the Revolution itself. Wen, for his part, got to reminisce about his early years on the farm in the mountains. The business of the state and the state of business began to fade from their conversation.

The old farm came into view under a rising mist, as they came down the last road from the Dabie Mountains. The fields were full of winter wheat, peeking up in tufted rows laced with wet snow along the north side of each row.

Someone rang a bell and people started appearing from behind the barn and in the fields. When they pulled up inside the fence in front of the house, the Civic Guard who had been left to work the farm gathered around to welcome them. The last of the Taiping and their bandit friends had been dealt with, and they were happy to report that the farms on Fang's lands were once again producing at prewar levels.

The house was warm inside because the men had maintained a small fire in the potbelly stove in the living room, 'Just to keep it dry,' they said. The windows had been repaired and someone had even made curtains. There were rugs on the floors and new wooden chairs and tables set about the main room. Oil lamps had been purchased and set out around the room and in Lao Fang's office, which now doubled as a bedroom. The kitchen had new ceramic bowls and chopsticks. The main room had new futon beds with a real mattress, pillows, sheets, blanket, and down comforters. The chest in the main room contained sleeping mats and blankets for visitors.

"All the comforts of home!" said Lao Fang delightedly, as they made the grand tour of their beloved farmhouse.

"It all smells so new; fresh cut pine and varnish!" Madeline smiled. "The men did a wonderful job. I just wish it were bigger. We can't really have all of us here for any period of time."

"I'll look into having them add a second floor," Fang said, "But, I think that we'll be just fine for now!"

They unpacked their pots and pans, suitcases and chests, and soon had a dinner of chicken, rice, and vegetables set out in large bowls at the large new table in the main room. By now, the sun had set with a warm glow of its own. The house had become a home again, and there followed three days and nights of family bonding.

The following day, they visited the graves of the boys, up on the hill. With a basket lunch, they spent the afternoon tending the graves and talking to the boys as though they were still there, alive. Despite the cold, they stayed till the sun dropped behind the Dabie Shan range.

In the morning, Lao Fang and Wen went into town to pick up a list of things that were still needed and to check out the city. Now that the Taiping were gone, Lu'an was once again a flourishing river trade center. Tea from the mountain farms, fish and crawfish from the river were traded in bulk, both for export and local consumption. The main street, however, still had only one really good restaurant and it seemed there was some cause for excitement inside. Zeng Guofan, The Viceroy and Governor General, was seated at a long table in the back with his entourage.

As Wen and his father-in-law entered, and their eyes adjusted to the dark, they stood for a moment at the doorway and looked for an open table. Through the glass bead curtain, Wen and Fang could see that the room was packed with men. "Please, come in and join us!" came a voice from behind a beaded curtain. A waiter pulled aside the strands to reveal a large table, surrounded by several Kwan. At the head was an older man in a yellow riding jacket.

"Nimen guo lai!" he said, waving them in to a place opened up along the side nearest the curtain. Wen and Fang took their seats and Wen made the introductions.

"Father, this is General Zeng Guofan. General, this is my father-in-law, Fang Laogai."

"I know Wen," Zeng Guofan explained to the group. "He is a friend of the Empress." There was a murmur of surprise around the table.

"Please, Sir," Wen demurred. "I have served her, but I wouldn't say I am her friend. That would be presumptuous of me."

"In Beijing today, you are either a friend or and enemy," Zeng said with a snarl. "You, my friend, are a friend. Now tell us how you come to be in this little town, so far from home."

Wen told the General about their visit to Lao Fang's farm and their living with him in Xiangfan. The General also did not know about Lao Fang's role in the River Campaign, of his technical help with understanding the breach-loading rifles, which Wen now told him proudly. He also recounted many of his own stories of establishing trade along the Han and Yangtze, and how Fang had created the banking empire needed to complement and foster that trade. "But, my father-in-law has endured the greatest loss for any father -- his two sons died in the war against the Taiping."

Zeng stood up and bowed toward Fang. "I regret your loss of both your boys." he said solemnly. "We have lost so many! But, each one is a grave personal loss to the family. I wish it were otherwise." He sat down and fell silent for a moment.

"Sir, what have we accomplished with all that?" Fang asked him, tears running freely down his cheeks. "Is China any greater for our loss?"

Zeng reached across the table and put his hand on Fang's shoulder. "China has survived! I can only hope that we will live to see it become greater. But, at least, we have passed through the abyss. The younger men will have to carry on from here. There are still a few as loyal and committed to The Way as Xiao Wen. And Li Hongzhang over there has raised and is leading his own army of Huai Braves. When the fighting is done, I am sure that these two, and others like them, will make China great again."

When they finally finished their meal and prepared to get on with their day, Zeng insisted they meet for a private dinner that evening. Wen and Fang did their shopping and loaded the cart with things for the farm -- more down blankets, candles, honey, and some pastries -- and they finally took a short ride around town to see what had changed in their absence. As the sun set, they returned to the restaurant for their second meal with the General.

***

A New Assignment

After greeting each other again, Zeng quickly shifted the tone of their meeting to serious business. "China needs you both! There is no way around it! We need you two in the lead, with the millions of other capable men of influence. The Confucian Way has suffered as great a blow in our lifetime as it has ever known in the past. We are in the midst of a cultural contest, a contest that the Europeans have won, so far. Our plan is to learn enough of the barbarian ways and technology that we will be able to use it against them and regain control of our own land. The name of this process is 'self strengthening.' You both have unique and highly successful pasts which will help to build that future."

Both Wen and Fang waved off what the General had just said as though it were mere flattery. "No! I am serious about this," Zeng said. "This is a campaign of construction that will be greater than all of our military campaigns of destruction put together. We are going to rebuild the country!"

"I need you." He said, looking at Wen. "I need you to build the machines that will physically build the infrastructure that we need."

"And I need you," he said looking a Fang. "I understand that you are a man of letters who knows the enemy. You speak his language and know his ways. I need you, most of all, to raise the veil that the old ways have laid on our eyes. The Manchurian era is passing. The Han era will be greater than all of the dynasties of the past. The new Emperor is young and given to liberal ideas; so you will be able to help bring those ideas into reality. I would like Wen to talk with Li regarding the local manufacture of firearms and war materials. Meanwhile, I would like to get to know Fang Xueshang here a little better, and talk him into teaching us about Europe -- their languages and their culture."

The young General, Li Hongzhang appeared at the curtain, waving for Wen to follow him, leaving Lao Fang to talk with Zheng. "The General is quite the salesman, isn't he? But, you know he is right; he is always right! He graduated in the same year as my father. But, of course, the General was the first in their class. He passed the Metropolitan Exam the first time and with the highest scores ever. His mind is awesome. But, the strength that he speaks of must be enforced with armies that are better equipped than the barbarians'. That is where your experience could be of real value. I understand that you are already making weapons in Wuhan and Xiangfan."

"That's right," Wen answered, "We have two primary factories and have been making and shipping that technology out to the other provinces as quickly as we can. I believe we are able to make rifles and handguns the equal of any made in Europe today. They are inventing new technology all of the time -- which we can copy. But, soon we will be innovating as well. There is nothing supernatural about the Europeans. We not only can match them -- we can best them!"

"I should be done with this campaign against the Nien soon," the general said, "And I would like you to get started in Hefei as soon as you can. We moved the provincial capital up there when the Taiping took Anqing back in '53. Now we are moving the governmental offices back down to Anqing. Hefei will need the new industry to maintain and grow their economic base."

Wen looked up with a fresh excitement he hadn't known for a long time. "We have been talking about moving to Lu'an for some time; my father-in-law wants to retire and this visit was going to be our chance to evaluate the prospects. Now I see how fate is turning my life to new uses," he mused with a smile. "How should I pay for this new venture? If it is to be strictly military, I would expect to be paid from the army or from the Province. But if there is no funding, I would have to set up a more varied manufacturing facility that would make and sell civilian materials, then use the profits to fund the military output. It would just take longer."

"I appreciate your honest approach," Li said, laughing at himself and his own impetuousness. "These are economic issues in which I am not so well versed. The General always taught me to press those with a vital interest for the money needed to underwrite their own defense. But in this case, the city is both the source and recipient of the money. I am afraid I don't understand that kind of banking very well."

"This is where my father-in-law has directed me. The money always comes from the people; who else is there? There is value, not only in the silver itself, but also in the exchange of the silver. 'Buried in a vault,' he would say, 'silver had no value; it only has value in exchange. An outsider's money will buy something from a village; then that seller turns around and buys something else from within the village. And then that seller will buy something else. In the end, one bar of new silver has paid for labor and materials several times and has produced a value worth five bars of silver.' He learned all this in England when he studied there and worked in a bank. We will be the outsider, by setting up a factory and employing the local people. The people's taxes are fed back into the local economy as though it were outside money and all that activity becomes wealth."

That night, Wen and Fang took a room in the hotel over the restaurant, but they slept little, instead talking by the light of a candle till early morning. The new ideas challenged many of the old ways. General Zeng talked as though the Emperor were not necessary to the Empire; he would just be a figurehead. The Kwan had always run the country, anyway, they agreed, while the Generals protected it. And other states in the modern era had adapted to this form of Constitutional Monarchy, they reasoned; even though England had never had a constitution, they did have an agreement called he Magna Charta and a body of common law, which bound them to principles of shared responsibility between the people and the Monarch. France, too, had established the Republic under the Napoleonic Code to include the Church and the people in governance, and then they invited a monarch back to represent them.

When the men got back to the farm, Madeline and Meixing rushed out with worried looks on their faces. "Where were you? We thought that you would be back yesterday."

"There is nothing wrong!" said Fang. "We just ran into the Viceroy and his generals and -- we were invited to help create a new China." he finished dramatically. "There was no problem!' They then spent the rest of the day and evening explaining the turning of history in which they had just participated to a rapt audience.

Madeline and Meixing had been busy as well while they were gone. They showed Fang and Wen plans they had drawn up for a new addition to the old house.

"We will have to take off the roof and build a platform to overhang the old walls," Madeline began excitedly. "It will sit on a new sill plate that supports the walls and a new roof for the addition."

"And there will be three more bedrooms upstairs," Meixing continued. "A staircase that opens into a hallway upstairs will run down the back wall with a door at the bottom into the living room."

"And there will be a storage room on both the top and bottom floors," Madeline finished proudly. "The downstairs store room will open right into the kitchen, so in the winter you won't have to go outside for wood or preserved food."

The women stood back and waited for the men's reactions.

"Then I will sit at my desk and look out at my fields from under the bottom of your staircase?" Fang asked sarcastically.

"You won't even see it," Madeline chided him. "Look." They had several drawings which showed the elevation and perspective views of the proposed work. "Dao Liangai is a carpenter and he said that he could build it for us."

"Hmmm," Wen mused. "It looks like we have to be out of the house for them to do this building work. I had hoped that we could spend some more time here, but maybe it is a good thing. I will need to get things organized for this new assignment. If we are going to live out here, we will have to pack up what we'll need from the houses in Xiangfan."

Lao Fang said, "I think we will stay here a little longer and set up an office in Shanghai. I may have to work a deal with the bankers, just in case this 'New China' thing hits a snag or two. We will join you in a couple of weeks. Why don't you and the children take the coach back and we'll come back up the river. Evidently Zeng and Li will be busy for a while. We have time."

***
Return to Xiangfan

Wen and his family returned to Xiangfan. Meixing worked with her schools and worked as a mentor to her friend and protégé Wan Xiaolu, who would run the school in her absence. Wan had started her own project; she was making colored glazed tiles with the characters. The tiles were mounted to the classroom walls and became a permanent display of poems and aphorisms, both art and teaching aids.

Wen took advantage of the time to specify and order the machinery they would need in the new plants in Hefei. But, the spring extended into summer and word had not yet come from the farm that the renovations were done, or that the war had been concluded.

It was late in the Fall of 1862 when the word finally came that the addition to the farm was done; they could move in. Zhenli was seven-and-a-half years old, and his sister Meiliang was almost six. They had grown to be Grandma's little girl and Grandpa's little man because their parents were involved in their business ventures and had little time to spend at home with them. Zhenli had started martial arts classes in town and dragged his grandfather with him as often as he could persuade Fang to accompany him.

When the time came for the family to leave, Zhenli was not happy, and let it be known with disrespect and sulking. "I don't want to go to that old farm!" he pouted. Meixing rubbed his head. "Oh, you'll like it, now! The new upstairs will have rooms for us all." But, he still sulked and had to be prompted to do his part in packing up for the move.

The new house had a room for the children with their own beds, another for Wen and Meixing. The larger one, for Grandma and Grandpa, was in the front over the main room. All of the rooms were fully furnished with a large rug on the floor. There was a large closet room at the top of the stairs, and on the ground floor beneath it was a large storage room with shelves for canned goods, bags of dried potatoes, yams, and tobacco. There were also six filled porcelain crocks with close-fitting porcelain lids, the symbols glazed on their fronts indicating that they contained oil, salt, wheat, corn, rice, and millet. Skeins of onions, garlic, and dried peppers hung from the walls and rafters. There were glass jars filled with preserved fruits, vinegar, sauces, and meats produced on local farms. Madeline loved being back in her old kitchen and bringing up the grandchildren, as she had with Meixing

But Meixing had known the rewards of teaching older children as well as her own. And, only two miles away, the city of Lu'an was an inviting new blank page for her. Soon, she was spending more of her days in town, talking with the young women about education. She started distributing posters and organizing gatherings for women interested in learning to read and write. She also read out loud from the Book of Poems to groups who might gather in the city park, and read the newspaper to interested knots of young ladies. She searched for a storefront that could be made over into a school and finally found an older house on the west side of town, close to the farm. She put a sign in the front yard: "Girls School". The Civic Guard came out to help her with shelves and supplies, and soon, the smell of ink and wet paper drying filled the rooms on the lower floor and the shelves started filling up with the copied works of her students.

Wen was gone for days at a time to Hefei, about thirty miles to the east. He had taken over an old foundry where metal had been smelted to make farm implements. The local mines supplied all of the components and fuel to smelt out and cast malleable bar stock. He then made a reverberatory furnace to puddle high-grade steel. The lathes, line boring machines, shapers, and grinders then turned the steel into rifle and pistol barrels. The mills cut out the rest of the firing actions and the wood shop turned out matched stocks and receivers. The assembly process occurred in a plant that copied the ones Wen had set up in Xiangfan and Hankou. He also imported several of his more experienced craftsmen to turn out high quality weapons and to teach the craft to the local workers.

Lao Fang was busy closer to home, visiting the farmers who worked his lands. Some of them had been there before the Taiping, but he wanted to make sure the new arrivals felt comfortable with their relationship. For those who had little or no equipment, Fang would advance it on credit. He asked only that he be the one to gather, sell, and ship each farm's grain to market. The larger combined quantities could command a better price. He taught them newer techniques, and helped them get fertilizers where they were needed. Sometimes Wen would come home from his visits to Shanghai with technical publications in German or French. Fang would translate them and explain the new techniques, so Wen, too, could get his workers to implement the latest technologies.

***

Farm Boy

Zhenli had a problem. Not quite eight years old, he had to make a long hike from home to school in the nearest town, Lu'an. In addition, it was obvious that Zhenli knew almost as much as the teacher in the school, who was, as was common, someone who had failed the lowest exam and therefore worked for next to nothing except the title and could teach only the most rudimentary skills of writing. When not in school, Zhenli had to make his own social life with farm boys whose parents worked his grandfather's land -- not that there was anything wrong with being a farmer, but their home life was different from his own.

To fill the boredom, Zhenli became a teacher of the martial arts routines which he had learned back in Xiangfan. He did them all from memory because there were no books on the techniques. Instead, each master had a following and the moves and techniques the master taught were considered secret routines among that close knit group. So

Zhenli became known, among his friends at least, as Master.

While this was an honor of sorts, Zhenli was a boy in search of himself, and was soon attracted to another, more knowledgeable, seeker, the local Buddhist monk who lived in the mountains. From time to time, the monk would come down from his retreat to beg for food. Zhenli would feed him and listen to the wisdom that he carried from a distant land.

"Why do you have nothing?" he asked the monk.

"To have nothing is to have everything," the monk replied. "To 'have' something is to be possessed by your possession. To be free from possessions is to have yourself. Beyond that, wanting what you do not possess is one of the three causes of suffering in this world. Possessing only my inner self is quite enough."

"Suffering? What causes suffering?" Zhenli asked.

"You make yourself suffer from fear -- fear of getting something that you do not want, for example, like a disease or bad a relation," the monk answered. "You suffer from want -- as when you want wealth or beauty, but you only see yourself as poor and ugly; you bring this on yourself! The last cause of suffering is not understanding your self and the world." The monk placed his palms on either side of Zhenli's face. "To be consumed with the attempt to know yourself and the world is the hardest suffering. The answer, to all of these, is learning to let go of the self and become one with the Dharma, which is the way of the world."

These discussions went on through the summer -- and during their course, Wen Zhenli went from enthralled to confused to disenchanted. 'Having nothing' was, in the end, just that.

Grandpa just smiled when Zhenli came to him, yet again, trying to figure it out.

"Life has many 'answers,'" Fan reassured him, "And you will have to sort them out as you go along. Our whole country is going through changes that challenge us to understand these matters. Some answers lead to embracing poverty, some to amassing great wealth. The Confucian Way leads us to live for the common good. In that view, fortune, influence, even life itself, are just tools we use to promote that common good. Understanding what the common good is and how we work toward it -- these are the problems of our time."

* * *

Mama?

Meiliang had a secret, and she could only share it with her very best friend. They would run off, giggling, and covering their mouths. They held the door open for Grandma Madeline when she came to see them perform a puppet theater play. After the show, Grandma would reward them with steamed dumplings filled with a bit of fig paste.

Meiliang's friend's family was of the Hok ethnic group. Because of that, her parents were shunned by many of the locals for their accent and their ways. They, in turn, worried about their daughter's friendship with Meiliang, a Kwan's daughter.

To Grandpa, her friend's parents were just a hard working farm family. When a mild drought came that summer of 1863 and much of the crop was damaged, Fang treated them like every other family, providing credit to cover their losses and seeds for the next planting. Meiliang and her friend were totally oblivious to all of that.

Grandma helped the girls learn to cook, to sew, to weave, and all the other things that a girl should know. She listened to their stories and discussed boys with them; she knew all of the mysteries.

"Where is Grandma?" Fang asked the girls, who were playing in the front yard when he returned from his farm visits one day.

"She went inside to take a nap," Meiliang answered.

Fang shot a look at the door which stood half open. "Stay here!" he said to the girls, and quickly went to the house.

"Madeline?" he called, pushing the door fully open.

Inside, he saw her foot on the far side of her chair, a bowl of knitting spilled out across the floor. She lay on her side and Fang knelt beside her, shaking her gently. Her half-opened eyes were unresponsive.

It took all his strength, but he dragged her into the living room and laid her on the futon bed that was kept for visitors. He was still sitting there when Meixing got home. She found her daughter wandering around the still open front door with tears running down her cheeks.

"Where is your Grandma?" she asked.

"Grandpa put her to bed. He is in there crying!"

"Oh, God!" Meixing ran in and saw her mother on the bed, her father sitting beside her. She wrapped her arms around her father and they rocked and sobbed together.

One of the men saw the open door and Meiliang outside. He went in and learned what had happened, and was sent to Hefei to tell Wen. Zhenli learned about the death of his Grandma when he got home, late for dinner. There was no dinner that night.

Wen met with his staff at the foundry to tell them the news. He would have to be gone for up to three years for mourning, and so, resigned from all his posts, turning everything over to others. The plant manager was a competent man, but could only be expected to carry on the projects Wen had initiated. The financial affairs were left in the hands of the banker, whom Fang had schooled. It was a sad and lonely trip back to the farm.

Madeline was buried on the hill next to her sons, and would be visited by each member of the family alone or together throughout the year. Fang built a fieldstone fireplace so they could cook meals when they went up for one of their all-day picnics at her gravesite. The marker stone was made by the same mason who had done them for her sons. Fang had him make one for himself as well, for when that time came. It was sad in the house now, and the children spent more and more time with their friends or alone.

A letter of condolence on Yellow Silk came from the Emperor by special courier; it was stamped with the official seals of both of his mothers, the Empress Cixi and the Empress Ci'an, the new titles of the former Lady Yi and The Lady Lin in a deathbed proclamation from the Xianfeng Emperor. He had appointed them co-regents with his brother, the Prince Kung, to guide his son, the new Emperor. Other letters came to Wen from military and governmental officers, as well as from commercial 'friends' and foreigners. Almost lost among these many letters were reports from the factories and news of a more general nature.

Shi Dakai, the last of the original Taiping Kings, had been cornered, captured, and killed, along with the rest of his western army, somewhere in Sichuan Province. Li Xiucheng, current head of the Taiping Army in Nanjing, tried another breakout campaign to gather food, but was driven back inside the walls of the capital after losing almost all of his army to the combined Qing and foreign forces. Zeng Guofan and his protégé, Li Hongzhang, were joined by an old friend General Zuo Zongtang, who had defeated the Taiping in the south. The three proceeded to divide and destroy the forces that held the high ground around Nanjing, and to drive tunnels for explosives under the walls. Hong Xiuquan finally succumbed to the effects of starvation in June 1864, and his son, Tiangui Fu, held onto the crown for an additional six weeks. But, the walls of Hong's dream fell to the sapper's explosions on July 16. Tiangui Fu managed to escape during the confusion. The young Monarch was chased almost a thousand kilometers south, before he was captured and killed on October 25, 1864. The Taiping era ended in exhaustion on both sides.

The Europeans had, by force of arms, dictated the terms of the treaties and the new peacetime economy. The official Chinese response was to 'learn from the barbarians in order to beat the barbarians.' However, dissident factions within the highest levels of the Qing government, as well as patriotic citizens at the lowest levels, were spoiling for a fight to regain control of China.

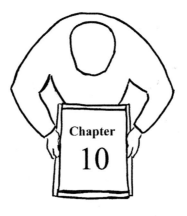

Chapter 10

Into A New China

***

The Book

An Imperial messenger delivered two packages to the farm the morning of April 13, 1865. Meixing had never met an Imperial messenger before and she insisted that he take his morning meal with them. "Have you recently been in the capital? And what news is there of the Emperor and of his mothers?" she asked him excitedly, half in awe and half in relief from the boredom of rural life.

Since her mother had passed on, Meixing was officially in mourning, but spring was well along now and the messenger was a welcome breath of fresh urban air. As she engaged the hungry soldier with food and idle conversation, Wen opened his package.

It was from Li Hongzhang, now at his new offices in Tianjin, and contained a letter and a book. Li's military career had become a political one, his rank going from B4 to A3. He was now working directly with Prince Kung, the third regent for the Tongzhi Emperor, Zaichun. The letter stated that the Emperor's ninth birthday, on the 27th of April, would feature celebrations throughout the capital. Under the guise of the celebration party, Wen was invited to attend a meeting with other military and industry leaders. It was to be a planning session for the progressive leadership. The Grand Council was still deeply divided between cooperation and confrontation in foreign policy. The Emperor was mainly influenced by his mother, the Empress Cixi, and Prince Kung. The Empress Ci'an was generally nonpolitical, tending toward conservative views.

The book Li had sent was *Elements of International Law: With a Sketch of the History of the Science,* a volume only recently translated into Chinese. "Please familiarize yourself with this book before you arrive," Li had written. The book lay heavily in Wen's lap. He opened it to a page called 'Advertisement' (prologue), and read:

> "The object of the Author in the following attempt to collect the rules and principles which govern, or are supposed to govern, the conduct of States in their mutual intercourse in peace and in war and which have therefore received the name International Law, has been to compile as elementary work for the use of persons engaged in diplomatic and other forms of public life, rather than for mere Technical Lawyers, although he ventures to hope that it may not be found wholly useless to the latter."

"The first sentence is almost a whole page," Wen muttered to himself. "This will not be a light read!" He noted that the book was originally published in 1836 in Philadelphia by Cary, Lea & Blanchard. Written by Henry Wheaton, the text had been translated into Chinese by Rev. W. Martin, DD and published at the expense of the Imperial Government.

A second package, which looked identical to Wen's, was addressed to Lao Fang. Wen wrote a response to Li's letter, accepting the invitation for both of them, to send back with the messenger. Then, he settled in his chair to begin reading.

***

10 Years Old

As Wen sat reading the opening chapter, Zhenli ran into the living room and directly into his chair.

"My doll!" Meiliang shouted angrily, also crashing into Wen's chair and wrapping her arms around her brother's waist and dragging him to the ground. "Give it back!"

"What is going on here?" Wen demanded, setting his book aside and pulling them both to their feet.

"He took my doll and won't give it back!" Meiliang said, her black bangs, lower lip and crossed arms forming three parallel lines.

Zhenli held the doll high, out of her reach, giggling maliciously, as he pulled against his fathers grip. "It is my birthday present!" he said.

Wen shot a look at Meixing; obviously, they had both forgotten Zhenli's birthday. "That's right! Why, you're.... You are ten years old today! Happy Birthday!" Wen tried to give him a hug, but Zhenli struck him with the doll and ran to his mother.

"All right! Let's settle down, here!" Meixing said, taking the doll and giving it back to her daughter. "This is a special day and you may have a special treat. What would you like to do?"

"I want to study Wushu (martial methods). There is a school in Lu'an." he answered immediately.

"Today we will go into town and see this school, if that is what you want," said Wen. He looked at Meixing and shrugged his shoulders.

***

Wushu School

In town, they were directed to a Buddhist temple built on a high plateau overlooking the city. The temple's tall pagoda and some trees appeared over the outer wall. Through the entrance, they could see a yard with a large brass bowl filled with sand and holding several sets of three joss sticks, smoldering on the ends.

"Pretty smells!" said Meiliang, watching the white smoke as it carried someone's prayers to heaven.

The roof over the entryway was covered with rows of round, grey tiles cemented together in convex rows down the pitch of the roof. Between and under the upper tiles were shallow concave tiles to conduct rain off into rivulets which cascaded down onto the flagstone laid around the building. The roof line flipped up at the ends like a bird's wing in flight. The inner yard had stone walkways that meandered around stunted bushes planted in gravel- filled boxes.

As they began walking around the grounds, a young monk greeted them. "You are looking for the Wushu gardens? Please, follow me."

Around the back of the buildings on the right side of the courtyard was an open grassy area. Several boys were gathered there, dressed in Han-style robes with great sash belts, all in white. While the rest watched, two of the boys stood up before the others. They bowed three times, and then took a pose. Suddenly, they rushed at each other and shouted, each grasping at the other. One managed to take hold of his opponent and threw him to the ground. Then both stood up, bowed to one another, bowed to the teacher, and sat down with the others.

The teacher was dressed in a dark red tunic with sandals. When he caught sight of the family, he smiled broadly and walked over to them. "Our son would like to join your class," Wen said. Wen Zhenli stepped forward and bowed to the teacher.

"That will be fine," the teacher answered. "There is always room for another student. Would you please wait here till the class is over? Then we can talk." He returned to his class and the family sat on a wooden platform under the trees at the side of the yard.

Wen glanced around the yard and recalled his own early training in the old Daoist temple in Xiaohexi. How poor and primitive it seemed next to all this! He felt like he was standing next to himself for the rest of that day, silently hearing a running commentary going on in his mind. Mechanically, he went through the process of signing the papers and paying the fees for Zhenli's class. But he was not completely there, not inside.

As they rode home, Zhenli sat in the back of the carriage and looked at his new Wushu school uniform. "Well, you were quiet!" Meixing remarked. "I thought you would have at least objected to spending so much money on gymnastics. But, he does seem to be happy with it."

"It's more than gymnastics," Wen answered. "I have talked about this with several men who had taken the military path in life. Wushu training is about finding your center in many ways. It is a physical analogy that teaches balance in many other aspects of life."

"I don't want him to go into the Army!" Meixing answered sharply, looking suddenly troubled.

"Come on, he is only ten years old. He has a lot of growing up to do before he makes any commitment. I will work with him on the scholastics, but he may be inclined, by nature, to follow another path."

"I don't want him to become a Buddhist either!" Meixing said.

Wen laughed, "Oh, I think we'll avoid that. Between your father and me, I think he is already too well grounded in Confucian principles to go off and live in a cave."

Meixing thought about it all the way home. When they arrived, she watched her son show off his new Wushu uniform to his friends at the fence by the side of the house. Wen returned to his chair and passed the day totally immersed in his copy of _The Elements of International Law_ -- sometimes he didn't even sit down to dinner, but paced around like an actor silently rehearsing his lines.

Three days after Zhenli's birthday, Lao Fang returned from a trip to Shanghai. "Papa, a package came for you," Meixing said, handing it to him excitedly as soon as he got in the door.

"I have presents, too!" Lao Fang said. Indeed, he had remembered his grandson's birthday and that Zhenli had a sister who needed attention as well. "But I like the wrapping on your gift more. What is this?" he asked, looking over at Wen.

"A messenger from Li Hongzhang brought it a few days ago."

"Heavy enough!" Fang said as he held up the book.

"Heavier than it feels! Wait till you read it."

Standing by the window, Lao Fang unfolded the letter and read it, then folded it back up and tapped it on his lower lip while he looked out over the flat expanses north of the farm. "I hope this leads to some real change in Beijing."

"I wrote him that we would be there. Is that all right?"

"I hope so," said Fang, as he slowly unwrapped the book. "What is this thing?"

"We are going to town, Papa," Meixing interrupted the men. "I left food out for you. Is there anything else that you want?" She had decided that what she really needed was to return to her school and her mission of women's education; it would honor her mother more than any form of mourning. Starting, this week, she would begin her new schedule. She would get up early and make breakfast for the family, set out lunch for Wen and Fang. Then, while the men harnessed the horse to her landau carriage, she would get the children ready to set out for Lu'an. She would drop Zhenli off at his school and take Meiliang with her to the Girls School.

"Oh no, thanks," Fang answered his daughter. "What is this rig?" he asked, pulling on Zhenli's uniform.

"I am in Wushu training, Grandpa!" Zhenli said proudly. Before Fang could ask more questions, Meixing had hustled them off to the carriage and they left for Lu'an.

***

A Conference

The house fell silent and the two men sat reading, intent upon the books before them. It was near midday when Fang broke the silence. "You know? This reminds me of the *Wealth of Nations* -- just a century later, -- more politics, but the same economics. I don't see how they are going to get the Manchurians to accept this Western thinking," Fang said, rocking slowly in his chair.

"They are going to have to. Don't you think they'll see how much we can improve our position in the world?" Wen looked surprised.

"NO! I really think they are still looking out through the same blinders," Fang retorted. "There are fundamentals at work that the Qing mentality has no way to understand. The whole humanist movement is as foreign to them as Brazilian headhunters. No, that may be too close. Their whole worldview is from the top of some mountain of delusion. There is this tribute obligation fantasy that they still believe in -- even though it hasn't existed since their predecessors in the Ming Dynasty. They still can't seem to understand the corruption and degradation that has permeated much of the Kwan system during their rule. I doubt whether the whole Taiping rebellion taught them anything!"

Fang laid his book on the chair and paced around the room. "How do you shift from this false belief in the perfection of the Emperor to the Rights of Man? Is all truth given only to...whom? A nine year old child? And that greedy bunch around him? I wouldn't trust half of them to sell my grain at the market! They are just self-serving politicians."

Wen stood, too, his face almost ashen, and followed him with his eyes. "Are you now saying that the Confucian Way is a false belief?" he asked, obviously shaken.

Lao Fang wheeled around, pulling his gaze from the bright light outside the windows back into the darkened room where Wen stood. "Oh, Heavens no!" he said. He realized then that Wen had given his words more weight than he intended. "The truth of Confucius is, and always will be, true. It is the practice of the teachings that I feel have failed in the hands of lesser men. If all Kwan acted as you do, it would never have come to this. Your whole administrative life has been a testament to following the virtue of the Middle Way. I believe that you don't see the others as I do, because you so thoroughly accept the principles and practice them. I don't expect to see the bureaucrats perform their functions in the future any better than I have seen them perform them in the past. There are many, like you, who live the tenets of The Way. But, sadly, there are enough who take advantage of their power and influence that they have sapped the life out of The Heavenly Mandate." There followed an awkward pause, as Wen composed himself.

"Let's get out of here and take a walk." Fang said. He went to the kitchen and put the fruits and sandwiches Meixing had left for them into a picnic basket.

They hiked to the high ground, where the family always picnicked, and sat for a while on the bench. Behind them, above the stone monuments, the mountain faded into the mist that still clung to its northern slope. To the north, fields of light green shoots were accented by walls and irrigation ditches, patiently built and maintained by the tenant farmers who could be seen working the fields here and there.

Fang pointed out across the fields. "Are they any less 'persons' than those generals and ministers we will be meeting with?" Fang dragged on his pipe and looked out at the small figures working among the crop.

"They don't know as much!" Wen answered. "Certainly, there is something less about them."

"True, they are unschooled. And I'm sure that most of them are not as capable of understanding as the learned men of our time. But, could such learned men stoop all day to raise the crop that sustains the nation? Is there not a humanity that they have, wherein we might be less? You remember being behind a plow with numb feet in icy mud. Isn't the dirt-poor farmer as noble as anyone? Didn't Mencius cite Confucius for us, and say that it was the people were the most important; then the ministers, and lastly, the Emperor?"

***

The Meeting In Tianjin

The three weeks leading up to the supposed celebration for the Emperor passed quickly; Wen and Lao Fang set out to meet with Li Hongzhang and the others in Tianjin. The city resonated with fireworks, to ward off the evil spirits. Red banners and bunting were on all of the buildings. The Emperor's birthday was especially gay because he was so young and the past few years had been so miserable.

The men met at the town house of Zeng Guofan. He had not yet arrived and Li was acting as the host for the meeting. Li had been delegated by Prince Kung to marshal the civilian and military forces who would implement new and progressive initiatives. And, they knew that the Anti-Reformist movement would oppose these initiatives whenever they found an opportunity.

The overall program was known as the Self Strengthening, but it relied on the very real efforts of the hated foreigners to help China to grow strong. The English, French, and Americans had taken over many Imperial functions, while the Qing attention was consumed by the war against the Taiping. The Post Office, the new Telegraph System, the Customs House, Police and Fire in Shanghai were all reorganized by the "barbarians." The European gunboat diplomacy of the 1840s had been replaced with Western bureaucratic systems, under the coercion of the 'treaties' which left China weak and pliable. By the mid 1850s, much of the Chinese Civil Service had been taken over by the Europeans. The central government strained just to survive the indemnity payments for reparations, failing crops, natural disasters, and the wave of rebellions and criminality of all sorts.

In 1853, the rebelling 'Short Sword Society' burned down the old Grand Custom House, which was rebuilt, only to be burned down again by the Taiping. In 1854, the British, French, and Americans took over the collection of duty payments for imports and exports, as 'neutral' parties between the Taiping government and the Qing government. The Qing later agreed to appoint a British Inspector General over the Chinese Maritime Customs Service; at the time of this meeting, the Inspector General was Sir Robert Hart, appointed in 1863.

Prince Kung established the Zongli Yamen, or Foreign Office, to represent the Imperial court in dealing with any foreigners in 1860. Under the then-current 'co-operative policy', trade with America had grown from $82,000 to $300 million per year. That year, Mr. Burlingame, the American Minister to China, received a grant for the first submarine telegraph line to connect all of the treaty ports from Canton to Tien-tsin. At Mr. Hart's suggestion, an American College had been opened in Beijing under the direction of the venerable Chinese scholar, Seu Kiou and the American, Dr. Martin.

Prince Kung was most adamant that all participants at this meeting have a clear and consistent understanding of the *Elements of International Law*. "This text is like a pair of glasses," Li said in his opening remarks. "It helps us see the fabric on which the Europeans have embroidered the Treaties we have been forced to sign. If we are to grow strong and independent, it will be by re-doing much of that history through their own laws. We must use all the diplomatic tools at our disposal."

Despite the general agreement on the direction for China, each of the delegates had come with his own vision and agenda. Li's intent was to put them through a common experience, analyzing the book, and ultimately to bring them into closer agreement on how that book could be of value to China.

Additional memoranda were submitted to frame the discussions. Feng Guifen published his argument, called *Western Learning*, under a pseudonym because of the current hostilities against such thinking; he had, for example, advocated adopting "Western technology while retaining Chinese values."

In rebuttal, Yan Fu insisted that Western science could only be learned within a framework of the Western democracy that spawned it. The Chinese had always considered successive periods of order and disorder, periods of prosperity and decline, to be the course of nature. Westerners, however, saw continual growth and progress as the norm, and believed that disorder can, and should, be held in check indefinitely with good government.

Feng Guifen countered with a citation from the famous historian, Sima Qian, 'Take the later kings as models, because we are more alike than we are like the ancients.' The implication that a change in government was needed was left unspoken.

After the meeting's opening arguments and discussions, the attendees were sent off in smaller groups to consider individual chapters of the book. Each group was to re-read and analyze, without drawing conclusions, the content of their chapter. When they re-convened, a representative from each group would present its understanding of their chapter. The overriding admonishment to these groups was to not be judgmental of the work, but simply to summarize the information offered.

"This is a book of observations on the conventions of international trade, government and conflict resolution which controls international commerce," Li said. "It is descriptive; it is not prescriptive. We are not bound nor advised to adapt its method. We are only to be aware of its content."

For the Imperial court, the concepts in the book were as foreign as the language it was written in; for any merchant, it was as familiar as the trade they engaged in every day. For the attendees, it was important that they have both an understanding of the book and how it was viewed by the court as well as the market. Prince Kung was trying to use the moment to direct the future, and shared knowledge was only the first step to agreement. They would meet again.

Zeng Guofan would arrive on the day after the meeting had been adjourned, but had sent word ahead that Wen and Fang should remain for a breakfast meeting with him. The Court had already recognized these two men from the heartland for their initiative. But Zeng had also recognized another useful quality in these two men; they were both blessed and hampered by their lack of familiarity with the politics within the Imperial Court, and neither of them came from a Great Family.

***

Another Commission

In the morning, when Wen and Fang came down to breakfast, they were shown out into a garden at the rear of the house. Zeng rose to greet them and showed them to chairs at a round table. Across the table was an older general, roughly the same age as Zeng.

"Allow me to present my oldest and dearest comrade in arms, Zuo Zongtang, Viceroy of Fujian," Zeng said. Together, the two old generals had only recently overrun the Taiping in Nanjing. "What we are going to discuss here, today, must not leave this room," Zeng cautioned, "But it is of such importance to China that we must start even before it is approved by Beijing."

The plan he laid out would create a facility for making military arms, large and small. They would establish, both in Shanghai and in Fuzhou, shipyards that would vertically integrate all of the stages of manufacture, taking the ore and coal from Anhui and developing each of the manufacturing steps to produce ships for China's new navy. In Shanghai, the new facility would be named the Jiangnan Arsenal

A second arm of the plan involved Li Hongzhang and his subordinate, Feng Guifen. They were setting up a school to teach Western languages and badly needed the help of men like Fang Laogai, who had been educated in England, France, and Germany. Both the school and the factories would be in the Shanghai area.

Once Zeng had presented the overview of their plan, he and Zuo assumed the role of teachers. Neither Wen nor Fang had grown up in a Great Family; neither had the traditional Confucian/Daoist upbringing which centered everything on 'the ancestors.' Whereas that made them well suited to the future of China, they would have to learn the traditions of the past. To a large degree, that past was the greatest impediment to the future. The Emperor was a young man, eager to embrace the new world order; his mother, the Dowager Empress Cixi, was not. The Empress was the 'voice behind the curtain' that reminded the young Emperor of his duty to the ancestors.

The Emperor, despite being the head of the government of China, was not the head of his own family; that role belonged to the ancestors. Everything he did, every directive he issued had to honor the principles laid down by his ancestors. The pressures of honoring the past versus accepting the future had crushed his own father and grandfather.

The expression, "incompatible with T'i chih," which reoccurred in almost all Chinese rejections of European proposals, had been translated as "incompatible with basic institution"; it should have been translated "respect for the ancestors." To the Chinese, conformity with T'i chih was as axiomatic and inviolable as the concepts of Humanism or Common Law were to the English. T'i chih was based on 'li' (propriety) and 'jin' (benevolence); these were the warp and weft binding the members of the Kwan together. Europeans had no way to appreciate the enormous weight it carried. Guardianship of this T'i chih was entrusted to the 'censors', 'ultra-right wing' watchdogs who pervaded the whole country and reported directly back to the Emperor any plots, impropriety or malfeasance within the system of Kwan administration.

Zeng Guofan and Li Hongzhang were faced with the same problem, as they were representatives both of the Emperor and of Prince Kung's agents for change. "The Book which your group just reviewed has already been of service to the Emperor," Zeng offered. "Last year, Prince Kung tested it without authorization from Beijing. It was a delicate matter, one which could have set a very bad precedent for our relations with the West for years to come if it had been handled in the old way. But the situation was defused, using their own "International Law." Zeng stood up and pointed at a map on the wall behind him.

"The Russians were engaged in a war with Denmark. Three Danish trading ships were in the 'Inner Ocean' when the new Russian Minister, Van Rehfues, arrived on his warship. He took the Danish ships as war prizes. Prince Kung protested that 'these waters were not the open seas, and that he could not allow the Europeans to bring their war into Chinese territorial waters.' His argument employed three principles of International Law. He claimed the waters to be Chinese, cited treaties with Russia which described them as such, and refused to recognize the ministerial status of Von Rehfues until the matter was settled. The minister acknowledged his mistake, freed the vessels, and paid a compensation of $1,500 to the Danes. Only by knowing these conventions can we deal with the Europeans. Only by knowing our own historic lack of direction in dealing with the barbarians can we frame the new conventions to deal with other countries of the world."

"As for your new assignments, you will find that the Europeans are open to sharing almost any established technology. The newest technology may be held secret while they take maximum commercial advantage of it, but they very quickly share it when it is no longer novel. In this way, we can catch up to them in fields where we are weak -- mining, mineralogy, casting, and forging are all industries we will need in order to convert the minerals we have in abundance into the materials that we lack. Your small factories, in Wuhan and Xiangfan, will be the models for our larger ones in Shanghai and in Fuzhou. Till then, you should return to settle your families on your farm in Lu'an, and make arrangements to make yourselves available for long-term assignments at these facilities."

***

Separation

Wen and Fang returned to the farm and the domestic side of their lives, but the news about the new assignment did not sit at all well with any of them. Zhenli was ten-and-a-half years old, and had become pugnacious and combative. He was doing well in his martial arts classes, winning acclaim in the contests among the students, but he was quickly growing less respectful to his teachers in the academic subjects. "He really needs you in his life!" Meixing insisted. So, Wen took Zhenli up to the picnic grounds for a father-son talk. Actually, he hoped the spirits of the uncles and his grandmother might help in his brief instruction, but like many such 'talks', it only opened old wounds and vented the hurt.

"You are working for the Foreign Devils!" Zhenli accused him. "You should be fighting them, driving them out of our land! Why are you not taking up arms against them?"

Wen tried sitting next to his son, but the distance between them was growing. "Ah, Zhenli, Zhenli…. We have taken up arms against the foreigners and thousands have died in the attempt. They are stronger than we are. That is why I am building factories to make weapons for our armies that are the equal of theirs. At the same time, we are trading with them because they have much to offer both as customers and as suppliers. It is not a simple or comfortable answer."

Zhenli held his arms stiffly at his sides in anger, the sleeves of his sam covering tightly clinched fists. "I will not accept their ways! I will be strong and I will drive them away. You will see!"

Wen put his hands on Zhenli's shoulders. "To do that, you will have to become a serious student. Physical strength alone will not do what you want. Return to your studies and grow strong there."

In the weeks that followed, Wen included Zhenli in a trip to some of the factories and stores, while awaiting his orders from Zeng Guofan. But Zhenli was distant and disrespectful, even of young men twice his age. Once, he got into a physical fight with a French sailor who was working on the docks. Initially, his clever moves defeated the sailor's fighting stance. But, when the sailor abandoned his Marquise of Queensberry Rules, he picked up the boy and threw him into the water. Mortified and smelling of river backwash, Zhenli crawled up the bank -- now armed with yet another reason to hate the foreign devils. By the end of the trip, Zhenli returned to school more hardened and resentful than before.

Meixing and Meiliang continued their daily commute from the farm to the school for girls in Lu'an, dropping Zhenli off at his Wushu school. Meiliang had her ninth birthday and was now a student in her own right. She already knew more of the academic subjects than her brother, but she had learned to keep that to herself. She was given the rare opportunity to study the classics and could write several hundred characters. She was enthralled to be learning the poems of the Song and Tang periods. But, she had also taken to reading the Western books which her father brought from Shanghai as well. French villages and the seacoast of Brittany filled her imagination. She played out the *Tale of Two Cities* in her dollhouse theater. English and French were 'kitchen languages' in her life, and she would shyly respond to French missionaries in town, reading from their Bibles and hymnals. Meixing was torn about her daughter's new interest; her own mother was a Catholic and had taught her a lot about that religion. But, they lived in a Confucian house in a Confucian land, and she didn't want Meiliang to be too different -- at least, not in public.

Wen made several subsequent trips, alone, all the way back up the Han River to Xiangfan, and beyond to the string of stores and banks he had left in the keeping of his local associates. He was surprised by the growth in trade throughout the river system. Cheap goods from Europe had replaced local handcrafts, but new industries had grown up in their place and new trades replaced the old. He placed orders with his own factories for machinery to be used in the new facilities in Shanghai's Jiangnan Arsenal. He also transferred much of the wealth he had accumulated in his local banks to the same local towns for public works projects.

Too soon, it seemed, a messenger caught up with him with a directive that he return to Shanghai. Meixing was stoic as he prepared for the new assignment; they didn't know how long he would be there nor how often he could return. But, he would return, he kept reassuring them all. Zhenli was proper, but obviously restrained in his good-byes. Meiliang wept openly, but promised to write to him in three languages. All too soon, Papa and Baba were waving from the carriage window as they rolled down the road from the farm toward Shanghai.

Map of Southern Provinces

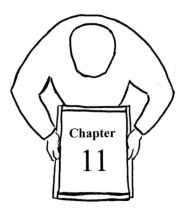

Grandfather, Wen Zhenli, and Sister Meiliang

***

Return to School

Above the entrance to Zhenli's school was a sign, 'School of the Six Harmonies'. He paused and read it out loud to himself, as though he had never seen it before. Harmony was not what he thought of as he remembered his fight with the French sailor and the humiliation he still felt. He rubbed his eyes with his clenched fists before he started up the stairs.

"What's wrong, Shao Wen?" asked his monk teacher, who had just caught up with him.

"I was shamed by a foreign devil! I have failed your teaching. I have no right to call myself your student!"

The monk directed him to a bench, off at the side of the yard, and Zhenli told him about the encounter. "You only lost a fight; there is no shame in that. That you let yourself get into a fight, which you could not win, should help direct your studies."

That advice was as close to anything 'spiritual' Zhenli received at the school. 'Wushu' training was physical, not spiritual. The Harmony, mentioned in the sign, referred to the coordination of the parts of the body; hands and feet, hips and shoulders, elbows and knees. Each pair should move in coordination, or harmony. Martial arts schools of that era taught systems called "Tixi," which advocated a style, or "Pai"; these systems emphasized one of three major areas of concentration -- striking, grabbing, or weapons. Each style had its own practice exercises, called "fist routines" or "quan tao" which were performed like acrobatic or skating programs are performed today. These schools took their names from the family name of their founder, from the place where the school started, or from an animal which the school emulated.

The style form Zhenli had learned in Xiangfan was called a 'Village Kung Fu'. As often happened, the teacher was someone who had recently left the army, where he had received some training. Mixing that training with other moves he learned, through usually bitter experience, he developed a style of his own. Most often, the goal was to intimidate and drive off an attacker, rather than to cause injury. The method involved demonstrating either your own mastery of your quan tao or your opponent's vulnerably. Fancy footwork, such as 'Bagua', might show your opponent that you could get around him, or manipulating a weapon like a staff or a sword could make him loose heart. But it was the training of the inner self that Zhenli had to work on.

***

A Visitor

Meanwhile, along the river path southwest of town, a woman named Wei Xiaohua sat down, heavily on the side of the road next to a stone marker which read, "Lu'an five li". The straps that held her pack were cutting into her shoulders. She slid them down over her arms and let the pack slip to the ground.

Down the slope she had just climbed, was her son, Dong Bainong. "Hurry up! I'm almost there," she called to him in a mockingly husky voice. He stopped to look up the slope and leaned back to rest on the long handles which ran back to a cart. The cart held several large boxes filled with books. Drag sticks, which hung from the axel between the wheels of the cart, dug into the ground and keep it from rolling back down the hill behind him. They both rested for a few minutes; then she went down to him. "We'll never get there by being here!" she said, as she walked past him to the back of the cart. "Ready?" She pushed against the back of the cart while he pulled on the poles, and they slowly mounted yet another grade.

The towpaths along the river from Shanghai were a blessing; they were flat and long. Wei and her son were taking books that her husband had printed to find markets in smaller towns of Anhui. Clearly, they would rather have taken a river boat, but that was expensive. So this would be another night on the road, under the oilcloth that they draped over the books to keep them dry.

The big printing firms in Shanghai could afford to send their salesmen along the big rivers to the stores in the larger towns. But, Xiaohua's husband, Dong Guaiji only had one very old hand press, which he had received in lieu of wages from his previous employer. That old printer had abandoned his own shop to take a better job with one of the big printing houses in town. Now, Dong Guaiji was learning that the big city market would not even buy his books, because they lacked the high quality of a modern press. There was too much competition in Shanghai. Xiaohua's trip with her son was a desperation measure to recover at least some income from Dong's months of working the press.

From the window of her school, Meixing saw the woman and young boy come over the last bridge into the town.

The school was in an old farmhouse, with several outbuildings for the chickens and a cow that provided food for the students. Wei Xiaohua turned up the pathway and knocked at the farmhouse door. "I saw your sign," she said when Meixing opened the door. "Are you the mistress of this school?"

Meixing invited them into the front room and Xiaohua showed off the books they had brought. The girls and teachers flitted in and out as Meixing listened patiently. Dong Bainong was ten, actually only three months older than Meiliang. He sat in a chair in the corner and pretended to be napping, but his eyes opened as the girls came and went.

Meixing invited her two visitors to lunch; they both seemed quite hungry. Then they spent the afternoon looking through the books. That evening, when all the girls left for home, Meixing invited the mother and son to come home with her. They obviously needed to clean up and get some rest from their travels. Dong Bainong brightened up when he found that Meiliang would be joining them. He stored the cart and the books in the old barn in back of the school, then came back out front with their clothing bundles. Meixing drove by the temple school to pick up Zhenli and they headed out the West road to the farm. Happily, the carriage had a back seat large enough for the children, while the two women sat in the front and talked all the way home.

At the farm, Meixing showed her guests around the house and had Xiaohua put their things in the master bedroom upstairs. The boys went out to the barns, where Zhenli showed his new companion the barracks for his grandfather's tuanlian soldiers. Some of the soldiers had stayed to maintain the farm and work with the tenant farmers. Others had been contracted to serve the City of Lu'an as a police force.

The boys took out two horses and rode to the picnic grounds, where Zhenli pointed out the grave stones and told

Bainong about his uncles, who had died in the war, and about his Grandmother. Zhenli told him how his grandfather ran the farm and had helped his father in the battle on the river, back in Xiangfan. Now they were in the capital at some conference, he said.

Bainong's grandparents had all died in the rebellion. One side of the family was killed by the Emperor's own Imperial Bannermen, because a member of the family had joined the Taiping army. The other set of grandparents were killed by the Taiping because they wouldn't give all of their food to the Taiping Army. Bainong's parents ran away from Guangdong, and traveled up through Fujian and Zhejiang to get to Shanghai when he was just a baby.

While Meixing worked in the kitchen, Xiaohua took a bath in a tub in the back yard and then washed their clothes. When the boys got back, Bainong was sent out back for his turn at the tub and finally, they had dinner. After dinner, when the children were at last in bed and everything was cleaned up, the two women sat before the open hearth fire and compared their family backgrounds. Xiaohua's family were landlords in an area west of Canton, and had been killed when they refused to supply food for the Taiping's "Heavenly Army". She and her husband were then living in Canton, just five miles away, and ran for their lives when the Imperial Army identified her husband's granduncle as a Taiping official. Most of the family was executed to set an example.

Meixing told Xiaohua about her own father's reluctance to get involved as an Imperial Kwan, and how the farm had always been run as a service to landless tenant farmers. She told her about Wen's service as an administrator and magistrate in Xiangfan, and how he dealt with the Hakka rebellion when they invaded his area on the Han River. She explained how the two men in the family were currently building factories and schools in Shanghai, as part of the new Self Strengthening movement. Xiaohua told Meixing about the family's adventure of running away from the war to Shanghai, more than a thousand miles away.

Dong Guaiji was a good worker and knew how to fix machines, so they were able to live from one small job to the next. In Shanghai, he found a job with a printer who was going out of business. In the end, he left the business to Dong and took a good job with one of the larger printing houses in town. Since then, she and her husband, and now their boy, were printing handbills, signs, and books. Most of the books were left -- abandoned on the shelf; their authors couldn't or wouldn't always pay. So, Xiaohua and Bainong packed them onto a cart and were selling them in the small towns, along the banks of the river. The women talked late into the night, finding more common ground in the raising of their children and maintaining ambitious husbands.

In the morning, they all ate a large breakfast and went off to town, dropping off Zhenli and Meiliang at their schools. Meixing took her new friend around town in her carriage, and introduced them to local merchants who might wish to become her customers. Meixing herself had bought more books than she could really justify for her school, and they were able to sell some of the rest in town as well. Most of the books, however, were left at local shops under a consignment arrangement, with Meixing acting as agent for Wei Xiaohua.

Over the next few days, the two families enjoyed their visit together, but then Xiaohua insisted they had imposed long enough and it was time to head back to Shanghai. Meixing suggested they could share a ride together to Hefei; she could see her husband and do some shopping -- the stores in Lu'an just did not have the range of goods that were available there.

For the trip to Hefei, the men cleaned up the old heavy coach that the family used when they had returned from Xiangfan; it was larger and much more comfortable than the carriage for the seventy-kilometer trip -- and it could carry much more on the trip home. Because Xiaohua and Bainong had come around the southern side of Lake

Chaohu from Shanghai, they had missed seeing the larger city. This trip would be a treat for them.

When they arrived in Hefei, Meixing found that Wen and her father had not stopped there on their return from the meeting in Beijing, but had to report directly back to Shanghai. So Xiaohua and Bainong set out to sight-see the capital city. Meixing, meanwhile, went shopping for supplies for the farm and posted a letter to Wen in Shanghai, telling him all about this family that she had met and asking him to see if there was any way he could get work for Dong Guaiji. She sent a similar letter to her father. That night, Meixing put them on an overland sleeping coach which would take them directly from Hefei to Wuhubei on the Yangtze. From there they would be able to book a cheap passage on a river steamer, home to Shanghai. It was hard to say good-by to her new friend, Xiaohua and her son. They waved from the windows of the coach, and then their faces quickly disappeared as the coach rolled away from the light of the gas lamp.

Inside, passengers were tightly packed into the small space. Once the road left the city, the coach's swaying and bouncing shook the passengers against one another and soon they no longer felt the need of distance between themselves and the strangers next to them; they all fell asleep. At the city of Chaohu, everyone got out of the carriage to freshen up. Some new faces replaced old ones. Then they resumed their seats and soon everyone was again fast asleep.

At the end of the coach line, in Wuhubei, they clambered down from the coach and made their way to the river for the ferry ride to the other side. Wuhubei was a smaller version of Wuhu, the large commercial town on the other side of the river. Wuhu's big claim to fame was that it was the hometown of the Empress Dowager Cixi. Aside from that, the town was unremarkable. Xiaohua had decided not to take the passenger boat downriver to Shanghai. The cost of the tickets was more than she could earn in a month-and-a- half of washing clothes. Better, she thought, to walk for two weeks and bring home as much of the book money as she could.

***

New Work for an Old Press

Meixing's letters to Wen and her father did take the boat downriver, and as a result, they knew about Xiaohua and her husband before either had met them. In the letter, Meixing had said that Xiaohua was 'intelligent and well-read for someone from the south.' "Thinking like her mother again," Wen thought. 'Her family was gentry, landed, and evidently prosperous before the rebellion. The Imperial Army killed her husband's whole family, because some uncle was a Taiping official,' Meixing wrote. "And the Taiping killed most of her family to take their food. What a waste -- and, how sad for Xiaohua and her husband!"

Wen read on about her flight with her husband and baby up to Shanghai and how they were struggling with his printing business. He re-read the lines asking him if there were something he could do to throw some business their way. 'Maybe they could print up flyers or books for you,' Meixing suggested.

Wen called in his assistant. "Don't we have some investigators to check out new employees?" he asked. So, unknown to Xiaohua and Dong Guaiji, the wheels were set in motion.

Under a large tent with several long tables, the investigator stopped and scanned the area, looking for someone. Lanterns flickered at intervals between the poles. People came and went from the vendors' stands to the tables. The investigator asked a man who cleaned the area between the tables, "Is that him over there?"

"Yea, regular as clockwork, since his wife left him."

"What? I understood he was still married."

"Oh? It is just talk, you know. A couple of months ago, his wife took their boy and all the books and lit out. No one has seen them since. He doesn't seem to be all that sad about it. Maybe she'll come back."

"What does he do when he's not here?"

"He has some kind of shop down the alley, over there," the man pointed down the street. "I think he prints signs and stuff."

Usually, the investigator would not have taken such a personal interest; he would have sent one of his helpers to get some statements from neighbors and checked out the man with his friends in the police force. But this request came from a high Kwan, directly. He was curious why this fellow would be of any interest to him. Nothing that he had learned so far would set the man apart. There was nothing on file with the police; he dealt only in cash; the banks knew nothing. But there was a note on the file not to talk directly with the printer. Reluctantly, the investigator sent back a report that was so bland that he wanted to spice it up a bit with the rumor that the man's wife had deserted him. Cautiously, he included it as a footnote; "unsubstantiated local speculation" he called it.

Lao Fang had also received his letter from Meixing and brought it up with Wen over lunch several days later. "Did you check this fellow out?" he asked, knowing full well his son-in-law's penchant for details.

"I did," he answered. "I already have the investigator's report back. I don't see anything negative in it, except he evidently didn't tell everyone about his wife going on the road to sell his stock. They think she just ran off. He keeps to himself and does odd printing jobs on an old hand press. Why do you ask? Do you think you would have any work for him?"

"As a mater of fact, I do," Lao Fang answered brightly. "We are doing a lot of translating. Everything we do has to be edited, so the workload is killing us. The big printing houses want a fortune to set up and do these small runs. This might be just the thing for this man. If he can print up fifty copies, we can send them out to the proofreaders before it's reviewed by the Censors and the Hanlin Academy. Of course, after it passes all that, it must be sent to the best printers for publication, but still, there is a lot of work before that. I'll see if I can't get him to give us a price on something small."

And so it was that Dong Guaiji, much to his surprise, received an order from the new Translation Bureau. He was first visited by a young Kwan of the ninth rank who ran errands for Fang. They went over the handwritten notes and the specification of form and quality of the printing to be done. The young man mentioned a price which was more than twice what Dong thought it was worth, but was half of what the Bureau was expecting to pay. Both sides were quick to come to agreement and the order was placed.

Dong spent the next few days setting character blocks in their trays to make the mat impression from which the Babbitt plate would be made. Once completed, the plate was wrapped around the drum, inked, and hand cranked onto the paper that Dong fed through the rollers. He took the first five pages back to the Bureau for approval and they were well received. The turn-around time and price were better than what they had received from the established printers and the work was quite sufficient for the editing process.

Xiaohua and Bainong arrived home after seventeen days on the road. Shanghai was bustling, as always, as they made their way through the old French Concession. Each of the treaty partners had taken a section of the city as their own. They each had their own characteristic way of dealing with resident Chinese. The French Concession was more casual than the others and it was now their home. Guaiji was stringing up a new line for drying the printed sheets when Xiaohua and Bainong came in. "Busy, busy, busy, little Bee?"

He looked up, surprised, and they ran together in a long embrace. It had been over two months since she had left and she was surprised by all of the work on the drying racks. "Where did all this work come from?"

"The new Translation Bureau needs rough copies for editing. They have money and an endless need. I am exhausted! How did it go with you?"

Xiaohua told of the long march across Anhui and the difficulties of getting the heavy cart up and down the slopes. Then she told him all about this family she had met in Lu'an, and how she had unloaded the entire balance. They counted out what she had brought back.

"I was hoping for more, but this will take care of us till we get paid for this work," he said, waving his hand toward the drying papers on the racks.

"There is more, maybe. I had to leave some of the books on consignment -- at stores in Lu'an."

"What do you know about consignment sales? Aren't you the bright one!"

"I met a woman in that city who runs a school. She bought almost half of what I hadn't sold. Then she took me around the city and introduced me to some of the local store owners and we made arrangements to have them try to sell the books 'on consignment'."

"You trust her? Tell me about her."

"She is very rich and has a farm outside Lu'an. Her husband and her father are Kwan, working here in town for the Jiangnan Arsenal."

"Does that have anything to do with the Translation Bureau? I wonder.... I think I smell a rat!" he said, smiling, and looked around at the racks filled with the new work.

"Do you think this is because of my visit?" Xiaohua asked. "I must thank her." She looked perplexed.

"What is the matter? If I am doing a good job for them and they want to pay so much for the work.... What is the problem?"

"I should find a way to thank her. Remember, they are quite wealthy. I can't imagine any gift that I could buy that would be good enough."

"I'll try to remember to thank her husband, if I ever get to meet him. But for now, I'm hungry. How about dinner at the tent?"

***

An Introduction

Dong Guaiji was sent for; the newest batch of printing needed some minor corrections, the editor from the Translation Bureau told him. Many words in European languages were totally new to Chinese, and had to be represented by either several common characters or by a new character accompanied with an explanation. Any new character had to be judged by the Hanlin Academy, as not being offensive to the Emperor or the T'I chih of the court. They also needed to decide whether to use footnotes or a glossary presentation of new words. Dong offered his opinions well and took instruction without any problem; this was Fang's first impression at their initial meeting. After the meeting, he asked to speak with Dong alone.

Dong entered into the smaller office with some trepidation. Although Fang was not dressed in his full official robes with the insignia and buckle, the white shell button on his cap let Dong know he was a sixth level Kwan -- reason enough to wonder why he would want to talk to this lowly printer.

"Please, make yourself comfortable," Fang said, indicating a chair near his desk. "I understand your wife is a friend of my daughter."

"Oh! It is you!" Dong said, standing and bowing from the waist. "I thought she said it was her husband that I would meet here."

"Well, you would have to go to the shipyards to meet him -- maybe another day. He is building the industry -- and I am writing and translating books. You, on the other hand, are young and just starting this business. I hear that you have one hand-crank press?"

"We have only one very old press; that is true. I hope it lasts long enough to print up all of your orders."

"How would you like a newer one?" Fang offered. "I have connections with all of the printing companies around town and they are always upgrading their equipment. As a result, they have to sell off the older equipment they can no longer use. It is good stuff. I could probably get you something affordable and you could print up some of my writing, on the side, for me. What do you think?"

It was the sort of business relationship that made Shanghai the trade center that it was. Their agreement was all the contract that either needed.

Months later, Meixing received a parcel from Shanghai -- several volumes of a collection of poems her father had written. In a letter accompanying the package, he suggested she might try to sell them through her bookstore friends. She read the book and was mildly surprised that it was quite well done. She decided to distribute them around town on consignment. At night, she even tried to share some of it aloud with Zhenli. He tried as hard as he could to commit some of it to memory, but he was not the academic his parents had hoped he would be. His Wushu training program was the only part of school that he really liked. Though mathematics and language still held some interest for him, the classics were like a switch that shut down his brain. His eyes drooped and he sometimes drooled on his composition book, running the ink onto his lap.

***

A Student of Life

Zhenli had taken an interest in at least one other non-academic thing in school -- not at his school, but at his mother's. Many of the girls were only a few years older than his eleven years, and proved a constant source of amusement. The girls, of course, did not find his attentions at all amusing, and had complained to Meixing. His eleventh birthday was coming up and his father would be home. Meixing would ask him to have a long talk with his son.

Wen received a detailed letter from Meixing on the subject and he discussed it with Fang. "The boy has always needed more of your time than you could give him," Fang agreed. "Maybe if he were here, in Shanghai, it would give you both a chance to grow that part of your lives. It is good that you are successful in your work. But he needs to have you see him growing up in his world. He needs to receive approval or disapproval from you, directly. "And," he added, "You would also benefit from a close relationship outside your work."

Over the following weeks, Wen interviewed several of the better schools in Shanghai that also had a program in Wushu training. By the time of his visit back to Lu'an, he was prepared to present the idea to Zhenli. Fang had arranged to go home with him, to make it a true family event. Neither had been home in almost a year. Seeing the old farm would release a lot of pressure for both of them.

One of the first things they did after arriving home was to have a picnic, on the rise where the monuments were. Then they toured the farm and met all of the new tenant farmers. Wen was tempted to go back upriver and see the shops and factories along the Yangtze and Han rivers; but that would take too much time. They were only here for a short visit and needed to make arrangements for Zhenli's move to the new school. Zhenli resisted the idea of moving to Shanghai, but his was the minority position.

The Shanghai apartment that Wen and Fang shared had several storage rooms; they had always thought they would make them into their home offices. But in truth, they pretty much lived at their offices and only slept at the apartment. So, Zhenli was given the task of clearing out one of the rooms and fixing it up as his own.

The new school was not a monastery, but a professional institute for directed learning. Most of the boys were a problem at home and the staff ruled them with a heavy hand. Zhenli would not be allowed to sleep in these classes! Happily, the school just used the Wushu training to burn off the students' excess energy and to keep them fit. School uniforms answered any question as to dress, and homework was required, expected, and done. But, the subjects that Zhenli liked least were the ones in which his father and grandfather were most able to offer help. After a while, this regimen held them all together.

***

Samurai

One day at school, all of the boys assembled in the great hall for an announcement. The head instructor said, "Today, we are honored to add a new member to our teaching staff." The boys had formed a close horseshoe around him, and he stepped aside quite suddenly revealing a boy, perhaps fifteen or sixteen years old, wearing a headband and colored robe held with a sash. In the sash were two swords. He glared at the boys through eyes masked with eye shadow. He bent at the knees and pivoted on the balls of his feet.

"I am Samurai!" he hissed menacingly. The boys' eyes widened. Then the visitor laughed.

"My name is Akiro Manashi and this is the casual dress of the old warrior class in my hometown in Japan. Our family has been Samurai nobility over many generations. We ruled our farms and villages under the 'Taiho' rule for two hundred and fifty years as the lowest rung in the Tokugawa Clan Shogunate. That period of isolation ended when the Americans forced us to open our country to foreign trade in 1854."

The boys relaxed and started looking more closely at his clothing, and especially at the two swords. "Since then, our focus has been outward and many are now studying in Europe to modernize our military. I have come to China to study your traditional martial arts and to make something of a pilgrimage to the Daoist Temple at Shao Lin in Henan Province. While I am here at your school, I will teach you about our classical forms of martial arts and our warriors' Bushido Code. You will find many parallels, in honor, respect, and duty, to your Confucian teachings. Bushido is, however, more concerned with the warrior's personal honor, rather than with public office. Is there anything that you would like to ask me right now?"

"Why do you wear two swords?" one boy blurted out.

"A Samurai has the authority to kill any commoner who would insult him or do harm to others. Of course, with that authority is the responsibility to justify his acts. If a Samurai acted in a way that did not honor the Bushido Code, he would be obliged to kill himself in a ritual that we call Seppuku. Using his short sword, the Samurai would cut open his belly and would soon die. As this would be a very painful way to die, and because his honor had been restored by inflicting his own death wound, a friend would stand at the ready and would cut off his head, to end the pain."

"What is your religion?" another boy asked.

"Our religion is a mixture of teachings, as is yours. We have the Confucian loyalty to our Emperor and all of the lords in between. We follow the Middle Way, and believe in the Buddhist cycle of life. We believe in the spirits that inhabit everything -- rocks, mountains, animals, wind and rain, lightening. It is very much like your Daoist teaching. In fact, it came from China. It is called Shinto; our word 'Kami' (spirit) means 'Shin' in Chinese and 'To' came from Dao. It is a religion of The Way of The Gods. Individually, we are Zen Buddhists. In Chinese, you would say Ch'an (meditation) Buddhists. We believe that, as in all things, our Buddha spirit lives deep within ourselves. To know that inner spirit requires introspection and deep meditation."

"Who is your father?" a third boy asked.

"My father has lost his name. We are a proud family -- intellectual Samurai, in the Mito Domain. Our people are very conservative; some say that we are fanatically militant. The Samurai of our clan opposed, on principle, the rationality of the Shogunate that lets him bow to the foreigners. We see our Emperor as the direct descendent of Amaterasu, the Sun Goddess; we felt that the Shogun was neither protecting the Kokutai (National Essence) nor the moral leadership of the Emperor. A movement called Sonno Joi (Revere the Emperor and Expel the Barbarians), grew more and more violent in the rural domains -- especially during recent draughts, famines, and changing politics. In 1860, my father was one of a group of seventeen "Shishi" (Young Lions), who were self righteous and rabidly anti-Western. They attacked and killed Ii Naosuke as he was entering the Edo Castle. Emperor Komei later pardoned the assassins because they were acting to protect his honor against the forces of change. But short of Seppuku, to protect his honor, my father chose to retire to a Buddhist monastery and became a monk with no name."

Akiro Menashi's Japan and Wen Zhenli's China came from remarkably similar histories, but had an equally remarkable difference in their response to the changes that were thrust upon them. Both cultures had an Emperor with a mandate from heaven and a bureaucracy that ran the affairs of the state. Both had allowed foreign commerce and religion to enter, but limited and controlled their influence with a strict body of law and convention. The differences were, in no small part, due to the differences in the sizes of the two countries.

In China, the foreigners were dealt with by the Kwan who administered the port cities or border crossings. The Emperor was almost always isolated from the foreigners by several levels of administration, as well as by vast distances. The foreigners were of only occasional amusement for the Imperial Court. In Japan, however, the coast was everywhere much closer, and the clans that ruled the provinces were tightly controlled by an increasingly more intellectual and pragmatic military Shogunate administration. The Chinese, in their capital, disdained all things 'barbarian' as official policy, although in the far provinces, which had to deal with the foreigners directly, accommodation was easier and more profitable. The Japanese people, with the exception of the Emperor himself, were less isolated from the foreigners.

In Japan, the Dutch traders had a long history of promoting their trade and missionary work while on a very short rein; conventions of interaction were strictly maintained, so as not to offend the Kokutai (national essence). Similarly, the Japanese had learned about European technologies under the name "Dutch knowledge" and, as a result, knew a great deal more about the Europeans and their ways than their Chinese counterparts. Against this background, affairs changed rapidly in Japan when the Shogun died. In 1858, Ii

Naosuke was appointed Tairo, or Grand Councilor, and effectively became head of the government. He quickly took control and eliminated his opposition. For the most pragmatic reasons, Naosuke signed the Harris Treaty with America and similar treaties with the other large powers, actions that opened a few large port cities to trade with the West.

Akiro was torn between his father's Japan and what he saw it evolving into. He had no grand passion for politics or religion; only for the art of bushido. In China, he was not looking for a new life, but for a better understanding of his Japanese roots. At this point in his life, it seemed a good thing to travel, study, and teach his art.

***

Parental Bonding

Meixing was happy to finally meet Dong Guaiji on a visit to Shanghai. Xiaohua was still embarrassed by the difference between the two families' fortunes, despite the flood of work that was passing through the shop. Dong had hired twenty-three workers, and was making them into printers as fast as he could. He was also buying up the shops next to his and installing additional presses as quickly as he could afford them.

Two years had passed since the women's first meeting. Meiliang was growing into quite the cultured young lady, a fact that Xiaohua's son couldn't help but notice. Bainong had little time for schooling, as he worked with his father in the shop every day. But Meiliang had developed an interest in the printing business, and soon became familiar with all aspects of the new presses -- bed size, paper feed, and inking. She could simply glance over a frame filled with character blocks, and although seeing it in its reverse image, was able to do some on-the-spot editing before it went onto the presses.

One evening, when the two families had gone out for dinner together, Xiaohua expressed a wish that surprised her husband. "I would like to visit our old farm in Sundak," she told her husband.

"Old times, bad times," muttered Dong from across the table. "What would you like to see now? We left for a reason!"

"I still have property there, don't I?" Xiaohua said firmly. "My uncle, on my mother's side, is watching it for me, I think. Besides, we have relatives around there who are still having a hard time of it. We should help them out."

"I don't think I can get away right now," Dong argued. "There is just too much work!" He looked up at Wen and Fang and smiled broadly. Then he said to his wife, "But, Bainong might want to go with you. I'm sure he doesn't remember it at all." He looked across the table at his son, who was looking back and forth excitedly between his parents.

"Would it be a long trip?" Meixing asked, looking over a pea pod held at the end of her long chopsticks. "I have never seen that part of the country...."

"It is more 'country' than up north," Xiaohua answered, blushing as she recalled the rustic background she had known as a young girl. "The land is flat delta, full of rice and mulberry trees. And they don't speak as you do around here."

"Mama, the pressmen are from the delta. I have to talk with them all of the time." Bainong said a few things in the dialect and his parents laughed out loud.

"Don't use that kind of language around my relatives!" Xiaohua admonished him. She looked over at Dong. "Do you really let the men talk like that in the shop?"

"I just put them to work!" He shrugged and looked at Bainong. "That could be just a bit course for your relatives. You might want to make a better impression on them."

Meixing saw her daughter blushing; "Did you understand what they were saying?" she asked her.

Meiliang looked up from her plate. "They don't always speak that way. They talk half in their home dialect and half in Shanghai Shuohua. And when they talk with me, they are usually polite. But, yes. I understand them."

"Well, I think that it would be an interesting vacation. What do you think, 'mon amour'?" Meixing said flirtatiously, batting her eyelashes and vamping her own husband.

Fang looked at his daughter, and reminded her, "Maybe you should take a few of our soldiers. That is still a pretty rebellious region." Conversation stopped and Meixing blanched.

She reached over and put her hand on Xiaohua's, next to her. "Father, I am sure that we will be quite safe with Xiaohua."

Dong looked toward Fang, though not directly at him. "In that part of the country, you don't want to appear 'Imperial' in any way. They are not anti-Emperor, but they are still sensitive to the treatment that our people received at the hands of the Bannermen."

"It was a long war! Hard on everyone, I fear." Fang said, apologetically. "You're right. It is probably better not to draw attention." He sat back, pensively.

"Still, you think that it is safe to travel there?" Meixing asked Xiaohua.

"It is as safe as anywhere. As long as you speak the language and respect the customs, we should be all right.

The last time we made the trip, we were running for our lives all the way across the southeast. This time I think I will book a passage on a coastal freighter, down to Canton. Then, from Canton, we can go by boat upriver to the high ground to the south. We will have to hike over some at the top and then get another boat into Sundak. Our farm is on that side of the mountain."

"Why not get off along the Pearl River before Canton, at the mouth of one of the southern tributaries, and go by boat straight up?" Dong asked.

"I have some maps at the office," said Wen. "Is this something you really would like to do, ma chéri?" He tried to affect the same eye batting she had used, but it came off more comic than her version. They all had a good laugh at his expense.

***

A Trip to Canton

The idea became a plan and the women went out shopping for the event. It was not new clothes they were looking for; instead, they searched for shops that carried used clothing and picked out several outfits that would fit in with the area they were to visit. Typical local samfus were darker and featured the work apron of the Hakka. The cloth was lighter weight, and two of them were even silk.

"We raise the silk worms down there, and the cloth is not a luxury as it is here." Xiaohua explained. "Everyone has several trees around the house and we harvest the cocoons for sale in Canton. There are always extra ones that the girls work on at home. Sometimes two cocoons are interwoven on the twigs of the mulberry tree and separating them is too much work for the commercial silk houses; they just won't buy them. The girls use boiling water and pull off the strands of silk by hand and wind it onto reels so it can be spun later into thread. It is a lot of handwork. But we were poor and that is what we all did."

Next, the two women worked on their hairdos. The delta women wore their hair in a stylized bun that showed whether they were married or not, and identified the area that they came from and the class of their family -- as did the cut and cloth of their samfus.

Xiaohua also led Meixing and Meiliang through pawnshops all over town. They bought up a large quantity of good jewelry -- not the finest, but neither was it cheap. They took it all back to the shop office to show to Dong. "The idea is to not carry large amounts of money but to have something of value we can sell for currency or trade for things of value along the way. Here in the city in such shops, the price is quite reasonable and in some cases an outright steal. We should be able to at least make back our money, if not make a profit besides," Xiaohua said excitedly.

Bainong laughed out loud. "Mother, you have been too long on the road selling books."

The four of them boarded a coastal trading boat; it would be fast and they commonly took on passengers, as passengers were more profitable per square foot than trade goods. When they landed in Hong Kong, they were dressed in their mainland Hakka outfits and were treated as though they were from the back country. Meixing was outraged by the dockworkers' slighting attitude, and even more outraged when they encountered the British duty inspectors. They were definitely seen as second-class citizens. The duty inspectors made insinuations in English and were surprised when Meixing quipped back that they were not only ill-mannered but out of uniform.

Xiaohua pulled her away before the situation got out of hand and convinced Meixing to laugh about it. Surely there was better trouble to get into on the island! They had their bags transferred to a river boat and paid to have them checked into a secure hold and guarded while they went to explore the busy streets and shops. That night, they slept on the river boat, which was much slower than the coastal trader as it worked its way up river.

In the morning, they changed boats in Panyu and commissioned a small sampan to take them inland to Fo Chyun, a small market village. In one of the stalls, Xiaohua broke into an animated discussion with the woman who was weighing out vegetables on a stick scale. The pan holding the vegetables was suspended by strings from the short end of a stick that was marked on the longer arm like a ruler. A weight was hung along the markings. The woman picked the whole thing up with her left hand, as she moved the weight till it balanced. The price was reckoned by the weight and then argued according to the quality of the produce.

After a few minutes, the woman stopped arguing and looked intently at Xiaohua. A look of recognition swept over her wrinkled face like a cloud passing. She dropped the scale and took hold of Xiaohua's hands. There were introductions and a tour of all the local stalls as they encountered one relative after another.

That night, the women and their children were guests at the house of Xiaohua's mother's brother. Their family had been down on the river trading on that terrible night when the Taiping came for all the food and men they could find. They all agreed it was better just to forget the past and to live a quiet life. Another family that had been displaced had taken over Xiaohua's old home, and was paying rent for it to her uncle. He had saved some of the rents against the possibility of her return. It was such a pitifully small amount that Xiaohua decided to abandon her claim to the property and to any rents.

The next day, Xiaohua showed Meixing and Meiliang around the village, where they met many old friends and more distant relatives. "Let me show you the Girls'

House," said their guide. "I don't think you have these where you live."

***

A Custom of Marriage

The women walked to the edge of the town, where an older style building had been converted to a house for girls.

"Many girls choose to sleep here rather than at home," the guide told them. "Some are embarrassed by the changes in their bodies and the attention of the men, even in their own families. Here they are among friends, girls of their own age. Most of them return in the morning to their own families to perform their chores and whatever work they may have to do in the fields or the shops. But in the evening, they come here to bathe and clean their clothes. They can talk and bond with other girls and they are comfortable."

"How do they learn about boys?" asked Meiliang.

"That is sometimes a problem.... Well, it is always a problem! But there are many other things to learn about life in these years, about themselves and their position in life. Many of these girls do have a difficult time when it comes to marriage. The husbands are chosen by the families when the girls are in their early teens. Even after the marriage, the girl may stay with her own family for three to five years."

"Why even get married?" Meixing asked, afraid of what her daughter was hearing.

"Oh, a girl must be married before she is twenty years old or she will be a disgrace and a burden for her family," the guide answered. "And, a girl's soul needs family ancestors to serve in the next life. Without another family, her ghost would be lost and wander forever."

"Then, she does eventually live with her husband?"

"Sometimes.... If a girl is afraid of what kind of a man she has married, how he and his mother would treat her, she could run away and only come back to die. But, that is rare. More often, if a girl has talent and can earn money of her own, she can buy a second wife for her husband. The second wife would have the children and work for the mother. That way, the first wife could have children to call her 'mother' and a place among her husband's ancestors for her soul."

Meixing looked at her daughter's face, which was filled with incredulity. "Not something you'd be interested in?" she asked wryly.

"I think I would rather love the man I marry and build a life with him," the girl answered simply.

Meixing beamed. "Well said! Let's see the rest of the village then." She turned and went out the door with a sigh of relief.

They went down the pathway with their guide, who promised a special treat. "We will be having a celebration this afternoon. The men have finished building a new trading boat."

Several hours earlier, Bainong had gone to help the uncle and some other villagers launch a large trading boat they had built. He swapped his secondhand clothes for a more comfortable set from 'one of the cousins'. The air by the river was humid and unexpectedly warm. Bainong found he was using muscles he rarely had to exercise in the print shop.

The large flat-bottomed boat was built on the shore, then rolled to the water on logs. Each log then had to be carried by ropes and shoulder poles by rotating teams of men, from the high side down to the lower side. The boat moved slowly down to the bank. The sand, as they neared the bank, was soft; under the weight, the logs did not roll easily, like a wheel on a hard road. To make it more firm, bamboo was laid on the sand, pointing toward the water. Side by side, as the large logs rolled over them, the bamboo crushed into splinters which sank beneath the weight of the boat and logs, pushing the splinters into the mud. But then, the boat and logs began to float on the mud! And then on the water! The whole village let out a cheer, as the boat floated freely and the logs bobbed out from under it.

The boat was later loaded with bamboo and made ready for its maiden voyage to Hong Kong. Xiaohua and Meixing agreed that the trip had been a huge success, but that it was time to return to the lives in which they both felt more comfortable. They left most of the clothing and jewelry as gifts for relatives, and looked forward to buying more fashionable clothing on the British stronghold of Hong Kong.

***

A Visit to Hong Kong

In Hong Kong, it was Meixing's turn to play host. The first stop was at the Bank of England branch office. Initially, the clerks were put off by her clothing, but out of that soiled bag she kept behind the work apron came the proper identification. This was the daughter of Lao Fang, the Shanghai banker! A letter of credit was on file in anticipation of her arrival. With the letter came bank notes that could be spent anywhere in town. Their bags were delivered to one of the better Chinese hotels, and packages from the Chinese shops began arriving at their rooms. Bathed and dressed in more familiar Shanghai fashion, the four travelers set out to enjoy the Hong Kong nightlife.

After a lavish meal, they took a ride on a public horse-drawn carriage up the hill to Victoria Park. Foreigners in the park were somewhat taken aback seeing these 'native people' in their park. A young officer in full uniform with a feathered hat, who was attending his superior, politely, but pointedly, questioned them.

"My lord was wondering if you had been taken to the correct part of town, Madam?"

Meixing responded in French, "Ah, C'est lui là-bas? Je ne le connaît pas." She looked him straight in the eye, as if expecting a response.

He swallowed and glanced back uncomfortably at his superior.

"Oh, I am sorry, Monsieur" Meixing said. "I said, that gentleman over there? I am afraid that I do not know him. Please inform him that we are from Shanghai and we came to see the sights. My husband and father are both Kwan, working for Li Hongzhang. Perhaps they would know him. Please give him our regards." She nodded in the direction of the older officer and then turned and walked her group over to an observation platform to see the lights of the city below. When they were ready, they hailed a cab and returned to the city.

A Growing Family

***

The Printer

Upon returning to Shanghai, Meixing and Xiaohua found Dong in his office in a state of utter exhaustion. The shop foreman was with him and explained that Dong had been working, day and night, for three days straight.

Bainong and Meiliang went directly out into the shop and talked with the manager, who was excited and almost as incoherent as Dong. The new contracts had finally exceeded the capacities of both the presses and the operators, and problems seemed to cascade, one on top of the other. "One machine would go down and then another. Dong was shouting orders and running around like a madman. Nothing was getting done. We had to put him in the office and insist that he get some rest."

Bainong talked as calmly as he could to each of the pressmen, and looked over their machines. Two machines had simply been turned off in the confusion; there was no good reason for them to stand idle -- so he got their operators to start them back up. Several others were only out of ink or needed some small adjustments to get running again, and they were quickly put back into operation. Only two of the machines had actual broken parts, but were quickly fixed and restored to operation.

Meiliang, meanwhile, sorted through the orders and updated the schedule of work for each machine. By the next morning, they had a better idea of the situation -- Dong had just overextended himself and the shop. To take some of the pressure off the staff, Meixing talked with her father and found it was a small matter to reschedule most of the outstanding orders. Bainong was able to further prioritize the schedule so that the most important work was being worked on first. The rest could be done in order. Although just fifteen, Bainong had taken charge of the situation and, with the help of his mother and Meiliang, the drying racks started filling up and work was again being delivered.

Wen visited Dong two days later at his home, where he had been ordered by Wen's doctor to take some extended bed rest. "Feeling better?" asked Wen. "Don't worry. The shop is in good hands. Bainong is a good manager and he has the confidence of the men."

"I just wish he didn't have to come home to all this!" Dong was impatient and fidgeted with the edge of his blanket.

"You'll have to relax. I tell you, everything is fine. It is you who needs repair. Doc told me you came close to a breakdown -- that is serious stress. Take the rest, you have earned it and you can afford it. I'll work with Bainong and see if there is anything I can do."

"No, no! You don't have to ...."

"Oh, relax! It is nothing -- just a little look-see. Did you know that he has already set up a repair facility in one of the old store rooms? He is training some of the printers to be mechanics, so it doesn't all have to fall back on you."

"It's not just the shop. I haven't really kept up things in the office either."

"We know," Wen laughed. "Xiaohua has taken over the office. Lao Fang really likes the way she handles the billings and shipping. She is quite good! What I'm trying to say here is, you're not in this alone, you know. But, the work flow through your shop does need to be improved. What I see is a lot of little shops stuck together. If you want to do this volume of work, you will have to admit that you are no longer a little shop."

There were several interfamily meetings and they developed a plan. The larger building would be retrofitted to contain all of the presses in a pressroom. And the smaller buildings would be converted for use as stock, maintenance, office and shipping. A flow of paper and ink was established for unified production, and parallel flow of paperwork would track the orders from one door to the other. Dong reluctantly agreed to being relegated to an office, in charge of sales and purchasing, and to leave the stress of the operation to the younger people.

Within a few months, Wen's construction company had completed a new facility, with Dong's office located in a building, down the street from the plant itself. Intercom and phone lines kept Dong in constant contact with the plant, without making his heart race. Bainong's office was at the plant, but when there were problem calls, his secretary redirected them from the floor supervisors to the repair or shipping offices. That left Bainong free to plan and control production scheduling.

Even Meiliang had an office at the plant, where she would review proof sheets before they ran them through the presses. She was also compiling a dictionary of the new characters for the new foreign concepts that appeared in the translations. As this required knowledge of the concepts themselves, Meiliang and her grandfather were in frequent conferences over lunch.

One day, for example, Xiaohua, came into Meiliang's office with a book, in English, titled *Elements of Analytical Geometry and of the Differential and Integral Calculus*, by Elias Loomis. It was submitted with a hand-written translation into Chinese by Li Shanlan, who gave it the title, *Zhongxue* (middle school). Li was a Chinese mathematician who lived in an era that frowned on science as nonacademic. Despite the practice of advanced mathematics and celestial navigation in China dating back centuries, science did not enjoy the respect of the classics. "Before I can give them a price for publication," Xiaohua said, "I thought you should look at all of the new characters to make sure they are approved and in our dictionary."

"I'll show it to my grandfather," Meiliang told her. "I'm sure I wouldn't understand it at all." She took the book with her when she and her father met him for lunch the following day. Wen joined them for lunch and brought with him a letter from the Viceroy, Zeng Guofan.

"We have been invited to a dinner!" he said. "They are celebrating Li Hongzhang's victory over the Nien rebels in the north, and his appointment to be the Viceroy of Huguang. Li is also hoping that you will find time to help in editing and publishing a collection of 154 writings of Zeng Guofan."

Li's appointment was one of those techniques that were used to keep the higher Kwan aware of their reliance on the whims of the Emperor. By never letting any Kwan hold power in a region for long, no Kwan could harbor illusions of grandeur, or build up the loyalty of an army to enact them. Li would, for years to come, be the most trusted and powerful advisor to the Emperor and his mother, The Dowager Empress. Even so, he was not Manchurian and he would always be under their surveillance and sufferance.

As it turned out, the dinner was more a meeting than a social event. All of the mid and upper management in the Self Strengthening movement and some government officials in related agencies were invited. It was a chance for the new bureaucrats to speak out, to listen, and to hear from the top about their performance and achievements so far, and the next goals for the Self Strengthening movement.

Behind the agenda of the meeting were the political tension and interplay of two still-powerful factions within the government. Like mismatched horses, the reactionary school of traditional Chinese learning pulled against the progressive school of Western learning and visa versa. The tension between the two diminished the force of either to advance its program. Perhaps Yan Fu was right; perhaps 'Western Learning' could only be useful in the context of the Western style of democracy that spawned it. The issues were not settled.

***

Zhenli Graduates

Zhenli had transferred from his city school in the Fall of 1864 to the new School for the Diffusion of Languages, set up at the Jiangnan Arsenal. Li Hongzhang created seven new divisions for the curricula of study in the new program; Mineralogy and Metallurgy, Metal Casting and Forming, Wood and Iron Fabrication, Mechanical Design, Navigation, Naval and Land Warfare, and Languages. Upon completion, students were sent to Beijing for Provincial-level examinations.

Zhenli had grown into a more serious student and had passed the examinations, third in the class of 1870. He received a commission in the service of Zuo Zongtang, the old friend of Zeng Guofan and the current Governor General of Shaanxi and Gansu, far west of the capital. Zuo had recently been assigned to reassert Chinese control over Xinjiang, "the New Frontier" in the northwestern-most corner of China. During the Qing Empire, Muslims had expanded their influence eastward into Xinjiang, and it had become known as Chinese Turkistan. The Russians had come south across the Altai Mountains, past the treaty boarders into the Ili Valley between Kazakhstan and Mongolia.

In a letter dated July 23, 1873, Zhenli wrote, "It was with the utmost sadness that I learned of my grandfather's death. So much of who I am and who I would like to become is rooted in my love for him. I wish that I were not so far away. My unit is involved in the suppression of the Yakub Beg Muslims. Here in the desert plains, we are so very far away that we are not allowed to return home, even for the rites of death. I will come as soon as I am able." The letter was forwarded to the old farm in Lu'an. Fang Laogai had been laid to his final rest on the hillside, next to Madeline and their two sons.

Wen had taken the mandatory three-year retirement from all of his governmental positions, starting in 1873. They lived quietly on the farm with their daughter during this time of mourning. However, Meiliang did manage to return to the printing plant in Shanghai for longer and longer visits, while Wen and Meixing developed a growing interest in the bucolic joys of running the farm.

Then one day, a package arrived from Zhenli in Xinjiang. On the outside of the package, he had written the characters "I am fine." Inside were his diaries, some drawings, and a long letter explaining that he remembered when a package had come from his uncle, who was dying in a hospital; he wanted to assure everyone, immediately on receiving the package, that he was not dying. He had been injured when he and his horse fell down an embankment and into a river. But, it all seemed to be healing well, he said, and he had taken up an office position in a supply depot in Turfan, at the eastern end of the Tian Shan range. Zuo had used his solders as farmers as his armies had advanced to the west against the Muslim Turks, under Emir Yakub Beg. In this way, Zuo's supply lines were kept short and he was always in control of his food source.

By the spring of 1878, Zuo and his armies had taken control of the far western borders of the province of Xinjiang, and had sent Ch'ung-hou to St Petersburg to negotiate a treaty with the Russians. The treaty would establish trade and restore the border as it had been since the treaty of 1689; it would also restore the Ili valley to China's control. Zuo was anxious to return to the comforts of the capital and he brought with him key members of his staff, including Zhenli.

***

The Prodigal Son

Wen looked through the packet of notes that was stuffed in with his son's diaries, and was surprised at the quality Zhenli's art work. He had drawn local people from the areas the army traveled through, as well as buildings and individual houses of the most remarkable style. There were sheep herders and their horses, women setting up a circular house made of sticks and cloth, and drawings of some sort of underground tunnels. There were also several engineering drawings for four-wheeled, horse-drawn carts with a lot of computations and endless schedules of materials, distances, and maps. The packet had taken almost as long to get to the farm as did Zhenli, who arrived a week and a half later.

"Zhenli is coming!" Meiliang shouted from the yard where she was hanging out laundry. They all hurried from the house to welcome him and wave at his arrival, but their smiles turned to wonder.

"What kind of Rag-tag army are you in?" Wen laughed, as he took the bridle of Zhenli's horse. Zhenli was wearing a turban and a long robe, tied with a sash over his new uniform. One of Wen's Civic Guard came out and held the two packhorses that were tied on behind him.

"What? Have you never seen a Turk, Father?" he laughed. He climbed down from his horse gingerly, obviously favoring his left side and he took a cane out of his saddle pack. They watched him do a slow spin, which showed off his sheepskin-lined boots as well.

"Get out of that robe right now!" his mother said, running up to hug him. "It's much too hot for all that. Oh, that smells terrible! Do they all live in a barn, out there?"

Zhenli did, indeed, get out of the costume and left it to air out on the fence in front of the house. Under the robe he wore the new uniform issued to him when they got as far as Xian. The uniforms were modeled in the European fashion and looked a lot like those of the Japanese soldiers who visited Shanghai. Even the uniform was hot, and Zhenli could hardly wait to get into his old clothes. His mother was determined to wash everything before she would be comfortable with any of it in her house.

More than eight years had passed since they had all been together and Zhenli didn't know where to start. "Well, you have grown into quite the woman," he said, grabbing Meiliang and spinning her around; he couldn't help but noticed her blushing. "What have you been up to?" They all went inside and sat down in the living room. His sister, obviously, had something to tell.

"We wanted to wait for you to get home," she blurted out first thing. "Bainong and I are going to get married."

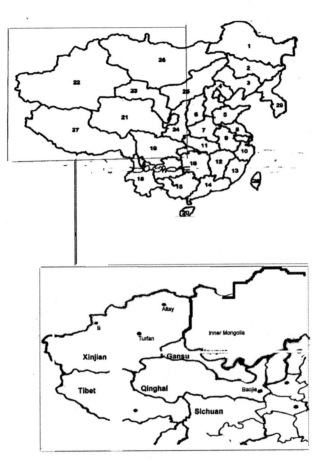

Map of Northwest Territories

"Wow! You have been growing up." He glanced at their parents and could see that it was already a settled matter. "Well, where is the young master, anyway?"

"He is fixing up an apartment in Shanghai. From the window of the apartment, you can see all the ships in the harbor and along the Bund. It's on the second floor and he is having a telephone line run to his office so we can talk anytime."

"Oh, I'm sure he'll love that! When do I get to see him?"

"He should be here in a few days. I haven't seen him for a whole week! But I came home when I heard you were on your way. I want to know all of you adventures."

At the table in the main room, Wen placed the packet that his son had sent in front of him. "It looks like there is a story or two in here."

Zhenli folded back the wrapper and took out the books and drawings. "Yes, there are a few in here," he agreed, nodding slowly with a wispy sigh. He opened the oldest diary and flipped through the pages. "I.... I was so young; look at how carefully I made my characters. It is like block printing." Some papers fell out of the book and he carefully unfolded them. "When I finally passed my examinations, I was given these orders to join Zuo in the Northwest Territories." He spread out a map that was attached to the orders. "They gave me a supply company of young officers and a consignment of new European weapons to take out there."

"We hauled the equipment down to Tianjin and put it on river boats. That was a mistake! The boats almost capsized in the sea swells along the shore at Bo Hai. Just picture these top-heavy, shallow draft river boats trying to cross open water! But we lashed them together with bamboo poles and rafted down to the mouth of the Yellow and then upriver to Xian. From that ancient capital, we followed the old tea trade routes.

"Which reminds me.... Have you heard the new name for the tea routes?" Zhenli pulled out a tattered German newspaper, dated November 1877. "I picked this up a year ago in Xinjiang. Grandpa would have loved it! They are calling it 'The Silk Road. Look. 'Die Seidenstrasse'. It's still just an old dusty trail, but the Europeans are romanced by the name. I don't think they realize that almost all shipments of silk have gone by sea for the last four hundred years.

"Anyway..." He pointed back at the map. "From Xian, the river goes up here past Baoji on up to Tianshui. At that point, the river flows much too fast, and we couldn't pull the boats against the current. So we repacked the cargo onto carts and went the rest of the way, up through Gansu, in wagons and on horseback.

"Along the north side of the Qilian Shan range, the trade routes make a wide, flat road all the way out to Wuwei. From there, you can see the Great Wall. Then, following that along, just before we got to Jiayuguanand, the western wall ends. There is a huge fort, called the Jiangyuguan Pass that commands the narrow valley. At that point, we had been traveling for three months, so we took a week to rest up at the fort. Here, I've drawn a picture of it."

Drawing of Fort Jianyuguan

"The supply officer at the fort made sure we traded out our oxen for camels and draft horses. That added a lot of weight, in water and supplies, but he was right. We soon left the north end of the Qilian mountains and marched several days over a high grassland with occasional sandy desert. Sometimes there wouldn't be enough grass for the livestock and we were glad they had packed grain for them.

"One night, I found a strange man in a turban and robe, standing at the flap of my tent. 'Good evening, sahib,' he said to me, touching his forehead and making a graceful bow. 'Do you know that you are my prisoner?' With that, he pulled out a huge sword and pointed it at me. I don't recall ever being more frightened."

Meiliang caught her breath and put her hand to her mouth. Wen put his hand on her shoulder. "Well, he must have gotten out of it all right." They all laughed.

"But, I wasn't sure that I was all right. I was scared cold! I called out, 'Guard?' The man just laughed and waved me out of my tent. All of my guards were on their knees in a row in the center of the camp. Many men, dressed as the stranger was, were scattered throughout the camp. They all had long guns, knives, and swords.

"'Well?' said the man with the turban, 'What is next, you are wondering? Are they going to kill us? I assure you, if that was my intention, you would not be alive to wonder. Sahib Zuo has sent me to make sure that doesn't happen. But you made it so very easy!' He laughed in a friendly sadistic way. 'I hope that you will forgive me for my little theater. My name is Armal, and I am your servant.'

"I laughed with him, but my knees were not yet steady. We went to the center of the camp and he introduced himself and his men to our men. Everyone got off their knees and jostled one another. Actually, it was a good thing! We had left the civilized part of the world, and this was only our first lesson in the hard logic of the New Frontier (Xinjiang).

"During the next week, we paired off with our counterparts in the guard and learned defense and aggression on the open plain. We scouted the land to the north and west of our trail and found out we were not alone. Fresh tracks from other horses and camels were close by. We would never be caught sleeping so soundly again.

"We had seen mountains in the distance; thin grey lines on the horizon. My map indicated a town at the base of the mountains called Kumul. It was a natural oasis, a low point that the winds had carved out, 200 meters below sea level. In summer it could get over 40°C and in the winter it would drop almost 40°C below. We arrived at a more temperate time, but the days were still very hot and the nights were quite cold. We had come to a point, almost within a day's travel from Kumul, when Armal ordered the caravan to stop in a particularly high and open plain. 'I think that we should make camp here,' he said, 'Rather than push on to the oasis.'

"It was so early; I was astounded at his suggestion. We were still fresh enough to get much closer. But, he was in charge of our security; that point had been made. So, we unloaded the pack animals, spread out the tents, and fed the animals, using almost all of our extra supplies and water. The cooking fires were particularly bright and the men were playing around, not as tired as they would have been had we traveled a full day. Armal called his men and my lieutenants into my tent for a meeting. 'The oasis is a trap,' he began bluntly. 'It has always been a trap because it is the only water in the area. Coming from Gansu, it is almost certain they will think that we will stop there. We must not!'

"The men buzzed with questions and Armal quickly brought them to focus again with answers and reassurance. 'We will rest this evening and strike camp in the middle of the night. We'll need to move quickly to get around the town and into the foot hills on the other side before they realize that we are gone. In the hills, here is water and natural grazing. It will be enough to get us safely to

Qijiaojing, in Bogda Shan, the next range. You must remember we are transporting weapons that would be of great value to our enemy, weapons that would drag this war out for many more years than you would like to spend out here.'

"His plan worked," Zhenli continued, "And we made our way to Zuo's field headquarters in Turfan. He remembered Father and Grandfather and it was good to see his familiar face! He was also very happy to see the new weapons and ammunition. Even though he's very good at providing for himself, arms are almost impossible to make in the field. We soon put them all to use in the action against Yaqub Beg."

Drawing of Yakab Beg

"What kind of name is that?" Meiliang asked.

"He came from Uzbekistan, a country further to the west." Zhenli held up a map and pointed to the left side. "He was a soldier who rose through the ranks of the army to become the ruler of the kingdom of Kashgaria with the title of Emir.

Unfortunately, he was a really unsavory character and he died last year at the hands of his own soldiers. I think they poisoned him. Anyway, we made a deal with his successor and the war came to an end."

"What are all of these drawings?" Wen asked, pulling out several pencil sketches.

"These are people who lived in the area. I tried to sketch the clothing and faces of as many of the minority peoples as I could. These are Hui, Bai, and other Chinese who were in rebellion when Zuo went out there. The whole area had been without Qing protection for most of the last hundred years, and that vacuum of power sucked in the Kazakhs, as well as the Turks, Tibetans, Tatar Mongols, and even the Russian Tsar's armies. They all resisted the return of the Imperial forces, but eventually we brought them all under our control."

"Why the Russians?" Wen looked at his son curiously.

"Oh, the Russians were trying to expand to the south to get an unfrozen seaport for shipping. They did get down through Kyrgyzstan into Afghanistan," he said, indicating the Russians' movements off of the map. "But that threatened the British who were in India, and their neighbors in Persia. The Russians were looking for a soft spot and the English want to keep them away from the Arabian Sea; there were spies everywhere. In an article in a London paper, a British newsman called it 'The Great Game'. In Russia, it is called 'The Tournament of Shadows'. But, for the Russians, it was a real problem -- they needed access to the seas to be a part of world trade. They have a huge country with most of its ports frozen for more than six months of the year."

"The Russians got their port in the Sea of Japan with the Treaty of Aigun in 1858," Wen snarled, "And their Treaty of Beijing in 1860 -- they are both are unequal treaties that should be reversed! They took away the Outer Northeast -- from the Stanovoy Mountains down to the Amur and

Ussuri rivers -- a huge tract of land that the Treaty of Nerchinsk established as Chinese back in 1689. The British are right to stop such aggression!" Wen was obviously quite familiar with the history.

"That's true," Zhenli agreed. "They have an open water port at Vladivostok. It is about the same latitude as Sapporo, Japan. But, to get there they have to cross all of Siberia. Transportation to it is restricted by rivers that freeze over in the winter, and roads that are almost impassable mud bogs in the summer. They have been digging a canal system for many years, but that also freezes over in the winter. I understand they are working now on a system of railroads, like the British have. But, they have factions and cliques in their government as well, and not everyone thinks the expense of laying rail lines would be worth it. Anyway, Zuo got them to respect our frontiers in the Ukok Plateau," he said, pointing to the point on the map between Kazakhstan and Mongolia, "And we took back the border city of Ili."

"What are these women doing?" Meixing asked. "They are women aren't they?" She held out a drawing labeled, 'Kiyiz Uy (felt home, Kazakh); yurt (Dwelling place, Turkic)'

Drawing of Yurt

"Yes, they are women, but they wouldn't let me draw their faces." Zhenli answered. "They are setting up a Yurt. It is a kind of tent that can be set up quickly, moved easily, and is comfortably warm on a cold night on the steppe, the grassland in Mongolia. Yurt walls are made of split willow saplings. The crossed pieces of wood are tied with rawhide at the tops, bottoms, and in the middle to form a lattice." He crossed his forearms and moved them like a scissors. "The enclosure can be rolled up when they move, or unrolled and stretched out to form an open lattice. To set it up, they stand it on edge and unroll it into a circular wall. They use a framed doorway to hold the wall and make a closed circle. Inside, these tents can be from three to ten meters across. To help hold the circle rigid, they use two bands of horsehair rope. One is run all the way around the top, woven through and tied. A second one is run around, midway down, and tied to the sides of the door frame.

"The roof is made of many split saplings which run from the wall to a ring at the top. Each roof piece rests on a notch cut in their lower end which is fitted over the top of the lattice. The upper ends of the roof pieces fit into a slot in a ring at the center top of the structure. The weight of the top holds the sides out, symmetrically. Then they cover the frame with large cloth sheets. The walls and roof are then finished by stacking layers of felt blocks around the structure. They make the blocks out of cotton and animal hairs. They beat the wet fibers into rectangular frames and dry them into light blocks that insulate the walls and roof. Sometimes, they put up to eight layers of the felt -- which can build out the wall a half-meter or more. The felt layers continue up the wall and over the roof. Then they cover the felt with an outer cloth wrap and tie it with bands, all around and over the top."

"That sounds like a lot of work! How often do they do that?" Meixing was looking at the size of the room they were in.

"It only takes about a day, if everything is ready. And they don't move unless the pastures burn over or there is a war.

The grass lands are usually a reliable place to graze the animals."

"What is it like to live in there?" Meiliang was looking through the lattice wall at the inside.

"Inside, the walls are finished off with tapestries and shelving, hooks and racks for art work and utensils. A fire ring is usually built in the center of the floor with the smoke going out through the top ring which has a moveable cap. The door faces south and the place of honor is across the fire to the north. Men sit near the west wall and women near the east wall. Mats and carpets cover the floor and the door may be solid or cloth. It is a remarkably sturdy, roomy, and a warm form of housing."

"Why are the women on one side and men on the other?" Meiliang asked with a giggle. "Don't they get along?"

"I think they get along just fine. Women just know their place out there," said Zhenli, with a smirk and a shove at his sister. "Actually, it has to do with their religion. They are Muslims."

"What kind of religion is that?" asked Meiliang "Is it like the Buddhists?"

"Their religion is more like the Christians', I think," Zhenli answered. His mother leaned forward and gave him a hard, questioning look.

"Well, originally, there were many tribes that lived a nomadic, pastoral lifestyle out in the deserts between Egypt and Persia. Some of them claimed a common ancestor, Abraham, and they worshiped one God. But even though their God was supposed to be all-knowing and all-powerful, he was unable to keep them from going astray. Consequently, their own history is one of reoccurring punishments. One of those punishments was being captured and made slaves to the Egyptian Empire. A prophet named Moses led some of the slaves on an escape out into the desert and gave them a law to live by; these people were known as the Jews. Eventually they grew rich and powerful and built great cities.

"One of the later Jewish prophets was a man named Jesus, who preached that love was a better basis for human interaction than the laws. He claimed that the God of the Jews was a natural part of all men. He said life was eternal and material existence was a passing phase. Many of the problems and illnesses of the people, he preached, were caused by their own beliefs in death and disease, sin and punishment. He may have learned some of his ideas from the Buddhists, because when he was a young man, he traveled abroad. Later, he returned to his homeland to begin his ministry. But, the leaders of the Jews were afraid he was taking the people astray, away from their influence and reliance on the laws, and they had him killed. However, the teachings of Jesus lived on and many of his followers have experienced both great conquests and contemptible failures. The leaders of the Taiping Rebellion are an example; they clamed to be following that teaching."

"Wait a minute!" Meixing said, waving her hand in front of her. "Who are the Muslims in all of this? We have a large area with a lot of nomadic sheep herders. Some share a belief in one God and have one common ancestor, named Abraham. Some of that group follow a Prophet named Moses and are called the Jews. Then one of the Jews, named Jesus, tries to break away to form the Christians. The rest of the Jews kill him; and then what? Somehow we still have the Jews and the Christians, but I still don't have any Muslims."

"OK. The Christians were an underground sect for many years. But their popularity grew and they won a lot of converts among the other Jews and non-Jews called Gentiles. Eventually they grew in power and influence and made converts in high government office in the states where they lived. It became the state religion of the Romans, but that empire declined and split in two. The Catholics were the Christians of the west, based in Rome, and the Eastern Christians were Greeks with a capital in Nicomedia, Anitolia (Turkey). Later, they moved it to a city named Byzantium, which controlled the trade routes at the Bosphorus. They changed the name of the city to Constantinople, which is its name today.

"Still no Muslims!" Meixing said, baiting him with a smile.

Zhenli laughed. "Just wait. Seven hundred years after the Prophet Jesus, and about 300 years into the Byzantine rule, another Prophet, called Muhammad, came from one of those tribes of desert peoples. His people were neither Jews nor Christians, but called themselves Bedouins. The name -- their own self image, means 'those who come from nothing'; they are people of the sands, the wisps. They had no great cities, no great kingdoms. And, they had no unifying beliefs as the Jews and Christians did. They worshipped many gods in no particular hierarchy. Muhammad saw that the Jews were held together by their shared history and laws. The Christians had the history of the Jews and their Prophet's promise of life everlasting as a reward for living a life of loving acceptance. Both of these communities had money and power, compared to the Bedouins."

Zhenli's mother walked around the room, refilling the tea cups and offering dumplings; all the time with a look of mock suspicion on her face.

"Muhammad, this Prophet," Zhenli continued, "Had dealt with both the Jews and the Christians. He married a widow who owned several caravans, which he drove. He traveled along the western end of the early tea routes, and had learned the stories of the Jewish traditions. He had also seen how their teachings held the believers together as a people, and how that brought them money and power. Muhammad returned to his home town of Mecca and retold those historic story-lessons of the Jews, to his own people in a series of Suras (revelations). He claimed the Angel Gabriel had told the stories to him directly, so that his people could know God and prosper as well. They were, after all, people from the same deserts, also sons of 'Ibrahim' (Abraham).

"Muhammad claimed that they had a common family link to the Jews through Isma'il (Ishmael), the son of Ibrahim and his maid Hagar, who were driven off into the deserts to die when Abraham's wife gave birth to Isaac. After his death, Muhammad's Suras were collected into a book called the Qur'an. The name 'Muslim' refers to the submission to the faith of Islam."

"So why aren't they just Jews, and be done with it?" Wen was getting restless.

"The Jews didn't want to adopt them -- a bunch of rag tag desert people! They had gotten pretty uppity. Besides, Muhammad didn't want to be a Jew. In his eye, they were a people who had erred by making God's law into laws that suited man more than God. The Christians erred by deifying a man who was no more than a messenger. Muhammad reiterated to his followers that there is only one God, 'La ilaha il ALLAH!' (No Deity there is except The Deity), and that he was just the messenger; the Suras were 'Bismillah ir Rahman ir Rahim' (In the name of The God [known to the Jews as 'The Beneficent'] and [known to the Christians as 'The Merciful']). Muhammad claimed only the title Warner or Messenger from that same God."

"Hold on! There are three religions and only one God -- the same God?" Meixing was shaking her head.

"Right! Muhammad was going to set the record straight! The others had gone wrong and his people would do it right." Zhenli looked up a little apologetically. "But, he did have a little problem in his own community. Muhammad lived in Mecca, in a town where the people worshiped many gods, and each effigy collected substantial donations from passing caravans. These were a good source of income for the local merchants. So, they were not at all happy with Muhammad and his one God. The good folks of Mecca became so irritated that they offered a reward to anyone who would kill him or drive him out of town.

"Muhammad and some of his followers escaped and went to another town, to the north, called Medina. The Jews of that town were of two factions and they hired Mohammad and his men to be the Sheriff, keep the two factions apart and bring an end to their fighting. They had no problem with Muhammad's beliefs because most of what he preached was so familiar. His popularity and followers grew and he formed his own army. He was later able to sweep back down to conquer Mecca, impress his religion on them, and go on to conquer large areas of the western world. In 1453, The Ottoman Turks conquered the Byzantine Empire and Islamic influence followed up the Tea Routes to our western boarders. They are there, even to this day."

"You still haven't answered my question, why are the women separated from the men." Meiliang was not going to let him off with a history lesson.

"Because, my dear sister, you ladies are so dangerous and irresistible," Zhenli countered, "We must keep the men away from such temptation and their inevitable demise. Even in the home, men feel unsafe sitting next to the women."

"I don't think you'll get yourself out of it with that one!" laughed Wen. "And, it would take more than the thousand years since Muhammad to explain all the customs and variations that religion has developed since. But, let me interject one thing that is of more current importance. It has to do with larger trends that developed after the Prophet died."

Wen explained, "When Muhammad died, the elders in Mecca needed someone to lead the movement; there was money and power to be had. Ideally, they thought, the leadership should fall to the closest relative in the same Quraysh tribe. Their candidate was a cousin by the name of Ali, who had married Muhammad's daughter, Fatima. They had a son named Hussein. But, Ali was assassinated by a rival relative and a second Caliphate, the Umayyad, was formed. There have been four such Caliphates over the years, and many religious or political contests. Today there are two primary factions. The moderates, called Sunnites, or Sunni Moslems -- they are followers of the Sunna, 'the way of the Prophet' and the Caliphate, which was based on it. Members of the smaller faction are called Shiites, from 'Shiat Ali', or partisans of Ali. They rejected the Sunni authority. They also claim to follow the Suras of the Qur'an and the Hadith, a collection of sayings of the Prophet which direct the life of the believer and his relations with other members of the faith. They are given to more mystical and fanatical acts, even martyrdom and self-flagellation in the name of the faith."

Wen was caught by the stares of the others in the room. "Well, I did read some things beyond the classics and the law!" he said. "Let's try another drawing; what are all these wells and tunnels?" He held up a cutaway view of the side of a mountain, with holes dug down to intersect a horizontal tunnel.

Drawing of Quant

"Well, that is just what it is!" Zhenli said. "They are called Quants. The well is actually the horizontal tunnel, and the vertical shafts are only dug to give ventilation to the tunnel diggers. The windless at the top of each shaft is to haul up the dirt from excavating. Even though there is no rain at the base of the mountain, some does fall at the top. The tunnel will become a well when it intersects the water that flows over the bedrock face, which is under the ground on the side of the mountain. Then it is collected and flows down the horizontal well, all the way to the town. It provides a pretty reliable supply of fresh water."

"That is pretty clever. Are there many of these wells?" asked Wen.

"Anywhere there is a desert town at the base of a mountain, they usually have one."

Meiliang then took up several drawings that were tied together. "Who are these men? I like their hats!"

Drawing of Cossacks

"They are Cossacks; the Tsar's border guards," Zhenli explained. "They have a long and colorful history as well, but I'll try not to tell it all. Suffice it to say, they are a very independent bunch. They call their armies 'Hosts,' and can have 120,000 or more men fighting together at one time! And, they will fight anyone for anyone, if they want to. They elect their leaders and everyone votes on treaties -- like the one they have with The Tsar in Russia to act as border guards, or the treaties that they have with the Polish-Lithuanian Commonwealth, and the Ottoman Turks to not attack one another. They love to fight with their long swords, and they have also adapted to the cap-lock pistol and long rifle. Even so, the weapons they use are obsolete next to the arms of any modern army, like ours. They still ride their horses like the Mongols. And they sing, dance, and drink -- and are just a lot of fun to be around."

Drawing of Mounted Turk and Oriental Sword

"This guy was not so fun!" Zhenli said. "The Turks had a great cavalry and they used these swords very well."

Wen was still looking over the drawing of the quants and asked about the wagon and the attached pages of calculations. "All right, what is all this? Are you doing engineering now?"

"Yes! That was my last assignment," Zhenli answered. "We had to take Zuo's war booty back to the Emperor. There was quite a lot of it, some tribute, and some, just souvenirs. We went mainly by horseback, but the heavier things came back on wagons. So, I had to design a wagon that could roll across all the various terrains -- the grass, desert, and mountain passes -- and yet be light enough and water-tight enough to float down rivers as we got to them. This is all weight and buoyancy calculation. I watched the wagons all of the way to Xian and they worked well. From there to Bo Hai is an easy float, and from there to Beijing should have been no problem. But, I just felt I should get my leg in shape before I take on any more duties. Zuo agreed and told me he would send word when I should rejoin him."

Zhenli enjoyed the next three months as a lay-back gentleman farmer. The family visited the graves, had their picnics, and watched the crops grow. In May, Meiliang and Bainong were married and moved into their apartment in Shanghai. Several times during the next year, Zhenli visited them there, and began making the rounds of the nightlife in the big city. There were rumors linking him to one of the hostesses who worked in a bar in one of the rougher neighborhoods.

Wen had a little talk with his son about this relationship, how it could adversely affect his career, and the problems it could engender. Zhenli was polite, but still drawn like a moth to a flame. Then, fortuitously, a letter came from Li Hongzhang regarding Zuo Zongtang; he had been appointed a Grand Secretary to the Grand Secretariat while still fighting in the northwest, and in January 1880, he was elevated to a Marquessate. Zhenli was summoned to attend the celebration and to take up an assignment as Zuo's adjutant in his new office in the Grand Council.

Growing Older

***

Zhenli's Beijing Assignment

Zhenli quickly discovered that Beijing life in the early 1880s was neither the restful bucolic pace of the farm nor the carefree madness of the Shanghai nightlife. He was, in fact, in awe the moment he stepped off of the boat. His orders were to familiarize himself with the city and be ready to assist General Zuo with information on a wide range of topics. For him to become the newest 'expert' in courtly affairs at age 25 would take some fancy footwork. So, footwork it was -- and he set about it with a walking tour of all the neighborhoods of Beijing.

His first contact was not with the general, but rather with the family of the Empress. He presented the letter from his father to the guard at the door and waited outside for a long time. Suddenly, the door burst open and an older woman rushed out to greet him. "Oh, you are certainly the son of Wen Fulian! You have his jaw," she exclaimed, "But those must be your mother's eyes. Please come on in and tell me how they all are doing. It has been almost twenty years since your father's last visit. How is he?"

Zhenli was shown in through the street door to the courtyard between the apartments, and into the family's living room. The older woman would be the Empress' mother, he surmised, but he had no idea about the others. He told them all about his father's and his grandfather's involvement with the Self Strengthening movement, about the industrial and educational projects that they were working on. But, to his surprise, all of that was remarkably distant from the concerns of this household. Even outside the walls of the Forbidden City, the people of Beijing were concerned about the power struggles which had brought war to their doorstep -- the ones inside the court. On the one hand, the reactionary faction was almost exclusively interested in expelling foreigners and their influence. On the other, the progressives saw their only future choice as emulating the 'foreign devils' and using their 'practical knowledge' to develop China. Throughout the north, outside the capital, the ultra-nationalist organizations, called the Boxers, were gaining both popularity and militancy, emboldening the reactionary members of the Emperor's High Council. For Zhenli to be of any value to General Zuo in his new position, he would have to know the exact political position of each and every member of the Council.

Another, not-so-minor, fact of life was that there was yet another new Emperor. Zhenli had been so far removed from Beijing that he had all but missed the fact that, even though the Dowager Empress Cixi was still the power 'behind the curtain', the young man on the throne had changed.

Shortly after she became a member of the royal household, the Empress Cixi had introduced her sister to her husband's brother, Prince Chun. The matchmaking might have been dumb luck or farsightedness, but the fact was that Cixi had the Emperor's only son, and her sister had the son of his brother -- a plausible successor to her own and one whom she could control. Some said that she saw a weakening of the males of her husbands' bloodline, or at least progressively shorter life spans. Be that as it may, Zaichun, her son, was stricken with a fatal disease and died at age eighteen; Zaitian, his cousin and soon-to-be successor, was waiting in the wings.

In a deft deployment of raw power, Cixi summoned Li Hongzhang, at that time Viceroy of Zhili, the Metropolitan district around Beijing. From his post eighty miles away, he and his army literally came in the middle of the night to dispose of or detain anyone who might challenge her choice of successor to The Dragon Throne. The anointment of her nephew, Zaitian, as the Guangxu Emperor, pushed aside any aspirations of Prince Kung's son and assured her of de facto control of this latest government.

The Dowager Empress Ci'an was not well; in fact, she was dying. Old traditional medications and Buddhist monks could only comfort her. With her death, the most influential voice of the reactionary faction would be silenced.

It had turned into a long day. Zhenli took a common room at a local inn before going to meet with General Zuo in the morning.

***

The General at Home

Guards at the gatehouse outside of the Forbidden City directed Zhenli to the General's villa, on a hill in the east end of the city. A rickshaw took him there, clacking down the cobblestone streets of the main part of town, and then gently hissing along the damp dirt paths further out of town. On the flat stretches of the road, the man pulling the rickshaw slid back down the poles, nearer to his passenger, and balanced his weight against Zhenli's, so he could pull up his feet and coast for a time before sliding back out toward the ends and resume running. Leaves stuck to the soles of his sandals and the smell of early winter filled the air.

When Zhenli arrived, the General was wrapped in a blanket with his feet in a pan of hot water. "Sorry, I don't seem to be able to get rid of this cold. How are you? You look well rested!"

"Yes Sir. Life on the farm is very slow. I had to get into Shanghai just to find some night life. How is the war going here?"

Zuo laughed, "War indeed! First, tell me. What is the news from Shanghai? They are so full of themselves around here, you have to talk with the English just to find out what is going on in the world."

They brought each other up to date for most of the day. Zhenli talked of the death of his grandfather and his own father's retirement back to Lu'an. But, the General was most keen to hear about the progress at the arsenal and the shipyards. He had worked with the French to build China's first navy when he was the governor of Fuzhou Province.

As the afternoon wore on, Zuo began instructing Zhenli on the politics in the capital. "You'll find that we do our fighting with memoranda around here. It is all jockeying for the attention and favor of the Empress. She, on the other hand, has to pit one of us against another to get any sort of a balanced view of any situation. Everyone has an ax to grind. It is a fine art of one-upmanship. You will also have to exchange that old uniform for the latest thing. It's all about appearances, you know!"

The next day, Zhenli was tailored into his new uniform -- the latest fashion, with a German pistol holstered at his side. He had a 'man's man' to keep his uniforms cleaned and polished, and a secretary to do most all of his paperwork. He only had to know everyone who was anyone on sight, and be prepared to whisper prompts into Zuo's ear about anything important about them -- from personal to criminal details. Not infrequently, these were hard to separate. He also kept the social calendar and, at a moment's notice, could find things or make contacts that the General needed. It turned out to be a natural fit for him. He did have his father's eye for details.

Zhenli maintained every contact that he made, and stopped often at the house of the Empress's mother. It was there that he met Prince Chun and his wife, the Lady Rong, the younger sister of the Empress Cixi. She was mother of the Emperor, but her big sister was the Dowager Empress, and Rong knew her place. But, it was through her, the court gossip flowed freely.

At the other end of the power structure, Zhenli met Bingzi. He was the young boy who had helped his father come to the attention of the Empress by having Wen wear The Empress's mother's bracelet. Bingzi was a character. He was now in his mid-thirties, but still fascinated by the goings on in the capital; he was an endless source of information and rumor. He currently ran a transport company with access to the port and all its goods, as well as the 'side door' through which he delivered all sorts of things for the Imperial household. It was at that side door that he talked with many of the younger eunuchs who, in turn, moved around freely inside the Forbidden City. Zhenli and Bingzi exchanged useful and interesting tidbits almost daily.

Zhenli's information-gathering network also included the coolies who serviced the Legations of the English, French, Germans, Russians, and Americans. For a small favor or fee, he could learn almost anything that went on in the highest diplomatic circles. And, he could, and would, procure and deliver things or favors anonymously to those with even better access. All of the walls in Beijing were permeable.

Zhenli made it his habit to have lunch in a public house between the Meridian Gate of Forbidden City and the ceremonial 'Great Qing Gate' in the park, to the south. It was there he received and delivered notes and payments for favors with his army of informants. Information, though, was a two-way street and occasionally, some member of a Legation staff would stop by and introduce some new diplomat or currier who would, in turn, become part of the network. Zhenli had a seemingly limitless memory for names and faces, as well as for their current duties and who could get what, for a price.

His first test came at an embassy dinner for the Englishman Robert Hart. He was being honored for his service representing China as President of the Chinese Government's Commission at the Paris Exhibition in 1878. Mr. Hart was the Inspector General of Customs, and for the past twenty years had actively promoted a postal system to be installed as part of the Custom Services. Delivery of the post had traditionally meant the Imperial Post, but that service needed a wider vision -- for commercial reasons and for access by the whole population.

The General was presented to a lovely lady in her mid-thirties, a Mrs. Jenny Taylor. As she was being introduced to several other people, Zhenli whispered in the General's ear that this was the second wife of Dr. James Hudson Taylor, founder of the China Island Mission. She had left her husband to his duties in England, and had just spent the last two years leading other women in famine relief work in Shanxi Province. She was now returning to England.

"We appreciate all of your assistance in Shanxi," the General remarked to her later in the evening, "And I am sure your husband will be pleased to see that we have returned you in good health." She beamed at him and took his hand, thanking him for making the evening so memorable for her.

Throughout that evening and many to follow, Zhenli's whispered words that filled out an introduction made the General a welcome guest. One night, the General anxiously tugged at Zhenli's sleeve. "Who is that man with Li?" he asked. "I knew him once." "That is Charles

Gordon," Zhenli replied. "You fought with him against the Taiping, remember? He took over the Ever Victorious Army when that American, Frank Ward, got killed. Since then, he has been in India and Africa. Brilliant solder! Retired now, but Li invited him up to Beijing to intercede with the Russians."

"Well, my old friend; back to help us out of another sticky spot?"

"Zuo, you old angler; I see you're just as sharp as ever."

And so it went for a year and a half.

Unfortunately, Zuo was facing his seventieth birthday; the politics of the court was a younger man's game. He requested and received a transfer to become the Governor General of Jiangnan and Jiangxi, which covered the lower Yangtze, including Shanghai. Zhenli, of course, went with him and set up his offices in a recumbent suburban area, well away from the commercial, political, and military excitement of the Bund.

New duties and old habits drew Zhenli back down into the business district and its seedier nether regions. He was soon involved again with his hostess, Sui Chuhng, known to many on the Bund as 'Charlie'. She was, without question, one of the most attractive girls in the clubs along the wharf, and was also quite talented; she could both sing and play the pipa. She played Zhenli, as well.

Charlie's father remained out of view, but he kept a close eye on this young man. Sui Gaodi was a part-owner in the bar and ran a brisk trade in opium in the back room. His main claim to fame, however, was as an enforcer for the Fujian Hall. The 'halls' were large, older structures which were renovated to provide a place for meetings and social functions for one of the many ethnic minorities. Shanghai supported many halls for each hometown area, where people could speak their hometown dialect. The hall would 'protect them' in much the same way that the 'Black Hand'

Mafiosi 'protected' Sicilian immigrants in New York during the same time period.

The Fujian Hall was a spicy collection of grafters and drifters -- and Gaodi fit right in. His family ancestors were in the pirate trade, before the British threw their navy against the pirates in the middle of the nineteenth century. The pirates just moved inland and learned to steal alongside the foreigners; it was an easy transition for the Sui family. His father ran opium through the city of Fuzhou -- Gaodi just followed the trade up to Shanghai. Now he was a respected and feared member of the community, who counted his treasures and family dear and would protect them as he felt the need.

Charlie's mother was dead. Gaodi had won her mother as part of a pot in a card game -- he only knew she was Japanese and her fingers were stained yellow with opium smoke. She stayed around long enough to give birth to Charlie. But, 'she must have got hold of some bad stuff,' they said. Gaodi found her on her mat, looking lazily at her pipe. Charlie never really knew her.

"Zhenli, you would probably have liked her," Charlie said to him. But he didn't pay much attention to most of what Charlie said, and he never saw the analogy.

Zuo was getting busy, so Zhenli was getting busy. The Chinese Navy, which Zuo had built with the help of the French back in the late sixties, was now being readied to fight the French. The Empire of Annam (Viet Nam) was under the protection of China, but the French wanted to expand their colonial forces north into the Red River, from Hanoi up into Yunnan Province.

Zhenli was too busy learning about the terrain of that distant area to notice the more subtle changes in undulations of his girlfriend's figure. "Gaodi wants to talk with you!" was all he heard, as men on either side lifted him off his stool and helped him out the back door of the bar into an alley filled with Gaodi's men. He was roughly thrown up against a telegraph pole and his hands were held behind him. Zhenli could feel several knife points pressing on his arms and throat and Gaodi stood directly in front of him.

"Charlie is going to have your baby!" he hissed. "The only question is whether you will live to see it." His face was twisted with anger and indecision. It was not a comfortable way to meet your in-laws.

Their wedding was performed by a civil clerk and the reception was at the bar. Wen and Meixing only found out about it a week later. The new couple just presented themselves at the farm and made their little announcement. Meixing was reserved but invited her new daughter-in-law into the kitchen for a talk. Wen took Zhenli out into the barn for a less restrained talk.

"Are you crazy?" Wen was beside himself.

"Please, Father, she's really a nice girl."

"What kind of marriage is it -- at knife point?" Wen was storming around in the barn. Between the epithets and glares, Wen had managed to kick almost everything around him. "You are an idiot and probably deserve anything that you get! But, your mother doesn't deserve this!"

Meixing was inside the house with Charlie, trying to understand and adjust to this new situation. Charlie was doing her best not to be intimidated by the proper lady before her, who had served her tea in fine porcelain cups with matching saucers. The cakes were fresh baked and the house was much larger than her father's bar. Charlie, in her best dress, felt tawdry, and for the first time felt a deep shame in who she was. It was not a comfortable way to meet your in-laws.

On the ride back to Shanghai, Charlie wept almost the whole way. "Don't worry, honey," Zhenli tried to comfort her. "They will learn to like you. You will just have to be patient. They were just caught by surprise. I couldn't really give them any advanced notice, you know."

It was a week later before Meiliang had a chance to visit with her mother, but things had not changed very much. Meixing was still walking around with a hankie and burst into tears from time to time in the middle of dusting the same table for the third time or trying to find the broom that she held in her other hand.

"That girl is just using Zhenli to become something she can never be." She sat down heavily into a chair, exhausted with the futility of the situation.

***
Sister ?

Meiliang had no time for this 'stuff'. Zhenli and Charlie stopped by for a social lunch, but Charlie's shallow understanding of the world and the resulting banality of the conversation was more than Meiliang could tolerate. Once was enough. Her stomach turned cold when the boy who watched the front door came in with Zhenli's card.

"Your brother is here to see you, ma'am."

That, in itself would have irritated her. She thought "'Ma'am'? What am I? Doesn't he know that is how you talk to an older woman? That's my mother, not me!" She bit her lower lip as she picked up the card and unconsciously crinkled it in her hand. "Is that woman with him?" she snapped.

"Oh, Miss Charlie?" he smiled. "No, he came alone today."

"All right, tell him I am busy, but I will see him just for a short visit."

The boy left and, after a few minutes, Zhenli came through the shop, loudly greeting everyone, and opened her office door.

"Good morning, Meiliang. How is my favorite sister?"

"What is it, brother?" She sat back and crossed her arms.

"What do you mean? I come in peace. Is that a problem?" He stood before her like a schoolboy in mock contrition.

"At least you came alone. How is all of that going?"

"I wish you all would give her a chance. She is what she is because of her family -- just as we are who we are because of our family. She had no control over all that. Give her a chance and I think she'll grow into a fine person. OK, not a refined person, but she has to see us as a proper family; like we were her school. She can do it! I'm sure she can."

"I don't know if I'll live that long," Meiliang grumbled.

Zhenli half sat on the edge of her desk and talked over his shoulder at her "I want to set up a picnic with her and our family. You know, out of the house and walking around the farms. Maybe she could meet some of the tenants and see that we are not such a bunch of stiffs. She needs to smell the place and feel the soil. She never had all that."

"And I suppose that means that you want me to sell the idea to Mom?"

"Oh, could you?" He stepped back, as if she had surprised him.

"Oh, you're too pathetic to turn down, and this has to end somehow, some day. I'll see how she feels about it," Meiliang agreed. Then added, "Could you at least get her to dress like she wasn't hooking sailors?"

"Now, that was mean!"

"You're right! I'm sorry about that; but it is something that she'll have to fix."

"OK, I'll work on that and you talk with mom. Thanks! Now I'll let you get back to your drudge. Love you." He blew her a kiss and stepped quickly beyond the door as she reached for a paperweight.

***

Propaganda

Down the hall from Meiliang's, was her husband's office. Bainong looked up from his paperwork as one of the printers popped his head in the doorway. "There is some guy out back talking to the men."

"What do you mean?" he asked. "Do you know what he is looking for?"

"I have no idea. I never saw him before. It just seemed strange. They are taking their lunch break. Thought you might want to know."

"All right! I'll go see what is going on; does sound strange." He went around to the alleyway behind the building, and saw a man talking to a small group of his workers.

"Did someone extend lunch time?" he called out to the group. The men put away their things and quickly went back inside.

"What was that all about?" Bainong asked the man.

"I was just telling the men about a new movement that is sweeping the world -- Communism. Have you heard of it?"

Bainong looked at him blankly. "What is it? Another rebellion? A new religion?"

"You are a printer. You might want to consider publishing this." The man handed him a modest book with the title in German, *'Manifest der Kommunistischen Partei'* (The Communist Manifesto). "I'll give this copy to you if you promise to read it through. When I come back in a week or two, we'll discuss it. If you then have a grasp of what it has to say, you may keep it. If not, I will want it back. Is that all right with you?"

"That is good," Bainong said. "We will be with my in-laws this weekend; they can read this language." The man smiled, they bowed to each other, and he left.

That weekend, everyone met out at the Farm. In addition to their normal visit, there would be an arranged picnic with his brother-in-law and his new wife. Bainong took the book with him and presented it after the picnic. Wen and Meixing looked it over and started writing out the text.

"Oh, you don't have to translate it," Bainong said. "I just wanted to know if you thought that we might be interested in printing it."

Wen looked at him intently. "Were you able to understand any of it?" he asked. Bainong shook his head. "This is very powerful stuff," Wen said. "Do you remember me telling you about the manifestos that the Taiping wrote back in the fifties? This is very much like that. It describes class warfare in Europe -- and I'm sure they mean to branch out here in China. I think you would be playing with fire if you published it. On the other hand, I still think that you should read it, so you know what these people are saying, since they are talking to your workers." Wen turned the paper around, so Bainong could see what they had written.

> A specter is haunting Europe -- the specter of Communism. All of the Powers of Old Europe are entered into a holy alliance to exorcise this spectre....

"What are they? Do they worship ghosts?" Bainong couldn't make anything out of it.

"No, it is a political movement. Think about the factions in our own government. A faction is made up of men who think a lot alike on most issues, and try to promote changes or prevent changes depending on their point of view. These people who are talking to your employees are trying to have us envision the world without any government; no Emperor, no Kwan, no High Councils, none of that," said Wen.

"Then, who would run the country?" Bainong asked.

"That is just the problem! They think the country would somehow run itself. No person would own anything and there would be no property inheritance."

"That is crazy! This is a crazy book. I will not publish it!" Bainong said angrily and pushed it back across the table toward Wen.

Wen picked it up and looked at it thoughtfully, "It may be crazy," he agreed, "But there are many people who think such a world could exist. There is a whole school of thought like that called the Utopian Socialists."

"Where is this school? We should burn it down!"

Meiliang laughed. "No, Wodeai (my love), he means...."

"I know what he means. I'm not that stupid!" Bainong stood up and walked away from the table.

"Come on, now. Nobody thinks you're stupid." Meiliang went over and stood and talked with him quietly.

"Well, it all seems like a nice theory," Zhenli chimed in. "I just wonder how they plan on changing things to get there." He sat down and looked across the table at Wen.

"Look in the back," said Charlie, sitting down next to her husband. "There is a section called 'A Call To Action'."

Everyone stopped what they were doing and stared at her.

"What do you know about this book?" Zhenli asked, with a curious smile on his face.

"I have seen them discussing the book in my father's bar. There is a section in the back...."

Wen flipped the pages. "Here we go:"

> The communists disdain to conceal their views and aims. They openly declare that their ends can be attained only by the forcible overthrow of all existing social conditions. Let the ruling classes tremble at a Communistic revolution. The proletarians have nothing to lose but their chains. They have a world to win. WORKING MEN OF ALL COUNTRIES, UNITE!'

"Well, that sounds like a fun bunch," Wen said sarcastically and laid the book back on the table. "They sound like Hong Xiuquan and his Taiping rebels, but without the justification of God."

"They are not crazy people!" Again, all eyes turned to Charlie. "You think they are crazy because you have everything. These are people who have nothing, just this dream. Maybe it is a long shot; but it is better than no shot."

Wen pulled back from the table, and glared at her. "You are too young to have seen the Taiping. I'll grant you that. But, didn't anyone ever tell you about the horrors of that time?" Wen stood up and shuddered at the ignorance that he saw in her. The lessons of so recent a past were lost on yet another generation.

Meixing crossed the room and stood directly in front of Charlie. "I would like you to move out here to the farm," she said. "We have so much to discuss, I think we need that time together."

Wen turned and left the house, without a word.

"Father, wait!" Zhenli looked around the room of faces in shocked silence, and quickly followed his father out into the yard.

***

Retirement

Dong Guaiji was still listed in the prefect's record as the owner of the print shop, even though it was his son who had grown it into one of the leading print houses in Shanghai. But recently, Dong had been approached by two groups, outside the family, who had interest in his business. And after several meetings with them, he decided to retire.

Bainong, Meiliang, and Xiaohua were called to Guaiji's office, down the street from the print shop, and sat across from him. He wore a curious smile. "Well, I had an interesting visit from a man from the Fujian Hall a few months ago," he said. "He was very polite, in a rough sort of way. And he explained to me they are concerned about our workers; most of them come from there, as you know. He pointed out that they work in the older buildings, which are made of wood and could easily burn down That would put them out of work -- and might even kill some of them. I, of course, had to agree. Then, he offered me a proposal -- well, more like an ultimatum, really." Guaiji stood up and looked out the window toward the harbor. He sighed heavily before he could go on.

"I would have to come up with twenty-five cash per worker per day for protection to be provided by the hall. 'It is like an insurance policy,' the man said. They would have their men come visit us every day to check out the 'safety' of the buildings and to pick up the policy payments. Last month, they doubled the fee."

"Why didn't you tell us?" Bainong gasped. "That is just robbery!"

"Of course it is, but it is hard to resist -- because it is also impossible to get any help from the police. They are probably getting a little taste of it themselves. Anyway, there is also a carrot to go with that stick," he smiled. "The Daily Shipping and Commercial News made an offer to buy us out; our presses, trade accounts, and our 'good will' as an ongoing business. The offer was too good to turn down and we made a deal."

"Father! What are you talking about?" Bainong gasped. "We are doing so well, now. We could fight them." Bainong slid to the front of his chair. Meiliang put her hand on her husband's.

"What better time to cash in?" Guaiji sat back on the window ledge behind him. "Xiaohua and I have talked this over, but we didn't want to make this your problem until we had a clearer idea of what we wanted to do. And, we want out. Now, we understand and appreciate all of the time and effort that you two have put into making this the success that it is. We would like you to take half of the proceeds of the sale for yourselves."

Meiliang and Bainong looked at each other and she squeezed his hand. They were shocked by the suddenness of the offer, but intrigued at the same time. Meixing sat quietly, looking at them all anxiously.

"When were you thinking that all of this would happen?" Bainong asked, sitting back in his chair. He listened as his father laid out the details that had been worked out so far. They paid particular attention to the details of the financial settlement. There were options, as to 'how and when', but the numbers were good and they would never be poor again.

It was past midday when Meixing suggested they go over and tell Wen the news. His office was a good walk across town and they all could use the fresh air. When he heard of the plan, Wen also needed some fresh air, so they all walked back to Dong's office.

"Well, they tell me that you are taking an early retirement, Dong," Wen said.

"Oh, not so early really," Guaiji flashed a smile. "I have already outlived most of my friends. And Xiaohua wants us to go back to the Delta and be big shots in our old hometown. We'll have enough to be comfortable. It won't be like starting over. We can just lay back and enjoy!"

"You didn't tell us that!" Bainong said. "When are you planning to do all this?"

"It has all come together rather quickly," he laughed. "I'm not sure I've absorbed it all, myself."

During the next few weeks, there were several exploratory visits between the new and old management, while Bainong worked out the turnover of the company and all of the records were stamped and filed. But, these tasks were finally accomplished, hands were shaken, good byes were said, and gifts were exchanged.

When the last of the paperwork was completed, Bainong came home in the evening to find Meiliang looking down from the window of their apartment at the Bund and the harbor -- toward the corner where Bainong would first appear on his trek home each night.

"What is this? Tears for Shanghai? We are free to do whatever we want. Canton is not so very far away; we can visit them any time." Bainong stood behind her, his arms draped over her shoulders and their hands holding each other's forearms. Together they stood by the window, as the sun set and the room grew dark behind them. On the streets, the lamps came up to full brightness, making the evening streets seem even darker, and the endless flow of people slowed into night.

***

The French

"You are going to fight the French?" Meixing chided Zhenli. "They are almost my people! Remember, your own grandmother was French. Would you kill your own grandmother?" She was teasing him, but it was a little over much.

"Oh Mother, give it up! Grandfather had the French pegged for what they are long ago. They're just a bunch of money-grubbing colonialists and you know it!" he retorted vehemently. "Ten years ago they forced us to give up Annam in the Treaty of Saigon. Now they are forcing their way up the Red River into our back yard. They would have succeeded, too, if the locals in the Black Flag army hadn't beaten them. Now they're trying to intimidate our own navy in our own port. Don't you dare take their side; you're half Chinese as well, you know!"

Meixing laughed at her son's combative response. "When you're on solid ground, you don't give an inch, do you?"

Charlie stood at the kitchen door wondering what she had just walked in on. She could tell Zhenli was more shaken than he showed. "Let's go for a walk," he suggested. "I have to tell you something and I'll get no support from her!" He smiled back at his mother and opened the door for Charlie.

"I'm starting to show, did you notice?" she said, smoothing out her apron over her stomach. "We will have a baby by summer. Isn't that wonderful?" She tried to catch some feeling from his controlled look.

"Well, I hope I can be back here by then," he said. His words were aloof, but his arm was around her waist and his hand was on her apron.

"You can't just go away and leave me, here, with them," Charlie teased him with the uneasy peace that had been worked out.

"What is wrong with them? Besides, I'll be in a war zone. That is no place for a baby, much less his beautiful mother."

"Don't give me that guff," Charlie laughed and spun around to look him in the eye. "I never thought she could be such a Chinese mother-in-law."

"What did you think she would be? You should appreciate her for who she is. She can teach you a lot about being the mistress of this place. That is what you are in line for, one day, you know. Besides, if she were a 'regular' Chinese mother-in-law, you would be on your hands and knees, day and night, baby or no baby, scrubbing floors. You ought to thank your father, one of these days; he married you off well. Don't you ever forget it!"

"I don't want all of this," She said, smiling coyly and waving her hand lazily across the view of the farmlands that stretched to the horizon. "That is a lot of responsibility. You will just have to come back and help me."

Zhenli was not fooled for a moment. His new wife knew every coin in her own purse and had a good idea about everyone else's as well. The estate that his grandfather's family had labored so long and hard to amass would cost her only nine months of labor. And her husband would also, some day, take hold of the sprawling system of manufacturing and mercantile facilities, which alone would have made them rich.

"Well, I don't know when I can get back. Yunnan is a long way off." He gazed off at the moon in its first quarter in the western sky and stroked her hair. "And nobody knows how much it will take to turn back the French. You'll have to promise to listen to mother and make the best of it -- alright?" She nestled her head into his chest and hugged him.

Zhenli had already been looking over the General's war plans for months. The French had taken the citadel of Hanoi, the capital of Tonkin, in April of 1882. Unfortunately, their leader, Capitan Henri Riviere, died in a battle with the 'Black Flag' local militia, and pro-war sentiment had increased in France. The Emperor of Annam signed the Treaty of Hue in August 1883, ceding Tonkin to France as a protectorate. The Qing government, however, rejected the treaty and ordered General Zuo to move his forces into the Tonkin. Despite there being no declaration of war, France and China deployed forces that Fall, as though war had been declared. French Prime Minister Jules Ferry wanted to avoid involving the other colonial powers, but ordered a measured blockade of the Chinese navy in their ports in Fujian and on Taiwan.

General Zuo Zongtang, who had built the Fujian Navy with French engineering in the 1860s, was relieved as Governor General of Jiangnan and Jiangxi and was once again called back to active duty. In 1884, Zuo was made Lord Admiral and Imperial Commissioner of an expedition force to fight the French in the South China Sea. But, while Prince Chun played the politician and ordered Zuo not to fire the first shot, the French Navy sailed their ships into the port of Fuzhou and anchored them along side of the Chinese fleet. In August 1884, in a thirty-minute 'battle', the French opened fire and sank the Fujian Navy.

Even though the Treaty of Tianjin had acknowledged the Hue Treaty which made Annam a protectorate of China, in

May of 1884, the French were just waiting for the monsoons to subside before they went back on the attack in the Red River area. This would make the mineral deposits and crops in the Yunnan Province available for the expanding colonial ambitions of France. However, in March of 1885, they were beaten by the local Black Flag forces and Zuo's land forces. The French lost much of the ground that they had already taken and suffered a humiliating loss of face among their Fellow colonial governments. The French government, under PM Ferry collapsed under the weight of the scandal. The strain was also too much for General Zuo; he died in September. Zhenli had the sad honor of returning the body of his commander to his ancestors for burial in Wenjianlong in Hunan.

***

Home Again

Zhenli once again came home from 'the war', but this time received a much more subdued homecoming. Meixing was tired and the lines on her face made her look older than her fifty-two years. It was also a quieter house despite his year-and-a-half-old daughter, Yili. On the day Zhenli arrived, Charlie had gone to town to do some shopping, Meixing told him. "She does a lot of that! She is quite the woman of fashion, for a farmer."

They had a quiet lunch and his mother brought him up to date on the family news, such as it was. Lao Wen had taken to reading the classics again, and spent a lot of time at the picnic ground on the rise. Meixing had taken up the pipa, with some instructions from Charlie. But, the big news concerned his sister; she was expecting a baby in the spring. They were also were getting restless in Shanghai. Bainong had invested most of their share of the sale of the printing business into commercial paper, which funded trade along the coast down to Hong Kong. But having to deal with the criminal element in the trade made Meiliang uncomfortable and it limited their profits. Bainong was thinking about joining his parents back down on the delta around Canton, but Meiliang was pulling for Hong Kong.

After lunch, Zhenli walked up to the rise to greet his father. "So, this is where you are holed-up!" he said as he approached

Wen looked at his son over his reading glasses. "Oh, so you're back again! Well, you seem to have all of your parts. The war went well then?"

"The General died. He was over seventy and the war was just too much for him. I had to take him home and I decided they could run things without me. Actually, my commission ended with his. So, I am unemployed again. How are you doing?"

"Oh my war isn't over yet! I just come out here to get away from it all, now and again. "

"Your war? Is it Charlie and the baby? Now that I'm back, I could get them out of your hair, if you want."

"No, it's not just the baby. It is your mother. She wants so much for her family, but Charlie is satisfied with so much less. I tell her, the girl is not interested in… you know, in life -- the histories, the arts, books, that whole world outside herself. She is still the product of her life before you met her. I doubt that she will ever rise much above it. The whole thing is wearing on your mother."

"I'll get them out of here," Zhenli decided without much hesitation. "I'm really sorry about leaving her here with you. But, mom did want to try to change her. Maybe if we move back to Shanghai, Mom will get back her spark. Does she still have her schools?"

"Oh the schools are still there, still running with the teachers that she trained. She just lost interest. She seems to see Charlie as her own personal failure and it is sapping all of her strength. I think you're right, if they were separated for a while, she could ease up on herself. It's letting go of the granddaughter that will be more of a problem."

They sat for a while looking out over the farms. When the sun set, they returned to the house.

***

The Lady of Fashion

Charlie wheeled into the front yard and threw the reins to a man who had come out from one of the barns. "You'll have to walk him," she said excitedly. "I just heard in town that Zhenli is back and I had to hurry home! And, bring those boxes inside when you're done."

Zhenli was standing by the door when she made her grand entrance. "Well, you have made a full day of it," he said with a snarl, standing with his hands on his hips.

"Oh, there is so much to see!" she answered happily. "And, you are worth seeing, too!" She ran to him and kissed him with her brightly painted lips. "Have you seen our daughter? Isn't she the most precious thing?"

"Why wasn't she with you?" Zhenli asked coldly? "Or, more to the point, why weren't you here with her?"

"It's because your mother likes to have her here with her! I can't say that I blame her. She is so well behaved. I never saw a girl so quiet!"

"We will have to come back and visit sometime. But I am back, and we are going to live in Shanghai from now on." Charlie may have changed several shades of color, but it was dark and Zhenli could only hear her gasp at his announcement. "Now, come in. Mother has been holding dinner for you."

Zhenli found a place, in the suburbs of Shanghai that was as far from the old bar and her father's cronies as possible. It was in a clean and respectable Dutch community -- not as lively as the French quarter, or as fashionable as the English/American enclave, but Zhenli had made it clear to his wife that he was in charge of the money and that her days of free-wheeling in the stores were over. He proceeded to sit on his house, and all in it, like a mother hen.

The Shanghai Municipal Council was in the middle of a long struggle to revise its Land Regulations. Since the 1880 Ratepayers Meeting, which brought foreign and native residents into a common forum to set a Municipal Budget, the affairs of the city were left to the Council, made up of foreigners. At a meeting five years ago, they proposed sweeping changes to their constitution that would make them a "free city". However, any changes to their constitution had to be approved first by the Consular Body in Shanghai, then by the diplomatic corps in Beijing, and only then submitted to the Supreme Chinese Government in the Forbidden City -- and they were masters of indecision. Shanghai needed someone to take charge of its Municipal Police force which controlled the Chinese enclaves in town. Zhenli's name was submitted by his father's old friend, the Viceroy Li Hongzhang, and the Council approved the appointment out of hand. Zhenli wore his military uniform from his days as adjutant to the General in Beijing, and ran the Municipal Police Force office with an iron hand.

Chapter 14

Hong Kong and Shanghai

***

The New House

On the southwest end of Hong Kong Island, the newly named Bay of Aberdeen had grown to accommodate the British Navy, set well back up into the deep water harbor. The original small fishing village still clung to the north shore at the mouth of the bay, facing the open sea. Its floating market was an odd mixture of sampans and junks tied off to the shore and to each other. People walked from one boat to the next in an ad-hoc open air market. But by night, the lamps glowed inside each boat, illuminating a family home where dinners were cooked on charcoal woks, while above, men smoked their pipes in hammocks slung between the masts, silhouetted against a sunset over the South China Sea.

Bainong and Meiliang built a large house on a hill, overlooking the mouth of the bay. It was more than they really needed for their growing family but, they reasoned, "We can have the rest of the family come and visit." After the congestion and noise of Shanghai, the tranquility and the vast view of the open ocean was a relief.

The market was peopled by an endless mixture of Cantonese (mainland natives), Nyin-hak (Hakka people of northern origin), Miao tribesmen (who came down the rivers from Guangxi), Tanka boat people (traditionally landless, who lived in 'the Hok' along the seacoast), and any number of Indian, Javanese, and local islanders. Everyone took everyone else for what they proved to be; and the cast of characters changed daily as boats came and went. The seafood was kept and sold, live, from baskets that floated by each boat. Passing fishing boats sold their fresh catch to the people in the market and dead stock was cast out of the baskets back into the open bay.

The town of Aberdeen was named by the British after the Earl of Aberdeen. It serviced the British navy with its deep water bay and natural shelter from typhoons. It was a busy and growing area -- and that is why Bainong had picked it for his next printing venture. The city was growing to the east; land prices were going up and labor was scarce. But, that left older buildings on the west end available for sale. Bainong decided to buy a building near the house. It was made of mud brick, sheathed with baked tile grouted to the outside, and had a tile roof on wooden trussing. The property next door was also for sale, but it was in much worse condition. Nonetheless, Bainong settled on both properties and tore down the more dilapidated one, using its bricks to build a wall around both of the sites for security.

Meiliang liked the location because it was close enough to Canton to visit Bainong's parents and her own, by costal trade vessel. A good Sampan could make it to the mouth of the Pearl River by sundown and up to Sundak by noon the next day. They had their first baby in the new house. It was a boy who they named Shaodai.

The following month, a new printing press from Germany was delivered to the shop to join the older, lower-volume presses that Bainong had shipped down from Shanghai. His two employees were being trained on them and orders started coming in. The start-up went surprisingly smoothly and the presses began cranking out the new work.

From time to time, Bainong took the coastal trading boats up to Shanghai to meet Wen. Zhenli, of course, was also there, but he was getting bogged down in local politics, and often could not make even a casual luncheon. He explained that the city was building a system to pump clean water, under pressure, through a processing plant for drinking and for fire control. In the past, 'fire wells' were maintained throughout the city to supply fire brigades with enough water to dampen down large fires -- or at least keep them from spreading to adjoining buildings. There was also a movement in the city to install electricity to replace the old gas lamps. The city council listened to rumors that the new power source might kill people and burn buildings, but they ran trials and nothing happened. The gas company, which had opposed this new competition, started selling gas for cooking and heating and the pressure against the energy change abated. Also, the electricity plant started selling off steam and distilled water that were byproducts of the generation process -- the operation actually became a revenue source for the city.

Meixing occasionally came down to Shanghai with Wen, and spent the bulk of the day with her granddaughter. But, at the end of such visits, she was exhausted by Charlie's banality and triviality, so she eventually prevailed upon Wen to extend their visits to include a sail down to Hong Kong to see her other grandchild. There, on a hill overlooking the town and busy harbor, she could also indulge her new-found love of painting with water colors in the European style called Impressionism. The view to the west, the same perspective each time, held infinite variations and she hungrily attempted each nuance.

On other days, when it rained, Meiliang and her son, Shaodai, would take Grandma into town for a short shopping trip. On one such trip, they found that the English had established a public coach line to the north side of the island. They had been there once before when they visited Xiaohua's village near Canton. The north side was the more commercial side of the island, but more importantly for Meixing, there was a branch office of the Bank of England. Meixing led her daughter and grandson in through the great doors, which bespoke the grandeur of the British Empire, and went directly to one of the officers in the Trust Department.

"We would like to speak to someone regarding an account I have here, please," Meixing said to the bank clerk. They sat and waited, looking at the vaulted ceiling and huge, windowed walls that formed a bright gilded cage. The hollow sounds of footsteps and muffled conversations came and went like waves breaking along the coast.

After a while, a curious officer came out and inquired if indeed they had any business with the bank. Meixing almost bit her tongue through, "Imperious bastard!" she thought, but maintained her composure.

"I have a letter of credit which I would like to augment," she said coolly, pulling herself to her full height in front of him. She stood almost as tall as he. "Could you help me with that?"

He stepped back and showed her inside the gated railing to a desk. "May I see the Letter of Credit, please?"

She laid it on the table and sat back, a smile playing at the corners of her mouth. He read it, looked up, and then read it again.

"I'm sorry, Madam, what is it that you would like to do?"

"I would like my daughter, as well as myself, to have access to these funds," she replied. Meiliang looked at her curiously, obviously taken by surprise.

"If you will excuse me, I would like to show this to our Director," the clerk said.

Meixing held up her hand. "Could you bring him here, please? Such an important paper; I would just feel more comfortable not letting it get out of my sight."

"Of course, madam; I will be right back." The clerk laid the letter back on the desk in front of her and scurried off into an inner office.

"What are you up to with all this?" Meiliang was starting to get an idea this was more than a simple transaction. The man returned and ushered them into an inner office. It was a large room, with windows along the far wall that looked out over the inner harbor between Hong Kong Island and the Kawloon peninsula of the mainland. A massive desk dominated the center of the room and chairs were drawn up to it for Meixing and Meiliang, who held Shaodai in her lap. Once they were seated, the man from the outer office excused himself and left them with a large man, who sat across from them. He wore a swallow-tailed coat and a vest that sported a watch on the end of a chain.

"Now, how may I be of assistance to you ladies?" he began importantly, his voice was a very controlled baritone and his manner impeccable. Meixing laid the letter of credit on the desk. "Oh yes. Let me see." He studied it and sat back. "All right then; what is it that you would like to do?"

"My father gave me this to cover my finances, and I would like to include my daughter as a precaution against my age." Meiliang looked alarmed.

"This letter permits you to draw funds against the account, without limits." He looked back over the letter again. "That is an odd thing! It is a blank check. Is your father available to confirm these arrangements?"

Meixing produced other papers from her case. "My father died in 1873, but left this warrant to manage his business affairs and monies, which he had invested with your bank." The letter was written in Chinese, English, and French and was festooned with several seals and official stamps. "This is his official death certificate and this is his will," she said, handing the man two more documents.

"Shouldn't all of this be for his sons?" he asked under a furrowed brow.

"His sons, my brothers, died in the war against the Taiping. But we are under English common law in this arrangement, are we not? My father explained all of this to me before he died."

"Quite right you are! And it seems that you have all of the necessary paperwork to affect the transfer. Was it your plan to continue to allow our bank to manage this estate?" He had obviously become uneasy at the thought of the alternative.

"Yes. I think that is still the best course. For the moment I would only like to establish and fund an account here for my daughter, and to arrange to transfer control of the balance of the account to her in the event of my death."

The papers were prepared and Meiliang was instructed how to make withdrawals, should she have a need. Leaving the bank, they went to a restaurant and spent most of the afternoon discussing what had just happened. Lao Fang had spent all of his life operating the farm and investing the proceeds -- he had amassed a sizeable fortune. His trust in the English banking system was well founded and the investments had grown quite large.

"Under Chinese law, only the sons can inherit their father's estate," Meixing explained to her daughter. "But, my father died with no sons, so he entrusted me to manage his cash estate. Under English law, I can assign that control to you. And that is what I just did. Your brother, of course, will have the right, under Chinese law, to inherit the farm and your father's businesses along the rivers. There is more there than your brother knows -- but I am sure Charlie has that amount figured out to the last penny. I try not to think about that. But, when I die, you alone will control this cash estate; as long as you are in an English extraterritorial area or anywhere outside of China, you will still have that control."

***

Sensei

Zhenli's gaze went from the yardarm of a ship on the other side of the harbor to a fly that had avoided his riding crop all morning. It settled on the calf of his boot, and he was taking aim when the door burst open.

"Captain; there's a problem at the jail! I think you should be there."

"Don't you knock at my door any more?" He righted himself behind the desk and glowered at the anxious jailor.

"My apologies, sir! But our night patrol has put us in a problem."

Zhenli stood up and tugged his tunic coat straight under the pistol belt. "What have they done now?"

"There was a fight at the Qingshan bar. It must have taken all of the night patrol to break it up and they dragged everyone into jail. They really had to bust some of them up pretty badly to get them to stop fighting. The doctor is over there now."'

"What is the problem? They often have fights at the Qingshan."

"This time they picked up several Japanese sailors!"

"Are they crazy? You know that is a treaty violation! We could loose our heads over this." They both ran down to the jail and into a storm of indignantly cursing Japanese. The doctor was already sorting out the Japanese sailors from the rest of the inmates and tending to their wounds first. Two Chinese nurses were cleaning cuts with tincture and bandages while being groped by their patients. The sailors were alternately taunting and demeaning, solicitous and abusive. Their officer sat in the corner, awaiting a more worthy adversary who would receive his anger.

"Are you the one in charge of these coolie thugs?" He hissed at Zhenli when he entered. "You will die for laying hands on Japanese Imperial Sailors! You know that, don't you?" He had a cruel laugh and stood up to face Zhenli directly. There was a moment of silent recognition as each man focused on the other.

"Sensei Manashi! Shitsumashite!"

"Abunai! Your Japanese never was good enough to get you out of something like this." They both broke out into smiles and circled each other.

"Well. You're commander of the police? They must be in more trouble here than we were led to believe."

"And you. Captain of a ship? They must have trained you well at the Shao Lin Temple."

"Oh, today the better military academies are in Japan! You must come there and study someday. You know that we have a new treaty with the British. My whole crew and I will soon be leaving to train in the British Royal Navy."

"I have never wanted to leave China. From what I have seen of foreigners.... "

"Oh, you Chinese! What is it? This dung heap! You realize that the whole place is rotting from the top down, don't you? China is like an overripe piece of fruit and the worms are having a feast. That crazy lady that you call Empress surrounds herself with advisors who pull her this way and that. The whole system is at odds with itself. Wake up!"

"We are growing stronger," Zhenli countered defensively. "It is true, we are taking our time doing it. But, we are building, using the barbarian's tools to defeat him in the end."

"Oh come on now! The end is here! Your progress is like waves building onto the shore only to collapse on top of the remains of the one that collapsed before. The shoreline remains in the same place."

"We have a navy and an army of millions."

"What navy? The French sank those buckets of rust in Fuzhou. And the army that you claim -- it would be blown away just by the wind from our new weapons. China is living a delusion."

They both sat down on the bench and watched the nurses and sailors in the other room. "What do you plan to do about all this?" Sensei asked.

Zhenli shook his head and looked at his boots. "If I can get past this, I'll have to do more training with the night patrols."

"No, I mean when our diplomats take another bite out of the plumb. They will want some heads to roll -- and money, lots of money. Face it. You're in some hot wan-tan."

"I'll have to go back to Daddy. My father is in league with the higher ups. He'll get me out of this, I hope. By the way, how did things work out with your father? Did he ever get his name back?"

"No, not while he lived. He got consumption in the monastery and died. But the emperor did restore the family to nobility. My eldest brother was the only one to get a title and peerage. Now he sits in the Diet and makes the laws. The rest of us have to work for a living," he laughed.

"How is the new government working out? You have an Emperor, but he is not all- powerful?"

"It is bumpy. But if you remember, the Tokugawa Shogunate started to fall apart when the Shogun died; at that time the Emperor had no power. Ii Naosuke took over the government, got rid of his opponents, and signed the treaties that opened up our ports to the west. He exercised too much power and did not honor our national essence. Then, I think I told you, my father and several of the other members of the Samurai Bakufu killed Naosuke in 1860, and forced the government to restore the Emperor to a more central role with many advisors.

"They didn't really mean to put the sixteen-year-old Meiji Emperor in charge; they were the older ones, each of them only in their thirties and forties. They felt older and full of power. What they did was to write up a Charter Oath of five parts that gave our leaders a common goal and pathway toward a Western-style government. The Domains were abolished and samurai feudalism was replaced with Prefectures run by a bureaucracy. The armies were formed by conscription; that way samurai and commoners serve alongside each other.

"The last uprising of the Samurai was in 1873. Saigo Takamori and other powerful men wanted to war against Korea for its minerals and agriculture. But, Iwakura Tonomi, a noble, and his study group had just returned from a tour of Europe and America, and had seen Western strength. They would not allow a war with Korea till we had become stronger. The rebellion ended with Saigo's death at his own hand. Now, the government is formulating a constitution, which will bring Japan in line with the Western governments. Hopefully, we will soon shake off the last of our old-world thinking."

"But, if you make war on Korea, you make war on China," Zhenli pointed out. "They have always been a tributary state to us."

Akiro Manashi stood up and smiled. "Not so! In '76, we negotiated a treaty with Korea in Ganghwa. They are free from Beijing's meddling and have opened trade with Japan. Now, we are playing Europe's game."

"Game indeed!" Zhenli shook his head ruefully. "Your games left many dead in '84, when your henchmen took over the government in a false revolt. And then many more had to die returning the government to the people of Korea. The Treaty of Tientsin now keeps both our countries from sending in armies, just to prevent such interventionist games."

"History will be written by others," Akiro said solemnly. "For the moment, I must take my men back to our ship. We are being sent to England to study in their military academies and to serve on their ships while they build modern cruisers and torpedo boats for our new navy. I hope this does not go too harshly against you." They bowed and parted.

***

Contrition

Lao Wen was sitting in front of the farmhouse, watching the sun set and listening to his new wind-up Victrola when Zhenli rode up. One of the soldiers was headed back from the fields and took his horse.

"Could you walk him and give him some water?" Zhenli asked him. "I'm sorry to put the chore on you, but I have to talk with my father."

Wen looked up curiously, hearing the urgency in Zhenli's voice. "Please, tell me it is not as bad as it sounds," he said, as he lifted the needle off the cylinder and the music stopped.

"You will have to tell me," Zhenli responded, wringing his hands. "I hate to dump this on you, but my men may have put me in a bad spot. They rather forcibly arrested some Japanese Imperial Sailors in a bar fight last night."

"I hope they made it worthwhile. How bad was it?"

"Well, no one died," Zhenli said, sinking into a chair next to his father. "And they were playing with the nurses while they were getting bandaged up. As it turned out, I knew their Captain; he was one of my teachers in school."

"Will he bring charges against you?"

"I don't know. He might have to. But, he seemed all right about it when he left."

Wen stood up and started for the house. "We should probably visit their legation in Shanghai and make our apologies -- just to head off any problem."

The carriage ride was long and bumpy, but it gave them a chance to talk. Wen had been keeping up with the changing events in Japan -- and the growing concerns in Beijing.

"The Japanese are melting a lot of iron, much more than they need for domestic consumption," he said to Zhenli. "Their shipyards are also busy making state-of-the-art vessels with twin screw propellers. Someday, they will be faster than anything we have and much better armed. They use the latest German blast furnaces to smelt the ore, and reverberatory furnaces to alloy it. So they can make naval guns to challenge anything afloat today. For us to go to war with Japan is a perilous option. Even the reactionary bunch in the capital has to realize that."

When they reached the Japanese Legation in Shanghai, they found it a foreboding old building in a remote section north of the main harbor area. Unlike the other legations in town, armed soldiers stood guard with bayonets fixed to their rifles. The attitude of the guard in charge was also pointed. "Where are your papers, Chinaman?" he growled.

Although Wen wore his official robes and Zhenli his uniform, they still had to wait in an outer office all that afternoon and much of the second day, before even a third-level clerk would see them. "What is your business here?" the clerk asked coldly. He was dressed in a black robe with a cap over his wire rimmed glasses.

"We came to express our regret for an unfortunate incident which involved some of your Imperial Sailors," Wen said humbly.

"We know about your stupidity! We don't need your groveling as well!" the clerk snapped. He waved some papers in the air over his head. "The matter is closed and you would do well to punish your own men and let it rest." He turned and stalked out the room.

On the street, Wen removed his cap and looked at it. "I thought he might have melted my button!" They laughed and went into a quiet restaurant for tea.

***

A New Book

Meiliang invited the man into her office and he put a book on the desk in front of her. His rough sailor's hands politely removed his cap and he pulled up a chair on the opposite side of her desk.

"Is this a book that you wrote?" Meiliang asked. "No, I see it is not. I don't believe I know this author; Mary Baker Glover Eddy. Has she written many books?"

"She has written many pamphlets and sermons, but I believe this is her only book," the man replied.

"Sermons? Is she a preacher as well?" She opened to the title page and read 'Science and Health, Volume II.' "Well, I see that she has some readership already. Is she quite famous?"

"Her teachings are growing in America and she is called upon to lecture quite often throughout the country."

"Which scriptures is she talking about?" Meiliang asked.

"Her teachings are all based on the New Testament of the Christian Bible. In particular, she advocates a thorough familiarity with the works of Jesus Christ and how he brought healings in his time through the spirit of the Holy Ghost. He admonished his disciples, and all future members of the faith to continue healing through faith and understanding."

"But she is not rewriting the Bible, is she?" Meiliang looked concerned. "We had one of our own people use the Bible as a pretext for rebellion. He did a lot of evil in the name of God. Over the course of fifteen years, tens of millions died from all that!"

"Oh Lord, she is nothing like that," the sailor said, shaking his head. "This book is about how Christ's teaching has shown us how to heal, using the inspired word of the Bible."

"Did you mean to have us publish this book for you? I mean, who would pay for it?"

"I have no authorization or expectation about all that. I certainly don't have much money of my own. I was hoping to put this book into the hands of someone who might study it and perhaps help spread the word of Mrs. Eddy. In any event, you will certainly benefit from reading this book as well as the Bible," he said.

Meiliang thanked him and added the volume to her stack of things to take out to the farm. She was a voracious reader, as was her mother, and the farm was the perfect setting to enjoy the leisurely consumption of new ideas. The titles of other books and pamphlets in the stack ranged from flower arranging to political movements of the time. There were also many pamphlets and letters advocating the formation of a constitutional monarchy patterned after the Meiji restoration or the American model. "Ah, seditious material!" she mused, "But, I think Mother will like this one better."

Meixing had gotten weaker this past winter, and couldn't make the trip to Hong Kong as often as she had in the past. But it was now Spring. With one baby in a perambulator and another just starting life inside of her, the daughter would make the trip instead on the next coastal ferry.

Things were going so well that Bainong was reluctant to leave his shop, but Meiliang persuaded him. With bags in tow, they made the evening ship and took a sleeper compartment -- quite the luxury for the times. In the morning, when they arrived in Shanghai, they were surprised to catch her father in town. After cajoling them to join him, they all went out to Zhenli's house in the suburbs for a visit with Charlie and her daughter. Yili was almost two years old and talked all the time. Shaodai, Meiliang's son, was only fourteen months old and could form only a few words. Charlie just had to make jokes about the 'little Englishman's' accent. They stayed about as long as they could stand, and then returned to town to resume their trip out to the farm.

Meixing was feeling better, Wen told them, and the sight of everyone in her living room would be the best medicine she could have. But, the best of all would be the baby, Shaodai. During their stay at the farm, Meiliang noticed that Meixing asked Wen a lot of questions about the outside world, as though she were taking notes for her father; she often found herself thinking about him these days. In the evenings, they read the stacks of books and pamphlets that Meiliang had brought with her.

But the weekend was running out and Bainong and Meiliang had to return to Hong Kong. "Why don't you come with us?" Meiliang said. "The sea air always makes you feel so much better." Wen protested that he had too much to do to get ready for the first harvest and he would have to stay home, but he urged Meixing to go, promising that he would join her in a week or so.

***

A Lecture

The Hong Kong College of Medicine had sent a flyer to be printed at Bainong's shop. Meiliang showed it to her mother. "Why don't we go over and hear this speaker?" she suggested. "I understand he is an advisor to the Emperor and quite a reformer. It should be interesting to see how much 'reform' he is willing to talk about."

Meixing read the flyer and sat back with a sigh. "This man is only forty-two! It's not that I feel so old, really. It just seems that everyone else is getting younger and younger." She picked it up again and said, "Your grandfather would have loved this. They may finally be getting rid of 'That Bunch' up in Beijing -- the pity is that he's not here to see it," she said sadly, looking out beyond the flyer with tears glistening in the corners of her eyes.

Meiliang sat next to her and took her hand. "Then, you'll go for him. He would like that. And, you can tell him all about it."

Meixing slapped at her daughter's hand with the paper. "You know me too well!"

The first day of the lecture series included long laudatory speeches about the founding of the college in 1887, only two years previous. Then they presented the members of the two attending classes, who stood for recognition. Faculty members were almost all Westerners;

understandable, since they were, after all, teaching Western medical practices. They also stood and were acknowledged with a round of applause. Then the laboratory assistants were called upon to stand. "Good heavens, they will be calling out the janitor before long!" Meixing said, laughing at her own joke.

Finally, Kang Youwei, the featured speaker, mounted the platform. His voice was clear and strong, but the two women were glad that they had come early enough to get seats close to the stage. His accent was clearly from Guangdong, but his thoughts were, just as clearly, not traditional Chinese. Carefully, he wove a picture of a new China that would incorporate some of the 'benefits' of the Western models of 'governmental administration' and 'higher liberal education'. He was particularly careful not to make statements that might come back to haunt him -- or get him killed when he returned to Beijing. He advocated equality of the sexes and participation by the public in political affairs. It was an interesting dance.

When the lecture was over, there was a luncheon on the lawns of the college. Meixing and Meiliang had an opportunity to meet some of the students. The top student in the first class was Sun Yat-sen. He and his friends, who called themselves the 'Si Da Kou' (The Four Great Gangs) were always together -- and today was no different. They went from table to table, making sure to talk with everyone, asking attendees where everyone came from and why they had come to the lecture. Meiliang flashed the promotional flyer. "I am the printer who made this." she said. "And, this is my mother."

"You are from the land of "Liberté, égalité, et fraternité, n'est pas?" he asked.

Meixing laughed and looked at her daughter. "Yes, I guess we still have the eyes. Actually, my mother was from France," she answered. "The rest of our family are all Chinese. Mais, vous parle très bien la langue de ma mère."

Sun laughed self consciously. "No, we learn only what we must. I did learn English when I was living in Hawaii with my brother. He enrolled me in the British Anglican Iolani School and the Oahu College. But, he shipped me back as soon as he could so I wouldn't become a Christian -- he failed. I received my baptism three years ago."

"And now, you are studying Western medicine! How heretical is that?" Meiliang blushed to tease a stranger so boldly and threw up her fan to hide her smile.

"It is a new age. I am more concerned with the future of China."

"How do you envision that future?" Meiliang ventured.

"That would take more time than I am allowed here today. We are obliged to circulate and talk with all of the guests. I hope to have the opportunity to go into that with you at length some other day. Do you attend a school here in the city?"

"No, not now," Meiliang said, her voice trailing off as she thought about it. "Do you have many girls in your school?"

"No, actually there are none in the medical school. But, there are other schools in the city that teach girls. You might want to look into one of them. Now, we really must go. Thank you for attending the lecture and I hope to meet you again."

"What an intense man! Did you see his eyes when he talked about the future of China?"

"Watch it, my daughter! Intense young men can be quite distracting."

"Oh, Mother!" Meiliang laughed, waving off the idea. But she blushed again, just a little.

***
A Letter from Zhenli

"Look at this," Bainong said, waving a letter from her brother in Shanghai.

Meiliang smiled and held it ceremoniously at arms length. "Well, this is a first! I can't remember him ever sending us a letter before. Are they having another baby?"

"No, he wants me to meet with him on my next trip to Shanghai. He wants to introduce me to some missionary who is getting into printing bibles. Maybe I could sell him some of my old presses."

"Oh, now that would be cruel!" Meiliang laughed. "Aren't there enough bibles around already?"

"I don't know. Zhenli says the missionary is only twenty-six, but he was educated in America and thinks he wants to get into business now. I guess the ministry doesn't pay all that well."

"When will you be going?" she asked.

"Not this month; there is just too much at the shop. But, you'll be going there with your mother. Why don't you check this out while you're in town."

***
The Minister

Meiliang met the Minister in front of his church. It was a small building in the French Concession, not at all like the Catholic edifice down the street, with its bell and brass fittings. Charles Jones Soong was a short young man with piercing eyes and dressed in Western clothes. When he spoke in Chinese, his accent was from the Island of Hainan, off of the southern coast; when he spoke his American form of English, the accent was a mixture of Bostonian and Virginian. But he was dashingly handsome and had a quick banter that was engaging.

He had married a fellow church member, Ni Kwi-tseng, shortly after he returned to China in 1886. They had had their first child, a girl named Ai-ling, just this past summer. He was a Methodist minister, but his ministry was not as fulfilling as he had hoped, and he thought that he could do better by printing Chinese bibles for other missionaries.

"I know a bit about the printing trade and I hope you won't be offended if I warn you about all of the work involved." Meiliang said.

"I have no problem with the physical work," he assured her." He pointed at the paint brushes and tools in a box by the front door of the church. "A Minister must be a jack of all trades these days. But it is not the kind of physical work that pays the bills. It seems that there will be a lot more bills than I had thought and my family has only started growing."

"Well, I can empathize with you about the problems of a family. We will be having our second baby this fall," Meiliang said with a smile, instinctively stroked her belly. "Have you found any printing equipment? Or selected a location to get started?"

"Actually, I found a printer who is ready to retire and I thought that I could work for him and then buy his business out of my earnings. Would you be able to go there with me and look over his operation? You said you grew up in the trade, so perhaps you would be able to see things that I couldn't."

Later that day, they stood on a side street in front of a small shop with a hand-lettered sign over the door, 'Meihua Printing Press'. An old man, with a paper hat rolled up like a collar around the top of his head, opened the door. The smoke from the cigarette which dangled off his lower lip licked up his face and across his squinted left eye. "So, you are back! You gunna buy my place?" he asked gruffly.

"I have brought someone to look it over with me, if you don't mind," the Minister answered.

The old man curled his lip as he looked sidewise at Meiliang. "Why not?!" He stood to the side and waved them in.

The light was scarcely enough to keep them from tripping over the clutter on the floor. The presses were old and there was nothing on the drying racks. The stock of paper was dirty on the edges and the room smelled of cheap ink.

"Do you work alone?" Meiliang asked, as their eyes became accustomed to the gloom.

"Yeah, this is my baby," the owner answered. "The young man could make a good living if he puts his mind to it!" He stood wiping his hands with a dirty rag, which could improve nothing.

"Do you have any work? Are there any orders waiting to be printed?" she asked.

"No," he said, pulling himself to his full height by tugging at his waist band. "I'm up to date. Got it all done, soon as it came in."

"How much are you asking for this?" Meiliang asked, looking him straight in they eye. The price dropped and dropped again as they spoke. "It seems to me you have taken all of the value out of this place already. The presses are old and there are no trade orders or 'good will' to speak of! I will give you the price of the building. No more!" She opened her handbag and took out three hundred Hong Kong Pound notes. She turned her head and winked at Soong. "Give him the key and let's be done with this!" Minister Soong stood speechless as the old man fumbled with the string tied to his pants that held the key, and the exchange was made. They watched him shuffle out the front door.

The minister turned to her. "Why did you do that? I didn't want you to get so involved. What if I can't make a go of it?"

"Then, I will sell the building and make a profit," she said with a smile. "All that I ask of you is that you clean this place up and get some lights. There are some men I know in this city who can help you to make these presses useful again. My husband trained them when we had our shop here years ago."

"But I have no money," he protested.

"None of us had money when we started our businesses. My husband and I were helped along by people that we did not know. Now it is my pleasure to help you. If you clean up the building for me, I will hire the men for you. And you can buy the building from me for what I paid for it, when you are able." They then went to her brother's office, and had the deal recorded in the town's record of property.

Chapter

15

Home and Abroad

***

An Imperial Mission

Lao Wen was happy to see 'his girls' and Zhenli returning to the farm. He had not been able to get everything done around the farm as quickly as he had hoped, and had not been able to get down to Shanghai as promised, much less Hong Kong. But he was excited and had news of his own to share. He had received a letter, wrapped in Imperial silk, from Beijing.

"Li Hongzhang has another mission for me." He beamed as he unfolded the letter. His wife and daughter were somewhat reluctant to join in his enthusiasm till they learned a bit more about the contents of the letter.

"Oh, come on now! This looks like it might be interesting - - you might even want to come with me." He explained the Emperor's commission, but the reluctance on his wife and daughter's faces did not go away. "The Emperor needs to know more about the Korean people's feelings on the growing Japanese involvement in their country. There are some members of the Emperor's court who want us to just drive the Japanese out of Korea, and others who are unwilling to engage the Japanese militarily. Our Beiyang Navy is supposed to be stronger than the whole Japanese Navy, and the Beiyang Army is larger than anything that the Japanese could field. The question is: 'Would the Korean people support us if we were to reaffirm our influence over the Korean Monarchy?'

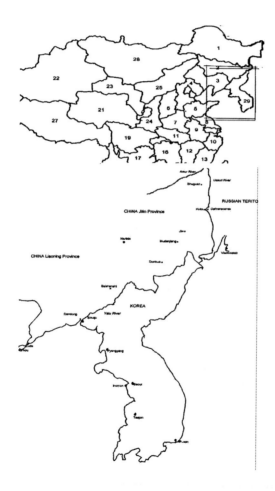

Map of Korea

"So, you see? It is just a trip, a vacation. We could sail across to the southern port of Pusan and work our way up to Seoul. Then, we could travel like tourists around the back roads and meet the people on our way up to Pyongyang. A little north, we will cross the border at Sinuiju and we're back in Chinese territory. From Lushun it is just a short sail across Bo Hai to Tianjin. Then I could show you Beijing!"

"I am exhausted just thinking about it!" said Meixing. "You go, if you must, but that is much more travel than I could tolerate. And I certainly do not want to end my days over there, only to become some 'hungry ghost' wandering around Korea for eternity."

"Oh I would bring you back to the farm. I would miss you in the afterlife." Wen wrapped his arm around her shoulder and poked her in the ribs.

"Why would you want to go to Korea?" Zhenli asked as he came in, banging the doorway with several bags and an armload of books. "I hear it's the new 'North Japan'."

"That is just the problem! Li wants me to check out our popularity with the Korean people. It will be more like a vacation with a purpose. I have been getting stale just sitting around the farm and I was trying to get your mother to join me." Wen folded the letter and put it back in his pocket with a sigh.

Zhenli shrugged, "After that Imperial sailor incident, I have to personally supervise the training of my men and run nightly checks to make sure they don't foul up again. That trip of yours sounds like a great adventure though."

The ladies worked on dinner as Wen and Zhenli brought in the rest of the baggage and shopping from Hong Kong as well as Shanghai. Then Wen and his son went outside to light up a pipe and discuss the problem that concerned the Emperor.

"Things are in a real state of flux over there," Wen pointed to the east with the stem of his pipe. "Korea still sends tribute to our Emperor, but the Japanese are up to their usual intrigues. They have trade advisors and emissaries from the Emperor of Japan bribing and manipulating the Korean ministers, who want to advance Japan's agendas and get the inside advantage at court. We have General Yuan Shikai over there advising the King; he is a good soldier, but a bit brusque for a diplomat. The people are caught in the middle -- overtaxed and under-protected. It is a powder keg in the middle of a grass fire."

"So, this is where you want to spend your retirement?" Zhenli asked. "It sounds pretty dangerous to me."

"It will be more dangerous to more people if we do nothing," Wen replied. "The Japanese government is seeing opportunity in the midst of the chaos. Not only could we lose the tribute payments, but our influence with a long-term ally. Furthermore, we stand to lose a buffer state, and that would put us much closer to a war with Japan. I must do what I can. It's my Confucian duty again." He laughed, but balled his fingers into a tight fist.

Lao Wen left for Shanghai two days later. "I'll try to make it back as soon as I can," he said to Meixing. "Take good care of the farm and try to visit the grandchildren. I know that it is tiring, but you should make the trip just for the exercise. And, try not to get into trouble," he teased.

***
Korea

The next day, Meiliang appeared at Zhenli's office door, ashen and sweaty as she burst through the doorway.. "Hello?" he said, surprised by both her visit and her appearance. "Oh, what is the matter? You look like a ghost. I know it's not that hot out there."

"Do you know what our father has gotten himself into?" she grumbled, setting a stack of books and newspapers on his desk.

"What is all this? I thought you went home yesterday."

"No, I wanted to find out more about where father was going -- and I am afraid that he is in real danger. I haven't really followed what was going on in Korea. That place is a war zone, just waiting to happen!" She was shaking and shaken. From her pallor, Zhenli assumed that she hadn't slept much, if any, the night before and probably not eaten either. She paced around his office looking out the window to the east.

"Sit down," Zhenli said, trying to calm her. "Where are you getting this information from, anyway?"

"I guess you don't read the Korean papers either. Look at these; 'Hanseong Hunbo' (the official government gazette, three times monthly), 'Hanseong Jubo' (the Seoul Weekly) and 'Ganjo Shimpo' (the Seoul News). They are a few months old, but translated and printed in Chinese. Korea is a country on fire. Do you know that they are modernizing faster than the Japanese?! Of course, the country is being run by a woman, Queen Min."

"Wait a minute!" Zhenli laughed. "There is a King over there, too, isn't there?"

"Yes, but he has been a playboy most of his life." She was putting on her serious face, and Zhenli was taking this all too lightly. "She is the one who turned things around. His family wasn't even royal, just a poor relative clan that they put on the throne when the last king died without an heir. His father was his regent till the king married and came of age. The father was such a bastard! He isolated the country, killed off the Catholic priests, and got into fights with the French for it. He wouldn't let the Americans search for a ship and its sailors, which were lost at sea in Korean waters a couple of years ago, and actually shelled their rescue ships. He raised taxes till families were selling their lands just to stay alive. He wouldn't even trade with the Japanese. He was just a ruthless tyrant, keeping alive the nickname 'The Hermit Kingdom'!"

"OK! But the Queen, she changed all that?"

"Yes, when they got married in 1866. She was from a family as lowly as his and everyone thought she would just follow along and look pretty. But, she was a reader and a learner. Most of all, she was interested in real politics -- the operation of the tools of power behind the scenes. In 1872, when he came of age, she got the court to recognize her husband as the king in his own right. The King's father was forced to relinquish the regency and retire to his estate. As much as she was political, the King was not. While he was still being the playboy, she filled all of the key political positions with her relatives."

"He sounds like my kind of guy!" Zhenli laughed.

"The next year, when the Japanese sent a mission to announce The Meiji Restoration, which put the Emperor of Japan in the constitutional center of their government, she refused to receive them. The Japanese then sent battleships into Korean territorial waters around Ganhwa Island, and were fired upon by shore batteries. At that time, Japan wasn't strong enough financially or militarily to pursue the issue, but came back in force in 1876, with six ships. They were able to force the King to accept the Ganhwa Treaty which opened Korea to trade, made them pay reparations for their last encounter, and disavowed any Korean subjugation to China."

"Wait a minute, they still send us tribute. They still are under our protection, aren't they?" Zhenli was shaking his head.

"Well, not exclusively. Queen Min was playing some games with the diplomacy. She didn't want to cut Korea free from China, but she had to sign the treaty to keep the

Japanese from an armed intervention in Korea. In 1874, she had sent a diplomatic mission to Japan to learn more about this new regional power and she was shocked to find that, outside of China, Tokyo and Osaka had become the preeminent cities of the east, outshining Seoul and Inch'on. With recent arms purchases from France and England and the products from their own shipyards, the Japanese navy had also far surpassed Korea's and, possibly, China's as well."

"She should have known about the naval program; that was no secret -- if she was paying attention," Zhenli kidded her. "But I can't believe that it's true about our Navy"

"Now, who is not paying attention?" Meiliang shot back. "Min's advisors, the scholars, and the members of the Yangban were isolationists and hid as much as they could from her. They advised rejection of the influence of the Japanese and all Westerners. When this became clear, she proceeded to restructure the government to expand trade. Military students were sent to Japan and China for training and familiarization with their Navies."

"That sounds like the same thing that the Japanese are doing in England and France."

"In 1881, Min sent a large fact-finding mission to Japan for an extended stay to further ameliorate the relationship between the countries. But, the reactionaries, led by Min's father-in-law, hatched a plot to overthrow the king and queen, who managed to escape the onslaught and called on Yuan Shikai and the Chinese legation force to put down the revolt."

Zhenli added, "I guess that was when Li Hongzhang and the Korean envoys in Beijing agreed to send 4,500 Chinese troops to restore order and arrest the King's father. I heard he was tried for treason by the Koreans, but they sent him back to China for imprisonment."

"Right, then Queen Min and the King returned to power and to their progressive programs. But secretly, the King signed a treaty with the Japanese for reparations for lives and property lost during the rebellion, as well as granting permission for the Japanese to station troops in Seoul at their legation. Min responded by opening ports to the Chinese, even though they were closed to the Japanese, and appointed a Chinese commander to take charge of the Korean army. The next year, in 1883, she had American instructors open an English language school, and also started a school for girls in her quest to put women's rights on a par with men's. That lasted only about a year before there was a palace coup, and our troops, under Yuan Shih-kai, had to crush it in order to return the King and Queen to their thrones. Again the Japanese bullied them into signing the Hanseong Treaty -- to pay more reparations.

"China started loosing ground diplomatically to Japan, and Li signed off on the Tianjin 'agreement' in April of 1885. That treaty supposedly removed the troops of both countries from Korea. But, Queen Min secretly kept 2000 Chinese troops, disguised as Joseon police and merchants, 'just in case'. The Korean Army was being trained by the Americans and the Germans. In 1888, the ports and customs were opened under a plan drawn up by the Englishman, Sir Robert Heart, who helped us so much."

"Then, what is the problem?" This was getting to be a bit too much for Zhenli. "It sounds like Father is there in boom times," he said.

"I'm afraid the only boom he will hear is from Japanese cannon," Meiliang retorted. "The Japanese thought the young King and Queen would just open the country to them, but it turns out that they would rather run their own country. The Japanese military is not taking this lightly. They need the minerals and food that Korea can supply, but they don't want to pay full price on the open market. And they make no bones about it! They want to 'protect' Korea and are more than a little afraid that Korea might be able to protect itself. It has been three years and the Japanese continue growing stronger and less patient. That whole thing might blow up any day!" Meiliang finally sat down.

"So you think that they are just looking for an excuse to get around the treaties?"

"Right! They have a small garrison in Seoul, as do we. But there are more and more indications that any opposition movement might give the Japanese all the excuse they would need to invade on a large scale."

Zhenli looked at one of the newspapers that she had thrown on his desk. "Well, you and I can't just rush over there and get him out. We will just have to keep our ears open and read these newspapers. Do you get them in Hong Kong?"

"I don't know. I never thought to look, but I will." She stood and gathered her things.

***

A New Student

Bainong was relieved when Meiliang and Shaodai waved at him through the window of his office. "Where have you two been? I was expecting you yesterday."

Meiliang told him about her father's mission and her research. "I can't really do anything for him, but I would feel more comfortable if I knew more about what is going on over there. I was thinking about taking a class or meeting some people from there. I'm sure there are Koreans going to school over here. I'm going to check it out."

"What does your mother think about all this?"

"She was concerned just about travel in general. She couldn't take on that much herself, but he was so determined. I didn't learn about the rest of this till I got back to Shanghai. I think I'll let her deal with what she already knows, and not add to her worries for the moment."

The next week, Meiliang found herself in the Admissions Office of the Hong Kong College of Medicine. "No, we do not yet have a program for young women." the administrator told her, looking somewhat bemused at her even thinking such a thing. "Perhaps one of the religious orders would be more receptive." He turned and went back to his desk.

She walked, somewhat stiffly, out of the office and out of the building. She took a deep breath and decided not to scream. There were food vendors in the large courtyard, and she went to one of the stands.

"I'll have an orange juice, please."

"I'll have one as well." The voice was familiar and she turned to find the student, Sun Yat-sen, at her elbow. "How very nice to see you here once again!" he said.

She looked down, feeling a warmth in her cheeks. "I'm sorry. I was quite within myself, there. Wherever did you come from?"

"I go to school here, you know." He was beaming, and waved her over to a bench nearby. He set his books down on the corner of the seat and dusted off the bench with a cavalier wave of his scarf. "Come! Tell me what it is that has you so 'within yourself.'"

They sat and talked for over an hour. She told him of her father's commission in Korea and her concerns for his safety. "Ah! So you are an Imperialist, then. I don't think your father would approve of your clandestine meeting with the rebel faction, now would he?" He laughed, and she caught her breath as he threw his head back.

"I actually wanted to start taking classes here myself," she said, "Or at least meet some Korean students, so that I could better understand what is going on over there."

"Do you really? When there is so much to be done right here in our own country?" He sounded amazed. "Korea and Japan are well along with their modernizing, while China strangles itself on its own past. We have a desperate need to break free, to drop the pretenses and the games. The court in Beijing is being isolated by its own intransigence. Look! Who runs the country? The real power, today, is in the modern systems of commerce and diplomacy. What do we have in China? There are petty criminals in every branch of the Qing system and they have debased Confucianism. Generals run their own armies, and admirals have their navies -- but they don't depend on one another."

"When the French wiped out the Fujian Fleet, did the Nanyang Fleet sail from Shanghai? Did the Guangdong Fleet come down the Perl River and help? And, let's not forget the crown jewel, The Great Beiyang Fleet. Did Li Hongzhang's navy get any saltwater on their hulls? NO! They represent their own interests. There is no one, great country anymore. Just a bunch of petty warlords tangled in the tatters of a rotting shroud." He had sweat on his brow and the veins stood out visibly along his neck. Then suddenly, he relaxed, sat back on the bench, and wiped his forehead with the sleeve of his robe.

There was a pause, and Meiliang leaned toward him. "What do you think we could do?"

Sun turned his head toward her and smiled. "Do you want to join a rebellion?"

"Well, no! I mean, I am Chinese! What are you saying?"

"No, no! It's not like we were taking up arms against a good king," he reassured her. "Our present system is rotten and has to change or be replaced. We have given them over two hundred years to get it right. I think we have to look at a change at the top. And that will have to start at the bottom. We have to align the body of the people through information -- to educate the country from within."

"And this means what, for me?" Meiliang asked.

"You are a printer, are you not?"

"My husband has a printing shop in Aberdeen. But, he is not one to give away his services nor the paper and ink. If there is something you need printed, I could help you pay for it. I just don't think he is ready to step out, politically."

"Pardon my lack of understanding here. You, but not him...."

"Oh, my family has money, down through my mother's side. I have access to funds that my husband doesn't know about. It is not treason, you know! Actually, it is still my mother's account, but I can draw off of it. "

"Ah ha! So there is already a rebellion in your life." They laughed and discussed the nature and content of the flyers that he might want to circulate.

"Hey, you lay about; it is class time!" A young man ran up to them.

"This is my friend Guan Jingliang," Sun said. "He is one of the infamous Four Great Gangs."

"I am Wen Meiliang. I believe we met at the lecture the other day."

"Oh yes, I remember. You were here with your mother. But, I must take this charmer off of your arm and drive him on to the study of Western medicine."

Sun stood and took up his books. "We will meet again, I am sure." And the two young men dashed off toward the school. Meiliang wandered around the bookstores and newspaper stalls, finally returning home loaded with reading materials on Korea.

***

Rebellion

Meiliang read through all of the papers, searching for anything on Korea. There was precious little, but there were several letters on the Commentary page regarding that other subject. "Have you read about all of this dissention against the Qing?" she asked Bainong.

He looked over from his chair. "Taxes again?"

"No, this is more fundamental than that. The people are really getting sick and tired of the Qing losing ground to the English and everyone else. All of the taxes go to pay off a phony debt to the English and the Emperor has nothing to run the country. A lot of people are talking about withholding taxes altogether."

"Now, that is the sort of talk that can get you in trouble. Bad as they are, the Qing are still the ones with their name on the debt. Throw them out and the English will be looking for somebody else to pay the old treaty obligations. So, what you're talking about is not just the Qing, but all the Westerners that hold our debts as well; they would resist any change."

"That was quite insightful, Bainong," she answered, surprised at her husband's knowledge on the subject. "We never discuss politics and I never knew that you even had an interest in it, much less such a grasp of the issues."

"Thank you for your one-handed applause," he laughed ruefully.

"Oops, a little condescending? I am sorry. But, we should talk about it; I mean citizen to citizen. Do you think the Manchurians can ever get us out of all of this?"

"No, I don't! They are so weak that the colonials will keep adding debt and protecting us from our own fate as long as they can milk us."

"Wow! That is quite a statement. Then, what is the answer?"

"It is a terrible answer, Meiliang -- it is war, civil war! It must be catastrophic, so sweeping that it will bankrupt the current order and make real compromise the only useful answer. Everyone knows it; that is what keeps the Qing in power. The answer is too terrible."

"What about education? I mean flyers and posters. What if we tell the people...."

"That is the first step in rebellion. And, I'm not sure that it isn't time for all that."

"I thought I was living with an old fuddy-duddy. Now you sound like some of the students at the college."

"I got all that from your father. The great family Kwan sees the cracks in the wall, and yet, he rushes off to Korea for the Emperor. His faith has sealed his fate."

"Don't say that! I just hope he gets back to us before things fall apart over there."

Several days passed before either of them thought about their conversation, but it came up again when Guan Jinglian came to the shop with a flyer in his hand. "Xiaojie Wen, Hao" He greeted her. "I have something from Sun."

Meiliang looked out of her office, where she was editing a recently translated book. "Hello, Guan, come in. Bainong, there is someone here you should meet."

Bainong stepped out of the press room, wiping the ink from his hands with a rag. "This is one of the students I met at the lecture, when Mother was here." Meiliang explained.

"What brings you all the way across the island?" Bainong asked.

"Our friend Sun asked me to bring you this flyer, to see whether we could get five hundred copies of it printed by next week." Bainong looked it over and gave him a price.

Guan looked over at Meiliang and she nodded. "We will have it ready Wednesday. Would that be soon enough?" He thanked them and left as abruptly as he had come.

"What was that all about?" Bainong looked suspiciously at his wife. "I didn't hear him say he would pay for it."

"They are just students. They don't have any money and I told them I would pay for the printing if they needed it." He looked quizzically at her and then examined the text a little more closely. "Mother gave me some mad money," she explained. "I'll pay for it."

"You do realize that this is for a political rally, don't you? Does this have to do with our conversation the other day?" She nodded coyly. "I think we should attend this rally," Bainong said, "And see what your mad money is buying. I may have to answer to your father for this."

The day of the rally, Bainong closed the shop and they took the coach line over to the campus. A rainstorm came and left, typical for the season. The speakers at the rally tried to move the crowd beyond lamenting the past or fearing the future, and instead, focused their remarks on developing a program of reform. The reforms needed, they said, would address local corruption and abuses of power. 'Other measures' were not what they were advocating, they said, but did not specify what those 'measures' were. Hong Kong did not want more conflict with Beijing, and the organizers were well advised not to use the rally to foment civil unrest.

Sun and his Four Great Gangs were once again working the crowd, and joined Meiliang and Bainong between speakers. She introduced her husband and Sun presented each of the Gangs.

"I don't believe you know Chen Shaobai, my right hand man," he said of a slight fellow-student with large round glasses whose robe looked slightly too large. "And this is Yang Heling. He and I came from the same village in Guangdong. I keep him around in case he ever gets his family money." Yang, who was more athletic, gave Sun a playful punch in the stomach. "And this is Wang Lie, another Guangdong expatriate. I believe you've already met Guan Jingliang."

"Is this rally your doing?" asked Bainong.

"Yes. Don't you just love that last guy with the megaphone? Bad enough that they are saying the obvious, now they feel that they have to yell it in your ear! We just thought it would be useful to have an open forum where anyone could say what is on their mind. I had hoped there would be more substantive information presented. Have you heard anything to which you would object?"

"No." Bainong shook his head as he talked. "Everyone is against corruption, graft, and abuse of power -- except the people who are directly involved, of course. And aren't they the only ones who have the power to change things, but probably won't?"

"We want to give the establishment time to change, on their own," Sun answered. "And we want the people who are not in power to know that they are not alone. We may have to act in unison in the near future. But, that is for later. Right now, we were going to a local restaurant. Would you like to join us?"

"Yes!" said Meiliang, before Bainong had a chance to answer.

"It's just a few blocks away, we'll show you."

The Heng Yin Lau Restaurant was an easy walk from the campus, and it was good to leave the noise of the rally. "Aside from printing, do you read widely as well?" Sun asked as they walked.

"Oh, Meiliang reads far more than I do," Bainong admitted. "I get quite enough words at work. What sorts of things do you read, when you are not studying medical texts?"

"In the last ten years, Hong Kong has really developed a world press," he answered. "We have the *Daily Press, The Telegraph*, and the *China Mail*, all in Chinese and not censored as they would be in Shanghai or Canton. The British are understandably anxious about the content of some of the articles, but as long as the pieces on reform are reasoned, and not just bellicose radical noise, they seem to put up with a wide range of opinions. We also have our own school paper which is more parochial. But it does sometimes have good articles as well. I just read one by.... Let's see...." He snatched a copy that Shaobai carried tucked under his arm. "Here it is. Page 3, 'Agrarian Reform Starts in the City', by Sun Yat-sin. He handed the paper, opened to that page, to Meiliang.

As they entered the restaurant, the owner moved other students out of a corner table and quickly drew up another table to accommodate Bainong and Meiliang. "I thought that you would be tied up all day at the rally!" the owner said to Sun and his gang as they sat down at their usual places and ordered tea and cakes all around. The owner came back with two copies of the *Hsiin-huan jih-bao*, a well respected leftist newspaper. "And here are your papers, sir."

"You are something of a regular here, I take it," said Bainong.

"Yes!" Sun laughed. "This is our hang-out, our escape from the study of the body -- and on to the body politic. Wang

T'ao, the editor of this paper, is a scholar-reformer who is promoting western learning and modernization. He always has good articles by prominent intellectuals. Last month, the paper featured my mentor, Dr. Ho Kai; he is the founder of the Hong Kong Medical College. He did his university studies in England and is not only a doctor, but a barrister as well. I had his class in medical ethics. He writes many articles for the English papers which are translated back into Chinese. He recently wrote that China's troubles lay, not so much in our weak military as in our 'loose morality and evil habits, both social and political.' He also is promoting new ways to fill government appointments, suggesting that we use people trained in a subject to fill the post that controls that area, like military men over the army and compradors over trade. Maybe even doctors running hospitals. How is that for revolutionary thinking!?"

"Is all of life that obvious to you?" Meiliang laughed. They finished their cakes and Bainong was obviously ready to go.

"I think we should be getting back to the other side of the island," he said. "We still have a business to run." They bid good-bye to everyone and left.

***

Charlie Speak

Zhenli came home at the usual time, but was stopped on the street by one of his neighbors, before he could get into the house. Neiles Hogart had been an importer who shipped Dutch products and missionaries into Japan and mediated with the shifting local politics. Now pretty much retired, he dabbled in investments in Shanghai. Tonight, he was on a different sort of political mission: "I must talk with you about your daughter."

When Zhenli finally came into the house, Charlie knew there was something wrong. "What kind of house are you running here?" Zhenli asked his wife. He was tired and this was not the sort of thing that he wanted to come home to. "Neiles stopped me on the street for a most uncomfortable conversation -- for both of us. What kind of language are you teaching Yili?"

"What did he say that she said?"

"He said he has a son in the navy who would not use the words that she used. What do you think he meant by that? She can't even play with the kids in the street without embarrassing me? And, where would she get that stuff from, if not from you?" He raised his hand as if to strike her, but waved it off in frustration.

"My father was here last week. I didn't want to tell you. I know how mad it would have made you. And, we had an argument -- you know how he talks. He was mad that he never gets to see his granddaughter. He was drunk and abusive. I got him out of the house as soon as I could. I told him never to come here again. I did!"

"I'll deal with him! But I thought that we were building a good life here. I don't want that side of your family around here -- ever! Respectability is not so easily earned as it is lost. You are going to have to be a better mother and teach that girl manners for this life or we will be forced to move. Maybe you should spend some time out at the farm again."

That weekend, with stifled protest from Charlie, Zhenli packed off his little family for a visit with Grandma. She received them, but did not relish the idea of dealing with her daughter-in-law and 'that child'. Meixing asked Zhenli to make it short or at least to allow her as much peace and quiet as he could. Charlie saw her opportunity and took Yili off in the carriage for a shopping trip in town. Both Zhenli and his mother were just as happy to stay at the farm and relax.

"You seem to be troubled. What has she done now?" Meixing asked her son, a sour smile playing on her lips.

"I can't really lay this one off on her. Her father decided to make a visit, drunk and disorderly. They had some argument and stuff came out of his mouth that Yili picked up and used the next day with her friends. One of the neighbors was very upset and I had to promise to clean up her act. Though, I don't know if I can un-ring that bell."

Meixing just shook her head. "You know my feelings on that family. But that is your bag of worms!"

"Any word from Father?"

"Just a letter that he sent back on the packet boat when he landed. He must be well up into the backcountry by now."

"Meiliang and I have been reading the Korean newspapers and it looks like he is there in 'interesting times'. I will be happy when he is out of there."

"Don't tell me any more. I am worried enough already," Meixing cautioned him. "I'm not feeling at all well these days. I don't think I have the strength to hear any really bad news."

"I wasn't going to mention it, but you do look tired. I thought that running the farm would keep your mind occupied and healthy. Have you been sick?"

"I just don't have the energy I used to have. I seem to wind down before I get everything done. There is grain in the silos that should be taken to market, but I just don't feel up to haggling with the brokers in town. Could you take it in?"

"Sure, I could do that. Maybe I can catch up with Charlie before she buys every ribbon in town."

A wagon train was assembled and loaded quickly, thanks to Lao Fang's systems. The men followed his established procedures and Zhenli only had to provide the authority to get the grain to market. Prices had gone up and Zhenli convinced himself he had done well in the sale. Once the deals were completed, the wagons were sent back to the farm and Zhenli wandered around the town. His mother's carriage was tied off at the local millinery. There were many packages in the back seat. Inside the store, they told Zhenli that Charlie had left a short time ago.

Further down the street was a public house with food and drink and a lot of noise. Zhenli entered and found Charlie and Yili at a table with two local men. As he approached, the men excused themselves. Charlie was obviously surprised and fidgeted with her broach. "I didn't know that you were coming into town." she said. Her smile was as made up as her lips.

"I can see that! If you are done here, we had better start back to the farm." He caught her up abruptly under the arm and almost lifted her out of her chair. On the way home, he made his point as clearly as he could; there would be no independent shopping trips and she would please her mother-in-law -- or she would displease her husband. It was on that visit to the farm that they conceived their second child; a boy named Naixin.

His mother's health was worse than he had thought and Zhenli felt he needed to move out to the farm until his father got back home. So, that would mean Charlie and Yili would have to stay at the farm, as well -- but just till his father got home. He pledged, to himself, that he would protect his mother from his family and yet keep up the farm.

On those occasions, when he had to take care of his other job in Shanghai, he would have to leave his wife's supervision to his captain of the guard. As long as he could monitor the situation via the telegraph and a messenger service, called 'chit mail', it was a workable arrangement.

***
Meeting Dr. Sun

Meiliang was a bit surprised to find Zhenli and his family so well established at the farm. She had come up to check on her mother and to get away from the printing business for a while. "Bainong couldn't make it this trip. We are happily over-committed, but my part is done for a while. How is all of this working out for you?" she asked her mother, plainly ignoring her sister-in-law across the room.

"It is all too busy for me," Meixing admitted. "I have been relieved of my duties running the farm; your brother seems to be able to handle all of that quite well. But now, I have to make up little things to keep myself occupied. I seem to be of no use anymore." Her eyes were tearing up and she dropped her hands into her lap.

"Would you like to come live with us?" Meiliang asked. "At least till papa comes home? We now have the two babies and you can spoil them both. You won't have to worry about them, though, because we have a full-time nurse to do the feeding and changing."

The suggestion brightened Meixing's face. "That would be nice," she agreed.

Zhenli came in from the barn and stood, brushing himself off on the porch as Meiliang came out to stand next to him. "I have invited mother to come stay with us for a while. The winter in Hong Kong is much milder, down by the sea." He nodded and sat to pull off his boots. "Are you moving back out here permanently?" she asked.

"I don't know about permanently," he said. "I thought I would just hold things down till father gets back. Having Mother at your place would probably work out best; she always likes the time she spends there and things have been a bit tense around here."

As the hoarfrost of winter settled on the stubble of the mowed wheat up north on the farm, the winds blew humid sea breezes over the island of Hong Kong. Meixing sat each day on the hill overlooking the mouth of the bay, wrapped in heavy blankets with just a hand protruding, trying to depict the sea fog with her paint brush. She had done more than thirty paintings of that scene, but had yet to capture that mist wrapping around the shoreline to her satisfaction.

Guan Jinglian, once again, came with another flyer. Bainong brought it, and Guan, up to the house for lunch. "I think you're going to buy some more printing," he said to Meiliang, as they came in from the road. She took the flyer and laughed.

"Well, I would sponsor this one, any day!" she said. "This is great news. It is official then? Sun will be a real doctor?" asked Meiliang. Guan was almost aglow. His friend and idol had graduated at the top of the first-ever class of 1892 from The Hong Kong College of Medicine for Chinese at Queens College. There were only two in his class, but he was the top student.

"We must throw him a party!" Meiliang looked at Bainong, then at Guan. "Do you think that you could get him to come over here with all of the Gangs? We'll get him away from that school, at least for a day."

The flyer, that Guan brought, announcing the graduation was actually drafted by Sun, ever the politician. He made sure that he would have something he could send out to friends and family, as well as to use for future résumés.

The party came several days after the actual graduation, but it was a welcome day of decompression. Wen had returned to the farm and Zhenli told him about the event. They sent their congratulations by telegraph, and promised to come along as soon as Wen had recovered from his own trip.

Dr. Sun had accepted a position with his mentor Dr. Ho Kai at the Alice Memorial Hospital, which Dr Ho founded and named in honor of his recently deceased wife. "But, for today," said Sun, "I am going to think of nothing academic. I will simply enjoy all of these pictures of the Bay... Why are there so many of the same scene?"

Meixing blushed at his attention to her work. "These are what keep me humble. Try as I may, I just never seem to get it quite right."

"I think Mother has painted a dozen very fine pictures and should be quite proud!" Meiliang defended her.

"Indeed! These are fine paintings. I would be proud to hang any of them in my office." Sun bowed theatrically.

"Well, you may have any one that you like. I must keep on trying till I am satisfied," Meixing laughed.

Sun noticed Meixing's heavy breathing and her tendency to sit down frequently -- sometimes suddenly. "Have you been feeling well?" he asked.

"No, not really. I just don't feel as young as I did, even five years ago."

"Would you like some professional advice?" he asked.

"Yes, do you know someone in the profession?" she teased.

"Let me look you over and see if there is anything obviously wrong. If not, perhaps you should get a more thorough exam at our clinic at the College. Come into the sunlight and let's have a look." Dr. Sun sat her down in a chair with the sunlight full on her face. "Now open your mouth and say 'Ahh'." His expression changed, as he looked into her mouth, belying his casual demeanor.

"Is there something wrong?" Meixing asked, picking up on his changed expression.

"There is a lot of blood on your gums," he replied. "Have you been cleaning your teeth properly?"

"I use an orange stick and rinse with boiled water."

"You will have to start using a stiff brush, with salt and baking soda. When you get over to the clinic, we will need to get you a professional cleaning and iodine treatments. I wouldn't wait any longer than the end of this week." She promised to follow his advice, but insisted on them both going back to the party.

As they passed Meiliang, he told her, "Make sure she gets down to our clinic in the next couple of days. She has a serious problem and it needs to be taken care of right away, OK?"

The clinic at the hospital was as cold and uninviting as Meixing had feared. Meiliang was there to hold her hand and fill in the paperwork, but she couldn't take her place in the dental chair. The treatments were as close to torture as Meixing had ever known. Despite the reassurances of the nurse, Meixing experienced pain -- and it seemed to go on for a very long time. Then they packed the opened gums with iodine-soaked wadding and lined her mouth with cotton padding. Finally, the nurse had her close her teeth on a pipette and wrapped a bandage under her chin and over her head to keep her mouth closed. "No food for 24 hours," she cautioned. "You may drink through this tube which fits onto the end of the pipette. But, just clear tea or fruit juice! Remember, keep everything where it is for 24 hours."

Meixing drew a scarf across her face and silently cursed the Western medicine. They went directly home and she spent the rest of that day and night in bed. In the morning, they took off the bandage and removed the cotton wadding and pads. Her mouth was dry and abused. Meixing would not talk or eat for the rest of the day, but sat at the window and looked out over the bay.

402

It was a week before Dr Sun visited his patient. He came in with Meiliang from the pathway that led up from the shop. "I understand you are not talking much these days; but you can talk with me, can't you?"

Meixing glowered at him. "It still hurts. Even my tongue hurts. Did they really have to cut me up so much?"

Dr Sun sat down next to her with his best bedside manor. "Yes, they had to cut out a lot of plaque and sick gum tissue. It will take some time to grow back the fleshy parts. Meanwhile, we have to keep you on a soft food diet and keep those teeth and gums clean with brushing and rinsing. You were losing the battle. You would have lost all of your teeth in no time if you had not had that treatment." He stood as Meiliang entered the room. "She needs to stay on soft food, soups and broths for a while. When she wants to try something more solid, her gums will tell her if she is ready."

Meixing had returned her gaze to the bay -- and the mist along the rocks on the shore.

***
Home from Korea

Wen finally re-joined his family in Hong Kong in the spring of 1893. He had spent a year working his way up through the Korean peninsula and a long winter in the north with Li Hongzhang. Then, he spent a seemingly longer month-and-a-half on the farm, with Zhenli's family, recovering from a deep cold.

Zhenli and Charlie had moved into the master bedroom upstairs and put their two children in the smaller rooms in the back. Wen moved his things into Lao Fang's old office on the main floor; he claimed it was more convenient for 'an old man'. But Meiliang was annoyed by her brother's presumption in taking the master bedroom. Meixing dismissed the whole farm thing with a wave of indifference; she was too sick to care.

Dr Sun was a frequent visitor that spring; his first patient was not doing well. "Your wife is suffering from a form of leukemia," he told Wen. "We treated the symptoms she exhibited early on, but the root cause is that she just cannot produce enough red blood cells. They are the cells that carry the food and oxygen out to the rest of her body. We are trying a new treatment with arsenic trioxide which is a poison directed at the cause, but she is weak and can tolerate it in only small doses."

As the family watched, Meixing was loosing her physical battles and seemed to grow weaker by the day. Finally, Dr. Sun started her on a series of morphine injections. The mist along the shoreline was her last view of this world; she passed on in May and was buried with her brothers and their parents on the hill overlooking the farm. After a short stay at the farm following her funeral, Wen moved all of his things down to his daughter's house in Hong Kong.

***

Requiem

Meiliang and her father eased their days and months of mourning, in part, by focusing on and discussing the problems of Korea. For all of his attention to the problems of China, Dr Sun had somehow failed to see the political storm clouds rolling in from the east.

Sun sat as a student, in the living room of the new house, as Meiliang and her father talked of the larger movements in Korean politics over the recent past. Starting with the death of the previous King, Cheoljong, who left the throne without an heir in 1864, Meiliang traced the selection and rise of his successors, Gojong and his wife Myeongseong, who was known as Queen Min. "Gojong's Father, Heungseon, ruled as regent till Queen Min forced him into retirement. His isolationist policies and repression of foreign missionaries perpetuated the popular name for Korea as the 'The Hermit Kingdom'.

"By 1872, Queen Min had taken control of the court. The King demurred to her, and his father was forced out by her faction of scholars, high officials, and clan members whom she had put in high places to pursue her progressive policies. She sent out emissaries to Japan, America, and Europe, but she tried to maintain Korea's historical protection through Chinese suzerainty (protection/ guidance). She was well aware of the colonial ambitions of Japan and the West, but tried to hold the world at bay while building up her kingdom." Meiliang was not holding back her gender-pride at all.

Wen added, "But, you know, she never did get the full cooperation of even her own relatives and hand-picked scholars. The implementation of reform would pit her own progressive faction, who wanted to change almost at once, against the old-line conservative ministers, the Sadaedang. The Sadaes advocated gradual change, within established Confucian principles and morals."

Meiliang took up the discussion again. "But it was the King's father who had rebuffed the Japanese. They came in 1873 to announce the Meiji Restoration, and were turned away by cannon fire from his shore-batteries. Then they returned in 1876 with six war ships to collect reparations for loss of life and property from the '73 incident, and forced the acceptance of the 'unequal Ganghwa treaty' which opened up Korea to Japan. It was King Gojong who caved in and paid Japan the reparations."

"Also," said Wen, "The next year, 1877, Queen Min dispatched Kim Gwang-jip to Japan to study their progress in Westernization. His report indicated Japan had pulled ahead of Korea domestically and militarily. China was no longer the only power in the area. Kim counseled the Queen to develop ties with the United States to counter the expanding Russian Empire. At the same time, he recommended that she send students to both China and Japan for training."

"Right!" said Meiliang. "She did what she could and things went well for a couple of years. Then in 1881, Queen Min sent another fact-finding mission to Japan for more than two months. This resulted in a far-reaching restructuring of her government and its policies. It also engendered opposition; in fact, a plot to overthrow her was uncovered. The next year, disgruntled military officers almost succeeded in overthrowing the government, killing many of Queen Min's supporters and some Japanese; the King and Queen, as well as the higher Japanese envoys, managed to escape."

"Li Hongzhang told me that he was already in conference with some Korean envoys then in Beijing," Wen offered, "And they agreed to send a force of 4,500 Chinese troops to quell the rebellion and reaffirm Chinese influence in Korea. But Japan forced another treaty on the King with payments for their losses and the right to station troops at their embassy in Seoul. Min countered with an off-setting treaty with China, expanding their trade advantage and the military training of Korean troops."

"Then, in 1883," he continued, "Min sent her cousin Min Young-ik to the United States on a cultural exchange mission. In her report she said, 'I was born in the dark. I went out into the light, and your Majesty, it is my displeasure to inform you that I returned to the dark.' The cultural lights that she saw were openness, freedom, and acceptance. She advised her Queen to press for even more rapid progress in 'this still ancient kingdom'."

Wen looked straight at Sun, "Changing a whole society is a perilous process. The progressive faction grew frustrated by the attenuated reforms which were concessions to the conservative faction, the Sadaedang. The Sadaes and the queen were afraid that more rapid progress would jeopardize their protection from China. The matter came to a head on December 4, 1884, when the Japanese and progressives staged a bloody coup, killing and replacing many of the Sadaes. The newly configured government had started issuing edicts in the name of the King and Queen, which they later refused to uphold and enforce."

Wen continued, "The revolt was put down in a matter of days by the Chinese troops stationed in Seoul, who were under the command of our General Yuan Shih-Kai. Many of the progressive leaders were executed and their edicts were made null and void. But, that left two camps of foreign armies, facing each other, in Korea. The Japanese took this opportunity to demand, and get, further reparations from the King. On April 18, 1885, Li Hongzhang met with the Japanese Prime Minister, Ito Herobimi, in Tianjin and signed an agreement to remove all Japanese and Chinese troops from Korea and to inform one another in the future should they be called upon to insert any again."

Meiliang added, "But, Queen Min responded by secretly keeping 2000 Chinese troops in Seoul, disguised as Korean Police, merchants, and boarder guards." She smiled broadly at Sun and summed it up. "For more than twenty years she has held to her course of progressive reform. Queen Min initiated modernization of the currency, the Customs and tax collection, and opened all ports to foreign commerce as well as to Western investment. She introduced many opportunities through education of both men and women. Religious freedom has been flourishing. Advancements in the arts and medicine are all growing at amazing speed. Korea is Westernizing faster than Japan! Queen Min is amazing!"

"And what is China doing, all of this time?" Sun asked, turning the focus of their history lecture back on an area more familiar to him. "We have a government torn between the future and the past. Compared to the rest of the world, we are standing still -- sliding back, into the past! Where is our leadership?"

Wen took a deep breath before responding. "If the Empress allowed the Emperor to listen to progressives like Kang Youwei, basic institutions like family and government would all be abolished. That is not an exaggeration; that is what he has proposed -- and that would be too much change. But, how much change is good? The Empress is the one 'torn between the past and the future'. If she acquiesced to any one of her advisors, the rest would clamor that she had done the wrong thing. She is doing well to hold the government together at all."

"With all respect, Sir," Sun responded, "Holding together the government we now have might not be the best answer. We may have to consider more basic changes."

"Hold your speeches for radical friends," Wen said, standing abruptly, shaken and glowering at the others. "You are talking of things perilously close to treason. Do not lose sight of the system which has endured harsher times than these. If you have lost faith in the principles of the Confucian system, perhaps you should live in a country not governed by them."

"I beg your pardon, Sir. I mean no disrespect to our ancient history," Sun said in deference. "But, I do see a reality which demands change."

"You are free to send memoranda to those who advise the Emperor. Present your ideas. But, be willing to let them decide on such matters. Remember, it is not a dialog. If they accept the proposals, they will act; if not, your ideas will be set aside and they will listen to other advisors."

"To whom should I present my ideas?"

"Send your memorandum to Li Hongzhang himself. He is the most skilled and liberal voice in our government at this time. Your letter must introduce you, cite your qualifications, and present your ideas -- which must be clear and useful. Remember to be brief; his time is limited."

Starting the next day, Sun and his friend, Lu Haodong, embarked on composing a basic letter, then took it to Cheng Kuan-ying in Shanghai for review. Cheng was an older revolutionary who had once helped revise Sun's article on agrarian reform and had it published in the *Wan Kuo Bao* newspaper. He was also an author who had written a book, 'Words of Warning in a Great Age'. In fact, Sun's letter covered little that was not already in Cheng's book. 'The land, the talents of the people, the natural resources and open trade must be employed freely,' were pivotal points in both. Cheng later introduced Sun to Wang T'ao, and through him, to Li's secretary. So, in time, the letter was presented to and ignored by Sun's best hope for change in the government at that time.

Chapter 16

The End of an Era

***

Conspiracy to Revolution

Early in January 1895, a visitor came to Bainong's shop. His tweed vest held a watch and fob over a growing mid-section that held his suit coat partially open. His bowtie hung half undone at his neck. "Good day, sir. My name is Charles Soong. I believe your wife might have mentioned me. I print Bibles in Shanghai."

Bainong had been cleaning up the office and dusted himself off as he approached the counter. "Ah, you are the missionary who wanted to get ink on his hands, eh? How is that project going?"

"Quite well, thanks to your wife's help," he responded, fanning himself with his fedora hat. Despite the coolness of the season, the climb from the town up to the shop had him perspiring, just a bit. "Now, I am in a position to make good my debts and expand into the Canton market. I hope that that is not a problem between us printers."

"Heavens, no! There is more work these days than anyone can handle. Is it still Bibles?"

"That is what I tell my wife." Charlie winked, mischievously. "We actually get into all sorts of things."

"I know what you mean. I just clean up one project and there are ten more to do. Say, I was just going up to the house to have some lunch. Would you like to join me?" They closed up the shop and went up the hill to find Meiliang with the children out taking in the laundry from the line. "There is someone here to see you, my love." Bainong called out.

"Charlie Soong! How long has it been? It must be three years. Come on in. I was just about to make lunch." She led the way into the house, holding her three-year-old daughter, Songmei, by the hand. Her son Shaodai was now ten and carried the folded laundry in a basket behind her.

As Meiliang busied herself in the kitchen, Charlie Soong and Bainong took up chairs in the living room, a few feet away. "I am looking into moving to Canton. The family is growing and Shanghai is no place to raise a family. Our Bible sales are good, down here in the south, and it just makes sense to print them out where you sell them. Besides, I hear life is slower in Canton." He explained. "And, I understand that we could get a large house cheaply outside of the city."

"Yes." said Bainong, "My parents live just south of Canton. They even think that this area is too big-city for the children. But, I know what you mean; we left Shanghai for the same reasons."

"What is this about a larger family?" Meiliang asked, as she sat down across from them in the kitchen.

"Oh, yes, that's right! You remember Ai-ling? She is almost six and is in boarding school now -- quite the young scholar. Since you last saw her, she got a sister and a brother. Ch'ing-ling is the middle one; she is two years old this month. And T'se-ven, their brother, is just a baby. It takes a lot of Bibles to float that raft!"

They talked about the printing business and the sorts of things they were printing. Then Charlie asked Meiliang about her father and brother, whom he had met before. "Zhenli is still running the Chinese Police in Shanghai, I know. I see him from time to time. But, what is this about your father and Korea?"

"Have you heard any news about Korea?" Meiliang was reluctant to reopen the subject in her mind. Her father had been home with her for the past two years. Though, her interest in Korea and her admiration for Queen Min were unabated, the thought that the Japanese were in control there, and that she could do nothing about it, made her very uncomfortable.

"I don't know.... That gets a little political," Charlie answered hesitantly, as though asking permission to speak freely.

"Don't worry," she assured him. "My father is no longer in Korea, and he is who he is -- an old-line Confucian Kwan. I can't change him, but I know that our generation must change China before the colonials take it all. Go ahead."

"Well, you know about a year and a half ago, our 'plenipotentiary' in Seoul, General Yuan Shikai, had a pro-Japanese rebel named Kim Okkyun captured and assassinated. And then he made an example of his rebellion and its consequences, by putting his body parts all over Korea. The Japanese were really affronted by that, and protested officially to Beijing."

"Then in June, the Koreans asked us for help to put down the Tonghak rebellion and we sent two thousand soldiers to help the General. The Japanese contended this was a violation of the Li-Ito agreement and sent 8,000 of their own troops, despite Chinese and Korean protests.

Regardless of all of the diplomatic efforts, the military fact was that more than 3,000 Chinese troops were trapped just outside Seoul and the Korean Government had fallen under Japan's control."

Meiliang's tears started flowing down her cheeks. "And the Japanese put the King and Queen under house arrest last July." she whispered into her hankie.

Bainong went to her side and wrapped his arm around her. "She has a great admiration for Queen Min and the Korea that she was building," he said, looking at Soong.

"Right, the Japanese navy sailed into the area and sank several of our war ships -- plus an English ship that was commissioned to transport replacements. On land, the Japanese troops encircled our forces at Seonghwan, near Asan. More than 500 of our troops died and the rest fled north toward Pyongyang. War was declared on the first of August." Soong found himself folding up the rim of his hat in his fist, so he set it down on the table.

"That was when I couldn't look any more," Meiliang said, blotting her cheeks. "I even stopped reading the newspapers; the news is so bad."

"Go on," Bainong said, in a low voice.

"In Pyongyang, the remainder of our troops joined with other replacements into a force of over 13,000, but the Japanese shelled them from land and sea and the city was lost. Our side lost over 2,000; the rest escaped under cover of darkness and a heavy rain. They made it to the fortified boarder on the Yalu River. But the Japanese ships blockaded the mouth of the river and sank eight of our ten Beiyang ships. Then our army dashed over into Chinese territory, and down to the harbor at Lushunkou (Port Arthur). By December, all of Gaixian and Liaoning Provinces fell to the Japanese First Army Corps. The remaining two ships and the last of our army sailed for the fort at Weihaiwei, on the other side of Bai Hai." Charlie threw up his hands and slumped back into his chair. "We may have to call upon the Western nations to stop this madness. But then, we'll just owe them more indemnities."

"So, that is it! The Japanese can just walk in and take over another country -- and no one says anything?" Meiliang was left wringing her hankie and looking at the others who were suddenly silent.

"It sounds to me like they tried to do something to stop the Japanese, but just couldn't!" Bainong shrugged.

"Any word about Queen Min?" The color drained from Meiliang's face.

"As far as I know, she is still being held prisoner in the Kyongbok Palace, with the King," Charlie answered.

In the pause that followed, there was a knock at the door. Dr Sun poked his head in. "What is this? Are you having a meeting without me?" he asked.

"Come on in!" Bainong invited him in with a wave. "We were just hearing about Korea. I knew we were at war with Japan, but I didn't realize that it had come so far into our country."

"Just maybe the Japanese will have our revolution for us. Oh! Hello!" he said, noticing Charlie for the first time as he got up out of his chair. "I hope I didn't misspeak."

"I'm sorry, you two haven't met, have you?" said Bainong. "This is a friend from Shanghai, a fellow printer, Charles Soong. Charlie, this is Dr. Sun Yat-sen, who is with the Alice Memorial Hospital on the other side of the island."

"Not a professional visit, I hope," said Charlie, as he shook his hand.

"No, just a visit. But you were telling everyone about the Japanese? Did they take Beijing yet?"

"Not yet, but they did get up to Weihaiwei. Sounds like the British back in the forties."

"Yes, it does! So, now what?" Dr Sun wiped his forehead. "Do we now sit back and let the Japanese set our course for the next fifty or a hundred years? At what point do we set our own course? This is what I have been talking about with our countrymen who have already left our shores. There are wealthy, intelligent, well educated Chinese, men and women, out there who want to embrace their country's history and could lead it into a better future. They are tired of living in the shame of our past weakness and corruption; but they will not come back as long as the country is in such a state of confusion and subjugation.

"There are also the poor hapless peasants," Sun continued. "They are starving in a land of plenty, yet they are literally ready to die for a better form of governance, one that would give their children food and hope. We are the ones at the doorway to that future. We can open the portal for that reunion. I am asking all of my new and old friends for help to do just that. Re-evaluate your fortunate situation and reflect on the paths we have taken and the paths we can yet choose. We can change our fortunes -- and that is the path that I choose." Dr Sun stood with one hand on his hip and the other shaking a finger in front of him.

"Wow! Where did all that come from?" Meiliang jumped up out of her chair and clapped her hands in mock applause. "I know you are serious about the rebellion, but what was that?"

"I'm sorry for the oratory." Sun said, taking a long drink of water. "I've been all over the islands Malaya, Singapore, up to Penang. I get in groups, not much bigger than this, and out it comes! I just get carried away. I really didn't mean to preach at my friends like that."

"Well, I must say, you do it well," Charlie stood up and shook his hand, smiling. "I take it, then, you are ready for this to happen?"

"Oh yes! This <u>will</u> happen!" Sun unconsciously resumed his oratorical stance. "And, it will happen within our lifetime. The question is how and who. There is dissention and distress at such a level that it cannot be contained any longer. The Qing government is weaker than it has ever been, and the foreigners who protect them are loosing their patience. One more hiccup and they will be thrown out. The question is -- who will take over when they are gone? I think it should be us, a republic for the people of China."

"So that is what all this travel has been about? I was wondering where you had gone. We missed you." Meiliang wrapped her arm around his shoulders.

"Well, first I went back to Hawaii to organize some of the off-shore Chinese in that community. We have taken the name 'The Revive China Society'. They are raising funds that will be needed to conduct operations. I thought I would continue the operation here in Hong Kong with some of my old acquaintances." Sun waved his hand in front of himself, indicating the others in the room. "We will need men, money, and material to start actions against the Qing."

"I am on my way to move my family to Canton," Charlie told him. "I assume that is where you will be starting?" Charlie showed no emotion, other than an abiding interest.

"Yes. You will be setting up a printing factory there? I could use your help as a base for operations and for cover, when things get rough."

"I will make provision for that," said Charlie, nodding and making a mental note.

"I think we will be able to help with more than just printing...." Meiliang said, looking over at Bainong, who just nodded. Not one of them blinked at what had just been said.

"You must come down to our office," said Sun. "We have use of the back rooms at the Qian. It is an odd little bookstore, named after the ancient historian of the Han dynasty. It is just down the street from the Heng Yin Lau Restaurant."

The following week, Meiliang and Bainong did visit the Qian. Sun met them and led them inside. Behind the stacks of old manuscripts and newspapers, there was a panel in the wall that, when pushed in, would slide to the side. Behind it was a short hallway with doors on either side. The one on the left opened into a surprisingly large room, which actually ran behind three shops next to the Qian. There were small, barred windows along the upper part of the wall, to let in air and light. The hall door, on the right, opened to a small apartment where the owner lived. At the end of the hall, a door opened onto the alley that ran behind the shops; the door was also barred and locked from the inside.

In the large room, on the wall across from the door, hung a flag -- a field blue with a white circle having twelve rays. "Lu Haodong designed and made our flag! What do you think?" Sun asked his friends.

"It is quite impressive!" Meiliang said, and then walked over to a map on the wall, across from the windows. "This is only the second full map of China I've ever seen. Grandfather traveled all over the world and always saw things from up there." She pointed skyward.

The map included the west coast of Korea and a bit of Japan. Pins, with little red paper flags, dotted the coast of Guangxi, Guangdong, and Fujian. "Safe houses," said Sun, answering Meiliang's quizzical look. "They are just waiting for someone to lead them. We are organizing all along the coast, and as far inland as we can. I don't want this all to die in the harbors. The yellow flags are meeting places. And the blue ones are where we expect to have weapons and ammunition."

"How do you know exactly where these places are? That is a pretty large-scale map."

Sun laughed, "That is just for a general overview. The names and addresses are information that we have to keep separate so we don't lose everyone at one time. Lu handles our membership and all of our security. You never keep it all in one place."

"Where is your hometown?" Bainong asked and Sun came over to the map, pointing to an area close to where Bainong's parents live. "What? Not safe at home?"

"I am still not too welcomed back there." Sun laughed. "They didn't like my politics and I didn't like their religious idols. Lu and I broke some of them up when we were eighteen; they haven't forgotten it. But," Sun said, his hand sweeping across the map, "There are many other organizations, in Hong Kong and on the mainland that we are bringing together. The Huaxing Society, Restoration Society and others joined with the Revive China Society under the name 'Tongmenghui' (The Chinese Revolutionary Alliance)."

The first joint operation of the Tongmenghui, in October of 1895, was to have been an uprising in Guangzhou, (the city of Canton). Guns were shipped into the city in crates labeled Portland cement. Unfortunately, word got out and the Canton police were waiting for the conspirators. Sun and some others escaped the trap, but many were captured, tortured, and executed. One of these was Lu Haodong. On the night of the operation, Lu was in the back room in the Qian with the panel door bolted. Qing agents filled the alley and were breaking down both of the doors as Lu heroically burned the membership lists. "Lu was the first person to have been martyred for the Republican Revolution," Sun was later to say.

***

Trouble in the North

Wen had returned to Shanghai for a visit and was asked to give his advice to the young men who had taken over his duties at the arsenal. As it became a more regular habit, Wen decided to maintain a room in Zhenli's house in Shanghai. During the week, Zhenli would stay with him and then return to the farm as his duties would allow. The Triads, criminal organizations that originated along the rivers in Guangdong and Guangxi, had infiltrated the Chinese community in Shanghai, and were growing bolder as the Qing government withered into financial and leadership bankruptcy.

Shanghai's primary saving grace was the commerce that passed through it and the strength of the foreign interests that relied upon that trade. It was a bone-hard laissez-faire relationship. "If the Chinese want to treat each other like that, so be it! Just keep them out of our area." There was an infamous sign in the park, "NO DOGS OR CHINAMEN" Zhenli's main duty seemed to be keeping the two worlds separate.

Hearing that Wen was again available, the Empress Cixi summoned him for another investigation; this time, it would be in her own country. The French and German ambassadors were repeatedly and adamantly petitioning the court to protect the missionaries in accordance with the treaties. Wen's task was to find out whether the French and German protestations were based on fact and to make recommendations for remediation, if any were needed. For Wen, Shanxi Province would be a cool respite from the southern heat and humidity.

West of Beijing, through the mountains, he traveled by mule and on foot from one mission to the next, bringing medical supplies and some scrap of news from home, having a meal with the missionaries. Then he would ask what problems they were having, carrying out their assignments.

"The stories are outlandish -- totally without foundation, I tell you!" The Reverend Roberts was at a loss. He supervised three missions along the mountain trails and had heard the caravan drivers' stories. "We are thought to be witches and warlocks! The local people say we are obviously crazy to give good money for girl babies. And, 'Why would we want to buy small children, anyway?' Well, they say; we must be eating them or using their 'essence' for our medicines. And, the more bazaar the claim, the more they believe it. We try to invite anyone who is curious to just come in and have a look around at what we do here, but to no avail. I believe that there must be a source for all of this; someone is out there agitating against us."

Afterward, Wen would visit the local taotai, or magistrate, to hear the people's side of the story. "The foreign devils have brought this upon themselves," a local village elder complained. "Why do they come so high in our mountains? They bring sickness and hunger where ever they go. Look at the fields! We have had no rain for months. In the big cities, many are dying because they are here. Why don't they just leave us alone and go back across the sea? The spirits of the mountains are trying to destroy them, but instead, they are killing us. We must drive them all away."

Wen presented his findings in a memorandum which was read at court when he returned. Summoned from the waiting area by the main gate, he remembered his first time ascending these stairs and seeing the sea of senior Kwan in their splendid array. This time, as he came through the portal of the Gate of Supreme Harmony, there were far fewer in attendance and they seemed somehow less splendid.

He proceeded down the steps and performed his Kao-Tows, but before his second set was done, Cixi's dry voice called down. "Rise and attend his Majesty." Wen stood, but kept his eyes lowered as one of the ministers read his memorandum.

"The people are looking for answers within their understanding. They see the recent drought as proof of a present evil. Now there is an organization which is gathering all of this ill-will and bundling it into a new religion. The Yi He Quan (Righteous and Harmonious Fists) claims to be the answer. Your Majesties, I am sorry to report that they feel that the Emperor is part of the cause of their distress." There was a sudden hush in the courtyard.

"Pray continue!" The Empress's voice crackled from behind the screen; the minister continued. "The members of this new religion are exorcising their frustration in martial arts exercises and monk-like denial. They claim to be impervious to the machines of war that the western armies would throw against them. In the final confrontation, they say, the spirits of all of the wrongly martyred heroes of the past will rise from the grave to join them in expelling the foreign devils."

Reports like Wen's had cost the heads of many bearers of bad tidings and he was surprised to hear her say, "Rise and inform his majesty of your recommendations." He looked up cautiously. The Emperor sat upon the throne, behind him a tapestry screen -- and behind it, the Empress Cixi.

"Your Majesty, we should enlist the energies of the people to serve the Emperor," Wen said. His voice wavered slightly, but he spoke as one with authority.

"That is a bold statement. I hope it is not reckless." It was Cixi's voice from behind the curtain. "How do you propose to, 'enlist the energies of the people'?" she demanded.

"I would support their leaders with food and weapons, letting them know that it was from you, and direct their words away from the throne and toward the foreigners, Your Majesty."

"I remember that you performed a similar service after the British and French attacked the capital. You directed the hearts of the people to the service of the Emperor. So, then, that is your assignment. Work with their leaders and I shall look for results. You may leave now." Wen performed his Kao-Tows and left their Imperial Majesties.

Before departing the capital for this new assignment's long winter in the mountains, he wrote to his children. It was a long letter, filled with remembrances and apologies for things he had forgotten to do as they grew up; for the time that he was away from home, his own aloofness; his short time with Meixing, scarcely forty years; and only catching the early years of his grandchildren. "My age is catching up with me" he wrote, "And yet I still dream of my return to a peaceful life with you. But, I am again going into the unknown future and I hope to write a more cheerful letter when I return to the capital."

***

The End of the War

Almost lost in the headlines about the peace treaty with Japan was a short article about the assassination of the Queen of Korea. "Japanese agents, 'dressed in peculiar gowns', had entered her private chambers with photographs to identify her, and killed the Queen and her attendants with swords. They then took her body to a wood nearby and burned it. The ashes were later scattered and no grave monument is permitted. Curiously, no picture or photograph of the queen can be found in the capital today."

The main article lead was "Li Hongzhang Shot"; it covered an attack by a radical Japanese Nationalist who shot Li in the face. The bullet hit him just under his left eye and exited close by. The injury was not fatal to Li, but compromised the 'face' of Japan in the negotiations that followed. The Japanese were forced to accept fewer concessions as a result. Nonetheless, the Qing Government gave up land and silver to sue for peace. China gave up all claims to Korea, the islands of Taiwan, the Pescadores, and the Liaotong peninsula. China also was forced to open many inland ports to trade. In addition, they were to pay $300 million in silver in restitution over seven years.

Not to be left out of this opportunity, Russia, France, and Germany 'intervened' in the treaty of Shimonoseki, insisting that Japan return the Liaodong peninsula to China. Japan was to be 'compensated' for this by an additional indemnity of $30 million in silver. The reasons behind this maneuver were colonial: Russia moved in and took control of the peninsula as soon as the Japanese left, in December. They fortified Port Arthur and drove a spur line to intersect their Trans-Siberian railway in Manchuria; Russia had finally obtained the warm-water port they had always needed. France was involved by way of an 1893 treaty with Russia, and the fact that her bankers were directly involved in the financing of the Russian rail system. The Germans supported the Russians in order to draw their attention away from Germany, which had only recently formed a single union -- they also received more territorial concessions. The British and Americans, though not a formal part of the intervention, also moved to increase their holdings and concessions in China.

Li Hongzhang returned home to less than a hero's welcome. Many Chinese held him personally responsible for the military losses to Japan. The Empress was forced to take from him all of his honors and titles, but saved him from decapitation. His protégé, General Yuan Shikai, had been recalled from Korea before the onset of hostilities in 1894, and in 1895 was appointed commander of the New Army which protected the capital. Following the war, the Dowager Empress Cixi retired to the Summer Palace. It was again a time of peace, and the Guangxu Emperor took up the reins of Empire, -- facing only droughts and floods, starvation and rebellion.

The 'New' Emperor was, by nature, more progressive in his politics than his aunt Cixi. He was influenced by men as radical as Kang Youwei and his student, Liang Qichao, who advocated the constitutional monarchy form of government and believed China should emulate the Meiji Restoration in Japan. Other advisors who had the new Emperor's ear were less radical, but none were conservative. By June of 1898, the Emperor announced a program of legal, political, and social reforms which, he hoped, would remake China. He issued edicts to build railroads and universities -- all under a system of realistic budgets. Many of the former Imperial advisors, who were too conservative for the new reforms, were dismissed.

But, in September, the 'Hundred Days of Reform' ended abruptly with a military coup led by General Ronglu, organized and backed by the Empress. The Emperor found out about the plan and called upon General Yuan Shikai to plan a counter-coup. The night before the planned counter-coup, Yuan turned to the other side and disclosed the Emperor's plan to General Ronglu and the Empress. Ronglu took over the capital that night and arrested the Emperor. With Guangxu imprisoned on an island inside the Forbidden City, Cixi issued an edict declaring him a "disgrace and not being fit to be Emperor." His advisors were deported, executed, or escaped -- under threat of execution. Among these were Kang Youwei and Liang Qichao, who had escaped to Japan where they continued to advocate restoration of the Emperor and his reforms. Cixi resumed control of the throne, without pretext.

Wen stayed up in the mountains, well away from the politics of Beijing. His continuing reports of social progress and improvement in relations between the people and the Imperial court were well received and encouraged by both the Emperor and the Empress Cixi. The Emperor was kept alive because the Europeans still regarded him as the legitimate head of state; they felt that the Empress was too difficult and there existed a tacit toleration of her by the Europeans.

***
Letters Home

Zhenli and Meiliang read and reread Wen's letters. Though it was difficult to understand what exactly was going on within the Imperial family -- Wen wouldn't commit any personal opinions to paper. The British newspaper coverage of Imperial affairs was hopeful, while Guangxu was on the throne, but then turned decidedly 'anti' as soon as the Empress wrested control from her nephew.

Wen did write to the family of his successes in getting local farmers to try new techniques that improved crop yield. Among the locals in the mountains of Shanxi, there was still a strong resentment against the foreigners. But, at least in his area of the mountains, they had stopped including the Emperor in their protests. Wen was training the local militia in the use of modern rifles which had been provided by the Empress, but he reminded them that they were to be used only in the defense of the Empire. It made no sense, but it would have sounded good to the censors who would read his personal mail.

In January 1898, Wen sent a memorandum to Beijing reporting on the growing hostility of the Righteous Fists, or 'Boxers,' as the Western press called them, against the local missionaries. Mobs, led by the Boxers, assaulted the members of the missions in the streets and set fires along the main roads. When Wen confronted the gangs about the harassment of the missionaries, he was told about two German missionaries who were killed in Shandong province; the German response was to seize the port city of Qingdao. 'Yu Xien is Governor here now,' the leader of the mob told him, 'Let them come to Shanxi and try to take our cities. We will kill them all and their soldiers!'"

The increasing militancy of the mobs drove the missionaries into hiding and they were unable to function according to the assurances of the treaties. The Treaty of Beijing had guaranteed free access of the missionaries to all of China. Meanwhile, in the capital, the conservatives were emboldened by the Boxers, and convinced Cixi the time was coming for a confrontation with the foreigners.

Wen was reassigned to Shandong province to assess the respective strengths of the foreign armies and the Boxers in that area. Before he had a chance to do much investigation, however, the Boxers started marching on Tianjin, then on to Beijing. The foreigners' Legations were almost all in one area, just outside the Forbidden City. The Boxers began to move out of the provinces and toward the capital about the same time the Hundred Days of Reform came to an end, June 11 to September 21, 1898. In October, the Boxers tested themselves against the Imperial Bannerman Army and were badly beaten. After that, the Boxer banners said, "Support the Qing -- Expel the Foreigners."

The next year, 1899, there was wide-spread murder of missionaries and, much more frequently, their Chinese converts. With growing moral indignation, and fear that all the instability would be bad for business as well as the security of their trade ports, the Western powers started amassing ships and men along the northeastern seaboard. America had just fought the Spanish in the Philippines, as an extension of the Spanish-American War, and was done securing its position there. As a result, the Americans had military assets close at hand.

However, it was not until the end of April 1900, that the Americans received a request for assistance from the legations in Beijing. Seven hundred and fifty men started marching from Tianjin for the capital, but were brought to a halt by large bands of Boxers supported by Imperial troops. A second force, of two thousand soldiers from several national armies, was sent out on June 10th to rescue the first group and they were all repelled and driven back to Tianjin.

With the foreigners' communications to Beijing totally cut off, an international force of more than 50,000 was amassed and drove in from the sea to take firm control of Tianjin and to march on Beijing, 120 km to the north. The

Japanese supplied 20,300 soldiers, as well as the commander of the combined force. The Eight-Nation Alliance, as this international force was called, reached Beijing on August 14 and relieved the remaining Legation staff and soldiers who were still alive. Half of their number had died in the defense; the German embassy across town had been totally overrun.

Beijing, even the Forbidden City, was seized, sacked, and scourged by the forces of the alliance. Dressed as peasants, the Dowager Empress and the Emperor managed to escape. The "Final Settlement" stipulated ten Qing officials who were to be executed. The Kwan, A5, Wen Fulian's name was on the list.

Zhenli brought the last letter himself. He stopped by the shop before he went up to the house to ask Bainong to come with him. Meiliang's expression collapsed when she saw their eyes. It was obvious that they brought bad news -- just not the details.

"Oh, God! What is wrong?" Bainong caught her in his arms and helped her into the house. "It's about Father, isn't it? Is he all right?" Meiliang's hands were clawing the air for the letter as she burst into tears.

"No! Just sit down and listen," Bainong said, helping her to a chair.

Zhenli stood, ashen, in front of her. "He sent us this letter from Beijing. He was in prison when he wrote it. The Boxers and the Imperial forces were overwhelmed by the foreign armies. Both the Emperor and the Empress escaped, and the capital is in ruins. Thousands died and even the Forbidden City was looted. Now, they are taking their 'revenge' on us, once again. They held their investigations into the causes and have named ten Kwan for execution because of their involvement. Father was named."

"Will we be able to see him?" Meiliang pleaded.

"No. They were all executed last week."

Meiliang buried her head in her husband's arms and sobbed. Shaodai and Songmei came to the door, trying to grasp what had happened. "Mama, what is wrong?" They ran to her and threw their arms around her.

"Grandpa Wen died," she said, as calmly as she could, and pulled them to her.

Zhenli went to the kitchen and made a pitcher of lemon water. He stood at the windows looking at the spray from the waves on the rocks along the shoreline and the clouds rolling in from the west.

"Where is he now?" Meiliang asked, making the effort to put things back in order, as she had always done.

"The Empress's brother has claimed the body and will ship it down as soon as he can. The Empress's family had met Father several times when he was called to the capital on duty. I met them when I served General Zuo."

"What about the Empress? Is she still alive? She made this all happen! I would kill her myself, if I could." Meiliang said, sobbing with anger and loss.

"No, they want to execute her as well. But, I don't think they will. Li Hongzhang and Yuan Shikai are defending her. They claim that 'She wasn't in control of the Boxers'. "Ha! That old witch was in charge of everything!" Zhenli's eyes were filling with tears of frustration.

Why don't they kill Li and Yang? Aren't they just a guilty as she is?" Meiliang said.

Zhenli smiled, "Not really, they held their armies back and didn't join the fight on the Boxers' side, against the Europeans. It pays to know your friends!"

A month later, when the body arrived from Beijing, the family gathered at the farm. Lao Wen had had a stone monument made for himself when Meixing died, and the family used it to mark his plot next to hers, on the hill overlooking the old farm. As part of the service, they read the letter from grandpa. In it, after his abject apologies for his life, he willed his lands and business ventures to his son and acknowledged that his wife had already provided for Meiliang. "Tell the children of me...." And he closed with a poem, an ode to a fallen kingdom. "I will die as I have lived, in service to my Emperor."

***

Carrying On

Meixing performed her mourning duties quietly, privately, and with a minimum of public display. Zhenli, as an official, was 'required' to divest himself of his public offices and to take a year to three for his Confucian reflection on the life of his father. To Zhenli, that meant he was free to checkout the business affairs which his father had left to him in his will. Charlie could have told him almost exactly what that would be, as her mother-in-law, Meixing, had predicted. She had rifled through all of Lao Wen's personal papers just as soon as she took over the farm.

But Zhenli needed to get away from family, work, and restrictions of any kind. The first thing to go was his uniform; instead, he styled himself after his grandfather. He put on the black silk Samfu and leather boots, with a black silk cap. On the Cap was a worked-gold button, reflecting his rank under General Zuo.

Zhenli enjoyed the tour of Lao Wen's old plants. Everyone was anxious to meet and size-up the son. Managers were obsequious and fawned over every one of his observations. He was wined and dined in style; and, just as happily, sent off to the next station on his tour. Nothing changed, except that the managers' skimming from the profits would probably increase. Zhenli added nothing and changed nothing, and he left many shaking their heads over the passing of a great man -- his father.

Meiliang started taking a more active role in the Tongmenghui after her father's death. She didn't feel that it was revenge, but she believed more strongly that Sun was right. Sun was allowed to travel through Hong Kong, despite the Imperial price on his head, and it was enough time to meet with the leaders. Meiliang kept track of the finances and would, as often as not, fill in any shortfall from her own account. The years of the revolution were long; each battle left scars and lessons. The day-to-day running of the nation fell more and more upon the shoulders of local administrators, who readily took bribes, rather than attempt to quell the revolution.

Charlie Soong expanded his business as he expanded his family, and became Sun's mainland administrator and center for information. Soong now had the title of Executive Secretary of the revolutionary party. He maintained residences in Shanghai, Canton, and Hawaii. Charlie claimed Portuguese nationality, on the story that he had been born in Macao; this made immigration to the US one possible escape route -- should one be needed. He was a man living on the edge. His personal fortune was approaching a million dollars and as soon as he could, he started shipping off his children to America for their education.

Shaodai, Meiliang's son, was educated at his mother's knee, much as Meiliang's own mother had taught her. She taught Shaodai and his sister to be functionally literate in French, German, and English. They had read the Chinese classics, but had grown up with dinner table discussions of the modern world and its worldly affairs. Lao Wen lived on, in them, through their great appreciation of Western mathematics, business, law, and politics. Bainong helped them understand the physics of machinery through his presses and the ideas that were reprinted there.

Shaodai was totally home schooled in the normal academics -- but more so, the secret things about the revolution. Many things had to be learned and destroyed. No scrap of incrimination could be left whole, to be found later by the authorities. Security was the price of life, theirs and many others. In 1902, at the age of seventeen, Shaodai was ready to start a new phase of his life -- and that of China.

One afternoon, when Dr Sun came for one of his visits, he had a long talk with Shaodai. Organizations throughout southern China were springing up spontaneously with the same goal of revolution, but without any unifying programs. What Sun needed was a way to contact them without endangering them. Shaodai came up with a solution.

"My Uncle Zhenli has commercial interests all along the Yangtze and its tributaries," he suggested to Sun. "What he doesn't have is the drive to tend to their management. He has asked me to join him on his next tour so I can learn and, he hopes, take over the traveling part of the business. I would have access to wide areas of the country and to the people who live there. It would be a small matter to make contacts for you at the same time."

So it was, with some surprise, that Zhenli found his nephew a willing and eager student. It did not take long for the young and affable Shaodai to make friends and establish relationships throughout the vast Chinese interior. He came home between trips to pass on the messages that he had collected from his contacts inland and to memorize the messages to be sent from Sun. Nothing was written down until he arrived in a town along the way. Then, furtively, he would write a letter and deliver it to a drop point; sometimes he just posted it on a wall with all of the other public information.

With a price on his head, Sun left to travel in Japan, Hawaii, America, and Europe. He had lost the early battles, but gained an international reputation, as well as recognition as the head of the revolution. In his absence, men like Zheng Shiliang carried on the fight. On October 8, 1900, in the midst of the Boxer rebellion up north, Zheng led 20,000 rebels against the Qing forces in Sanzhoutain, Guangzhou province. They ran out of supplies, however, and had to abandon the fight. Over the next ten years, Sun and the Tongmenghui carried on raids and full-fledged battles on the Malay Peninsula and on up through the southwestern provinces.

When the Emperor and Cixi returned to the capital, they were forced to sign the "Boxer Protocol", a peace agreement with the Eight-Nation Alliance, on September 7, 1901. The agreement provided the West an "Open Door Policy" for almost total free trade, including open trade in opium, as well as 450 million teals of silver, to be paid over thirty-nine years for reparations.

The Empress was back in control, but had lost the backing of the conservatives with the suppression of the Boxers. The Self-Strengthening Movement was largely repudiated, since one of the terms of the Boxer Protocol was a suppression of arms import and manufacture. The Imperial Examination system was dropped in September 1905, and the liberal faction had it replaced with a European-style educational system. The idea of a constitutional-based monarchy with Prime Minister and cabinet was proposed the following year; but those selected to be in the cabinet were almost all members of the Imperial family. The proposed slate served only to disappoint many reformers and turn them into revolutionaries.

The health of the Empress was failing, as was her suppression of her nephew, the Emperor, who had continued his affront to her. In fact, the two both died almost simultaneously -- he on November 14, 1908, the Empress, the next day. But on her deathbed, Cixi made one last appointment: The successor to the throne was to be Puyi, a grand nephew. The new Emperor was not yet three years old, so his father, the second Prince Chun, became regent.

In London, Chinese agents kidnapped Sun and held him in the Embassy pending transport back to China for execution. During his incarceration there, a maid at the Embassy recognized him and contacted Sun's friend and teacher Dr James Cantlie for help. Cantlie managed to generate newspaper stories and community fundraisers until international pressure grew and eventually freed Dr. Sun.

On April 27, 1910, the Second Guangzhou Uprising, which was planned by Sun and his council at the Penang Conference, and which they had hoped would be the spark to ignite the revolution, turned out to be a disastrous failure. Huang Xing was wounded and 85 fighters were lost in an action. In later histories, it would be celebrated as the 'Yellow Flower Mound Revolt'.

Articles in the English and Chinese press appeared from time to time, speculating on Sun's travels. He had become too famous for the Qing to publicly assassinate him, so his fundraising in the Chinese communities around the world continued to filter needed cash into the many revolutionary movements back home. Meiliang and Bainong were questioned by the Hong Kong Police, but nothing was found connecting them directly to Sun.

On October 10, 1911, Shaodai was taking a late lunch at a restaurant in Wuchang. He had just returned from a productive trip; boats along the Yangtze were more numerous and his business was going very well. As he contentedly watched the leaves turn and twist in the gentle breeze outside, there was a sudden sound of thunder. The sky was clear, however, and he could see people at the adjacent tables looking around at one another. Then a second, and decidedly louder rumble filled the air. A plume of white smoke rose from the area of a garrison a few blocks to the north. Shaodai recalled the garrison as a site where dissident army officers were actively planning an uprising and had a bomb-making facility. Something must have gone wrong!

The sound of gunfire and alarm sirens filled the air. People were running through the streets, in no particular direction. "The revolution has begun!" he muttered to himself. Workers poured out of the factories, and soldiers in favor of the revolution took over whatever stores of weapons and ammunition they could. It spread like a grass fire. Whole army units quickly aligned themselves with the rebellion.

Shaodai made his way to the telegraph office and sent this message, "Mother, there is fighting in Wuchang. I have presents for our Doctor's friends. I will take the next boat to Nanchang and be home as soon as I can."

Posters were glued onto walls. Men ran through the streets with banners calling for people to join the rebellion. Loud, animated conversations were everywhere. Shaodai made his way down to the docks and boarded the first boat down river.

Dr. Sun learned of the uprising in Wuchang from a newspaper while he was raising money in Denver, Colorado. He instantly realized that his not being on the scene when the revolution broke out diminished his chances of taking control. Instead, he set out on a quest to get backing by one of the major Western powers, but was unable to forge the alliances he would need from America, England, or France.

Sun returned home on December 11, 1911, to a hero's welcome, but with faint hope of regaining his role in the center of things. However, the delay actually worked to his advantage. In his absence, the new revolutionary government was fragmented. Many of the leaders of various factions contested for leadership of the movement, but none could win enough support. In the end, they could only agree that Nanjing would be the capital.

Sun was elected as the Provisional President of the Republic of China, and his first official act was a visit to the Ming tombs, fulfilling the revolutionary goal "Fan Ch'ing fu Ming" (out with the Qing, up with the Ming).

His second act was to formally establish his party as the Kuomintang.

In Shanghai, Zhenli had a close association with "Big-eared Tu", leader of the Green Gang, one of the most powerful of the city tongs; it was the criminal element that ran the practical matters within the Chinese community. Among the young military students returning to Shanghai from training in Japan was a young officer named Chen Qimei and his sworn brother, Chiang Kai-Shek. They quickly forged links with the Green Gang and other criminal elements for an assault on both the city's arsenal and its garrison camp on Nov. 3, 1911. Chiang was put in command of an Army Brigade funded by local merchants.

Chiang had his first meeting with Sun at the house of Charlie Soong, where they adopted the new flag of the Republic for the new country and the Kuomintang flag for the party and the army. Charlie sent one of the first flags of the new republic to his second daughter, Ching-ling, who was away at school in Georgia. She displayed the new flag in her room, next to the white sunburst on blue of the Kuomintang. She explained that the five horizontal colored bars representing the unity of the five great people of China; the Han, Manchus, Mongols, Moslems, and Tibetans.

Unfortunately, it quickly became obvious to everyone in the movement, including Sun, that he had no real power to run the country. The center of rebellion's fervor was still in Wuchang, while the center of Imperial power, which included relations with the foreigners, remained in Beijing. The Northern Army, protecting Beijing, was commanded by Yuan Shih Kai. The Emperor and his father, the regent, continued to be dependent on -- and defended by -- the Northern Army. To Sun it was obvious; popularity and honor were fine, but to really control things, you needed that loyal army.

Dr. Sun resigned the Presidency under an agreement with Yuan and the rebels in Wuhan; terms of the agreement were that they all join the KMT and protect the Emperor, who would abdicate the throne, but remain in residence in part of the Forbidden City. General Yuan took over as the first President of the Republic.

Zhenli, though physically closer to the action, was far removed from that whole world. The revolution had changed little in his life, other than the speed with which things happened. Large sections of the city were being torn down and rebuilt. The sidewalk factories opened onto the street, and child labor became the rule more than the exception. The high death rate among the laborers and unemployed produced a steady stream of bodies to be hauled out of town for burial in communal graves. Huge fortunes were being made, while the life of the poor was cheap. Law was a matter of convenience and compromise, when it existed at all.

Dr Sun was made Director of the National Railroads, with Charlie Soong as his Treasurer and Ailing as his Secretary. Sun was living in a dream world; he could not see that Yuan was consolidating his personal power by appointment of his friends and eliminating competent rivals by assassination. Dr Sun had also fallen in love with Charlie's oldest daughter Ailing, who had the practical sense to let him know she did not reciprocate his attraction. This caused a rift between himself and Charlie.

By July 1913, Yuan's pretenses of power had become too much for many of the other leaders of the revolution; it was apparent that he would like to become Emperor himself. The Governor of Kiangsi Province publicly announced he would no longer accept the leadership of General Yuan. Dr Sun publicly proclaimed that the people should attack anyone who would try to become Emperor. Yuan dismissed Sun immediately from his government post and both he and Charlie were listed under an order of arrest and execution. The Second Revolution had begun.

Sun and Soong took their families and escaped through Shanghai to Japan. Charlie had his wife and the two eldest daughters, Ailing and Ching-ling, and his two youngest sons, T.L. and T.A. Soong with him; May-ling and her brother, T.V. were at Cambridge University while he finished his Doctorate in Finance. They all took up residence near Tokyo. Sun's only son was in school in America, but his first wife came with him.

Once again, Dr Sun was at the top of his game, organizing and fundraising, and took on Ching-ling as his new secretary. Ailing had met a very wealthy banker, H.H. Kung, who was heir to his family pawn/banking business in Shanxi Province. His family had a reciprocally advantageous relationship with the warlord, Yen Xishan, who 'liberated' Shanxi Province. After the Boxer uprising, it was H.H. Kung who negotiated with the Alliance for retribution of a financial nature, rather than a military takeover of Shanxi. Kung had been married to a frail woman who had died of consumption, and he had recently come to Japan to run the YMCA in Tokyo. H.H. and Ailing had met briefly, several years before, when he was a grad student at Yale and she was visiting her brother there. Their shared attraction to money and to each other resulted in their marriage the following spring.

Due to the lack of any unifying success of the second revolution and the lack of interest by any of the foreign governments to become involved, Dr Sun's role in government had become marginalized. Local generals and politicos had become warlords in their own areas in the north under a loose network controlled by Yuan.

World War I was killing off a generation of the European armies (10 Million) and everyone was holding tight till the colonials sorted out their affairs. The strain on Sun may have contributed to his shifting his romantic delusions toward Ching-ling -- and she was awash in the idealism of his cause. Charlie became aware of this budding relationship and decided it was better to tempt fate by returning to Shanghai, than risk his daughter to Sun in Tokyo. His family would be under the protection of his underworld friend, 'Pockmarked' Huang Chih-jung, who was both the French chief of detectives and the head of the Red Gang. He would be able to protect them, as long as they stayed in the French Concession.

Ching-ling was livid and had to be forced to move away from Sun. She did, in fact, escape from both Shanghai and from a quickly arranged engagement that her parents had set up. She sailed alone to Sun in Japan. When he found out about it, Charlie Soong was also livid, but late. He arrived after the ceremony that joined Sun and Ching-ling. But, he insisted as a Christian, the marriage was not valid; the bride was underage and Sun was still married to his first wife.

Though Sun had renounced his earlier marriage and told everyone that they were divorced, he had never gone through the proper legal channels. Sun had lived by his own rules for so long that he believed saying something was so made it so. Charlie ranted and raved, but the couple would not be moved. Sun claimed he could not continue his work without her. Ching-ling was in love with the man and his mission.

Charlie immediately disinherited his daughter and renounced his friend of so many years. The news, however, took months to get to Mei-ling and her brother T.V., who were still living in Cambridge, while he finished his education.

Meiliang and Bainong were shocked, as were the rest of their friends. Sun was forty-six years old and Ching-ling was only nineteen. Furthermore, although they knew Sun well, they only knew Ching-ling as the daughter of a friend. Sun's divorce problems were, in time, taken care of and the scandal subsided. After a while, Meiliang and Bainong would receive both Sun and Charlie in their house, but were careful not to overlap these visits.

One such day, Dr Sun and Ching-ling arrived with an escort, the dapper Chiang Kai-shek. Chiang was equally at home in his black silk samfu and skullcap or his Japanese style military uniform. Today, for this visit, he wore a Western, double-breasted pin-striped brown suit and fedora. The three were on their way up to Canton to check on the revolution, but Sun had insisted on this stop for a rest with his old friends.

Chiang was stiff and polite, but noticeably reserved. "He is somewhat single-minded and it's hard for me to get him to relax," Sun whispered to Meiliang.

The visitors had only been there for an hour or so when Bainong came up from the shop with Zhenli, who had also decided to take a day in the country. When they came into the house, Chiang rose from his chair, his eyes locked on Zhenli. For his part, Zhenli was relaxed as he entered his sister's home, but stiffened when he saw Chiang. Like two cats, with the hair on their necks up, they walked toward each other.

Meiliang caught the moment and said, "Well, I take it that you two know each other from Shanghai? This is my brother, Zhenli. And, this is Chiang Kai-shek, our guest who is here with Dr Sun."

"Yes," Zhenli answered. "We have met in Shanghai. I had to arrest some of his 'associates'."

"And you were quite right to do so!" Chiang answered. "They had become more belligerent than they had any cause for. I'm afraid the type of soldiers who fight revolutions is not as professional as we would like."

"They were gangsters!" Zhenli snarled. "I have seen them and their kind in the city for twenty years now."

"I am afraid that I must recruit from the cesspool of talent that is available," Chiang said coolly "We will try to make gentlemen out of them, or replace them, in time. For the moment, jail cells will do, just fine."

"All right, then!" Meiliang interjected. "Would you two gentlemen like to sit down and continue this visit over a glass of lemonade?" She pushed on her brother and indicated a chair for Chiang.

Sun filled them all in on what had been happening in the north. "Yuan Shi-kai had abused the trust and hope we had placed in him for the last six years. He dissolved the national and provincial assemblies, replaced them with his own military Governors, and caused the death of many good men. But, Cai E, a southern General, rebelled and the others followed. Yuan died of natural causes and the Beiyang Army split up into several cliques that followed their own local warlords. This is what we face today. Our country is represented to the world by whichever clique can control Beijing.

"The revolution has entered a new phase," Chiang intoned officiously, rising to his feet. With his hands clasped behind his back, he rocked up on the balls of his feet. "The Kuomintang will become the coordinating agency for both military and political activity. Doctor Sun is still the binding spirit of the revolution, but we will start now to gather under the KMT banner all of the military cliques in southern China, and then bring the north under our flag as well."

***

The Wens' Story Ends

My story-telling had lasted just long enough. We had pulled into Honolulu Harbor and from there, everyone would fly home, filled, I told myself, with a much better picture of China than they might have ever known.

As we lay in port, I stayed on with Captain Ellers and tied up some of the loose ends to the story. "Zhenli? Oh, he stayed on for a while as part-time police commissioner, part-time go-between with the government and his KMT contacts in the underworld, and part-time comprador in his own right. But, he died as he had lived -- playing one side off against the other. The Red Gang and the Green Gang were the two largest of the triad societies that ran the underworld in Shanghai. What exactly Zhenli's role was never did come to the surface, but in the end, he died leading his police into the midst of an inter-gang turf war.

"When Sun Yat-sen died, Ching-ling carried on his fight in the camp of the rising communist party, but was driven out of China by the KMT. She returned after the civil war, and was honored by and active in the New Communist Party structure. Her younger, sister, Mei-ling, had married Chiang Kai-Shek. It is said of Charlie's daughters, 'One loved money, one loved China, and one loved power.'"

"Meiliang and Bainong eventually moved out of Hong Kong, and retired on one of the smaller Hawaiian Islands. Their son Shaodai attended Stanford, and went into legal practice in San Francisco. His younger sister, Songmei, took over her grandmother's schools, and eventually retired in the old house in Aberdeen, overlooking Grandma's favorite misty, rock-lined bay."

"So the ancestors of your sailor friend were neither the Greedy Imperialists nor the War Lord villains that the communists claimed!" said the Captain, shaking his head. "Whatever happened with you and that sailor? And, how did Martial Lee play into all this?"

I looked around and, quite frankly, there was no good reason for me to rush off. I was in Hawaii -- with free room and board till the ship sailed again. I could play this out a little longer. "Well, that is a much shorter story," I said, leaning back in my chair.

Chapter 17

Nick's Travels in China

***

Welcome to China

"The last time I saw the sailor, Wen Gongshi, was when we landed in Luda. He had been helping me fill out the embarkation forms so I could off-load the equipment. The captain of that freighter was very nervous and didn't like the delay; he didn't trust the Chinese and I was as confused as anyone. My stuff turned out to be three, large, army surplus cargo trucks with huge trailer "pups" full of equipment. But, we said our good-byes, and I was escorted off the ship and through a gate in the fence.

"There was a lot of confusion and I couldn't understand a thing they were saying. Some guy grabbed me and started screaming in my face as though I was deaf. Another fellow started climbing up into one of my trucks and I tried to break free to stop him. The next thing I know, Wen is standing at my side, yelling back at them."

"They want to know how you are going to get these trucks off their dock!" Wen yelled, over the noise.

"I don't know," I answered. "There was supposed to be someone here to meet me."

"Let me see your papers." He read the part that was in Chinese and asked the men something. They all laughed, and a policeman stepped up and took the papers. After some conversation, Wen turned to me and explained, "This man, the one named in your papers, has been executed as a criminal. They don't know what you should do, but you must move these trucks off of the dock." The policeman was pointing at a parking lot adjacent to the dock area.

"Could you help me drive them over there?" I asked Wen.

"Sure, show me how. I never drove a truck this big before."

Wen and I got into one of the cabs and I started the engine. "I had to learn to drive these when I was in the Army in France," I told him. The motor belched out a black plume of smoke and we were off. "Six forward gears, two-speed axle, and highway overdrive; not bad!" I crowed, suddenly enjoying myself immensely. We got the first truck and trailer across the road to the parking lot and then went back for the others. We only had a little problem with the choke on one of them; but, finally, we got them all lined up in the parking lot on the other side of the road.

"Now I really need some help," I said aloud, beginning to realize my predicament. "What am I going to do with those rigs?"

Just as we got back inside the fence, the policeman stopped Wen. Their talk got more and more animated. Then Wen got absolutely panicky when the ship's horn blew three short blasts.

"I have to get on board," he shouted to me, "And this jerk won't let me go! They say I'm Chinese and I don't have the papers to leave." Panic swept over him and he struggled to get free of the policeman. The policeman pulled out his whistle and blew a long shrill tone. Very quickly, two more policemen were running toward us and took hold of Wen as well.

I followed them into their post-house by the main gate. Wen was ushered into a waiting room and set, forcibly, into a chair. The ship's horn blew again and Wen dropped his head into his hands. A man sitting next to him, who was not Chinese, said something to him, and Wen nodded. There was something that they silently shared, as they watched the lines being cast off from the dock and the ship slowly backing out of its berth. "This is a French sailor; been here forever!" said Wen, gesturing toward the man next to him. "He wants a ship as much as I do. Too much booze; no one would take him on."

"Prouve vous conduire un camion?" I asked.

"Oui, c'est sure!" (certainly)

"He said that he can drive," I said to Wen.

"Great, you two have fun then," Wen answered dejectedly. The policeman came back into the room and escorted Wen into an inner office. That was the last time I ever saw Wen Gongshi.

"So, what did you do with the trucks?" the Captain asked.

"Oh, I told the Frenchman I had to drive them somewhere but the authorities had executed my contact and I had no idea what to do with them. He started talking in Chinese with the guards. Then he told me to take him to the trucks. The guards marched us out to the parking lot and he got up into the driver's seat. I climbed up into the passenger's side and showed him how to turn on the ignition. He put it in gear and with a bit of jerking and few false starts, he managed to get it moving in a straight line. The guards applauded and whistled. I started feeling panicky, so I reached over and shut off the engine."

"The rest I can learn on the road!" he said. "Bien Sure!" (for sure)

I don't know why I was so concerned about the trucks. I had lost all contact with any reason for me being here, but I was the one they were looking at as though I knew what came next. I didn't have a clue.

On the street just outside the main gate, there was a sudden ruckus and three policemen were dragging a scruffy boy into the parking area. My Frenchman told me the boy had been arrested for stealing a truck.

"C'est merveilleuse, n'est pas? (that's wonderful) He could drive the third truck!"

"Are you crazy?" I exclaimed. "Look at him. He is only fifteen -- and he steals trucks!"

"We can work that out! Believe me, this is a sign from God himself." He reflexively made the sign of the cross.

The crowd on the street came into the area near the trucks where the police were holding the boy and swarmed all around us. The Frenchman talked with the policemen. Behind the Frenchman's blood shot eyes, I saw a conniving devil. You could see his manipulation, too, in his gestures.

All of a sudden, the policeman who was holding the boy, hoisted him onto the step of the truck cab and opened the door. I ran around to the other side and climbed up next to him on the passenger's side. The boy was wide-eyed and not anymore sure of all of this than I was. The Frenchman repeated to him, in Chinese, the instructions which I had given him. The truck's motor thundered into life and the crowd fell back, especially those in front of the truck. Then the boy pushed in the clutch, shifted into first-low gear, and released the parking break. The hiss of the air brake sent everyone even further back. Then he eased out the clutch, the motor lowered its tone, and we moved forward. I didn't let it go too far before I again turned off the key and the truck lurched to a stop.

***

The Escort

A young girl ran to the truck and climbed up onto the hood. All I could see were her military pants, stuffed into boots that were much too large for her. She started shouting to the crowd and they responded with cheers. The policeman in charge threw up his hands and waved us out of the parking lot.

The Frenchman leaned into the cab, laughing. "She will take us to the front," he said. "Her uncle is the Marshal in charge of our troops fighting the Russians."

"What are you talking about?" I exclaimed. "I didn't come here for a war!"

"Don't worry! They always run away," he answered blithely. "Then, they will take your trucks and you will be free!"

I had obviously lost any control that I might have had over the situation. Within five minutes we were a convoy on the move. The Frenchman took the lead truck, with the girl. The boy was in the middle, and I brought up the rear. Jerking and belching, we made it out of the parking lot and onto a main road, heading northeast. On the straight road we did much better; only occasionally did we bump into one another -- but, the bumpers on those old trucks were meant to take a lot of abuse. A short ways down the road, the lead truck pulled over and we joined it.

"We have to wait", the Frenchman said. "The girl must go to her home to get some things for the trip, but she will be right back."

"Where is her home?" I asked. She smiled a very pretty smile and pointed across a field toward some houses. "It is just over there," the Frenchman translated her gesture. "She will be back, Toute suite!" And off she went.

I walked over to the middle truck and introduced myself, "Hello, I am Nick Ramos, from the United States." It seemed a natural thing to me to make such an introduction; but all I got from the boy was a blank stare -- and the Frenchman was not even that responsive.

I tried again, in French, "Je m'appelle Nick Ramus de les Etats-Unis." I even extended my hand for a handshake, but none was forthcoming. "Comme vous appelez vous?"

I looked again at the boy. "Wo ja Nick. Wo shi Meiguo ren. Ni ja?" I said, trying my best Chinese.

He brightened and pointed to himself. "Wo ja Kong! Ta ja Marcel."

"Great, you are Kong and he is Marcel. Is he sick? Ta shi hou bu hao?"

Kong made a hand sign, indicating drinking. I responded with a nod and we ran out of communications, so we waited for the girl. The sun was starting to set so I looked over the manifest. Each truck had one, to cover everything that was in the truck -- right down to the contents of the first aid kit. My truck contained six barrels of diesel fuel and a Bridgeport mill, which could machine into existence almost anything mechanical you would ever need. There were also all sorts of smaller boxes, labeled and numbered with a corresponding page attached to the manifest. All seemed to be mechanical parts for the Bridgeport Mill or for some sort of wire harness. It must have been for the South American job. There also was a diesel generator for the mill, lights, and general power. The pup trailer had its own manifest, detailing a lot of wire, tags, binding materials, and instruction materials.

The truck that Kong was driving had its own six barrels of diesel fuel, as well as thirty large tanks of LP gas. The trailer contained a Korean War-vintage Mess, with all of the pots and pans, spices, twenty fifty-pound bags of rice, utensils, silverware, and cooks' uniforms.

The lead truck had the diesel fuel drums, twenty more LP tanks (must have been cheap), and an autoclave unit to sterilize medical instruments, plus twenty hundred-count bundles of wash cloths and towels. The trailer housed a whole M. A. S. H. clinic -- also from Korea of the 50s. It had the tents and scrubs, beds and desks, sheets and blankets, as well as an X-ray machine and another generator.

I decided to open up Kong's trailer and get out some of the rice. When he saw the pots and pans and all that rice, his eyes gleamed. "Me cook very good," he said.

So, we took out some of the rice and a pot and some bottled water and started making dinner. We didn't wait for the girl, but then, she never came -- not until noon the next day, anyway. By then, we were into our third bowl of rice and she went ballistic when she saw what we had done. She directed most of her anger at Kong, and he cowered in front of her. I just shrugged and indicated that I didn't have a clue what she was saying. Marcel finally came back to the world of the living and told me the gist of what was going on. It was the rice! We should not eat the rice! That would be for the men in the army. She insisted on locking the trailer again -- and she kept the key.

We drove on, late into the night until we came to a small village, where she had us stop along the highway outside the town and left us there. I remember watching the stars; such a dark sky -- no fog or mist or city lights to screen the night or break the spell. It was wonderful.

Then I saw a light, swinging along the path from town. The girl had hung a lantern on the forward end of a carry pole that had two baskets suspended from the ends. When she set it down, she gave each of us a bowl and two chopsticks. Then she uncovered six dishes in each of the baskets. There was fish and grain, several vegetables, and several spicy pots of some sauce they put on the food. She and the boy dug in and ate rapidly. Marcel was slower at the task and I was reluctant, but hungry.

In the morning, an old woman came up the path from town with two pots of ... I'd have to say it was gruel. She doled it out into each of our bowls and put everything else into the baskets. Then she deftly took it all away on the carry poles amid lots of chatter, smiles, and waving goodbye. It didn't really need any translation to participate. It was one of those golden moments of human interaction.

Then, our commandant in her oversized clothing jumped up, pushed her hair back up under her billed cap with the red star in front, and started giving instructions to get us moving again. I followed my comrades, and wiped out the bowl and chopsticks with grass along the side of the road. Then we rinsed them off with the boiling water from the pot, and we were off. Every now and again we passed a bay on our right, and we could see the ocean. At Zhuanghe, we stopped and I traded my Levi jacket to a local for his heavier Shepard's coat. I'm sure we both thought we had taken advantage of the other. I was cold at night -- we kept heading north. That evening we made it up to Dandong, the crossing bridge to North Korea.

I asked Marcel if this wasn't, indeed, the place where the Chinese soldiers had escaped from the Japanese at the end of the last century. He hushed me up. "Are you crazy? These people don't want to be reminded of all that! Don't even think of the Japanese. Those are Koreans over there -- and these are old American Army trucks. If you want to worry about something, figure out how we can get these things to the other side of town before they think another invasion is coming at them. Don't you see the watchtowers on the other side of the river? Pyongyang is just a hundred miles to the south."

It finally dawned on me the seriousness of what he was saying. The US and North Korea were still in a state of war; the armistice that we signed in the fifties had simply stopped the shooting -- for the last twenty years. We drove out of town as quickly as we could. North of the city were some mountains and we stopped for the night at a spot overlooking a great dam, probably a water supply for the city that we had just left.

The next few days we traveled up through the mountains. It was getting seriously cold! Baishanshi was aptly named, White Mountain Lion. It looked like a lion lying with its head up -- and I understand it was white with snow for most of the year. But as it was still summer, the mountain wasn't presently wearing its white coat. Lucky us! I thought. Brrrr!

Then the road went down, even though it still headed north. Rivers and lakes were the main features. There were more sheep herds and horses visible. Barley, millet, and wheat fields replaced the rice patties and fruit orchards in the south. The people we saw were thinner and more weathered looking than those in the south. And, the nights were colder. We stopped one night in Dunhua, and then drove on to the north, passing through Mudanjiang and back into the mountains.

At a place called Linkou, we actually started going east and then south for a very short time, before going north again. Over another mountain pass, we went into a larger town called Jixi. Most of the rest of our travel would be pretty flat land; just don't get off of the pavement -- the rivers, going north, started in those bogs. There was one interesting, wide spot in the road called Hutou; it was right on the border with Russia. On the other side was Dal'nerecensk, one of those ambiguous towns where half of the people were Russian and half Chinese. Yet, a little over a hundred miles to the north, Russian and Chinese soldiers were shooting at one another. Hutou was relatively prosperous due to its illicit trade in Russian goods, brought by the rail line on their side of the border, and fresh produce from the west in China. The rail line connected the Trans Siberian Railroad, which runs across Manchuria and down to Vladivostok, the port on the Sea of Japan.

It was May 16, 1978, when we ran out of road. The land was low, flat, and spider-webbed with rivers, draining the swamps which were all around us and extended fifty miles to the south. The Amur River ran to the northeast, just north of us, and the Ussuri River ran directly north, just northeast of us. On the other side of both rivers was Russian territory. Where the rivers joined was a disputed marshland, not well defined on the treaty maps.

The girl climbed to the top of the lead truck and called out at the top of her lungs. "She is calling for her uncle," Marcel told me. We waited and after several tries, a whistle came from across the swamp. By now, it was getting dark and the girl asked for a spotlight, which we had in the cab.

In about forty to five minutes, a voice called out from the swamp. The girl turned off the spotlight and we could hear people slogging through the marsh toward us.

When they got to the trucks there was a lot of talking. They had brought a couple of wounded men with them and all were helped into the back of the trucks. An older man was helped up into the seat next to me. The girl stood on the running board outside, talking loudly, and indicating we should turn the trucks around and go back.

The next town, south of us, was Shuguang about twenty miles away, and consisted of not much more than a few tent houses and a lot of sheep. She had us all pull off there. Marcel had a brief talk with the girl, and then told me that we had to unpack the M. A. S. H. trailer and set it up -- right now. I read the technical manual packed with it, and was able, through Marcel, to direct the setup of the main tent and to get the generator running. With lights and the heaters going, they took the old man inside and told me they could handle it from there. Marcel and I returned to our trucks and slept in the cabs.

In the morning, I saw that they were unpacking and assembling the Mess Tent, and had water boiling in the barrels for dirty dishes. It looked like they would not need any help from me. The girl seemed to be able enough to read English, even though she could not speak it very well. They had a water purification unit running and were very busy in the M.A.S.H. tent. I hung around the trucks, but there was really nothing for me to do except wait for them to finish cooking the rice. So, I finally had a chance to have a long talk with Marcel.

***

Getting to Know You

The girl decided to share the rice with us as some magnanimous gesture. Actually, there was so much rice we couldn't have made a dent in our stock if we tried. We sat on the running board of one of the trucks, and ate our bowls of steaming hot rice. Across the way, I noticed the girl reading a letter; there were tears streaking down her cheeks.

"I wonder what all that is about," I thought aloud. Marcel looked up and shrugged his shoulders.

Marcel, it seems, was a teenager in Marseilles, France who had run away from an abusive father. The father was a sailor himself, but he always returned home drunk and beat up on Marcel and his mother. When she died, Marcel lit out and never returned. He worked on a freighter and was in jail in Port Arthur when his ship sailed on, without him, in 1945. The Japanese had been thrown out, at the end of the war and the Chinese returned to power. Marcel got a job tending bar and was living with a sing-song girl; he thought he had found his ideal spot. But, in the early 1960s, when the Red Guard swept through there, the girl, the bar, and the good life were gone.

"They were a wild bunch!" he recalled. "They accused everyone of not being good revolutionaries. All of my friends were criticized for the way they lived. They closed the bars and rounded up the girls for retraining -- whatever that was. They dragged people into the streets with signs on their necks and beat the hell out of them. They sort of passed over me; I was usually drunk and I wasn't even Chinese. They did send me to cut trees in a re-education camp in Manchuria for a while. Later they had me in another camp tanning hides. It wasn't all bad. They fed us and, as long as you were out of their way, they didn't bother us."

We sat there, for a while, watching the vast sunset across the distant mountains. After dinner, we smoked some Russian cigarettes that someone had picked up and shared. The Mess tent and the M.A.S.H. tent seemed to fit right in; if anything, they were the upscale structures in the town. The tents that the local shepherds lived in were patchwork things, supported by cut saplings and tied with sheep gut, they were covered over with boards and scraps of leather. They saved the good leather and fur for clothing.

In the late afternoon, one of the soldiers waved me out of the cab of my truck. "Ni guo lai" (Come on), he said, motioning for me to follow him. He led me to the M.A.S.H. tent and stuck his head inside. Then he held the door open and waved me in.

"Hello?" The voice was weak as I entered. An old man was lying on a gurney across the room behind a drape curtain. "Please come in," he said, when I looked around the curtain. "I understand you are the one who brought this hospital to me. I wanted to thank you." His English was very good; he even had an American accent layered over the Chinese.

"I really wish I could take credit for that," I demurred, "But I'm just a tool of fate. This isn't what I signed on for. Actually, I was supposed to take all of this equipment to South America."

"Well, tell fate that I appreciate the delivery none the less!" he answered with a weak and raspy laugh. He was groggy from his wound and the medicine and he wrapped the blanket around his legs.

"It looks like we were on time for something. I didn't know that you were fighting the Russians."

"We are not, actually," he said. "It is just part of the game - - we spy on them and they spy on us. We try to hold the borders and they try to encroach a little more. This time, we were only up there as observers. I think someone must have told them we were there. They sent a helicopter and a couple of squads across the river to catch us. I wasn't going to get caught, but I did catch a bullet. We had a medic, but he didn't have anywhere to work on me. So, this was something of a miracle. I think I probably would have died before they got me back to Shuangyashan. That would have been the closest facility around here."

"Well then, I guess I did something right this year, after all," I said. "That niece of yours is quite the force. She actually rescued me from the port. The freighter, that dropped me off with these trucks, was going on to Korea; I couldn't have gone on with them if I'd wanted. The port didn't want us there and she helped us get out of town. Is she all right? I saw her crying over a letter out there."

"Oh she is all right," he answered. "She sort of lost her idol. Her older sister is in the Red Guard, and she has always adored her and everything she did. Now her sister is having second thoughts about her part in the activities during that early, crazy, part of The Great Proletarian Cultural Revolution. They were all running around with signs, 'Wage Civil War!', 'Overthrow Everything!' Anyone who knew anything was a reactionary. 'Struggle Against the Right!' Even Mao had the army supporting the left. 'Let them taste the power,' he would say. But they went too far. Often, they went too far. They killed and maimed people just for the sake of struggle; it was too much.

"The other day," he continued, "Her sister ran into her old teacher. At his trial, that was only ten years ago, to make him kneel down, she broke his kneecaps. They were all crazy then! But, really -- that was too much! Now she is a little older and sees how they made these mistakes. There is nothing they can do about it now. Her teacher will lurch around on two crutches for the rest of his life. And she will probably never forgive herself. Zhenzhu is feeling her sister's shame, probably more than her sister does."

"I think you have exhausted yourself," I said, noticing his breathing was becoming more labored. "Maybe I should leave you so you can get some rest."

"Yes, you are right. But please come back tomorrow. It is good to practice my English," he said.

"You speak it very well! But, I will be honored to help. Good night, then," I said, and left to watch the stars twinkle in a black blue sky.

The next two days passed in alternately short visits with the Marshal and pulling maintenance on the trucks for the trip back. Marcel told me they were going to be reassigned to Viet Nam. Marshal Lee was much in demand these days. He was one of the few old soldiers in the upper echelons, who would actually go into a war zone anymore. The rest of his comrades from the Long March were either dead or trying to stay alive amid the corrosive politics that followed Mao's death.

**

Marshal Lee and Mao

Marshal Lee first met Mao down south, under a pomelo tree on a rise over the banks of the Xiang River in Guangxi in the middle of a war. There had always been bandits and landlords fighting in that area, but this was unlike anything he had known or heard of before. The man on the ground was bleeding from a wound to his leg, in a field of men dead or dying from their wounds. The river was filled with bodies and the bombs had numbed his ears. Lee thought this was the same young soldier who spoke to his village only a week ago. He was tall and had the same mop of hair, but now he was wounded and his mouth was calling for help even though the words could not get into Lee's ears. He tied on a bandage that he made from the waist sash taken from a body not ten feet away. Mao pointed down the road and they hobbled off together.

Lee was twenty-two years old and had come back home from college to visit with his Aunt and Uncle in Guilin that winter of 1935 when he first walked with Mao. And, he walked at Mao's side for the rest of the 6,000 mile Long March. He had commanded troops and stood personal guard duty for Mao in the caves of Yenan, and later at the Zhongnanhai compound -- Mao's personal residence and the center of his government. Personal trust and loyalty were the qualities that the peasant farmer, like Mao Zedong, valued above all else. Lee had avoided the political traps of ambition and was content to serve out his career as a field commander.

"You come speak English?" a young soldier greeted me at the washtubs.

"Sure," I said, drying my hands on the towel and trying to think how to teach him to speak English.

"No, you come now! You speak English!" the young man said. He sounded urgent and waved me toward the tent.

"Oh! You mean Marshal Lee?" I followed him to the M.A.S.H. tent. "Well, good morning. How is the patient today?" I greeted the old man.

"I will have to use a cane till this leg heals," he winced as he alighted on the floor next to his bed. "But aside from that, I feel fine. I understand that the trucks are ready and we can leave tomorrow."

"That soon? Heck, I was just getting used to this place."

"You won't like it when the Fall comes -- and it can kill you in the Winter. Now is a good time to go. What would you like to talk about? I need to expand my vocabulary."

"Well, I don't know. Can we talk about things political?"

"Some things. What did you have in mind?"

"That whole Red Guard thing. Why was there so much violence?"

"That is a very basic question," he answered. "A very good question." He turned and said something to the soldier at the doorway. Then, he looked back at me, "How much of the history of China do you know?"

"Actually, a lot more now than I knew before I came here. But still, maybe it's not enough?"

"Well, you have read of our long Confucian history, right? And you know how that system worked?"

"I think I do."

"Well, the idea of a 'Mandate of Heaven' was just an agreement between the Emperor and all of the people, by which everyone would participate in running the country according to their abilities. Competition for the best positions was intense and lasted your whole life. The best scholars were given the most power, but they were never allowed to hold it long enough to make it their own. By constantly reassigning the Kwan to new positions of leadership, their loyalty was to the system that gave them power. But, the Mandate of Heaven was not a Confucian religion, -- it was a structure for administration." The Marshal worked his way around the room, testing is ability with the cane.

"Religion, according to Marx, 'is the opiate of the masses,'" he continued. In other words, any religion has a basic function of pacifying the general public. Even Mao himself knew the easing of pain through his mother's prayer at a Buddhist temple, when he was sick as a child. Yet he let the guard destroy many temples. Why?" He sat down on a chair and raised his eyebrows. "Because it is, even today, a class war and religion dulls the senses; it distracts the individual from that struggle against class distinction. From warlord to landlord, from city bourgeois to the country peasant, from any level to any other perceived level -- it is a process of 'unity, criticism, unity'. We must be clear-headed and strident to continue the struggle against class distinctions." The weathered face of the Marshal was full with color and he seemed rejuvenated by his own reiteration of Mao's words.

"But," I asked him "why couldn't they just go back to that Confucian system? It seemed to work and not so many would have died."

"But, that was only the veneer and lacquer that made traditional China look good from the outside. Just beneath that surface was a mean-spirited system of tough-minded functionaries who supported that outer shell. That under-side of advantage was not a pretty sight. The vast majority, who lived on the land, had no more influence on government than they did on the weather. To them, the old Daoist system of spirits counted the government as just another distant deity that had to be appeased with offerings. If rivers flooded and washed away their lives, if droughts killed off the crops -- and the people who relied on them -- or if warring factions ravaged their lives, it was all the same

458

to them. Hanging on to life was an individual matter. Rules for living were concessions to fact; you learned the hard truths of survival, not the etiquette of society. Millions would live and die by the whims of the spirits -- and think little of it.

"Still, over the centuries, things did get better. The Dynasties were stable for longer periods of time and the systems that supported their existence relied on increases in the population to support them. And yet, the vast majority of the population at any time was at the bottom, hanging onto life. The Buddhist religion offered a way to better cope with life, beyond survival. It came to China from India and took hold of the minds of many. The idea that there was more than one life helped many to cling to their bleak existence.

"Daoist and Buddhist ideologies held the people down, while the Confucian system tied the middle kingdom together for many centuries; they were the coping mechanisms of China's feudal period.

"It was the Ming Empire that sailed the many seas and brought tribute back to the center of civilization. Then the Qing Empire, later, received the backwash -- as the rest of the world came to China. Ground up in these shifting of powers were the tens and hundreds of millions of the peasant class -- always the poor at the bottom."

***
The Sand Wedge

The young soldier, to whom the Marshal had spoken earlier, came back into the tent with a shallow box, some rocks, and a bucket of sand. He set the box on the top of a table, with the rocks and sand next to it. Marshal Lee hobbled over to the table from his bed. He picked up the rocks and set them, one at a time, in the box on their flat sides.

"Think of this box as China," Marshal Lee said. "These rocks are the institutions of power which we have just discussed. This is the Emperor, this is Daoism, these are the Censors, these are the Kwan," he explained, picking up a rock to represent each group. "There are many more, but you would need an almost infinitely large box." Then he poured the sand around the rocks and patted it down. "The grains of sand represent the people of China," he continued. "The sand cannot move because the rocks hold it in place; the rocks do not move because the sand holds them in place." He set the sand pail down and pushed up his sleeves.

"Mao told us that, to change this picture, a violent revolution was needed. Not just a bump." Marshal Lee struck the side of the box with his cane. "You have to give it a good shake!" he said, grabbing the sides of the box with both hands and jerking it back and forth. "You see how, with a little shaking, the sand wedges under the rocks? Now watch!" He began to shake the box harder, until all of the rocks were moving freely on top of the sand.

"Now, just by tipping the box, many of the rocks will fall out," he demonstrated. "See how, with more shaking and tipping, almost all of the rocks will be made to fall out of the box? This is a violent revolution! But, it is not a complete revolution." He set the box down and picked up his cane. "To be complete, that is to say, for the people to be free from all bindings, we must look for the clumps that still hold the sand together. Only then can social equality be achieved." He stirred the sand with his cane and pointed out clumps of dirt in the sand.

"And, what are these clumps?" he asked, rhetorically. "They are the family, binding its members together with property and inheritance that stratifies the rich from the poor. They are the criminal elements, the triads, the capitalist ventures, and the social brotherhoods which segregate the people into classes, they all give advantage to some at the expense of the many. They are the religions which set members against non-members and give people false hope and take them away from their responsibilities for the whole of the people. These clumps must be eliminated," he repeated. "They must be broken up or thrown out of the box!" He took his cane and struck violently at the sand that was left in the box. "Only then will each grain of sand move freely -- only then can the people know true communism!"

His little demonstration had taxed him and he was breathing heavily. I helped him back to his bed and sat down on the stool next to him. "That was impressive," I said, as he regained his composure. "Did it really work?"

He started to laugh and, looking back at the box, he took a deep breath. "No! Does any of it ever really work? But we did give it one hell of a shake!"

"I notice a lot of the sand is on the floor. Many died in the violence?"

"Yes, and there are still clumps in the box. Mankind would not be bound by our poor thought-models. We could never rinse out all of the mud that is in the soil. When we took over the government in 1949, we had such idealism! We gave the country back to the people, but many became revisionists, capitalists and possessed with self interest. I'm sure many really bad people were thrown out of the box, but many remained inside as well. People took advantage of their freedoms. We had to institute a web of cadres to keep instructing the people and to root out the weak ones who would return to the old, dysfunctional social forms. And then, those at the top took advantage of the trust Mao had given them. Individuals and gangs coalesced, like so many droplets of oil on water. They had to be purged from power. Nothing offended Mao more than disloyalty to the ideals of pure socialism." He laid back and closed his eyes for a moment, then opened them with a shake of his head.

"I knew Mao well," he said, looking off into some distance of time. "Did I say I was with them from before the Long March? Mao and the rest were being chased by the KMT -

- even though the real threat to the whole country was the Japanese. Chiang Kai-Shek was against the Communists -- his own people. He liked to quote an old proverb, 'A mosquito in the house is worse than a lion outside.' He saw the political threat inside more clearly than the military threat from Japan.

"I met Mao in Tucheng, my home town in Guizho province. There is little there but the steep sides of the mountains. For Mao, that was a good thing -- and a bad thing for Chiang. The fly swatter couldn't get him there. But, the political committee had stripped Mao of much of his power. He waited it out and eventually got all of his power back. All of the other leaders fell to their own bad planning and arrogance. I went with Mao into the mountains and across the high deserts, all the way up to Yenan. He trusted me because I trusted him. Even in the really bad times, I knew he would be the best for China. Later, when Mao lived at the headquarters called Zhongnanhai, I was one of his personal bodyguards. I could hear it all, because we were just outside his room wherever he was. He even asked us about things -- even me, a peasant boy from Guizhou! Mao loved the peasant masses because that is where he came from."

***

Return to Life

Before we left, Marcel had a long discussion with the Marshal, and told me that when we got back to Hutou, he would leave the caravan and go over to the Russian side; that way, he thought, he could make it onto a French ship in Vladivostok. On the way down to Hutou, he would teach one of the soldiers to drive the truck. The other driver, Kong had been inducted, quite willingly, and was now officially a soldier himself. So, in the morning, we were on the road again.

As agreed, Marcel was relieved of his driving duties, and sauntered across the frontier at Hutou as though he owned the place. The rest of us pressed on toward civilization, or whatever lay before us. The next day we stopped at Jixi, which was a city large-enough to have a small factory that made farm implements. The Marshal donated the Bridgeport Mill, its tooling, the spools of wire, the generator, and two drums of fuel. The managers of the factory were so appreciative they threw a dinner for us all at the local restaurant. Sixteen dishes on 'Lazy Susan' rotating tops were served at each table, and each dish was replenished as it was emptied. We all slept well that night.

At Linkou, about thirty miles southwest of Jixi, the Marshal was asked to officiate at a trial. An old barn served as the courthouse. The trial was apparently just a formality, with presenting of 'evidence' of the complaint and pronouncing a suitable punishment. The whole town seemed to have crowded into the barn.

The accused, a peasant woman in her late fifties, was brought before the bench and made to sit facing the Marshal. The charge against her was read out in high, imperial tones that sounded almost operatic. Then several people were called upon to give testimony, and shook their fingers at her and rasped out whatever it was they had to say. Finally, the Marshal asked her to speak. As she sobbed and pleaded, the people in the crowd shouted out catcalls and threw things at her. Finally, the Marshal slammed his fist down on the table and pronounced his verdict. Two of his soldiers took her by the arms, which were bound behind her during the whole trial, and dragged her out to a waiting cart. They stood her in the front of the cart and held her there, as the horse slowly pulled the cart out of town to a field nearby.

The Marshal and I walked down a path with the town leaders, following the cart. "The woman was a notorious 'Capitalist Roader'," he said, "A revisionist who could not reform her ways. She took control of land and made poor peasants pay her to farm it for her. She would beat them for the slightest provocation, and took all of the harvest if they tried to get any relief. She has been warned and punished before. Today she will answer for her crimes."

Along the side of the fields, we followed the village leaders down a pathway, made of shallow boxes filled with stones, a construction that kept us above the sodden farmland. When we reached the destination, the soldiers took her down from the cart and walked her twenty feet or so into the field away from us. They made her kneel in the soft dirt, stood back a few feet, and shot her in the back of her head. She stiffened just before the shot, and then fell face down on the ground. I have to admit, I was sick. I looked down and saw the Marshal's boot flick a small stone out of the box upon which we were standing. I looked at him. He just shrugged and we walked back into town.

The rest of the trip, down to the port at Luda, was uneventful, but I couldn't get that picture of the woman falling out of my mind. When I did drift off to sleep, the next loud sound would wake me in a cold sweat. By the time we got to the port, I was sick from lack of sleep and unable to eat. I remember they were going on to Port Arthur to catch their ship to Hainan and then on to Viet Nam. But, I was a mess when they took me out onto the dock and your ship. The rest, you know."

"Well," said Captain Ellers, "That is one heck of a story! I must say, you made this cruise one that I'll remember for a long time. "What do you plan to do now?" he asked.

"I guess I'll go back to Michigan and pick up where I left off," I answered. "Maybe I'll write a book."

Suggested Reading List

Barons. Eds. F. Robertson and T.L. Davis. The Book of
    The Vedas. London: Piers Spence..

Becker, Jasper. Hungry Ghosts. New York: Henry Holt
    and Company, 1996.

Buck, Pearl S. The Good Earth. New York:Washington
    Square Press, 1931.

Buckley Ebrey, et al. Chinese Civilization. New York: The
    Free Press: 1993.

Chang, Iris. The Rape of Nanking. New York: Penguin
    Books, 1997.

Chang, Pang and Mei, Natasha . Bound Feet & Western
    Dress. New York: Anchor Books, 1996.

Chin, Shunshin. The Taiping Rebellion. Trans. Joshua A.
    Fogel. Armonk N.Y: ME. Sharp, 2001.

Cook, Michael. Muhammad, Oxford, NY: Oxford
    University Press, 1983.

Da, Chen. Colors of the Mountain. New York: Random
    House: 2000.

Dai, Sijie. Balzac and the Little Chinese Seamstress.
    Trans. Ina Rilke. New York: Anchor Books, 2001.

Eddy, Mary Baker. Science and Health. Lowell, MA:
    1886.

Fenby, Jonathon. Chiang Kai- Shek: China's
    Generalissimo and the Nation He Lost. New York:
    Carroll & Graph Publishers, 2003.

Garrett, Valery M. Traditional Chinese Clothing. Hong Kong: Oxford University Press, 1987.

Gascoign, Bamber. The Dynasties of China, A History. New York: (publisher?), 1973.

Gethin, Rupert. The Foundations of Buddhism. Oxford, NY: Oxford University Press, 1998.

Ha Jin. Waiting. New York: Random House, 1999.

Hearn, Lafcadio, Gleanings in the Buddha Fields. Rutland, VT: Charles E Tuttle, 1971.

History Dept., University of Futon and Shanghai Teachers. The Taiping Revolution. Honolulu: University Press of the Pacific, 2001.

Jean, Georges. Writing, The Story if Alphabets and Scripts. Trans. Jenny Oats. New York: Harry Abrams, 1992.

Lao Tzu. Tao Te Ching. Trans. Jonathan Star. New York: Penguin Group, 2001.

Kaizuka, Shigeki. Confucius His Life and Thought. Trans. Geoifrey Bownas. New York: Dover, 2002.

Kennedy, Brian and Elizabeth Guo. Chinese Martial Art Training Manuals. Berkeley: North Atlantic Books, 2005.

Kingston, Maxine Hong. China Men. New York: Random House, 1980.

Lattimore, Deborah N. I Wonder What's Under There. San Diego: Browndeer Press, 1998.

Li, Dr. Zhisui. The Private Life of Chairman Mao. Trans. Tai Hung-chao. New York: Random House, 1994.

Lippman, Thomas W. Understanding Islam. New York: Nal Books, 1982.

Menzies, Gavin. 1421 The Year China Discovered America. Great Briton: Transworld, 2002.

Menzies, Gavin. 1434 The Year A Magnificent Chinese Fleet Sailed to Italy and Ignited the Renaissance. New York: Harper Collins, 2008.

Min Anchee. Empress Orchid. New York. Hoghton Miffin, 2004

Min Anchee. The Last Empress. New York: Houghton Miffin, 2007.

Min Anchee. Red Azailea. New York: Berkley Books, 1995.

Morton, W. Scott. China Its History and Culture. New York: McGraw-Hill, 1982.

Nien Cheng. Life and Death in Shanghai. New York: Penguin, 1988.

Random House. Timetables of History. NewYork: Random House, 1996.

Ru Zhijuan, et al. (give all authors). Seven Contemporary Chinese Women Writers. Beijing: Chinese Literature Press, 1983.

Seagrave, Sterling. The Soong Dynasty. New York: Harper & Row, 1985.

Shi Zhengyu. Picture Within a Picture. Beijing: New World,1999.

Spence, Jonathan D. God's Chinese Son. New York: Norton, 1996.

Spence, Jonathan D. The Search for Modern China. New York: Norton Paperback, 1990.

Starr, John Bryan. Understanding China. New York: Hill and Wang, 1997.

Stockard, Janice E. Daughters of the Canton Delta. Stanford: Stanford University Press, 1989.

Sun Shuyun. The Long March. New York: Doubleday, 2006.

Sun Tzu. The Art of War. Trans. Lionel Giles. New York: Barnes and Noble Classics, 2003.

Tabataba'I, Allamah S.M.H. Shi'ite Islam. Trans. S. H. Nasr. New York: State University of New York, 1977.

The Classic Tradition of Haiku, An Anthology. Ed. Faubion Bowers. New York: Dover, 1996.

Three Hundred Poems of the T'ang Dynasty. Trans. W. Bynner. Santa Fe. NM.

Tsui Tsen-hua. The Sino—Soviet Border Dispute in the 1970's. Oakville, Ont. CA: Mosaic, 1983.

Watts, Alan. Eastern Wisdom. New York, MJF Books, 2000.

Wang Zheng. Women of the Chinese Enlightenment. Berkley: Univ. of California Press, 1999.

Wright, Daniel B. The Promise of the Revolution. Lanham, MA: Rowman & Lit1leiield, 2003.

Xueping Zhong, Wang Zheng and Bai Di. Some of Us. New Brunswick, NJ: Rutgers, 2001.

To order copies of "The China Sand Wedge".
visit www.thechinasandwedge.com

Place your order and pay via credit card or PayPal.
Copies are $24.95 US plus $10 S&H
Educational and Quantity discounts available